The Stubborn Season

Lauren B. Davis

The Stubborn Season

Harper*Flamingo*Canada

The Stubborn Season

Copyright © 2002 by Lauren B. Davis.
All rights reserved. No part of this book may be used
or reproduced in any manner whatsoever without
prior written permission except in the case of brief
quotations embodied in reviews.
For information address:
HarperCollins Publishers Ltd.,
55 Avenue Road, Suite 2900,
Toronto, Ontario, Canada M5R 3L2

www.harpercanada.com

HarperCollins books may be purchased for
educational, business, or sales promotional use.
For information please write:
Special Markets Department,
HarperCollins Canada,
55 Avenue Road, Suite 2900,
Toronto, Ontario, Canada M5R 3L2

Lyric from Bye-Bye Blackbird *by Ray Henderson*
and Mort Dickson, Warner Bros. Publishing.

Every reasonable effort has been made to contact the
holders of copyright for material quoted in this work. The
publishers will gladly receive information that will enable
them to rectify any inadvertent errors or omissions in
subsequent editions.

First edition

Canadian Cataloguing in Publication Data

Davis, Lauren B., 1955–
The stubborn season

ISBN 0-00-200502-6

I. Title.

PS8557.A8384S88 2002   C813'.6   C2002-900527-2
PR9199.4.D39S88 2002

HC 9 8 7 6 5 4 3 2 1

Printed and bound in the United States
Set in Dante

*This book is dedicated to my husband, Ron,
who never falters in his encouragement,
his support, and his love;*

*and to my mother,
who planted the seed for
this story with a story of her own.*

Part I

1

Sometimes ten-year-old Irene MacNeil lay in bed at night and listened. It was a weird trick of the house that the radiators and air vents acted as a kind of amplification system, conducting every sound, no matter how subtle, to every corner of every room. The heart-jumping thud of coal settling in the furnace. The gurgle of water in the pipes. The hum of the refrigerator. Her father's snore. Her mother's body turning, making the coils of the bedsprings squeak. She imagined the house was a creature in whose body they all lived, and the sounds were like those her own stomach made when she'd eaten something hard to digest.

For all the seeming order in the layout of the rooms it was a narrow, jumbled-up house, where even their small family of three felt like more. They were forever excusing themselves to pass in the hall, both people pressed up against the wall; or feeling as though a window should be opened to let in a little more air.

A concrete path led from the sidewalk to two wooden steps and the porch that ran the width of the house. The door opened into a small vestibule with hooks for coats, facing the steep stairs to the second floor. To the right was the living room, made cheerful enough by a rose-and-violet chintz sofa on one side of the green-tiled fireplace and a matching chair on the other. In the corner a radio stood proudly next to a potted split-leaf philodendron, and next to that, Douglas MacNeil's orderly desk, with neatly piled papers and envelopes and a little brass clock. In the dining room, no more than a dark nook behind the living room, was an imposing walnut table and a hutch containing the good dishes and two Toby jugs, which had been wedding gifts. The kitchen was in the rear of the house. Upstairs were two bedrooms, one for Irene at the back with a window that overlooked the yard, and one for her parents in front, as well as a summer sleeping porch.

This morning Irene was in the upstairs bathroom brushing her teeth. She was a deceptively sturdy little girl, her wrists thick and her face square and determined. Her nose was pug, her eyebrows sparse and her eyes nut brown. When she was finished brushing her teeth she ran a comb through her wavy hair, the colour of reddish earth. She thought her hair was pretty. It might even be what magazines referred to as a "best feature," except that her mother insisted on cutting it blunt and no longer than the bottom of her ears. It was parted on the side and held tightly with a hairpin so that it did not get into her eyes, although a stray wisp or two always escaped and sat rather ridiculously on her forehead. Such a curl now straggled out, no sooner than Irene pressed the pin into her scalp, and she hurried to wet it and pat it into place. Her parents' voices floated through the vent from the kitchen below, along with the smell of coffee and bacon.

Irene did not want to walk in on what was clearly one of her parents' "discussions." If she did, they would stop talking, and her mother's mouth would set in that way that made Irene feel as though she were a bother. So rather than interrupt, she brushed her teeth a second time, and although she knew it was wrong to listen to other people's conversations, she listened anyway. What choice was there? Sometimes she felt they were all mushed up together in the house and it was unclear where one of them ended and another began.

Douglas read the day's headlines. The news was bad, but he saw no need to alarm his wife further. She was far too easily alarmed as it was. The early-morning light made the red-walled kitchen look downright angry. It hurt Douglas's eyes, as he knew it would even when he had, on a benevolent whim, agreed to the colour two months ago. He held the newspaper up to block a shaft of light knifing through the black venetian blinds.

"We should have invested while we had the chance," Margaret

said. "The boom's all over now, isn't it, and we've lost an opportunity."

A banner across the front page of the *Toronto Star* read: "Stock Prices Crash." There were stories telling how the streets around the Montreal and Toronto exchanges were filled with crying men and women who pushed and shoved each other, losing their hats and bruising their shins, hoping to salvage something of their evaporating fortunes.

Douglas did not respond and so Margaret tapped the paper. "Put that down and talk to me, please, Douglas. We'll never get rich now, will we?"

Margaret's insistence upon wealth puzzled Douglas, for it was not as though they lacked for anything. They had an electric refrigerator as well as an electric cooking range. They had a radio. He'd given Margaret a fox stole for Christmas last year. They'd recently modernized the kitchen and painted it the garish red she'd insisted on. Douglas was a pharmacist, a professional man with a well-respected business. They lived a better life than their Scottish immigrant parents had ever dreamed of.

And Douglas loved his wife. She was the prettiest girl he'd ever seen, with her sleek bobbed black hair and smoky eyes and Clara Bow mouth. When he'd married her she was twenty, a tiny girl with a waist his hands could nearly span, and even now, ten years after Irene's birth, she had kept her figure. He wanted to make her happy. He had never given her the impression he would ever be anything except exactly what he was, take it or leave it. By marrying him he assumed she'd decided to take it.

"Margaret, there's a story here in the *Star* about a woman, a Lottie Nugent, who lost her entire life savings and went home and turned on the gas. Would you rather we had put all our money in the stock market and lost it? I don't understand you, my dear."

"No, you don't. I don't know if you ever have," she said and marched out of the kitchen, her heels clacking on the new linoleum floor.

Douglas carefully folded his newspaper. He ran his fingers along the crease, making it sharp. It was time to go to the drug store.

"Irene, stand still!" Margaret rubbed furiously at a spot on Irene's chin with a handkerchief on which she'd spit.

"Ow! Mum!"

"Oh, don't carry on. How you manage to get as much tooth-paste on the outside of your mouth as you do on the inside, I'll never know." She stepped back and surveyed Irene, who squirmed uneasily. Margaret hated it when Irene fidgeted, but bit her tongue. After all, she was annoyed at Douglas, not Irene.

"I'm going to be late, Mum."

"Hurry up, then. Hurry up! Get your books. Where's your sweater?"

Irene grabbed her sweater and dashed down the stairs. She picked up her books from the chair by the door.

"Daddy? Are you ready? I'm going to be late."

"Coming, Pet."

As he put on his coat, Douglas checked the inside pocket for his flask. Its smooth cool solidity reassured him. A little dram of rye whisky now and again kept him steady, especially after a spat with Margaret.

It was the habit of father and daughter to walk along the street together every morning, until Irene came to her school and they parted ways. As they left the house, neither of them mentioned that Margaret had gone upstairs into her room and closed all the curtains against the day's bright sunshine.

1929

The boy rests his head against the warm flank of the cow. His name is David Hirsch. He is half asleep still, as is the cow. Her name is Sophie and she smells of hay and manure and cream. The kerosene lantern throws a small pool of yellow light around them. Beyond it, the two horses, one dapple grey, the other roan, paw softly at the ground as they chew the feed he's poured in their trough. His hands work reassuringly on Sophie's teats, rhythmically, the milk hissing into the bucket. His breath and the cow's mingle in a steamy cloud, for the early-morning air is chill. Sophie lows and shifts her weight.

"Sophie-girl, there, there, Sophie-girl." David mutters the words as though speaking through dreams.

It is dark outside and will not be light for another two hours. The nights have grown longer, and it is harder each day to get up to tend to the cow and the horses and the chickens and the dogs and chop the kindling and start the fire and tend to the other thousand things a farm morning brings. Winter comes early on the Saskatchewan prairie and the wind warns the farmer of what's to come. This morning it is a slap on the cheek, delivered by a harsh hand, although it doesn't yet shock his breath away, as it will in deep December. He's already spotted the first few flakes of snow, dancing in a thin wisp along the side of the farmstead roof. The coming of the dark time, and perhaps another hungry time. There have been droughts before, but this has been a dusty year and the harvest was meagre and the cellar is not full enough to let them rest easy in the knowledge of plenty.

The wind has blown hot and dry and relentless all summer. Perspiration left a salty grit, drying on the skin before cooling it. Sand began to drift under farmhouse doors. The men whispered at the grain silo, at the feed store, at the barber's. "The crops are failing," they said, but did not say it loudly. They remembered other bad years. It will pass, they said, and turned their eyes to God.

The prairie sky is vast and moody and restless in the fall. The granite-coloured clouds shift and blur, the grey land, drifting to sleep beneath the thin blanket of frost, rises up to meet the air and the two become indistinct, inseparable, a huge arc of seamless space. Distance is distorted, everything seems farther away, while the soul longs for a warm, snug corner by the stove.

David is restless too, and moody, ill-fitting in his fourteen years. He is outgrowing his hand-me-down jackets and pants and pushing up against the tight seams of Sonnenfeld as well. One hundred and thirty-seven Jews on twenty-nine farms. It had been one hundred and thirty-eight, until his

7

mother died two winters ago of the influenza. There is only one road out of the settlement and it leads to the nearest railway stop in Estevan, fifty miles away. He lives on the farm with his father, Herzl, and his brothers Jacob and Isaac, and Isaac's new wife, Toba. Toba will have a baby in the spring. Then they will be one hundred and thirty-eight again.

It is a misconception that boys grow up more slowly in the country than in the city, or that they are more innocent. Death is kin. Accidents, the loss of an arm or an eye, not unfamiliar. Because the population in Sonnenfeld is so small, births and deaths, tears and pain, rage and despair, all are shared, and no one is too young to shoulder his or her burden. And they come from strong stock, these refugees from eastern Europe, from Lithuania, from Galicia, from Russia. They have fled, or survived, the massacres of Kharkov, Odessa and Kiev. They do not let their children forget.

David's father came from Bialystok to Canada with his parents in 1881, when he was six. His father's baby brother did not go with them. In the slaughter that followed the assassination of Czar Alexander, a soldier took little Asher by the heels and dropped him down a well where he drowned. The family buried him and, still mourning, fled.

It was a long journey, but they are settled now, here in the plains of western Canada, for the time being at any rate. But movement is in the blood, and the boy is distrustful of a place too-well loved. He has been taught that a boot can kick down any door, if there is enough hatred in the foot, and that hatred is also a creature that roams. The Ku Klux Klan operate in Saskatchewan now.

He pats Sophie and she turns to look at him, her great eyes trusting and calm. He takes up the pail of fresh milk and leaves the barn. The planks of wood laid down as a walkway across the yard creak beneath his boots as he walks toward the house. It is small. Three rooms. Kitchen, two sleeping rooms. Since the death of his wife, the boy's father has slept alone in one, but now that Isaac has married, he sleeps with his other two sons, and Isaac and Toba have a room to themselves. The roof is steeply pitched and the chimney rises from the centre. There are four poplar trees around the house, and by the door are two wild-rose bushes his mother transplanted from the prairie. His father cares for them now. Chickens peck at the ground in their wood-fenced pen. The dog, a yellow hound of indeterminate parentage, pads out from the shadows to meet the boy, its body wriggling with happiness as he reaches down to rub its ears.

He stops, picks up a stick and tosses it for the dog, who runs after it with a joyful bark. He watches the dog and then looks up to see the morning star in the charcoal sky. The earth sweeps out in a gently rolling sea to a sliver of silver promise on the horizon. He holds his head up and sniffs the air. Eggs and coffee from the kitchen, but more. David Hirsch is a child of the land and the scent is familiar. Something harsh and dry and brutal as a brush fire, rolling in across the earth on the northern wind.

2

It was so sweet to lie in the dark and pretend the day was ending, not beginning. Margaret arranged a cool cloth on her forehead and kicked off her shoes. The room smelled of the oranges treated with orrisroot, studded with cloves and hung in the closets to keep the clothes fresh. She closed her eyes.

Over the past few months she could count on her fingers the number of good days when she didn't need to escape to the dark refuge of this room. It used to be the other way around. Most days had been good. In fact, she'd been the Laughing Girl, hadn't she? Always ready for a party, ready for a lark?

She hardly recognized herself as that girl now.

Reverend Fuller said you should start every day with a commitment to God and that, should this commitment falter, you could start the day anew whenever you liked. You could simply say to yourself, This day begins now. Margaret knew that if she could make herself believe this then she'd stop obsessing about every harsh remark, every shrewish tone. She'd put whatever bad thing she'd done behind her and pretend the sun had just risen on a clean slate of possibilities.

It was as though some other woman lived inside her. The true Margaret was sweet and loving and caring, but this Other Margaret was a nasty, bitter piece of work who couldn't be controlled. She just popped up, no matter how Margaret tried to keep her under wraps.

She tossed the cloth onto the floor, rolled to her side and pulled the comforter over her face. She would not cry. She wouldn't think of the awful news in the papers this morning. She'd think of good things. Something to make her laugh. She closed her eyes and remembered a party long ago, before she'd married. The old gang had gone to a jazz joint and danced to the music of the saxophones and clarinets until three. Flat-chested Anne Franklin, tipsy on gin and lemonade, stuffed melons down her camisole and persuaded her brother to try on high heels. Why, she'd had fun that night, hadn't she? She'd laughed and laughed. Swirled and twirled and shimmied and shone, a glass of champagne in one hand and her arm around John Carlisle. Poor John. She thought about how the war had changed him. He had such terrible nightmares and couldn't seem to ever be still. He broke out in a sweat at every loud noise.

Margaret grit her teeth, the taste of frustration like iron in her mouth, and she clutched the comforter, willing herself not to tear it to shreds just to see the feathers fly. She must control herself.

Life had turned out to be so small. She'd had such high hopes and now it was all pinching pennies and saving for the future and not living beyond their means. A small house. A small savings account. A small future.

She twisted on the bed. I am an ungrateful woman, she thought.

But Douglas was so easy to nag. Why had she mistaken weakness for gentleness? Margaret's father had been a big, brusque man, all whisky and rough hands and a voice that could shake the windows. She loved him, but he was hard to handle, and her mother had always looked drawn and tired. In fact, she had never really seemed relaxed until after her husband died. It was a terrible thing to say, but it was true, wasn't it? Her mother had changed then, with a deep contentment in her widow's face that had never been there when she was a wife. With no disrespect to her father, Margaret had been glad to find a well-mannered man like Douglas, with his freshly pressed shirts and shiny shoes.

He had seen her at the Methodist picnic on Toronto Island and asked her brother, Rory, with whom he'd played a game of horseshoes, to introduce them. It was three months after John Carlisle had left for New York. Douglas seemed so refined, so unruffled, standing there in his straw hat, looking down at her. She now believed his calm masked an unmasculine timidity. He'd been thirty years old then, a whole decade older than she, and she found this reassuring. Surely a man, full-grown and responsible, with his own business, would never just up and leave. He had not been to war (an honour he said he was swindled out of by virtue of his age), and so did not wrestle with John's demons. She became engaged to Douglas six months later, although she had to admit that she hadn't taken the engagement altogether seriously.

"Don't mess with his feelings," Rory had said. "He's a nice guy."

"Of course he's nice. How can you think such a thing of me?" she'd protested. But in truth, she thought she'd stay with Douglas just until John returned. She planned to make John suffer a little, as he'd made her suffer. Then she would forgive him, and with deep regret, but with good reason (for hadn't John pledged his undying love for her first?), she would end her engagement to Douglas and things would go back to their proper place. But John Carlisle never did return.

Back in the spring of 1918, with the war raging in Europe, the world had seemed to offer so little promise or hope. So she walked down the aisle, wearing her cream silk gown, and beamed at Douglas. The war would end one day. They'd have a good life. He was kind and tall, with all that wavy brown hair and a soft moustache. She couldn't wait to see what he'd do once the relatives were gone and the lights were low and there was no longer any reason for him to be so careful of her. She thought he would shrug off the polite displays of gentlemanly behaviour and press her body to his the way that John had done, with a demanding knee between her thighs and his hand on her throat.

After the blur of the reception they arrived at the Queen Anne Hotel and went immediately to their room. The walls were pale blue and the carpet was ivory. Small cunning bunches of violets were woven through the bed's white canopy, and a gilt mirror hung from one wall. Margaret thought it the most elegant room she'd ever seen. Douglas uncorked a bottle of sparkling wine.

"Perhaps you'd like to get ready for bed now," he said at last, and his eyes were very bright. Margaret blushed, as was expected, and excused herself. In the bathroom she filled the tub and added fragrant oil. She lowered herself into the water, thinking of his hands on her hips. When she was done she smoothed scented cream into her skin and dabbed perfume behind her ears and between her breasts. She brushed her hair and slipped on the thin-strapped rose-coloured gown she had bought especially for tonight. Her breathing was shallow and her mouth was dry, but it was an exciting sort of fear.

She opened the door and stepped into the brightly lit room. She paused a moment so he could see her. How disappointed she had been to find him lying there, in his blue-striped pyjamas, with the covers pulled up to his chest. He had been reading a book.

"You look beautiful," he said. "Come here." He patted the side of the bed. She walked, feeling awkward. Douglas put out the light. She slipped beneath the cool, pressed sheets. He moved on top of her and pulled up her gown.

Afterwards, he'd asked, "Are you all right?" and patted her hair.

"Yes, I'm fine."

"I hope it didn't shock you. Did your mother talk to you?"

"I wasn't shocked, Douglas."

"Well, that's all right, then," he said. "I love you, Margaret." He put his arm around her and pulled her to his chest. She lay there, trying not to cry, while he fell into a loud and leaden sleep. When her arm became numb beneath her, she got up, went into the bathroom and washed her ruined nightgown in cold water, rinsing away the blood.

She spent the night in the armchair by the window, looking at the face of the man to whom she'd given her body and her future. In the morning she developed a headache and couldn't eat breakfast, preferring to lie quietly in the dark room while Douglas went down to the coffee shop alone. Over the eleven years of their marriage she'd come to rely upon the refuge of a silent, still room the way others relied on whisky, perhaps, or opium.

And so Margaret lay beneath her comforter now, a rattling bundle of irritable loneliness. The words from the newspaper accounts kept going through her head. *The market was completely demoralized ... Stocks were sacrificed ruthlessly ... Extreme declines ... Clients carrying cheques and cash in their hands to stave off ruin.* It shouldn't really matter to her—after all, they had no stocks, no bonds, no investments whatsoever. Douglas had been prudent. He was a deeply prudent man. But there was still a sense of ruin. She clenched her hands until the red moons of her fingernails left crescents on her palms.

The problem was that big things were happening in the world, and she was not a part of them. She felt that some great chance had been missed, for fortune or for failure, it hardly mattered. She'd felt it for weeks now, this itch of discontent. A shiver of something angry twitched at her body from her toes to her teeth.

3

April 1930

Homewood was a quiet, well-tended street. Although it was mostly a street of modest homes, boasting gardens of zinnias and marigolds and climbing-rose vines, there were several modern apartment buildings. Margaret did not approve of the apartments, nor their residents, single men and women, newlyweds, the elderly, and families too poor to afford a house.

Children played double dutch and telephone, using two tin cans and a length of string, while their mothers chatted with the fruit man who came by twice a week with his horse and cart, or the knife sharpener with his grinding wheel that sent out sparks. The women swapped recipes for angel food cake and jellied salads the way the children swapped the miniature playing cards that came in Turret cigarette boxes.

The residents bragged that Dr. Banting, the discoverer of insulin, had lived on the street as a boy. Dr. Banting, of course, had moved to a more fashionable district long ago, but still, they prided themselves on this badge of gentility, particularly now, when hope of moving off to Forest Hill or Rosedale seemed very slim indeed. Some of the families, such as the Gardners at number 19, the Lambies at number 25 and the Cantwells at number 36, had taken in boarders. The family who used to live in number 9 had moved out and the house was now carved up into four apartments, two of which were occupied by single men.

Still, the MacNeils' old neighbours were largely unchanged, although they were all feeling the pinch. The Steedmans, with two small boys; Mrs. Annie Dixon, a retired schoolteacher who'd lived on the street alone as long as anyone could remember. There were the Whartons, who had immigrated from England, the MacKays, the Boyers and the MacIntyres. All good Anglo-Saxon stock, most with a trace of Scottish in their backgrounds, a love of the King and a good cup of tea with toast. And there was Mr. Rhodes, who owned the butcher's across from Douglas's pharmacy, his overblown wife who had a hunger for gossip, and four noisy teenagers, three girls and a boy.

Inside the MacNeil house, at number 51, Margaret pored over news stories of unemployment and unrest from both near and far. In India, the nationalist leader Mahatma Gandhi opened a civil disobedience campaign by leading the Salt March, to protest the levying of a salt tax on poor people. In Columbus, Ohio, a fire killed 318 inmates at the state penitentiary, which was nearly two hundred percent over capacity. Margaret sat with her ear next to the radio as the voices spoke about the prairies drying up and blowing away and industry shutting the factory doors, leaving thousands to get by as best they could, living off their savings or their relatives if they were lucky, on the street if they weren't.

She sometimes sat for hours, her dust cloth in hand, rereading the paper. All across Canada manufacturing plants closed and men wandered the streets in rising numbers. Construction, in the middle of a boom just a year before, came to a complete halt. As the country grew more despairing and more desperate, Margaret kept pace. Like the winds on the drought-ridden prairie, Margaret's depression was invisible, guileful and exhausting. She began to scratch the back of her hands until they were red, and when Douglas told her to stop it, for it annoyed him, she looked at him blankly, and then at the back of her wounded hands, as though she had no idea where the marks might have come from. Her speech became peppered with negatives. Douglas teased her, called her Cassandra, prophetess of gloom, but no one laughed.

With every plant closing, with every layoff, she hoarded more food. When the massive layoffs came to the mechanics in Windsor, she put up cans of everything from tomatoes to plums. She was convinced that soon they would starve. She went to sleep grinding her teeth and woke up wringing her hands.

Irene came home for lunch one day and couldn't open the door. Puzzled, she rang the bell.

"You locked the door," she said to her mother when she opened it.

"And it'll stay locked from now on," said Margaret.

"Why? We don't lock our doors."

"There was a tramp at the door last week, and this morning I found another hanging around the back. It's not safe anymore."

"I'll have my own key, then?" asked Irene.

"No need for you to have a key. I'm always here, aren't I?"

Several weeks later Margaret drew all the downstairs curtains, saying she didn't want the men who came looking for handouts peeping in and spying on her. A few days after, the upstairs curtains were closed as well. Irene was confused at these precautions because none of her friends' houses were locked up this way, but when she asked her father about it, he simply said, "I'm sure your mother has good reason."

Irene was frightened by the strange woman who had come to take her mother's place, who looked like her mother but behaved so oddly. She hoped her father was right. She pictured her mother's depression like a shadowy fog that slipped around doorways and through plaster cracks and along the pipes. She couldn't escape it, and it made everything too close, too blurry. *Where did one person end and the other begin?*

"The neighbourhood's going downhill," Margaret said to Irene one Sunday in April. "I worry about you. I don't want anything to happen to you."

"What do you mean?" Irene said. "I don't understand."

"You don't have to understand," said Margaret. "You will stay home, where I can keep an eye on you."

When Irene looking pleadingly at her father, he only buried his head in the *Globe* and said nothing.

"Daddy ..." Irene stage-whispered. "Pleeease ..."

"Didn't Grandma send you a new *Girl's Own Annual?*" Douglas's parents had taken it into their heads last year to return to Scotland, and had sent Irene the book for her birthday.

"But, Daddy." Irene came to the side of his chair and clasped her hands under her chin. "It's so nice out. You always say I should be out in the sunshine, don't you?"

"Douglas!" Margaret hissed through gritted teeth. "Don't you dare undermine my authority. She's only playing us one off against the other."

"Now, Irene, you can't have looked all through your annual."

"I've read it all." She pouted, and then her face lit up again. "Checkers! Play checkers with me, Daddy."

"Maybe later, Pet."

Irene moaned and shuffled away to her room, dragging her feet in an exaggerated way. Douglas had begun to loathe Sundays, when he was stuck in the house. You could do nothing on Sundays in Toronto. Couldn't even buy a box of chocolates, let alone a bottle of beer.

He went out to the shed, where he kept a dusty bottle of whisky hidden behind the clay pots and rat poison. He took a good long swig. The whisky loosened the knot in his stomach. He lit a cigarette and leaned back on the doorjamb. Was it any wonder he'd begun to stay away from the house, preferring at the end of the business day to visit the Rupert Hotel at Queen and Parliament? There in a quiet booth a man could drink a beer and read his paper, or talk to his friends in peace. No women were allowed in the Rupert Hotel bar.

He was thinking how good a beer would taste just now and wondering if he could risk slipping out for an hour or two, when he noticed Irene looking out from her bedroom window; she looked as mournful as any kid ever had, cooped up on a fine day like this. Poor little mouse, he thought. But he didn't think it would hurt her to stay home and keep her mother company.

As he was looking up at the window, Margaret came out the back door.

"Douglas. Douglas." Her voice was small again. "I'm so sorry."

She came down the steps and across the garden to him. Her arms were held out and her head was tucked up to one side. Her face was tear-streaked. She put her arms around his neck and pressed herself against him.

"I don't know why I get so scared."

"I don't know why you do either."

"You'll take care of us, won't you?"

"Of course I will."

"I know you will. We're going to be all right."

"We're going to be fine, my dear."

"Do you love me?" Her lips pressed against his neck and he could feel the heat coming off her.

"I love you."

"I love you, too, Douglas, I do. You know I do."

"Of course you do."

Her display of affection and need, so raw, and out here where the neighbours could see them, made him uncomfortable. But he also felt himself harden inside his trousers. He drew her hands away from his neck and held them down at his side.

"Will you come inside?" said Margaret. "I'll make tea. Scones. With currants, just as you like."

"I was thinking I'd go for a walk."

Margaret felt the tears coming again. She did not want him to go for a walk. She wanted him to stay and have tea and they would be a family and she would be a gracious wife and he would see that and not disapprove of her. But there was no way to insist without being exactly what she did not want to be. The sour taste of resentment made its way up into her mouth.

"I could come with you," she said and was a little surprised to hear herself.

"Come with me?" Douglas said as though it was an odd idea. "Do you want to?"

"Yes," she said, and stood up straight. She would go for a walk, like any other woman, with her arm linked through her husband's, and they would talk of pleasant things and he would tip his hat at the neighbours. But her hair was a mess, and the neighbours would gawk and ask where she'd been and why didn't they see her these days, and she would have nothing to say. And there was the canning. It was so important to have enough food. She was tired then, thinking of all the things she had to do, and the idea of walking out on the busy streets made her heart beat a little too quickly.

"No," she said, her shoulders slumping. "I don't suppose I should go. But don't be long, will you? I'll be making supper soon."

"I won't be long," Douglas said, and tried not to sound relieved. He looked up again and saw Irene watching them. "Why not have tea with Irene?"

"We'll wait for you," Margaret said.

"As you like, my dear." He kissed her cheek. She smiled up at him, just as she should. He waved at Irene and told himself it would be just a short, quick walk, and his two girls would be fine together.

He lifted the latch on the back gate, stepped out into the alley and started toward Carlton Street. The Rupert was not open for business on a Sunday, but there was always a place or two in Cabbagetown where if a man knew the right people he could get something with which to wet his whistle.

A week later Irene had a nightmare. She was in the yard of a house where she shouldn't be, although she'd lived there once. It was an empty white house, filled with the kind of silence that made you think someone waited behind the door to jump out at you. She had to get out before anybody caught her, and she started to run up a great snow hill. She hadn't taken more than five or six steps when the crust broke and she plunged into a hole. She stopped, but could feel nothing below her but soft snow that could give at any moment. Her hands were trapped at her sides, and the daylight, the lip of the hole, was such a long way above her head. Someone was out there and she called softly, afraid if she filled her lungs to scream that she would push the snow aside and tumble down into the middle of the earth, or else the snow would fall in and she would suffocate. She whispered a thin "Help me!" A face appeared at the top of the hole, silhouetted against the unforgiving blue sky. It was her father's face, yet she was not reassured, for she couldn't tell from the look on his face if he had any interest in rescuing her.

She woke up crying, but she did not cry out. It was the first time she had not called for her parents after a nightmare. Soon she fell asleep again, and when she woke to the morning sound of sparrows in the hedge, she had no recollection of the dream.

1930

Just outside of Estevan, David runs alongside the moving train. His feet slip and twist on the gravel. He hears a voice hollering and looks up. A face, and hands reach out for him, and with a final burst of speed, muscles nearly snapping, he grabs for them and jumps. For a moment he dangles, legs dangerously near the churning wheels, and then, with a rasp of wood along stomach, he is in the car.

"Come on, young fella, you're all right now." The man is maybe thirty, maybe fifty, his face stamped with sleeplessness and hunger. He wears a cap low over his eyes and a lumber jacket that smells of wood smoke and long wear.

The boxcar is clotted with shadows, and his eyes will not adjust. He feels blind and a little dizzy. He lies gasping on the wooden boards, hugging his pack, too winded to say thank you.

"First time?" says the man after a few minutes.

He nods, swallowing hard. The man's voice is low and sounds kind.

"You gotta grab the ladder, boy, don't try and jump in an open door. You'll slip that way, lose a leg if you're not careful. What's your name?"

He tells the man and as he does his voice cracks.

Laughter comes from a pitch-dark space in the corner. He turns toward it, but can make out only a blacker shadow within the first one.

"Christ, how old are you?" This voice does not sound as kind.

"Old enough to take care of myself."

"Sure you are, son," says the man who'd hauled him through the door. He holds out his hand. "My name's Jim. That's Fred in the back there. We travel together. You just leave home?"

The hurt of it is still inside him. He had not told his father he was leaving. Could not bear seeing how his parting would add to the old man's worries, seeing new lines corrode his vein-threaded cheeks. His father spoke so little these days, just raked his fingers through his whitened beard, looked at the sky, rubbed earth between his fingers and shook his head. But staying meant worries, too. With Toba and the new baby and *no money to build another room. Jacob had now found a girl and would marry in the autumn. His father could move to the loft, but the boy would have to move to the barn. He'd told his brothers of his plans, and they promised to give his letter to their father after he was gone. He would be back, he vowed, and with some money in his pocket. He'd hire out as a hand for the season and return in fall, in time for harvest. Isaac squinted up into the cloudless, rainless blue and then spit on the ground. His brothers said there was nothing out there, shuffled their big feet in the dirt, but didn't try to stop him. They knew a bad year was coming. They knew they might be hard pressed to feed all these mouths. And they understood the road-lust. They'd never gone farther than Estevan, and he could see his own restlessness mirrored in their eyes.*

"Yeah, left a couple of days ago." *He shakes the man's hand. The grate of callus against callus.*

"Where's home?"

"Not far from here."

"Farmer?"

He says he was, and the man nods as though this explains everything. They are from Winnipeg themselves, they say, and warn him there is no work to be found in the cities.

"I'm gonna find work," *says the boy, and the man in the shadows laughs again.*

"Ain't we all," *he mutters.*

"Never mind, Fred. He's just out of sorts 'cause we ain't eaten much lately."

"I got a loaf of bread in my pack."

"We'd be obliged," *says Jim.*

The man named Fred steps out of the shadows. He is bigger than he'd seemed and his face is covered with pockmarks. One arm of his jacket is pinned up and empty. He stands too close and makes David uncomfortable. He can smell the sweetish, unwashed scent of him.

"I'd say you're no more than fourteen, boy," *he says.* "Young and pretty."

"Leave him alone, Fred. He's just a kid."

Jim puts his arm around David's shoulder and says, "Let's just take a look at what all you've got in there, son." *Then he takes hold of the pack.*

For a second they are both holding it, then Jim's arm grows tighter around his shoulder and the man begins to turn him toward the open door. The train has picked up speed and the ground is a blur.

"Nothing in here can be that important, now, can it?" Jim says, and Fred moves to the boy's other side.

He lets go. The two men kneel down and rummage in the knapsack.

"Well, looky here," says Fred. "Mama put a right nice parcel together. Cheese and bread and clean shorts and all. Bet she even told you to keep your money in your boot, now, didn't she?"

"That true, son?" says Jim.

Jim holds him down while Fred strips off his boots.

"My, my, my," says Jim. "There's five dollars here. We can't let you walk around with that in your boot. You might get a blister."

Fred laughs and bites into a hunk of cheese.

"You bastards," David hisses.

"Ah, now he don't like us anymore. And after you helped him up into the car and all. That's gratitude for ya."

"Guess you won't want to stay, then," says Jim.

The train comes to a bend and there is a long slope outside the door. As it slows down a little, they push him out. He lands on his shoulder and rolls. As he scrambles upright, tears streaming down his face, they throw out the half-empty pack and his boots.

He wants to go home then, but knows he will not. He knows this is the way the world is. He understands there will be many more moments like this one, when he will be aching for his brothers and for his own bed and the hay-sweet smell of the barn and the sound of the dog barking and the feel of his father's hand on the back of his neck and the lull of his father saying a blessing over the bread.

It begins to drizzle.

He limps down the line and picks up his boots and pack. He wipes the tears away with the back of his hand, leaving a smear of blood on his cheek. And to think he'd laughed at Isaac, who had insisted he pin two one-dollar bills in his shorts.

4

May 1930

It was Sunday afternoon, and Rory Cameron, Margaret's younger brother, sat on the porch with Douglas, while Irene and her mother made supper. Douglas sat on an old cane chair that he meant to repaint someday. Rory sat on the top step, his back resting against the support post. Rory had a wide forehead and thick hair that came to a widow's peak in the middle. He was dark-haired and blue-eyed, like his sister, but where she was pale as watered milk, his skin was ruddy, with the early evidence of lines around his eyes.

It was a warm day, thick with the smells of melting snow and the winter's debris that lay beneath.

"How are things going down at the factory?" said Douglas as he sipped his whisky.

"Not so good."

"Oh?"

"There's been some layoffs, and more to come." He took a long drink of beer.

"What about your job? Are you all right?"

"We'll see," Rory said. It was hard to explain, but he'd be almost relieved to find a pink slip waiting for him in his pay envelope. There were no other jobs to be had these days, but Rory didn't mind so much, if the truth be told. He hated the box factory. He hated the big building on King Street that looked more like a prison than a factory. He hated the enormous arm-eating machines, the noise, the poisoned fog of blue smoke that hung in the air, the acrid smell of the printers' ink. He hated seeing the children working there, no more than twelve some of them, working on "need permits," which meant the government recognized they had to support themselves. Rory's job was to feed cardboard flats into the jaws of one of the cutting machines and then to withdraw his hands before the press came down and pulled them in along with the paper. So far he'd been lucky, but the noise was deafening, and after only six months on the machines he had a ringing in his ears day and night. He worked from eight a.m. to five-thirty p.m. Monday to Saturday and earned ten dollars a week.

"What are you two talking about?"

Margaret stood in the doorway, wiping her hands on a red-and-yellow tea towel.

"Nothing, Peg, just moaning about the job." He didn't want to say more to her about his troubles. He could see the signs of strain in her face, the circles under her eyes.

"There have been layoffs," said Douglas.

"You're not going to lose your job!"

"Mum, what is it?" Irene peeked out from behind her mother.

The look on her face was so much like her mother's, thought Rory. His sister clutched the girl to her, in a gesture more dramatic than he thought necessary, and Irene stiffened, not pulling away but not clinging to her mother either.

"Now, Peg, it's all right. I won't lose my job." Rory hated it when his sister got like this; there was something selfish about the level of worry, like she wanted everyone to stop their own worrying and console her.

"What would you do if you lost your job? You'd have to move in here. How would we cope?"

"I haven't lost my job, for Christ's sake!"

"But you could, anyone could!"

He thought this would be a perfect time for Douglas to do something, but Douglas never seemed to do anything. Rory stood up and went over to hug his sister. Irene scuttled out from the embrace like a mouse narrowly escaping a trap.

Margaret clung to him for a moment, then stepped back. The angry look on her face surprised him. Her moods changed so quickly these days. She'd always been prone to fits of temper, even when they were children. He used to find it sort of funny, even though he had a bit of a hair-trigger himself. But he didn't think it was so funny now. She went back inside the house and

Irene followed her. Rory looked toward Douglas, but he was staring down into his glass.

As Irene left the house one morning a few weeks later, her mother's commands rang in her ears.

"You come straight home from school, do you hear me?" Margaret stood in the kitchen doorway, a copy of *Ladies' Home Journal* in one hand and a cup of coffee in the other.

"But Mummy ..." Irene would have stamped her foot had she not known it would lead to a smack on the bottom.

"Don't *but Mummy* me. You're too cheeky by far these days, my girl. If I tell you to do something, you do it."

"Yes, Mummy." Irene slipped on her plaid jacket and did up the toggle buttons.

"I won't have you out there with those ragamuffins. You are not to go to the lot. No baseball. Understand?"

"Yes, Mummy."

"Good. Now get along, you'll be late. And give me a kiss."

Irene trudged to school on the verge of tears. Something was wrong and nobody would tell her anything. How could her father say to go along with it for just a little while? A little while? It had been months and months and forever. It was so unfair. Something was changing.

Irene knew she was changing, and this was a strange thing to know. As her mother became more and more nervous, as her father referred to it, Irene became very good at several things. She made a list of them as she walked along. She was good at being small. At being quiet. And it was as though she had another set of eyes and ears, attuned to things outside the range of normal seeing and hearing. Like cats who could see ghosts or dogs that could hear whistles too high-pitched for humans. She was getting very good at being able to detect, from even the smallest signals, what sort of mood her mother was in. Because she wasn't always unhappy. She wasn't always mean. Sometimes she laughed and laughed and wanted to dance to jazz music on the radio. But when she was nervous it was important to know as quickly as possible, so that Irene could adjust herself accordingly.

Irene also knew that she must not speak to her friends about what was the matter at home, because, as her father kept telling her, nothing whatsoever *was* the matter. He'd made that very clear. Should anyone ask, nothing was wrong.

"There ain't nothing wrong with Mrs. MacNeil no way," said Jimmy Thompson, who tried to sound tough. He wore the same grey flannel pants and navy blazer as the other boys, but his trousers had a torn knee and there was a smear of jam on his jacket. There were rumours about what Jimmy's father did for a living. Some said he was a bootlegger, but most agreed he ran an illegal gambling operation. These things gave Jimmy Thompson a certain mystery and authority. "Nothing wrong in her body anyways. She's just nuts. Me and Charlie saw her burying something out in the garden late one night. I swear it to God."

"Don't swear, Jimmy, it isn't nice," said Violet, who always wore something to match her name. Today it was ribbons tied at the end of her thick brown braids.

"I bet it was a body," piped up Charlie, Jimmy's younger brother. They had the same freckled faces and might have been gap-toothed twins except that Charlie was so much smaller.

"Wasn't big enough," said Jimmy as he picked his grimy fingernails with a pocketknife. "I'll bet it was a box of money."

"Coulda been a baby," insisted Charlie, thrilled at the horror of it.

"What were you two doing out at night?" said Ebbie Watkins. "You live over on Prospect Street, you can't see Irene's yard from your house, and besides, your mother makes you go to bed at eight."

"We can get out if we want to. My mother don't have to know everything."

"Oh, you're just telling tales, Jimmy Thompson. You don't know anything about Mrs. MacNeil."

"I know that lady's crazy. My ma says so."

And nobody said much after that, because it was true that Irene's mother was different. It used to be that she would send out pitchers of lemonade to them as they roller-skated up and down the street on a hot day, or call them in for chocolate after they'd come back, half frozen and blue, from skating on the rink set up every year in the Allen Gardens. Now she wouldn't even let Irene out to play baseball. Their mothers told them not to talk about it, held their fingers to their lips and shook their heads, with a pitying sort of look on their faces.

Ebbie Watkins was Irene's best friend. Ebbie was tall for eleven, with curly hair so blond it was almost white and lashes and eyebrows that might just as well not have been there at all. Her skin was pale and her eyes protruded slightly, so that Irene's mother said she looked like a partly skinned rabbit. Irene didn't think it was nice of her mother to say such things about Ebbie. Had Irene said them herself, her mother would have given her a swat and a lecture about kindness to others. What Ebbie lacked in pretty, however, she made up for in smart.

As Irene rounded the last corner in front of Winchester Public School, Ebbie ran up behind her and jumped the last step almost on Irene's heels.

"Boo!" she yelled.

"Oh! You scared me half to death, Ebbie!"

"You looked like you were a thousand miles away." Ebbie's laugh was always a surprise. "What's the matter?"

"Nothing."

"Your mother not getting any better? I know maybe I shouldn't ask. Everyone says I shouldn't. Well, not everyone, it's not like everyone's talking or anything, but my mother says ... Oh, you know what I mean. But we're friends and all, so ... Whatever is wrong with her, anyway?"

"Nothing's wrong with her," said Irene, but seeing Ebbie's

eyes widen skeptically, she added, "Not really. Daddy says her nerves are bad and she's fragile. It's a sign of good breeding, you know." She paused and thought. "My mother's got awfully good breeding."

"Can you come over? My mother always asks why you don't come over anymore. She thinks you don't like me anymore, for heaven's sake." Ebbie pushed out her large lower lip in a mock sulk.

"You know that's not true, Ebbie! You are absolutely, positively my best friend!"

"Good, so come. Why not this Friday? We can have a sleep-over."

"I'll ask. I don't know, but I'll ask. I'd like that so much." Irene thought how her parents were always fighting now. She thought about her mother complaining the house was too small for the three of them. And so maybe, maybe, her mother would let her go. "She'll say yes, I'm sure she will. I'm positively sure."

Irene and Ebbie went the rest of the way to school together with their arms wrapped around each other, looking forward to that Friday, planning what they would eat and what radio programs they'd listen to.

5

Margaret passed the morning sitting in the living room. She could not rouse herself, although there were a million things to do. Beds to make. Laundry to fold. Dusting. Sweeping. Cooking. She kept saying, over and over, "Now, get up now. I will count to three and then I will get up. One, two, three." And then, nothing.

She saw her reflection in the mirror above the fireplace. Her eyes were wide and wild, her hair a mess, her knuckles in her mouth. She looked like crazy Mrs. Rochester, ready to set fire to the world, ready to be locked in the tower and replaced by Jane Eyre.

At last she walked toward this image. She leaned her elbows on the mantelpiece, pushing aside a purple porcelain dog whose hollowed-out stomach housed a wilting African violet. She put her hands on either side of her face and pulled back the skin. She stuck her tongue out and made a lizard face. Soon she would be old. All her chances at happiness seemed behind her. Before her the future loomed plain and comfortless.

If she could just find a point, a reason for her life. She had asked Reverend Fuller to see her after church yesterday. She thought surely he would be able to understand and offer her guidance. The Reverend was a huge heron of a man with a beaklike nose and thin lips. His hair was wiry and white, his skin laced with small red veins. His bony shoulders stuck up under the black material of his jacket, and his sleeves were too short. When she had asked for a few moments of his time, he smiled gently and told her to wait on his porch, next door to the church. Margaret did not want to wait there, in full view of the street. But she did as she was told.

"Masie," he called to his wife, "make Mrs. MacNeil comfortable, won't you, my dear. I shall be with her directly." Margaret refused the offer of tea and sat stiffly on the edge of the wicker chair. She told Irene to do the same.

"Stop fidgeting, Irene. Honestly!"

"But, Mummy, there's a piece of stick. It pinches." Irene was hot and miserable in her crinolines and hat and gloves.

"Shush. Be good. We won't be long." Margaret busied herself in her purse as a way of avoiding eye contact with other members of the congregation now on their way back home. The entire exercise of going to church was frightening. All those faces, all those well-meaning inquiries as to her health. She wouldn't go except she fervently hoped that here she might find answers to the questions she didn't even know how to form.

Before long the Reverend finished shaking hands and accepting compliments on his sermon. He approached her, his black Bible tucked under his arm.

"And now, Mrs. MacNeil, you have my full attention," he said

29

and led her to his office at the back of the house. She told Irene to wait outside.

His office was small. Just a desk, with a chair behind and one in front, where he indicated she should sit. Books lay everywhere and a cup half-full of cold scummy tea sat on his desk. Another cup rested on the floor, and yet another on a small table near the window. The Reverend Fuller perched on the side of the desk, facing her. He smelled of camphor.

There was so much of him, all height and limbs. The room seemed too intimate, like a closet in which they were hiding together.

"Now, what can I do for you, Mrs. MacNeil?"

"I need your help, Reverend. I'm not myself these days." She twisted the strap of her brown leather purse. How to phrase it so he understood?

"Well, these are difficult times." He held his head down, not looking at her directly, as though he were a priest and she a confessor. It made her fear he might not grant her absolution.

"It's just that I can't pull myself together. My head goes round and round with the strangest thoughts. Dark thoughts. I can't seem to stop worrying."

"We all have our worries."

"I find myself overcome with them, very nearly. Like I'm drowning."

"What do you worry about?"

"Well, the sorts of things that everyone worries about these days. Money, shelter, poverty, destitution, starvation." She heard a noise. Was he laughing at her? He must not be laughing at her! She couldn't bear that. Her palms were sweating, and her thighs stuck to each other.

The Reverend blew his nose with a handkerchief that was none too clean.

"Things are not that bad, surely? We must trust in the Lord. He will provide. Have faith, Mrs. MacNeil."

"I do try, Reverend."

"Of course you do, dear lady." He patted her shoulder. Then he turned his face toward the ceiling and began to recite. "'Be patient therefore, brethren, unto the coming of the Lord.' James 5, verse 7."

"I try to be patient, but I'm not, mostly. I can be"—she paused, unsure if she should continue—"peevish."

"Ah," he said, and looked severe.

"I do try. It's just that … sometimes … " She wanted to tell him about how lost she felt, how she knew the world was passing her by, how she was entombed in that little house.

"Yes?"

The conversation was not going the way Margaret wanted it to. She had hoped for solace, for comfort, perhaps even for a shoulder to cry on, just a little. She had taken such a risk coming here, telling him her secrets, but perhaps she hadn't told him enough.

"I can be impatient, irritable with Douglas, my husband."

"Does he beat you?"

"Heavens, Reverend! No, of course not." His voice, his big, sonorous voice, was terrifying.

"Does he commit adultery?"

"No, no, nothing like that." Margaret felt a little dizzy and couldn't catch her breath.

"Does he drink?"

"Well, yes, sometimes he does." There was that, at least. Surely now he would soften toward her, drop his disapproving stare.

"I see. Well, although alcohol's the Devil's cordial, I don't think your husband is an evil man, Mrs. MacNeil. It's your duty as a Christian wife to obey him and create a place for Jesus in your heart and home. Your husband is in danger, but that is our responsibility, is it not? To bring in the lost sheep? Impress upon him the importance of God in his life. Impress upon him the benefits of living his life within the boundaries of the Church. You must bring him into the fold."

"Douglas will never come to church. He's not that kind of man."

"Still, he is your husband and you must never stop trying. I believe you understand, Mrs. MacNeil. I will remember you in my prayers."

And with that she knew she was dismissed. Almost on cue, the minister's wife popped open the study door, and Margaret realized with horror that she had been eavesdropping. As she stumbled blindly to the front door her mind conjured pictures of the minister and his pigeon wife chirping with laughter at her as they sipped their tea. Back on the porch, her face burning, Margaret grabbed Irene by the arm and yanked her down the steps. It was only when the girl cried out that Margaret realized how tightly she was holding her. The red marks of her fingers were clearly visible on Irene's wrist. She knelt down on the sidewalk and hugged her and murmured, "I'm sorry, so sorry" until they both believed it. The pebbles under her legs cut into her painfully and this was just as she deserved. She ground her knees this way and that. When she stood, blood dribbled down her legs, and the little pieces of stone that had torn her stockings were embedded in her skin.

How hard she had prayed that night, to keep her faith, to hear some small voice of reassurance, but her words fell lifeless from her lips. It must be her fault. Reverend Fuller was a man of God, after all. Her rage and unkind thoughts had been no more than hurt pride. What had she expected him to say? She knew Reverend Fuller was right. She must try harder. She must be a better wife, a better mother, a better Christian.

But why should she? Ah, there was the voice again, the small nagging voice behind her left ear, always ready to whisper evil thoughts in her head, always ready to argue. Why humiliate herself in front of a man who was convinced of his own superiority with no evidence to support it except a black suit and a white collar? Surely that was no sign of divine inspiration. And so the question repeated itself. Why? Why get out of bed? Why get dressed? Why bother at all? And on days like this, days that stripped off her flesh and left her exposed, a throbbing burst of nerve endings in a needle storm, on days like this, she agreed. Why bother?

She could have sworn she heard laughter, a dry rasping giggle from a corner somewhere. She wanted to slap someone, to feel the solid crack of flesh on flesh. She pressed the heels of her hands into her eye sockets. *Crazy, I'm going crazy ...*

6

Irene took her time getting home for lunch, even though there was a chilly, persistent drizzle and she had no umbrella. Rainwater trickled down the back of her neck so that her arms broke out in goose bumps. As she walked she mapped out a strategy for asking her mother if she could stay overnight at Ebbie's.

She scuffed her shoes in the puddles and last year's leaves clumped up by the sewer. She walked heel to toe. *Step on a crack, break your mother's back,* she thought as she carefully avoided the fissures in the sidewalk.

The problem was complex. Should she ask directly, as though it was the most normal thing in the world? Should she try to provoke her mother into saying what a bother she was, and then offer to go to Ebbie's for the night? She didn't think that would be very hard. But then her mother might also be angry and say no to punish her. She thought of approaching her father first, but her father was never around these days. Perhaps Mrs. Watkins should call? No, that would only annoy her mother. Why did everything have to be so complicated?

She looked up and found herself in front of the house.

She stood at the door and chewed her thumb. She checked under the flowerpot for the key. Nothing. Irene hugged her history book tightly and thought. Perhaps she should wait for another day. She strained to hear sounds inside the house. You could tell a great deal from sounds. If the radio was on, that was a good sign. If the record player was playing Cole Porter, that was even better, unless it was "Love for Sale," which was bad. The smell of cooking was also good. Now the house was silent, and the only smell was the floury scent of paste from her own notebook. The curtains to her parents' bedroom on the second floor were pulled open, though, and that was a good sign. Maybe her mother was in the back garden. That would be good too.

She couldn't stand on the front step forever. The neighbours might see her and wonder what was wrong. She tried the doorknob just in case, just on the off chance it might be open. It didn't budge. There was no choice. She rang the bell.

It took what seemed like forever for the sound of her mother's footsteps to reach her. They were the wrong footsteps. Her mother was wearing her tired old leather slippers. They made an uncaring *slap, slap, slap* on the floor.

The door opened. Margaret wore her plain brown button-up-the-front housedress. Irene knew she wore it only when she didn't care what she looked like. Maybe she'd been cleaning? Sometimes she wore it for buffing the floors or cleaning cupboards. But she had a coffee mug in one hand and no rag, so that didn't seem likely. Her mother's hair had not been washed yet this week and she hadn't bothered to put it in pincurls last night and so it was lank and flat on one side.

"Hi," said Irene.

Margaret looked down at her for a moment, took a sip from the mug and without saying a word disappeared back into the dark house. Irene stepped in and closed the door behind her.

She walked along the hall into the kitchen and sat at the table, swinging her legs but being careful not to make any noise by banging the chrome. Her mother stood at the counter. She picked her cigarette up from the heavy glass ashtray and inhaled deeply, her eyes narrowing against the smoke. Through this veil she looked steadily at her daughter, as though trying to form a conclusion. Irene studied the hem of her tunic, waiting.

Margaret turned her back to Irene and opened the icebox to get a bottle of milk. Irene watched her. You could tell a lot of things by how loudly doors were closed, by how carefully things were placed on a counter. Margaret cut up a tomato, slopped butter onto bread and made a careless sandwich. After pouring milk into a glass, she put the milk bottle back in the icebox. She closed the door and leaned her head against the cool surface. Irene could not see her face, but noticed the jerky movements in her shoulders, as she was meant to. Then Margaret turned back and looked straight at Irene, knowing Irene would be watching her.

Margaret was crying. She rubbed at her nose and then wiped her hand on the seat of her housedress. She looked at Irene as though daring her to speak. Irene hated this part, when the charge built like a thunderstorm coming until you could almost see sparks on the end of your fingertips.

Her mother picked up her coffee mug and drank. She picked up the cigarette and took another puff. Then she threw the cigarette toward the ashtray. It landed on the counter and rolled onto the floor.

"I can*not* take this *any*more!" she cried. Her hands knotted in her hair. Her voice was that of a seagull shrieking into the wind.

Irene's heart was pounding. She quickly picked up the fallen cigarette and placed it carefully in the ashtray.

"I don't want *that!*"

Margaret snatched it up and threw it in the sink. Then she grabbed the ashtray and tossed it in the sink, too, where it shattered.

Irene's hands pulled up instinctively to her heart in small fists. "Are you all right, Mummy?"

"What the hell do you care. What does anybody care." Margaret slammed the plate with the sandwich on it in front of Irene. "Eat your sandwich. I made it for you. I'd never expect *you* to make your own lunch. I have to do everything."

Irene hated tomato sandwiches. The bread got all wet with tomato juice. She took tiny bites.

"What are you staring at? What are you *staring* at?"

"Nothing," Irene mumbled and lowered her eyes.

"He drinks, you know, your precious father." Her voice rose to a scream and her hands were back in her hair, pulling and tearing. "Weak and dirty, the bastard! Weak and dirty!"

Irene sat very still, while Margaret took another gulp from the mug.

"Well, cheers! This stuff's not so bad, after all. I might as well join him. That'd be a fine how-dee-do, wouldn't it? Both of us drunkards. If he doesn't care, why should I?" Margaret leaned forward. "Or maybe I'll kill myself. Then *he* can take care of you."

Irene tried to eat a little more of the sandwich and kept her eyes on her mother's hands, paying attention to what items were within reach. A wooden spoon. A plate. The bread knife.

Margaret sat down at the table across from Irene, banging down the mug. Irene could smell the liquor in it. It was sweet and sour at the same time, smoky and medicinal, mixed with the scent of the tobacco.

"You know, if it wasn't for you I could be free," Margaret said. She leaned back in the chair, her chin tucked coyly into her shoulder, a slight smile on her lips. But the look on her face, this tense but teasing look, did not match her voice, which was full of jagged ups and downs and uncontrolled cracks. It sounded as if she might spit glass. "If it wasn't for you, I could be long gone."

Irene kept her head down and said nothing. Try as she might, she couldn't think of a single thing to say, and the kitchen pulsed with silence waiting to be broken.

"I want to ask you something, Irene. Look at me." The hysteria was replaced with a slightly taunting tone, cool and low.

Irene looked up, warily.

"I've been thinking. How would you feel about going into the orphanage? Maybe you'd like that. I've been thinking about it for a while and think it might just be for the best."

Irene felt all the blood rush into her face. Intuitively, she knew her mother would not send her to an orphanage, but she also knew her mother required something of her at this moment. She must respond to these words in a particular way, a way that showed she felt the same thing Margaret herself was feeling.

Their gazes met. Irene knew she would lose something if she let herself slip down this hole. She also knew that if she didn't jump herself that her mother would push until she fell. She put her head down on the table, resting her forehead on her fist. She could hear herself, as though it wasn't her at all, sobbing loudly. "I don't want to go away! Don't send me away!" Hiccups in the sobs. "Please don't make me go away!"

"Oh," Margaret said, and then again, "oh." She placed her hands flat on the top of the table as though she needed to feel the cool surface to tell her where she was.

"I'm sorry, darling," she said, and she came around the table and stroked Irene's head. "What am I thinking? Don't pay any attention to me. It's just that I'm so mad at your father, you just don't know. I wouldn't dream of sending you anywhere. You're mother's little kitten. I just thought you might be unhappy here. You know I want you to be happy, don't you? You know I love you?" She spoke quickly, the words so light they almost flew out of her mouth.

"I love you too, Mummy." Irene's breathing slowed. Her tears dried. "It'll be okay. It will be. We'll be okay."

"Sure, baby. You and me. We'll work it out somehow." Margaret smiled, that glorious gleaming smile. She slapped at her hands, shaking off crumbs or dirt that only she could see. "Now eat your lunch. You were so late getting in from school, it's almost time to go back."

Just before Irene left the house her mother came up behind her.

"Listen, Irene, you and I have our little secrets, don't we, even from your father?"

"Yes, Mummy."

"And we don't need strangers knowing about our business, do we?"

"No, Mummy."

"Good girl. You come straight home after school, now. No lollygagging."

Irene closed the door and heard the lock turn. She walked down the street, her tunic and hair still damp from her walk home. The sidewalk felt uneven beneath her feet, but she didn't mind going back, because she could stay at school until three-thirty. Of course, she'd have to tell Ebbie she wouldn't be able to come over on Friday. It was quite clear her mother needed her at home.

1930

No.

The word waits for David wherever he goes. No at the gate, no at the door, no at the path, the portal, the window. A thousand faces, a thousand inflections, but always the same word. No. And sorry. How sorry they all are, these people who will not give him work, will not give him shelter, will not give him food or warmth or hope or comfort.

The boy knows it isn't that they will not, it is that these people can not help him, and he sees by the look in their eyes that it shames them to have to say no.

Sometimes he gets lucky, though.

"Any work I can do for you today, ma'am?" he says as he stands on the porch of the house, his hat in his hand.

"No work today. Sorry."

"Chop wood? Fix the roof? I noticed you got a fence post tilting. Chicken roost looks like it leaks. I could fix that."

"Can't give you more'n dripping and bread."

"I'd be obliged, ma'am."

And if he does a good enough job, his head dizzy from hunger and his arms weak with fatigue, then maybe the woman will let him sleep in the shed or on the porch. He wakes up in so many different places that every time he opens his eyes he is surprised. It is hard, sometimes, to tell which is the dream and which the waking.

He grows to need things less. He pulls his belt tighter. Sleeps in the hobo jungles. Sleeps in ditches. Sleeps in the rail cars and the roofs of trains, tied down so he will not fall and be crushed beneath the steel wheels. He sleeps in barns and creeps away like a fox, with a chicken feather hanging from his cap, before first light.

If good fortune smiles, David sleeps on bedbug-infested mission cots, eats their watery soup and stale bread and is grateful for it.

"Are you saved, son? Are you a lamb of Jesus?" says the man in the uniform of Salvation's army.

"Yes, sir. I am tonight," he says.

He eats beans and bread and beans and ketchup and beans and beans from a hundred different relief houses. He learns to eat fast and as much as he can, as much as they will give him at one sitting, for he never knows when he will eat again. More than once he eats from trash cans behind restaurants, brushing away the flies from half-eaten baked potatoes and pork chop bones. His father will forgive him, he knows, but the disgrace in him is deep sometimes. Only the sight of other men forced by circumstance to live the same stray-cur life saves him from falling into the pit of wretchedness.

David has been on the road for five months. He has travelled east until the land touched the sea, and then turned and started back again. He thinks about going home, and then he passes through Manitoba. Sees the skeletal cattle, the skyscraper-tall clouds of dust, and he keeps on going west. He finds a letter waiting for him in Vancouver, general delivery, where he's written his family they might catch him. Standing in the park at the corner of Hastings and Hamilton, the West Coast sky hanging iron-heavy and the air thick with humidity, he keeps his back against a tree to protect the ink on the page from the relentless drizzle and lets the tears spill from his eyes. Isaac writes there is another baby on the way and the land is cracking, mottling the earth like the back of a dying sun-baked turtle. They do not ask him to come home but send their love. His father says be careful. Be a good boy. He feels the weight of love behind those words. They mean he carries his father's dreams with him. And his blessing.

He folds the letter and tucks it inside his shirt.

The park is full of men doing nothing, the occupation they all share. They stand and smoke and try to stay cool in the steaming shade. He has learned a great deal about men in the past months. How frightened they can be, and how fear can turn to rage in the time it takes to swallow a mouthful of moonshine. How kind they can be to strangers, and how cruel. He has learned a man can fall into depths of depravity if he is hounded by despair. Drugs. Alcohol. The infliction of pain on the weakest. He learns how despair follows shame, which in turn follows despair, and it is a drowning whirlpool.

The older men, who have known better, prouder times, are most shamed by their circumstances, he can see that. They stand with their heads hung low, or sit on the wet grass. A few drink from bottles wrapped in paper bags; a group talks in loud voices, cursing the rich, the cops, the politicians. Most just stand their ground, silent and brooding, thinking of home, perhaps, or food.

They stay together for one reason more than any other: the hope of hearing something. They follow the ripples of rumour. Have become disciples of hearsay. Hear a farm wants hands down the road. Might be some track to lay up north. A truck of lumber to unload. A tobacco field ripening. A factory needs a guy to replace the one that lost his arm. There's forest to clear up the coast. Hear they're hiring out in Kamloops, in Grassy Narrows, in Sioux Lookout, in Mississauga, in Lethbridge, in Truro, in St. John's. Once in a great many days it is whispered that a truck might pass by the park looking for a few strong men for a day's work. Three were taken last time, nearly one hundred are left behind, pleading and resentful in equal measure.

David stays two weeks, but no truck ever comes. There is talk of the coal mines. No one wants to go there. Only the desperate. He listens to the stories of cave-ins and company bulls and bad air and shakes his head. He tightens his belt again and prays he'll never be that desperate.

7

August 1930

It was a sticky-hot August and even the flies buzzed at the window-panes without much interest. A ceiling fan moved thick air around the small drug store. Douglas arranged the bottles carefully on wooden shelves behind the register. He liked to have things orderly. There was a music to symmetry. Blue bottles of Epsom salts and bromides, arranged tallest to tiniest. Green bottles of foot powder. Clear bottles of headache tablets. Dental cleansing powders in tall yellow tins and Dr. West's toothbrushes. Odorono deodorant. Ointments and salves in flat silver tins. Bottles of cough syrup and small vials of smelling salts. Under the counter rested the items of a more intimate nature. Prophylactics. Feminine cleansing apparatuses. In the back room narrow shelves were lined with prescriptive medicine.

Douglas polished a small amber bottle of antacid. He didn't like dust, believed it was a disease that must be battled the same way he battled coughs and rashes and boils and bad nerves. The notion of bad nerves led him, as so many things did these days, to troubling thoughts concerning Margaret. He had tried every remedy possible on Margaret and nothing worked. Women, he knew, were prone to hysteria, and needed a firm guiding hand, but the firmer he was, the more she retreated into her private world. And so he had tried kindness, cajolery, but she only smiled weakly and gazed at him blankly, as though he were a stranger.

He straightened a row of Mistol Rub, making sure the edges were exactly even. He said to himself that perhaps Margaret was getting better after all. It had been two months since the day he had come home and found her in inconsolable tears, vowing she would be a better, more understanding wife and pulling out hair from her head, one single strand at a time. It had taken hours to get her calmed down, and he had been forced to resort to laudanum. Still, that had been the last truly bizarre incident. And she had stopped the endless canning and preserving, which was good, since their cellar and garden shed were packed to the rafters with more food than they could eat in three years.

She hardly ever nagged him when he didn't come home on time these days. He would not go so far as to say she preferred it when he stayed away, but she did seem to have accepted that a man was entitled to his own life outside the home.

"Good morning, Mr. MacNeil."

Mrs. Watkins was standing before him, all teeth and good intentions. She gave off a scent of eagerness, a slightly powdery, freshly scrubbed smell.

"Good morning, Mrs. Watkins. How are you this fine bright morning?" Douglas unconsciously folded his arms across his chest.

"Oh, we're all well at our house. Melting a bit in this heat, but surviving. Ebbie, Izzy, Lisa, all growing by leaps and bounds. Just like weeds, those kids."

"Ah, that's fine, fine indeed."

"And how about Irene? I haven't seen her lately."

"No complaint there. Grades through the roof last term. Smart as a whip, and yes, as you say, growing like a little weed."

"I'm glad to hear it. I thought maybe she'd been ill."

"No, touch wood." He tapped the oak countertop. "No more than the sniffles now and then. A robust child."

Mrs. Watkins opened her purse and then shut it again, the clasp making a sharp little snapping sound. "We don't see Irene around much anymore. Ebbie invited her over several times, but it seems her mother's feeling a little low these days. I have tried to drop by, to see if there's anything I can do, of course, but perhaps she doesn't hear me knock."

Douglas noticed several of the magazines on the rack were improperly placed. The *Ladies' Home Journal* was upside-down and the edges turned back. He frowned. He must stop the neighbourhood boys from coming in and looking without buying. This was all they were after, pictures of ladies in their slips and girdles. Little imps.

"It's not anything serious, I hope," said Mrs. Watkins, leaning forward.

"Serious? Is what serious?"

"Why, Mrs. MacNeil's illness."

"Mrs. MacNeil is just a little tired, is all."

"What a shame. Perhaps I can bring her by a casserole?"

"Is there something I can get for you today, Mrs. Watkins? I have some of that lavender water you're so partial to."

"Oh. Well, yes, I suppose I could use a bottle of that. And a small tin of aspirin, Mr. MacNeil." She raised her plump hand to her throat. "I hope you don't think I'm prying. I'd never think of prying, as I'm sure you know. I'm the soul of discretion, my husband always says. A secret would go to the grave with me. But some of the ladies couldn't help but notice that your wife isn't as social as she once was, and little Irene, well, it's not healthy for a child to be in the house all the time, especially now, in the summer weather. Don't you agree, Mr. MacNeil? A child should be with other children ..."

"I'm sure you'd never dream of interfering, Mrs. Watkins." Douglas put her purchases in a paper bag.

"Never! Of course not!" Mrs. Watkins blushed deeply.

"I assure you, everything at my house is as it should be. Your concern is appreciated, but quite unnecessary. Quite unnecessary. That will be ninety cents, please." Douglas held out the bag, with his arm straight and firm. "I'm sure you'll excuse me—I have inventory to arrange in the stockroom. Good day to you."

"And to you. Please give my best to your wife," said Mrs. Watkins, but Douglas had already disappeared behind the heavy dark blue curtain.

Nosy old bitch. His hands were trembling slightly. Why did people have to stick their nose in? That was exactly the sort of talk that must be nipped in the bud. A medical man, such as himself, almost a physician really, must be seen to have a healthy and well-adjusted family. The community expected it.

Douglas heard a dignified and indignant snort from Mrs. Watkins and then the tinkle of the bell over the door. He reached behind the *Annual Pharmacists Reference* volumes and dabbled his fingers about until they settled on the smooth glass of the whisky bottle. As he unscrewed the lid, the peat and heather scent made him feel better immediately. He raised the bottle to his lips. Just a little toot. And another.

Margaret would snap out of it, as she always did, and there would follow a period of gaiety and good humour. Douglas treated himself to a wee nip more. She was not terribly ill. Everything at home would be just fine.

He pulled the day's newspaper off the shelf where he kept it for quiet moments such as these, first pouring himself a last drop into a small tin cup he kept handy.

The paper had been full of economic encouragement ever since July, when the Conservatives had won the federal election. R. B. Bennett was, in Douglas's opinion, an arrogant blowhard whose predictions concerning the imminent end of the Depression were nothing more than election rhetoric. He sighed, chuckled to think how some people couldn't see their own hands at the ends of their sleeves, and turned to the comics, eager to see what Moon Mullins was up to today.

Ebbie plunked herself down on the stoop and munched on an oatmeal cookie, not caring about the crumbs that dropped on her overalls. She had hoped that after her mother's talk with him, Mr. MacNeil would let Irene come over and play, and she was mightily disappointed in her mother's failure. Ebbie was not the most popular girl in school, or out of it for that matter. Summer vacation was half over, and without Irene, Ebbie was left out. It had been bad enough when school was still in session and Irene had to go home every day right after school, but at least they'd had classes together and recess. Irene had taught Ebbie how to skip double dutch. Without Irene she would have stayed under the elm tree, picking the scabs on her knee and chewing the ends of her hair. The kids never asked her to join in on anything. Only Irene asked her. Irene didn't care what the other kids thought of Ebbie. Her mother had told her to leave it be, that there were some things you just couldn't change and that if people didn't want help you couldn't force it on them. Maybe not, but for heaven's sake, loyalty should be rewarded.

Ebbie finished her cookie, stood up and dusted off the seat of her pants. She marched along with strides as long as her legs would allow. Her hands were in fists and her arms bent, flailing at the air like a pint-sized prizefighter. She had made her mind up. She would march right up to the house and ring the bell.

Ebbie turned on to the pathway at 51 Homewood Avenue without slowing her step and mounted the stairs. She rang the bell and waited, her hands shoved deep inside her pockets, fraying the inside seams.

The door opened slightly and Irene herself peered around the doorjamb. Her hazel eyes looked bigger than Ebbie remembered. The dress she wore was as neat and tidy as if she were on her way to school.

"Irene! Hi!"

Irene put her index finger up to her lips. She came out onto the doorstep and pulled the door shut very gently. She balanced on the step, as though not sure she should come out. Her mouth was squinched as small as could be.

"Ebbie, I'm so glad to see you," she whispered.

Ebbie took her friend's hand. It was small and still, hardly a live thing at all. "Are you okay? How come you're all dressed up? Are you going somewhere?"

"We have to be quiet," Irene said, still whispering. She nodded toward the window. "My mother's lying down."

"Well, then, why don't you come out?"

"I can't. I just can't."

"She won't mind if she's asleep."

"No, not really asleep, I don't think. But she's lying down. She told me not to go out of the house. She might need something." Irene's eyes darted left and right, up and down the street.

"She won't mind. I'm sure she won't."

Irene bit her lower lip and her eyes began to fill up with tears.

"I can't, Ebbie. I just can't come out."

"Well, all right, then. Why don't I come in and we can play Parcheesi or checkers or something?"

Irene brushed away her tears with the back of her hand.

"We'd make noise. She'd hear us. She doesn't want anybody in the house."

"I'll be quiet as a mouse. Come on."

"Irene! Who are you talking to?" Margaret's voice was a sharp bark.

Irene jumped, and her hands curled up against her breastbone. She reached out with one hand and opened the door a crack.

"Nobody, Mummy. Just Ebbie. She stopped by. Just for a minute."

"Hi, Mrs. MacNeil!" Ebbie called out with a big grin on her face, even though she couldn't see Irene's mother. She craned her neck, trying to see around Irene's shoulder and into the dim house. She felt a thrill like when she sat up late and listened to radio plays about spooky houses. "I just came to get Irene and go play for a while. We won't be long."

"Ebbie! No!" Irene shook her head wildly.

"Irene can't go out" came back the flat answer.

"Oh, please, just for an hour? Please?" Ebbie wheedled as Irene tried to clamp a hand over her mouth.

Mrs. MacNeil swung open the door and looked straight at Irene, as though Ebbie wasn't even there. Irene instantly stepped back and stared down at her shoes, but Ebbie smiled up at Margaret like nothing in the world was wrong. Mrs. MacNeil wore no makeup, and her dark hair was dull and uncombed. Ebbie's mother would never come to the door this way. Maybe Mrs. MacNeil really was sick. Her skin looked grey, and there were dark circles under her eyes.

"How are you, Mrs. MacNeil?"

"Irene can't come out and play. I need her at home. Isn't that right, Irene?"

"Yes, Mummy."

"Well, how about if Irene and I just go into the back garden for a while? She'll still be home, then, in case you need her. And we won't disturb you at all. I can be quiet as a mouse. We'll just talk and be quiet and you won't even know I'm here at all."

Mrs. MacNeil entwined her fingers and held them together tightly, so that the knuckles became white and red.

"Is that what you want, Irene?"

Ebbie poked Irene in the small of the back and then took her hand, held it where Mrs. MacNeil couldn't see. Irene squeezed.

"It might be nice. Just for a little while."

"I see," said her mother.

The girls waited.

"Yes, I see now," said Mrs. MacNeil. Irene dropped Ebbie's hand. "It's very clear. Fine. If that's what you want."

"It's okay, Mummy. Ebbie doesn't have to stay."

"No. If that's the way you want it, I insist. Ebbie will stay today." She raised her eyebrow. "One hour. No more."

"Thanks, Mrs. MacNeil. We'll be so quiet you won't know we're there."

"Oh, I'll know." She stepped back and slammed the door.

Irene's lips twitched.

Ebbie took both Irene's hands in hers and jumped down the step, pulling Irene with her. She hopped up and down and danced around, her feet going every which way and her head flopping back and forth, her wheat-pale hair flying, until Irene smiled at how foolish she was.

"Okay, come on, we might as well. I'm going to get what-for anyway." Irene led the way through the side alley to the back garden, never letting go of Ebbie's hand, even when she had to reach over the gate to unhook the latch.

Irene said she thought it might be best if they made themselves useful, and so they began weeding the garden. They pulled out dandelions and milk thistle and stray clover and put the loamy-smelling scraps in a tin bucket between them. Ebbie jabbered on about the newborn kittens and the bat they'd woken up to in the house two weeks before that scared everyone half silly until her father had finally walloped it with a tennis racket, which was the only thing you could hit a bat with, on account of their special radar ears. She told Irene about the week they'd spent with cousins on Beaver Lake near Peterborough, where they saw a real beaver lodge and heard loons and it would have been practically paradise except for the outhouse and its terrible stink and the spiders that lived on the dock and were big as dessert plates.

Every few minutes Irene glanced up to the kitchen window.

"Irene, you're not listening." Ebbie sat back on her haunches in the dirt, wiped her forehead with the back of her hand and left a trail of dusty grime. Irene didn't sit in the garden. She bent over, careful of her shoes.

"Yes, I am. You said there were spiders."

"Yes, as big as oranges. Aren't you frightened of spiders?"

"No. They don't scare me."

"So what does scare you?"

Irene put down the trowel and rubbed her hands together to get the dirt off, being careful not to smudge her dress or her white socks. She didn't say anything.

"*Something* must scare you. Everybody's scared of something. Me, I'm scared of snakes and the root cellar. I hate the root cellar. I won't even go down there to get potatoes for Mum. I'd pay Lisa to go for me if I had to. Yuck. I heard about a boy once, he put his hand in the potato box and there was a snake in there! Can you imagine? I'd just die. So tell me. I told you."

"I don't know. I get nightmares sometimes." Her voice was very low and she kept glancing up to the window. "I dream awful things."

"What kind of things?"

"Things about people coming to get me. Someone ... It's awful. I dream it over and over. This lady ... she's terrible ... "

"What does she do?" Ebbie hugged herself. Irene stared off at something Ebbie couldn't see. "Irene?"

"Nothing. It's just a silly dream."

The back door opened and Margaret called to Irene. Their hour was up.

"Can I come back another day, Mrs. MacNeil?"

"Perhaps, dear." Irene's mother smiled. "If that's what Irene would like. Come in now, Irene. Say goodbye to your little friend."

"Goodbye, Ebbie."

Ebbie dusted off the seat of her pants and hugged Irene. "I'll see you real soon. I'll come back tomorrow."

"I'm glad you came by today, Ebbie. Real glad."

"I hope you're feeling better, Mrs. MacNeil. My mom says hi." She waved as she went out the side gate.

Ebbie stuffed her hands deep into her pockets. She didn't really think she wanted to go back there again. It felt like a betrayal to feel that way. She dragged her feet, scuffing the tops of her shoes without caring. She scuffed them for Irene, who she was sure would get locked up in her room for the rest of her life if she ever dared to scuff a shoe.

Irene knew she would have to pay for her hour with Ebbie. There was always a price to pay for nice things. She quickly put the trowels and the pail away in the shed. She patted her hair and smoothed her dress, then ran up the steps and into the kitchen. Her mother leaned against the kitchen counter, tying a red scarf around her head so the bow flopped down like rabbit's ears.

"Did you have a nice afternoon?"

"Sort of."

"With Ebbie Watkins? Really. I'm surprised."

Irene didn't want to play along. She pulled at a piece of dead skin next to her thumbnail, and a small spot of bright red blood appeared. She rubbed at it until it disappeared.

"Why?" she said finally, angry with herself.

"Well, she's such an ugly girl, isn't she? And so bad mannered. That whole family's low class. I've always said that." This was not true. Her mother used to say that Mrs. Watkins was a lady of good breeding.

"She's my friend."

"You don't really want to play with that girl, do you?" Margaret laughed. "She's the bottom of the barrel. Just look at her. She only wants to be your friend because no one else will have her. But I suppose you prefer being with her than spending time with your mother?"

"No, Mum."

"I can see it in your eyes. I always know when you're lying, you know. Well, now I know where we stand with each other. Stand up straight. Look at me."

Irene raised her face to look at her mother, but she kept blinking and her eyes skipped off to the right and left.

"Yes, I can see how duplicitous you are. You're not a very good girl after all."

"I try."

"Well, we'll see how hard you try." Margaret turned to the sink and snapped the ends off green beans. *Snap. Snap. Snap.* Like small bones cracking. "You may go to your room now, Irene."

Irene went up to her room. She knew that when Ebbie came knocking tomorrow, she wouldn't answer the door. But she hadn't cried today. And that was something to be proud of.

8

September 1930

Rory Cameron and Joe Fleischman sat in the Blue Tulip Restaurant at the corner of Spadina and College.

"Son of a bitch," said Rory. "Son of a bitch."

"It's for the best. They were bound to sniff you out. You can concentrate your efforts now." Joe was a former boxer known on the street as Joey Onions. He and Rory had met at a May Day march two years before. He had a mound of curly black hair that lay back in a series of waves, shimmering with pomade. He rarely smiled. He cracked the knuckles of first one hand and then the other.

"My efforts," said Rory, "are going to be concentrated on getting some grub on a regular basis."

"We're all in the same boat."

Rory scowled, but he knew Joe was right. The truth was, he'd been in a stinking mood for two days, ever since he'd opened his pay envelope and found the pink slip waiting for him. It hadn't come as a surprise. He'd been lucky to keep his job as long as he had. At least he'd left with all his fingers attached, which was more than he could say for some. The boss was sorry and all that, but what could you do? Since Rory had hated the job for such a long time, the fact that he was upset surprised him.

"I'd hoped to get the shop organized before they pink-slipped me," he said. "It would have looked good to the higher-ups." The Communist Party was like anywhere else. There was a hierarchy. There were guys in the know. "I don't know what I'm going to do. If you weren't paying for this meal, I'd be eating air."

"I thought the Party was talking about sending you up to Sudbury."

"Yeah. To the nickel mines. Sounds like a godforsaken place."

"It ain't so bad. Besides, if the Party wants you to go, comrade ..."

"Yeah, I know. You go where the cause needs you." And Rory believed that, even through the haze of his anger.

"When they sending you?"

"*Sending* me? You make it sound like I'm going to be riding on the *inside* of the train." Rory ran his hands through his hair.

Joe's family ran a bakery on Baldwin Street, and although they weren't putting much butter on their bread these days, at least they had bread, and some assurance that they'd ride out the Depression without finding themselves on the street. Rory swallowed the words threatening to bust out. *Fine for you, you've got a roof over your head. You won't end up with a train bull's nightstick up your ass.*

"The thing is, I gotta go and tell my sister and her family I'm leaving. She's been kinda squirrelly lately. I ain't looking forward to it."

"Best get it over with quick as you can, then," said Joe, and Rory figured he was right.

Margaret stood at the sink, wiping the same plate over and over again with the red-and-yellow tea towel. Her eyes were swollen with crying, and now and again she wiped at her face with the inside of her wrist. Irene stood near the sink, scuffing her shoes on the tile floor. Douglas had excused himself to the living room, where he listened to some radio play.

"Irene, stop that! You're leaving marks on the floor." Margaret put the plate down and tossed a sponge at her daughter. "Wipe those scuffs off."

Rory watched his sister and niece. There it was again, the weird similarity between them, the mirroring of emotion. Margaret turned to him and put her hand up to her mouth.

"I can't bear to lose you."

Rory sat at the kitchen table, leaning forward on his chair with his elbows on his knees. He wrung his hat in his hands. His sister was making him crazy. He'd expected her to be sad and worried and all that, but she was carrying on like she was the one with no job and no place to live and a long hungry journey ahead of her.

"You could stay here. You could get another job. Douglas, come here!"

Rory slapped his hat down on the table. "There aren't any jobs. I'm not going to go around with a bucket and a rag like some of the guys do, asking if they can clean windows for a few slices of bread. I ain't gonna stand on the corner with a sign around my neck: Will Work for Food. I won't do it." He would not, of course, tell her that he had a job with the Party, even if it paid no more than a living allowance that wouldn't feed a cockroach and often not even that. For her sake, the less she knew the better.

"What is it, Margaret?" Douglas stood in the doorway.

"Take the car and drive Rory over to his room. Get his things. He can sleep in the solarium for the time being."

"You could stay, Rory, if you'd like. We could make the room," Douglas said, somewhat hesitantly.

"Now you listen to me, Sis. I know you mean well and I appreciate it. But I can't hang around here."

"I don't know what I'll do if you go," said Margaret. "I'll be all alone."

"What're you talking about? That's a fine thing to say. You've got Douglas and Irene here. You've got your family."

"You can't go. You don't even have any money, I'll bet."

"I have a few dollars, and you don't need much, a man alone."

"I hear terrible stories about what happens to young men riding the rails."

"Nothing's going to happen to me, and it won't be forever. I'll land some work. Things here will change in a year or so. I'll be back before you know it."

"You haven't even tried to get other work here. You don't care about me."

"Now, you know that's not true."

"Do I?" she said. The tone of her voice put a knot in his stomach.

Irene watched them from the corner of the room, pressed as far up against the wall as she could get.

"I want to do this," said Rory.

"And what you want is all that counts, of course."

"Come on now, Peggy. Let a guy sow some oats before he settles down, eh? See some of the country?" He put his arm around her and she didn't move away, but he could feel how stiff she was. She looked up at him with such desperation he wanted to shake her.

"You'll come back, won't you?" she said. "And you'll write? And come home for holidays?"

"'Course I will. In the spring things are bound to pick up and I'll be back home. In the meantime, think of it as me going off to camp."

"I don't like it, Rory. I don't want you to go." She had taken to wringing the dishtowel again and scratching at the back of her hands. He took her hands in his to stop their restless movements.

"Let's make this a going-away party. Send me off in style, eh?"

"That's a good idea. Yes, a very good idea," said Douglas. "How about drinks all round? Little celebration, indeed."

"When are you leaving, again?" said Margaret.

"Tomorrow."

"I see," she said, and then, "Bastard." She pulled her hands away. She walked out of the room, and they listened to her footsteps on the stairs and the slam of the bedroom door.

"Goddamn it!" said Rory. He looked at Douglas. "What the hell's wrong with her?"

"She's just upset, is all."

"She's not just upset. She's not goddamn normal! You're her husband! What the hell are you doing about it?"

Douglas went over to Irene and gave her a quick hug. "She'll be fine. Just fine."

Rory had almost forgotten Irene was in the room.

"Yeah, course she will." He smiled at his niece and she smiled back. "I'll go see if I can talk to her."

He knocked on the bedroom door and opened it without waiting for an answer. Margaret stood looking out the window, but she turned to face him. She was crying again. He went to her, sat on the edge of the windowsill and took her hands. He swung them back and forth like when they were children.

"Jesus, Peg, what're ya making such a fuss for?" She tried to pull her hands away but he wouldn't let her.

"I should have gone with John. I'd be in New York City now. The big life, you know what I mean?"

It took Rory a moment to figure out who Margaret was talking about. *Christ! Was she still pining over him?*

"Peggy, I didn't know John'd asked you to go with him." More than that, Rory knew he had not asked his sister, had never had any intention of taking her with him.

"He didn't, not in so many words, but then he wouldn't have, would he? He thought I'd say no, that I'd have to be married, that I just wouldn't run away with him. But I would have." She looked at Rory. "Are you going to New York? Could you find him?"

"No, Peggy, I'm not going to find him. We don't know where he is. What do you want to find him for, anyway? After the way he treated you?"

"Maybe I could go with you."

He looked into her face to see if she was joking, to see if there was something he was missing.

"Gee whiz, Peg. I can't take you with me. I'm travelling rough. Sleeping in freight yards, riding the rails. You don't want to go with me."

Her shoulders sagged and she dropped her head.

Rory tried to laugh, as though it were a silly joke she'd made.

"Leave this pretty house, leave your daughter? Come on, you wouldn't do that."

Margaret's head snapped up again. "In a minute. I'd do it in a minute."

"Margaret ..."

She laughed then, shrilly. "Don't pay me any mind. I'm just a little depressed, is all. I need a good night's sleep. I can't seem to sleep. But Douglas gives me these pills. They help."

"Things bad between you and Douglas?"

"Bad? No. Not bad, I suppose. They're just not anything. He's simply someone who lives in the house. I want to be a better wife to him. I've made my bed, after all. I have to learn to lie in it. But there are days when I look at him and see him more like an annoying lodger than a husband."

"I'm sorry, Peggy."

"Things didn't turn out like I'd planned. I'd planned so many big things."

"Be patient. Times are hard right now. Give it a few years."

"Now you sound like him."

"Is that a bad thing?"

"It's nothing. Nothing at all."

Irene crept upstairs after her uncle. She didn't want to sit with her father pretending nothing was wrong. She stood in her bedroom, listening. At first she had tried not to listen. She even closed the door so that she wouldn't hear the things her mother said, but the words slithered through the thin walls and the heating vents and found her even there.

She heard them opening the door, going downstairs.

"Irene," her mother called, knowing exactly where she was. "Come down and say goodbye to your uncle Rory."

"Coming," said Irene. And so she did as she was told. She ran down to the kitchen to get the parcel of sandwiches and tins of coffee and sardines she'd wrapped up. She gave them to her uncle and he thanked her and hugged her and she hugged him back. Mother and father and daughter stood on the porch and waved goodbye and watched him walk away. Irene couldn't help thinking that all three of them were making an effort not to run after him.

1930

There is always the fear of cave-in, even though the men say methane is more dangerous. It makes him hunch his shoulders, and every few seconds he turns his eyes upward, scanning the malevolent weight above him for signs of instability. Water splashes all around and makes footing uncertain. Shadows fall on faces, and the dim gleam from helmet-lamps flickers on glistening stone. David feels as though he has stumbled into some circle of Hell reserved for those who squandered the pleasures of sun and space and solitude and silence. Riding down on the "man trip" every evening at the beginning of his shift, his knees and shoulders pressed against the fellows on each side of him, the contraption like a perverse version of a midway roller coaster, is an exercise in self-control. He keeps his eyes glued to the retreating entranceway as long as he can, until the small rail takes him into the belly of the Alberta foothills. They are only 250 feet down, but it might just as well be a thousand.

He works next to an Icelander named Ingvarsson, whose hands are hammer-heavy, hanging at the end of his arms. They share a tiny shack made of straw, mud and manure with two other men, sleeping in shifts on two bug-infested cots. The big Icelander has taken him under his muscular wing.

He looks down at the water, nearly at mid-calf.

"Don't usually go any higher," says the Icelander, but David doesn't find this information consoling. A squib blows from down the line somewhere and he jumps as the percussion hits his eardrum with a thick pop. He coughs, tries to take a lungful of air and coughs again.

"Fans shut down again, I guess," says Ingvarsson.

"*Kinda hard to breathe,*" *David says, holding a filthy rag up to his mouth.*

"*Long as you're breathing, you're doing okay,*" *says a voice behind him.*

He swings his pick, chipping away the coal as best he can. The blisters on his hands have broken and the wooden handle is slippery. The muscles in his back and shoulders burn. David has been down in the mine for seven days. He knows he's taken a job away from another man, probably one with a family to support, but he had been hungry and taken it anyway. They'd hired him because they could pay him nine dollars a week, four dollars less than a full-grown man. He'd asked to be paid by tonnage, at twenty-five cents a ton. The more experienced men said if he worked fourteen to sixteen hours maybe he'd do better. Now he wishes he'd stuck to the wage. David bought his used, too-large boots from a guy who'd broken his leg, saving himself three of the five dollars the company charged, but he still had to pay them a dollar and a half for the doctor, and another fee if he actually visited him. He'd borrowed a pick and shovel from the same injured guy but had to pay to get it sharpened and for squibs and lamp carbon. Already he's in debt to the company for six bucks. For as long as he can stand it, he'll skip the fifty cents for a bath, but has paid the three-quarters of a cent for a gallon of water. Only halfway through his shift and he's drunk it all.

"*Look out!*" *The Icelander pulls him back from the mine wall. A live electrical wire swings perilously close.*

"*Thanks,*" *he says.*

"*Don't mention.*" *Ingvarsson's face looks ghoulish, covered in black except for his eyes.*

David works another two shifts before a muscle in his shoulder tears. The night after, he lies on the floor of the miners' shack, his arm bound to his chest with an old shirt, trying not to scratch at the bug bites, when the siren goes off. The two men sleeping in the cots before their next shift spring up, grabbing their picks and shovels.

David pushes himself up on his elbow. "What is it? What's happening?" He hopes it is not what he knows it is.

"*Accident,*" *mutters one of the men, stepping over him.*

He hauls himself up and goes to the open door. Everywhere he looks men run to the shaft entrance. He seizes his pick and runs with them.

They stand around the opening in the earth, waiting for the first trips to bring the men out.

"Anybody know what the hell happened?" someone asks. "Cave-in? I didn't hear no explosion."

"Naw, the lamps went out's what I heard," says someone else.

"Fucking fans been out for days," a man growls and throws his pick in frustration.

The air is always bad down below, thick with smoke from blasting, and then there is the black damp, air dense with carbon dioxide from old shafts. There are no alarms in the mines. When the lights snuff out it means there isn't enough oxygen to keep them burning.

They hear the rumble of the trip and the first men appear. Some are vomiting. He looks for Ingvarsson, but he isn't among them. Most of the men get out this time. Five don't. The Icelander is among them. His body, water-bloated and black, is brought up the next day, after the air is cleared out.

David waits until night falls again, then slips out of the camp, crawling on his belly until he reaches the fence that runs around the limits of the compound, then digs under with his bare hands. He tries not to cry out when his shoulder snags on the wire, afraid the company's security guards will hear him and drag him back. He still owes them the six bucks.

9

October 1930

It was Wednesday evening and Douglas sat listening to the Palmolive Hour on the radio with his vest unbuttoned and a cup of tea on the small table by his chair. He looked so smug and content, Margaret wanted to smack him.

Margaret had shooed Irene off to bed early. All through dinner her nerves were so on edge she feared she'd bite through the fork. Douglas thought he was hiding the extent of their money problems from her, but he wasn't. The first hints had come a few weeks back, when he began complaining about little things she bought.

"Do you really need new handkerchiefs, Margaret? And more gloves? Surely you have a drawer full of gloves." He had stood in the doorway of the bedroom, with his hands in his pockets, jingling his keys, watching her fold her purchases and put them in the dresser. "For someone so very fond of pointing out how difficult times are, you certainly seem to be selective about where you economize. I don't mean to scold, my dear, not to scold at all, but merely to draw attention to how important it is not to live above ourselves."

"Above ourselves? What are you talking about? I'm the one who's scrimped and saved and done without while you waste your money on booze. You've got your nerve, mister."

He had looked blankly at her and turned heel.

Now, in the living room, Margaret said, "I went into Mrs. Munsen's today."

"Uh-huh."

"Yes, I had quite a chat with her."

"That's good, my dear. You should get out more often."

"I wanted to buy some cloth, to make dresses for Irene and me." She began to scratch the back of her hands without noticing she was doing it.

Douglas continued listening to the music on the radio.

"You can imagine my surprise when she wouldn't take our money." Margaret had the satisfaction of seeing his head snap around to look at her. She could hear the bones in his neck crack. He picked up his teacup and took a sip.

"What do you mean?"

"I think you know what I mean."

"If you have something to say, Margaret, then say it."

Remembering the scene in the yard goods store, she was embarrassed all over again. "Yeah, a fine cloth. Blue suits you fine," Mrs. Munsen had said, her arms waggling as she folded the cloth. "But you put your money away, missus. We owe your husband a penny or two. Not all the world's as kind as him."

"You've given them credit, haven't you?" Margaret said, and heard his startled little gasp. "I had to stand there and hear about it, hear how my husband had put me in the position of having to barter, for the love of God!"

"Not me, for sure, but Karl, my middle son, he's not doing so good now that Inglis let off everybody just like that," the woman had said, as though Margaret cared about her doltish son. "We help out where we can, but who's got extra these days? You feed the family and it's all gone, eh? You know how it is. Karl with the twins to feed, he's got his hands full, and your husband, a good man him, he says you pay when you can. So you don't pay here either, missus. We'll just make a note of what you take and tell the mister to set it down against what we owe. Like the old country, eh? When the newfangled ways all go to hell, the old ways are best again."

"There's nothing wrong with extending a little credit to a good customer, Margaret. It's good for business, in fact. Builds good-will."

"I know what you've been doing, Douglas. I've seen the books."

Douglas stood up, overturning his teacup.

"Douglas! Be careful!" Margaret knelt and mopped at the tea with her apron.

"Do not tell me, Margaret, do not tell me you've been going through my papers!"

It had been so easy to jimmy the flimsy lock on his desk with a hairpin and a nail file.

"Oh yes, I've been in your precious sanctum sanctorum. You've extended credit to almost as many people as have paid. How could you be so stupid? When do you think anyone's going to be able to pay? Next month? Next year? And what are we supposed to live on in the meantime?"

"You had no right!"

"I have every right," she said, standing. "You won't tell me things. All you say is, 'Buy cheaper meat, Margaret. Cook with beans instead, Margaret. Do without new shoes, do without new stockings, don't buy a magazine, can't afford this, can't afford that!'" She singsonged the words, her hands on her hips. She felt more alive than she had in some time, the fear for their future mixed with the red-hot joy of having him dead to rights, the perverse pleasure of having her fears confirmed. "We'll lose everything!"

"Things are not that dire."

"Collect that money, Douglas."

They stood facing one another, their laboured breathing the only sound.

"I'll run my business as I see fit," said Douglas. "Stay out of it."

And before she could say another word, he strode to the hallway, picked up his hat and walked out, not even bothering to close the door. Margaret wanted to run after him, to scream at him in the street, but the neighbours would see and she couldn't bear that. She stood in the doorway, all the passion of a moment before draining out of her feet onto the chilly floor. Then she slammed the door. She kicked over the chair, ran up to her bedroom, slammed that door and threw herself sobbing across the bed. Soon they would be out on the street, she knew they would be. They would starve.

Down the hall Irene turned her face to the wall and pulled the pillow over her head.

It was mid-October now, and they were blessed with a fine Indian summer. As the day ended, Douglas decided to take a long walk before going home. He was in a slightly bleary fog of whisky and goodwill toward men. He was thankful he was no longer burdened by an automobile. A brisk walk was good for the constitution. He stepped out into the lengthening shadows and took deep breaths of the muggy air. His flask rested against his heart. Although it was a balmy night, he whistled "God Rest Ye, Merry Gentlemen" and doffed his hat at ladies.

He decided to walk all the way along Queen Street, maybe as far as University, even up to Queen's Park and then back along

College to home. He strolled along, pleased with himself and the world. As he rounded the corner of Bay and Queen streets he came upon a group of perhaps twenty-five men and five or six women. They were a ragtag group; even in his jolly mood he could tell that. They were lean and serious. The man in front of him wore pants so thin in the backside they were barely decent.

Douglas did not like crowds, especially not crowds of dingy men and especially not on an evening when he felt so full of fellow-feeling. He tried to pass, but he was slightly unsteady on his feet, and someone bumped into him. A man reached out a steadying hand, and Douglas saw that the knuckles were covered in scabs.

"Whoa there, pal," the man said, his voice friendlier than his hard-luck face. "Steady," he said and smiled.

"Fine," said Douglas. "I'm fine."

"'Course you are. Can't blame a man for taking a snort to make hisself feel better in times like this." The man looked around and then leaned into Douglas, speaking softly. "Don't suppose you've got a taste thereabouts yer person, do you? For a pal?"

"Certainly not," said Douglas. He brushed imaginary crumbs from his lapels.

"Ah well, too bad, eh?" said the man.

Douglas was gently jostled into the centre of the crowd. Finding himself surrounded, he thought he might as well listen. No doubt some Methodist preacher calling on the Lord to bring on Armageddon. It might be amusing.

A young man stood on a crate, head and shoulders above the crowd. He was pale and wiry, and didn't look like he'd be much good at anything that didn't involve a desk and a stack of paper.

Douglas couldn't follow the man's words. He said something about the capitalists and how they didn't care about the working man, who was starving for lack of food and atrophying for lack of work. He waved his hands about a great deal.

"Now Tim Buck, he's a man with a difference, let me tell you. He'll not sell you out the way the Tories have, the way the so-called Liberals have. He's a man who cares, is Tim Buck. You support him and he'll support you!"

The man next to Douglas nudged him. "That there's Tom McEwen, and the guy behind him"—he pointed to a small, clean-cut young fellow who looked like a department store clerk—"that's Tim Buck. Great man. We's here for Tim Buck, eh? All of us. Ain't gonna put up with this no more. Not no more."

Douglas's head began to clear. There had been newspaper reports of this Tim Buck, a Communist. A rabble-rouser. A threat to the Dominion.

"Let's hear it for Tim, friends! Tim Buck!"

"Excuse me," said Douglas, starting to push through the cheering crowd. He did not want to be among Communists. Methodists were bad enough. He was too hot now and didn't feel well. He stuck out his elbows.

"Hey, watch who you're poking!" someone snapped.

"Sorry," said Douglas and tried to move forward.

"Oh Jesus," said someone else. "It's the cops!" The crowd became very quiet, everyone looking this way and that. The police had come off a side street and were upon the group before they knew it.

"We'll fix you sons of bitches." Several policemen shouldered their way through the crowd with far more success than Douglas, who was hemmed in on all sides. Over the top of people's heads he could see uniformed riders on horses.

"We have every right to be here. You have no legal reason to stop this meeting," said McEwen. Tim Buck stood at his side, his arms folded across his chest.

People began to mutter about their rights, but there was a hum of fear. A man grabbed a woman's arm and said, "Let's get the hell out of here."

More blue uniforms pushed through, their batons held out in front of them. The horses pranced nervously, their chests thrust out, driven forward by their riders, and people in front of them held their hands up, trying to quiet the animals and keep out of their way.

"This is a lawful street meeting!" McEwen called out.

"Shut that bastard's mouth!" yelled a policeman, and with that, another, thick-limbed and stocky, raised his elbow and used it to abruptly close McEwen's mouth.

In that instant people started running and truncheons began to fly. Douglas saw the man who had asked him for a drink cower in front of a mounted cop. He threw his hands up over his head and screamed, "Don't hit me, I'm an anti-Communist!" The cop cracked him on the back with his baton and said, "I don't care what kind of Communist ya are."

Douglas turned to his left and his right, pushing people who were backing into him. He found his path cut off in every direction and he pushed backwards, only to feel hands roughly upon him.

"Right then, Mac. Into the van with you," said the cop.

And although he protested that he was not a Communist, he was an Anglican, this only made the beefy man laugh. Douglas found himself in the back of a urine-rank paddy wagon with McEwen and Buck and several others. Three men bled from wounds to the head or face. One man's nose was broken and he cupped his hands against it gingerly as blood dripped onto his shirt.

"I'm not a Communist," said Douglas, looking from one man to the other.

"You are now, friend" came a voice from the corner. "Tom McEwen's the name," he said, extending his hand. "Welcome to the Great Repression."

Where the hell was Douglas?

Margaret smoked one cigarette after another and practised sending smoke rings into the sticky air. She got up now and again to check whether the telephone was working. She fiddled with the radio dial, listened to Chick Webb and his orchestra live from the Savoy Ballroom. At ten she turned to CPRY to hear Fred Culley and his Dance Orchestra. When that was over and the newscast began, she turned the radio off with a snap.

Where the hell was Douglas?

A month ago he had been brought home by Mr. Steedman, a

soft-spoken churchgoing man who lived with his wife and two small sons three doors down. Mr. Steedman had had to prop Douglas up in the doorway to make sure he didn't fall while he rang the bell.

"Just about made it home, Mrs. MacNeil. Found him asleep in his car at the end of the block. I thought for a moment he might be hurt, but, well, looks like he'll be fine." Mr. Steedman smiled. He had a wide, handsome face, clean and honest. He looked sorry to be embarrassing her this way.

"You're very kind to bring him home." Margaret threw Douglas's arm around her shoulder and began to wrestle him through the door.

"Hello, there," Douglas had slurred. "It's the little lady. Ain't she pretty? Prettiest girl …"

"I can't tell you how embarrassing this is. "

"No need to say anything," Mr. Steedman said. "I've been known to tie one on myself. Do you need any help? I could help you get him to bed."

"Thank you, you've done enough. I can handle it from here. Thank you." She closed the door.

"You idiot! Out there for all the neighbours to see. You're a disgrace." She had plopped him in a chair and left him. The next morning he woke with a neck so stiff he could barely lift his throbbing head.

"Serves you right," she said, and she hid his car keys.

She had wanted him to ask about the keys, wanted him to beg her forgiveness. But he only said, "Margaret, have you seen my keys? I have to get the car."

"I'll be getting the car, Douglas. And keeping it until you can prove you're fit to drive it."

"Suit yourself," he'd said. "Gas is too expensive anyway."

A week later he brought a man home after work. Douglas sold their Ford to him for $200. Walked into the kitchen smug as a feudal lord, riffling the money in the air like a fan. What he had done with the money she had no idea. She certainly never saw a penny.

If he was out squandering what little money they had left, she'd bash his brains in with the marble pastry pin. They'd never again brought up the subject of the credit he was giving out. She thought her silence might have pried some words from him, but there had been none.

She climbed the stairs now and went into her daughter's bedroom. A path of light fell across Irene's sleeping form. Margaret reached into the pocket of her housecoat and pulled out her tin of cigarettes and her silver lighter. She lit one, and then snapped the Zippo shut. Irene didn't stir at the sound.

"Sleeping, baby?"

Irene did not respond.

Margaret was about to sit down on the edge of the bed when she heard footsteps on the porch. She whirled toward the sound and rushed from the room.

As soon as Irene heard her mother's footsteps clattering down the stairs, she opened her eyes, just peeking through half-closed lids at first and then opening fully, staring fixedly at the point where her mother had been.

Douglas climbed the porch steps slowly. His feet felt encased in shoes of cement. He had spent the past several hours in a cell at the police station on College Street. It was a malodorous concrete space, crowded with men. Some smoked cigarettes and two played cards. One of these card players was a red-skinned Indian man. He was huge, at least three hundred pounds, with jet-black hair cut so close to his head that Douglas could see the multitude of scars on his scalp. He played some game that Douglas didn't understand and every time he snapped a card down on the pile in front of him, yelled "Shoot the dog!" and his partner laughed. Others hunkered against the wall, their eyes as flat as tin plates, giving away nothing. One man, the front of his pants stained dark with what Douglas's nose told him was urine, slept in a corner, his snores phlegm-filled.

Douglas sat primly on the edge of a bench near the bars where the air, he imagined, was slightly fresher. He remained very still, careful not to draw attention to himself, for who knew what these men would do if they knew just how little he belonged to their tribe. Only the conviction that they could turn on him at any moment, like hyenas tearing at the stomach of a weakened pack-mate, stopped tears from lining his cheeks. He willed himself not to pull the hem of his jacket away from the man beside him and thereby betray the intensity of his disgust. He sat still and silent and hoped this passed for assured self-containment.

He wanted to tell the police that it was a mistake, that he was not a Communist, but no one seemed to care. When he had been brought into the station, herded up to the desk and told to empty his pockets, he had tried to explain but was told to shut up and do as he was instructed. A hand had grabbed him roughly by the upper arm, and Douglas had been shamed by how scrawny his own arm must feel under such strong fingers. It made him aware of how weak he was and how vulnerable, and he then became afraid not only of the men with whom he had been arrested but also of the police themselves.

After they had clanged shut the heavy, barred cell door, the police brought in McEwen and began to taunt him, telling him they would take care of his kind. That they knew what he was up to. That he should go back to where he came from. McEwen said he was born right here in Canada and had a right to his beliefs. That he was a member of a legally recognized political party and that the police had no right!

A policeman had silenced him with a punch to the stomach. Douglas watched, horrified, as they beat him to a bloody pulp. McEwen kept his hands over his ears, his elbows shielding his face, until he became unconscious. Douglas thought they would stop the beating then, but they did not. They kept right on kicking him in the ribs and the back and the legs. What shocked Douglas almost as much as the beating was the fact that the police did not even try to hide what they were doing.

All the muttering, all the shouting, even the snoring in the cell had stopped.

When they were finished, they threw McEwen, nothing more

now than a sack of sharp bones and lumpy, multicoloured flesh, into the cell.

And now Douglas had to face his wife. He wondered which would be worse, but then shivered this thought away, because to joke about it, even to himself, was a betrayal to McEwen, a man he didn't know, didn't want to know, but to whom he felt he owed something.

Douglas drew a deep breath, ran his hand along the top of his shiny head and opened the door to his house.

"Where have you been?" Margaret was disgusted at the sight of him. "You've been drinking!"

Douglas moved past her, not quite pushing her but coming close enough to give her a heart-hiccuping start. She opened her mouth to say something, but then closed it again when she found no words ready. Douglas hauled himself up the stairs and disappeared into the bathroom. Margaret heard water running.

As she approached the bathroom door she made her hands into claws. She'd go right through the door if she had to.

Inside the clean space of the bathroom, Douglas looked at himself in the mirror over the sink, his face framed within the ivy pattern of the wallpaper. Behold the conquering hero, he scoffed at himself. Shock provided a window of weird objectivity, and it was through this portal that the sagging lines and pouches and rabbity eyes told the truth of who he was. Before this night he had believed himself to be no more or less brave than the average man. But now the truth was revealed. He was a coward.

The scene played over in his head like a newsreel.

He couldn't tear his eyes off the terrible spectacle of the man lying on the cold concrete floor, his face swollen and bloody, his left eye so puffed up it looked as though some parasitic creature had attached itself to his face. His shirt was hiked up, and Douglas saw the evidence of the beating: marks quickly going from red to purple, blood drying on boot-shredded skin. The men gathered close.

"Leave him alone," said one.

"See if you can wake him," said another.

"Should we try and get him on his feet?"

"Bastards did him in but good."

McEwen moaned and stirred, his arms and legs twitched. His eyes flickered open and then closed. A trickle of blood leaked from his mouth.

"Looks like he's lost a tooth or two," said a man with no more than three teeth in his head himself.

"Shoot the dog," said the big Indian, quietly, although what he meant was unclear.

McEwen made a wet sucking noise in his throat. He tried to push himself up on his elbows.

"Get him sittin' up," someone said.

"Perhaps we could lean him against the wall," Douglas said, and when eyes turned toward him, he pointed. "That wall, maybe."

Pairs of hands heaved the limp body into a seated posture against the wall. McEwen's head sagged on his breast and a string of pink-tinged drool stained his already filthy shirt.

With the injured man settled, the rest went back to their conversations, their pacing back and forth, their smoking, their cards, although now and then they glanced discreetly in McEwen's direction, as though to make sure he was not about to leap on them, or fall, or die. They acted as though the violence might be contagious, and Douglas was not so sure they were wrong.

Douglas resumed his post near the bars. He didn't like to think about what was happening to the other man, Tim Buck, who along with McEwen had been culled from their lot upon arrival.

It was very hot in the cell and sweat trickled between his shoulder blades and between the cheeks of his buttocks, places where he could not reach. The lining of his stomach felt ragged. He vowed that should he get out of this unharmed, he would never drink again. His muscles, cramped from tension, began to tremble. His shoulders began to shiver. He crossed his arms and tucked his hands beneath his soggy armpits, praying that the shaking would stop and that no one would see his fear.

He heard a terrible retching. McEwen, clutching his stomach, was going to be sick. McEwen's head lurched, and men scattered. He tried to get up on all fours, then gave up and leaned over on one arm. He vomited blood.

The men in the cell stepped over each other trying to get out of the way.

"Guard! Guard!"

"Get a doctor!"

"Jesus H. Christ!"

Douglas was pinned against the bars. He turned his face away. A young cop approached the cell.

"What the hell's the racket in here?"

"I think that man is going to die," said Douglas in a voice that he did not completely register was his.

"Goddamn it!" said the policeman. "Dan! Jack! Get over here!" Other policemen came running and the door was opened. Men were pushed out of the way. Douglas saw McEwen, held under the arms and knees, being carried out of the cell. His head was tilted back. Douglas thought, He'll choke. The man will choke.

"His head," he said. "Be careful of his head."

"Mr. MacNeil? Is that you?" A hand touched his shoulder. "What are you doing with this bunch? How did you get here?" said a dark-haired young cop. "Are you okay?" The young man waved his hand in front of Douglas's eyes.

"I'm not a Communist," said Douglas.

"What the hell are you doing in here?"

"I know you," he said.

"Of course you do. I'm Bobbie Patterson."

Yes, that was it. He was little Bobbie Patterson. One of the boys who had stolen candy from the counter and mussed up his magazines. One of the neighbourhood boys Douglas had chased out of the store for years. He reached up and put his hands on Bobbie's shoulders. He was afraid he might cry.

"I was walking. There were all these people. I wasn't one of them. I was just walking."

Bobbie Patterson pulled back and Douglas knew the whisky must be on his breath.

"'Course you were, Mr. MacNeil. 'Course you were. Let's see what can be done about this." And he pulled Douglas from the cell, amidst hoots of derision.

"Yer a yellow-hearted fellow," said a man. "Good riddance to ya!" And Douglas heard someone spitting.

"You know," Bobbie Patterson said as they walked down the long loud hall, "you should be more careful, Mr. Mac. These men in there, well, they're a bad sort. They're out to undermine everything we stand for in this country."

"Oh, yes, I can see that," said Douglas. "I'm just an unlucky bystander in all this. I tried to explain that to the other officers but they wouldn't listen. Although," he added, seeing a dark look cross Bobbie's face, "I can see how they wouldn't have had the time and all, given the situation. Ha ha. You men are doing a fine job. Yessir. A fine job."

"You wait here. I'm gonna have a word." Bobbie laid his finger alongside his nose and winked, then he went to talk to an older officer. The older man glanced in Douglas's direction. Bobbie put his hand on the man's shoulder, turned to look back himself, then mimed tipping a bottle to his lips. The other man smirked and nodded. Bobbie clapped him on the back and went behind the desk to a rack of lockers. From inside one he pulled a paper bag containing Douglas's possessions and walked back to him, grinning.

"Okay, Mr. Mac, you're free to go. And go straight home, huh?"

"Yes, of course, Bobbie, or should I say Constable Patterson, eh? Yes, straight home with me. It's been quite a night, quite a night." Douglas pumped the young man's hand. He was in a hurry to go. He needed the night air, clean, calm night air, to fill his lungs with the scent of something to wipe out the stench of the cell.

"Just one more thing ... " The young man held his hand firmly and wouldn't let go.

"Yes?"

"Well, let's be clear here. That man who got took to the hospital. That's a sad thing, I guess, but sometimes guys come in here all beat up, you understand. Don't have anything to do with the police department, you understand. Wasn't for us he'd of bled to death in that cell. You do see that, don't you, Mr. Mac."

"Of course," he said, smiling, looking Bobbie straight in the eye. "Of course. Like I said, you're all doing a wonderful job."

"To serve and protect. That's our motto. You have a good night, sir." And he let go of Douglas's hand.

Douglas fled through the doors. He emptied the paper bag and stuffed his pockets with his keys and change and stamps. The little silver flask was gone. He stood on the moon-bright street and breathed deeply. The smell of burning leaves and gasoline and sandalwood perfume from a dark-haired woman walking by filled his chest. He looked at the woman, strained after the scent and sight of her, as though she'd asked a question that was terribly important but spoken too quietly to hear. The woman wore a camellia in her hair, white as bone and pale as death.

"Douglas! You come out of that bathroom now! How dare you lock the door on me!"

The sound of her mother kicking the door made Irene want to crawl under the bed and hide. She hugged her doll, Noreen, to her chest and then the pillow too, so that Noreen would be protected. Voices became Other Voices. Similar to but not exactly the voices of the people you knew. It was as though there were violent and dangerous people hiding behind the familiar faces of your mother and father, waiting to emerge at unpredictable times like these.

"Margaret, for God's sake! Keep your voice down."

"You dare tell me what to do! After you've been out whoring around town? A common drunk?"

"Shut up. You don't know what you're talking about. You'll wake up the neighbours! You'll wake up Irene!"

"It'd be good for her, to see what kind of a father she really has."

"Margaret, I'll not have this, do you hear. Get control of your-self."

"Keep your hands off me. Don't you ever touch me again!"

Her mother's voice was completely gone now, replaced by the Other Mother, the woman who came and went inside her mother's skin. Sometimes you could tell just by looking at her; sometimes you had to hear the voice. The voice of the Other Mother was full of spit and sour with no laughter and no way to make her see you as you really were. Irene wondered what her father would do. He was as big as the Other Mother, bigger even. If Irene were bigger she would stop the Other Mother. Put her hand over her mouth and make the words stop coming out until the Nice Mother came back. Irene hugged her knees and held Noreen tightly.

Shadows crossed the threshold of her doorway and she closed her eyes, held her breath. Irene heard her parents descend the stairs. There was a cast-iron heating vent in the corner near the door. The words came through as clearly as if her parents had been standing in her room.

"You tell me, Douglas, you tell me right this minute. Who is she? Who's your little floozy?"

"I don't know where you get these ideas, Margaret."

"Oooh, don't you take that tone with me! I'm not the one who's out gallivanting all over town."

"No one is *gallivanting*. I worked late. I had a drink. I fell asleep over the accounts. There's no sin in that."

"You coward. You're going to add lying to everything else? A real man would stand up and admit what he's done. He'd take the consequences with his shoulders squared. But not you, oh no. Not the sorry excuse for a man I married. Tell me who she is!" The voice rose to a shriek, and Irene covered her ears with her hands. She pushed back in bed until she was in the corner.

There was a momentary silence and Irene held her breath.

"That's quite enough now," said her father.

Irene let the air out of her lungs. It would be all right now. Irene was very good at reading voices. She didn't have to even see her father to know what he was trying to do. His voice was reasoning, calm, a little afraid. She knew what that felt like. You had to be careful here, when the Other Mother was so close to the edge of the dark place.

"You're making yourself hysterical. I'm telling you there is no other woman. I admit I was thoughtless, I should have called."

"I called you. You didn't answer. You think I'm a fool. You're laughing at me. I can see that now. I hope you're proud of your-self. I hope you're very proud. You'll never be able to make it up to me. Everything is different now. Everything is very different." Her mother's feet on the stairs again, each step deliberate and measured.

"Margaret," her father called softly. "Come back here. Don't act like a fool." Her mother kept walking. Her shadow passed as she went into their bedroom and closed the door. Irene heard the sound of a chair being put under the doorknob. Her father would have heard that too.

"Oh, for God's sake," he said to no one.

Irene smoothed Noreen's sea-green dress over the doll's porce-lain legs. "Don't be afraid," she said. "I'm right here. I'm right here." She knew she was too old to be talking to her doll, too old by far. "Don't be afraid," she said.

After a while Irene heard her father make up a bed on the couch. She lay quietly, trying to fall asleep, but it wasn't easy.

"Good night, Noreen," she whispered.

Douglas pressed the heels of his hands to his eyes, trying to stop the flow of tears. He lay on the chesterfield and tried to under-stand why he hadn't told Margaret the truth. He tossed and turned, unable to exorcise the demons that haunted him. The smell of the unwashed prisoners, the metallic smell of his own fear, the reek of blood and urine. The implied threat in Bobbie Patterson's words and the cold grip of the young constable's hand. He wanted to talk to someone. He wanted to confess his fears. He wanted to confess his cowardice. He lay staring up at the ceiling, up to the room where his wife lay in their bed, from which he was banished, and deservedly so. Not because of what she thought he had done, but because of the things she didn't know about. She didn't know of his delight at saving his own skin, of his pathetic, salivating response to his own redemption, with nary a thought to the plight of those left behind. The tears squeezed from under his hands, rolled down the sides of his face, filling his ears, wetting his hair.

But he could not escape the horrifying fact that even though he had made the promise to God that, should he be released from the prison unharmed, he would never touch whisky again, he had no doubt he would break that promise. In fact, even as he thought this very thing, his legs carried him off the couch, down the hall and toward the closet. A voice in his head told him that after all he'd been through, it was only natural to have a drink to settle his nerves. He knew this was nonsense, but was powerless over it. He was a moral coward. In the back of the closet he found what he was looking for. He sat cross-legged in the closet and drank, and drank, and drank some more. The salt from his tears mixed with the taste of the whisky. He gave himself up to the soft warm lull and numbness of the liquor. He surrendered to it completely and drank until he had shut out the visions in his head and he could sleep.

Part II

10

By 1933, Margaret spent the better part of any given day poring over the papers. Douglas had tried stopping delivery, seeing how she became obsessed with the unending stream of bad news, but she'd kicked up an even worse fuss, saying he was trying to keep the news from her.

Conditions had deteriorated over the past three years. Prime Minister Bennett had been forced to back down on his vow that no government of which he was leader would introduce the dole, and more than a million Canadians were now on direct relief. The municipal governments, who had been given the bulk of the responsibility, buckled under the weight. All across the country, dissension roiled and seethed. Seven unemployed men in Edmonton went to jail for taking part in a hunger strike. There was a riot in Arborg, Manitoba, over a foreclosure sale. Marches were held all over the country by people demanding unemployment insurance. A system of geographically isolated relief camps had been set up in 1932, run by military law, where unemployed young men were warehoused.

In Toronto, the House of Industry on Elm Street had a constant line at its doors, a shuffling, weary mass of people looking for relief supplies and vouchers. Groceries obtained with relief vouchers were supposed to last seven days, but they rarely did. Often people lived on ketchup and water for the seventh day, if they were lucky, or just water if they weren't. Scenes of families sitting out on the sidewalk with their meagre belongings strewn about them, victims of eviction, were common. People averted their eyes as they walked past.

And there were even darker stories from abroad, where Adolf Hitler and the Nazi Party had taken power in Germany. In the *Toronto Star*, Pierre van Paasen, a journalist on assignment in Germany, described scenes of a Jew being beaten to death, of Jews being tortured, being drowned. On April 4, the paper ran a story headed "Nazis Cut Out Eyes of Berlin Lawyer Before Killing Him: Daughter Flees to Paris to Confirm Story of Horrible Murder: Mutilated Children: Communists Bear Brunt of Hilter's Terrorism But Jews Do Not Escape." Margaret fed on the gruesome tales.

"Listen to this one," she said to Irene or Douglas, whoever happened to be listening. " 'Erwin Wellner, arrested in Berlin, was searched and beaten. He was taken to an apartment in Prenzlauerstrasse, where 20 people, mostly in Nazi uniform, whipped the bare soles of his feet and put salt in his eyes.' " She did not tell them that she thought there were messages in the methods of torture. They were trying to tell the world something more than that they were simply cruel. There was alchemy in the medium. Salt. Judas spilt salt at the Last Supper. Salt to circle a house, protect it from evil.

The night after she read that story she put a tiny pile of salt on the table and left it overnight. In the morning a little had melted. Margaret knew this meant death coming, but she told no one. There were omens everywhere and she trusted them more now that she had decided God was treacherous.

At times she considered praying, as she used to pray and be comforted, but quickly discarded the thought. She had no faith left. God had clearly forsaken her, or perhaps He had judged her unworthy. She refused to go to church and listen to the sanctimonious lies of preachers like the Reverend Fuller. She could see through him, all right, see how he had nothing to offer her but disapproval. And she could see through Him as well, promising love and everlasting life, dispensing only sorrow, starvation and solitude. She wondered at times if she had failed to love Him enough and was being punished. Well, if God had banished her, then so be it. For all her prayers He'd given her nothing. To hell with her? To hell with God.

It had been nearly three years since Rory had been to see his sister. This didn't mean it had been three years since he'd been back in Toronto. In fact he'd passed through a couple of times, but each time he found an excuse to avoid going to see Margaret. He felt guilty as hell, but there it was. The fact was, Rory liked life on the move. At first he'd been reluctant to leave the city he'd known all of his life, afraid of what might be out there. It was true there were rough times, bruises and battered knuckles both behind and ahead, for life on the road was harsh, even for a strong young man like Rory. Still, he felt he had a purpose.

This time, though, he'd been back for a couple of months, and he figured it was only a matter of time until word got back to her that he was around. Toronto was a small town in many ways. Besides, he was sure he'd seen Douglas on the street not long ago, and he couldn't be sure Douglas hadn't seen him.

He stopped outside his sister's house. He took his cap off, smoothed his hair from his brow, put the cap back on and polished first his right boot and then his left on the back of his pants legs. It didn't help. All this time as a boxcar cowboy didn't leave much to shine on a pair of road-weary boots. He shifted the weight of the pack across his shoulders.

The little house looked sorrowful, but a run-down place wasn't unusual these days. He'd seen lots of houses worse than this. Places with the curtains flapping in the prairie wind, the sand piling up against the side of the kitchen door. A place could get buried like that. Just disappear. He'd come upon such a place once, what the boys called a suicide farm, out in Kincaid, Saskatchewan. A woman sat in the doorway, wearing a ragged shift on which the words Red Roses Flour were still faintly visible. He'd tipped his hat and asked if he might get some water from the well. The woman motioned for him to go around back. There were five graves out there, two with freshly turned earth and piled stones, but no sign of a well, so he told the woman he was sorry for her troubles and went on his way. She never said a word.

The cities were marginally better than the farming communities—there were no Bennett Buggies, the horse-drawn automobiles named in honour of the prime minister—but still, Toronto certainly showed the ravages of the Depression. Knots of hard-looking men in raggedy clothes loitered on the street corners. Lots of old battered-up jalopies. Lineups at the soup kitchens in the Ward and around the back doors of churches. To Rory's eyes, though, the street his sister lived on wasn't so bad. There was one house near the corner of Carlton with its windows boarded over and a foreclosure sign nailed to the door, telling passersby everything they needed to know. Like the black-cross mark of plague, people avoided looking directly at it, as though afraid the troubles were contagious. In one yard a car sat up on blocks. Here and there, Room For Rent signs hung in windows.

Margaret's house looked quiet, and for a moment he wondered if they'd moved on. Being on the move the way he was, there would have been no way for them to tell him where they'd gone. The place hadn't been whitewashed in a while. Spots of bare cement showed through where hunks of stucco had fallen to the ground. The flower beds, once his sister's pride and joy, seemed not to have been planted this year. Well, who had money for such things?

He scratched the back of his neck. Hot water and soap would feel mighty good. He walked up across the porch and knocked on the door and was relieved when after a moment Irene looked out of the curtain. When she saw her uncle's face, her own lit up and broke into the same crooked grin Rory saw when he looked in the mirror.

"Hey, Doodles! How about letting me in?"

Irene opened the door, and threw her arms around him.

"Uncle Rory! Mum, it's Uncle Rory! Uncle Rory!" She covered his face in kisses and held him so tight he started to cough.

"Don't kill me before I'm even across the threshold! Damn! When did you get so big, little girl? You're nearly a grown woman. How old are you anyway, eighteen?"

She blushed. "Oh, you know how old I am. I'm fourteen! Eighteen! Goodness! Do I really look eighteen?" She crossed her arms over her breasts.

"I'd have sworn it."

"Rory! Is that really you?" Margaret rushed onto the porch, grabbed his arm and pulled him into the house. "I can't believe it! I've been worried to death. Where have you been? Are you going to stay? Have you eaten? No, of course you haven't. Look at how skinny you are. When did you eat last?"

Rory laughed. "Slow down, sister, slow down. Guess you're glad to see me after all."

"Glad to see you! Why, I could just die!" She turned him round and round, reached up and touched his face. "Oh, Rory, you've grown old, older. Look at you, your face, all those lines."

As Margaret took stock of her brother, Rory took stock of her. She was thinner, he thought, although she'd always been a little bird of a thing. Her brown dress hung straight and loose, as though she'd shrunk inside the cloth. There were stains on the front. Her hair, once always bobbed and crimped and shining, was now pulled back into a plain bun. She had new lines, too, deep ones that ran from her nose to her mouth and made her face look severe. Well, how old was she now, thirty-four? A middle-aged woman.

"Yeah," he said, "but you haven't changed a bit."

"Liar." She patted her own face, then bustled him into the kitchen, made him sit at the table. She pulled out a half loaf of bread.

"Don't have too much in the house just today. Of course, if I'd known you were coming … but never mind. I've got some canned meat. Sandwich, do you?"

"That'd be fine, Margaret. Don't go to no trouble on account of me."

She put a pot on the stove. "I can't believe you're here. Coffee's mostly chicory these days, and we're lucky to have even that."

"How's Doug doing down at the store?"

"Douglas is an idiot," Margaret said bluntly. "Gives credit to everyone and expects his family to live on air."

Rory looked uneasily at Irene, who stood quietly in the doorway.

"You've got one smart Daddy is how I remember it." He grinned at her. "Not every man can be his own boss, manage his own business. That takes brains."

Margaret put a sandwich of bread and ketchup and canned meat down in front of Rory and turned back to the stove to get the coffee.

"And what kind of brains does it take to drink it all away?"

Rory was shocked at the grim harshness of his sister's voice.

"Come on, now, Peg. Maybe we should talk later, eh?"

"Irene," said Margaret, "I want to talk to your uncle alone for a while. Go on!" She waved Irene out of the room and turned back to Rory. "You know, Douglas came home a week ago and said he thought he'd seen you downtown. Told me he called after you, he was so sure."

"Well, mighta been me. I've been living in the shanty a while."

"In the shanty? By the viaduct?" Margaret's hands dropped to her sides and she stared at her younger brother.

"It's not so bad. Better than many." The way he smiled made him look older than his thirty-two years. "Better than lots of places I've been in the last few years. We've even got white-washed stones leading you through the lanes. I'm an elected official up there. We've got a committee to keep things organized. Keep the men outta trouble and keep things running smooth."

"How long have you been in the city?"

"Oh, 'bout two months, I guess."

"Two months! And you're only just coming to see us now?"

"I've been meaning to get by every week. But I've been mighty busy, Peggy."

"Doing what, for the love of God? What could be more important than your family?"

He took a bite of the sandwich and washed it down with the bitter, reheated coffee. "I've been doing some work."

"What kind of work? Nobody has work these days."

Rory put his hands around the mug and leaned back in the

chair, studying his sister's face. "You're right there, and the ones that do, they get taken advantage of. There's not much justice for the working man. You wouldn't believe, Peg, the way people get treated. In the coal mines in Glace Bay there's miners and their families starving to death, thanks to the Dominion Coal Company. They blacklist a man if he buys food anywhere except at the company store and there the prices are so high they can't afford to buy enough to feed a bird. Anti-slavery laws just don't apply up there, I guess. Housing so bad the snow piles right up on the floor and babies freeze to death in their sleep. And that's just one place. There's others, lots of 'em and not so far from home. Let me tell you, I've seen some things, travelling round."

"You sound like one of them Communists," Margaret said.

"There's worse things."

"Talk like that can get you thrown into jail. You want to end up with Tim Buck and those other men in the Kingston Penitentiary?"

"Listen, the cops raided Buck's house illegally. He and those other fellas were run up a tree on that. Unlawful association, my ass. Seditious conspiracy! A load of shit, I'll tell you."

"Rory, don't use that language in this house!"

"Five years to be served at that hell-hole penitentiary in Kingston. And I'll tell you, there's many say they shouldn't be in there."

"There's some say people talk too much. Look at how he started that riot in the jail."

"He never started any riot. The guards tried to kill him, shooting into his cell." Rory felt the heat rising under his skin.

"You seem to be in the know, Rory," said Margaret.

"Well, I guess you and me are just going to have to disagree on this one. But maybe you'd see things more my way if you'd seen what I have. Men living in shacks made from empty dynamite boxes and the company telling them that's company housing and they're lucky to have it. Men beaten bloody for speaking out against injustice. Men shot dead for taking a stand."

"Stop it, Rory. I won't have this kind of talk in my house. I'm glad to see you and all. I am. But you've grown hard, associating with God knows what kind of people, and you've had your head twisted around by these foreign agitators. They're the real problem in this country. Too many foreigners living off relief and draining the system. The newspapers say!"

"To hell with the newspapers!" Rory stood up quickly, knocking the table. The cup tipped over and the coffee spilled.

"Goddamn it! I'm sorry, Margaret. Give me a cloth. I'll clean it up."

"No, I'll get it. Doesn't matter. Sit down." She pushed him back into the chair and turned to get a rag.

He'd forgotten this, his sister's antagonistic side. She had always been able to rile him, even when they were children—to intuit the exact nerve that could be manipulated to make him explode, and then she'd back down.

"Let's just forget this talk," she said. "Let's have a nice visit. Can you stay a while?"

"I don't think so. I've got to get back."

She dabbed at the spill and didn't meet his eyes.

"Just thought I'd come by and say hello. Thought I might stay overnight. Just the one night, if that's all right. I could use a hot bath."

"Yes, you could." She smiled. "You stay as long as you like. We don't have much, but you're welcome to it."

"How are things with you?" He took her hand, made her sit down, let her know they would be friends again. "You seem, I don't know, edgy."

"Oh, Rory, you just don't know how it's been." She said this in a rush, then put her hand up to her mouth, as though to stop more words from flying out.

"Tell me," Rory encouraged her.

"We're a laughingstock. I can't set foot outside the door."

Rory pulled a package of tobacco and some rolling papers out of his shirt pocket. He wanted something ordinary to do.

"I feel like I'm coming apart at the seams," said Margaret.

"What do you mean?"

"It doesn't matter." She lit a cigarette and sucked the smoke into her lungs. "There was trouble last year."

"What kind of trouble?"

"I'm ashamed to tell you."

"Peggy, I'm your brother. You can tell me." He reached to take her hand again, but she pulled away. She stood and leaned up against the kitchen counter.

"Pharmacists shouldn't drink. They make mistakes."

"What kind of mistakes?"

"Mistakes that make people sick."

"He mixed up somebody's prescription?"

Margaret put her fist up against her mouth. "Everyone knows," she said.

"Knows what?"

She went to the window above the sink and looked out into the space between the houses. "The neighbours watch us all the time."

Rory got up. As he put his arms around her he noticed that her hair did not smell clean. He always thought of Margaret as smelling of lily of the valley, but now she smelled of oil and something yeasty and slightly sour. *It must be like this all the time.* The thought of his niece locked up in the house day after day made him sick to his stomach.

Two hours later, after Rory finally persuaded Margaret to go to bed and get some rest, with the help of some little yellow pills, he went into Irene's room. A bright blue-and-green quilt lay on the neatly made bed, and on the pillow lay a china doll in a torn green dress, the right leg broken. There was a plain desk under the window that looked over the back garden. A lamp, a few books, *Chatelaine* magazine. A bureau stood to one side with a long lace cloth over the top and a pink bottle of perfume, a paper fan, a string of amber beads. The walls were painted a dusty rose, but looked more dusty than rose. Two embroidered pictures depicted English country gardens. The room had the look of a place where

time was spent waiting for something, not a room where someone had settled in.

Irene sat at the desk, her back to the door. Her chin rested on
the palm of her left hand and she gazed out into the backyard.
Rory noticed her chewed-down nails; the skin around her thumbnail was raw and inflamed. She had grown up. Her face had lost
some of the baby fat and was squarer. Her chin was determined,
her mouth set.

"How about you and me go for a walk?" he said.

"I don't know. Mum usually wants me to stay in and help her
with dinner."

"She's sleeping. Come on. She doesn't need you."

Irene didn't move. "She always needs me," she said.

"We're going out. Now."

As they stepped out into the sunlight Rory closed the door
gently behind him so as not to arouse Margaret, unknowingly
adopting the household's habits.

"Someone's just cut their grass," Irene said. "It smells wonderful."

Rory put his arm around her shoulders. She leaned her head
back and let him lead her, and she watched the sky pass through
the leaf-laced branches overhead. They walked along the street in
silence for a while. He didn't know how to begin.

"Mom's been sick," she said, lowering her head.

"Has she?"

"For a while now."

"What's wrong with her?"

"Dad says it's her nerves."

"You don't sound convinced."

"She … She's … She's better sometimes."

"Is she better now? Is this better?"

"She's okay right now."

Rory could tell from the even and controlled tone of her voice
that she'd been told to keep secrets.

"And how are you?"

"I'm all right."

"Are you?"

"It's been difficult." Irene ducked under his arm, reached up and picked a perfect maple leaf. She twirled it and put it against her cheek. Rory wondered at her choice of words. *Difficult.* Such a grown-up word, full of understatement.

"Go on."

"Mum feels afraid, I think. She's angry, but I don't know who at, although lots of times it's me. She sleeps a lot, and she cries." Irene shredded the flesh of the leaf, stripping it expertly down to the fragile skeleton. "If she's alone she gets, I don't know, afraid of bad things happening. So then I stay home because she seems better when I'm there, because what if my leaving would bring on a bad spell again? It's going to start eventually, but why do anything that might make it happen sooner? It's so hard to tell what will set her off, what will make her turn."

She stopped walking and let the leaf flutter to the sidewalk.

Rory noted that although he'd asked her if she was all right, all she'd talked about was how her mother felt.

"What does your dad say?"

"What? Oh, Dad. He says she's fragile. And he's right, of course. She is. More sensitive than most. Then, too, it's hard on him. He has to run the business, doesn't he?"

Rory looked around, as though the answer to the puzzle of this family might be found in the trees or the wind. He noticed three girls about Irene's age. As they neared, the one in the middle, who had long braids and wore a bright purple dress, nudged the other two and they crossed the street. They stared, and the one on the left whispered to the others. They giggled and hurried along their way. Irene took no notice.

"You know those girls?"

Irene gazed back at them dispassionately. "That's Violet and her friends. Janet and Wendy, I think. They're in my class."

"You want to go with them for a while? See your friends?" He knew even as he said it that she would not go.

"Oh, no. I don't go with them."

"Irene. Listen to me. Has your mother seen a doctor?"

"No doctors. Dad's quite clear." She stuck her chin out, and he sensed she'd fought and lost that battle. "He knows about medicine. He gives her pills. They help."

"Maybe your mother needs to go somewhere where she can get the rest she needs." He brushed hair out of her eyes.

Irene's eyes flew open wide and she grabbed his shirtsleeve. "Uncle Rory, you must promise me, promise me, you won't say anything like that to them. You have to promise. They won't have it, and if they think I've talked to you about this! You don't know! It will make her worse!" She twisted her fingers in his sleeve. "Promise me! Or I can't talk to you. You don't know what it would mean. To have everyone know. A pharmacist's wife gone crazy! Why, no one would ever go to the store again. We'd be in terrible trouble. Even worse than now." Her eyes filled with tears.

He put his arms around her. "Okay. Okay. We'll think of something." He heard her mumble into his shoulder.

"Take me away with you."

Hadn't Margaret said the same words to him, the last time he'd seen her? He should have seen that coming. Should have known it would seem like the logical solution to Irene.

"You gotta understand, Irene. I don't live anyplace right now. My work takes me all over. I live too rough. You'd be worse off." He wouldn't tell her about what could happen to a young girl in a shantytown.

"I wouldn't be a bother."

"I know you wouldn't be, but I just couldn't risk it. Besides, I know, no matter how tough it is right now, your mum and dad love you and it would break their hearts to have you disappear like that. And this won't be forever. Why, in just a couple of years you'll be all grown up and married yourself." He smiled at her. "I'll have a wee talk with your dad. I'll go over there now. I won't say you and I talked at all. Just say I'm worried about things. You let us work this out, Irene. Let the grown-ups handle it. Okay?"

"Sure, Uncle Rory. It was just a silly thought. We're fine, really. Mum might be right as rain tomorrow. It goes like that. She might just snap out of it." Her voice was light with lies. She looked at her watch. "I really have to go back. It won't help if I'm not home when she wakes up. See you later."

And before he could say anything she turned and hurried down the street.

1933

David leans up against his pack, not so near the fire as the rest. He is tired and wishes the men would settle down so he can get some sleep. He is feeling low and dirty, even though he has $10 in his pocket. How long will that last?

It had only been three weeks' work, and it is over now. He still can't fathom the unbelievable luck of it. They'd thought it was a cruel prank at first. The train stopped, and he and some thirty other men had started to scramble off, afraid there was going to be a roust. It wasn't jail they were afraid of so much as the beating that might go along with it. But four men in overalls stood next to a couple of big pickup trucks. Said they were looking for hands to pick tobacco. Right off, nobody moved, figuring it to be a sick joke. When they realized it wasn't, the four men were nearly stampeded, and one of them fired off a rifle to make the men settle down. Everybody who wanted to work got picked, and that meant every man jack of them.

Picking tobacco was filthy, hot work. They lay on their stomachs on flatbeds, pulled by horses, leaning over the edge. This way they pulled the leaves off but didn't tread on the new shoots coming up behind. David had trouble getting the hang of it, and was afraid he'd be kicked off the gang, until the guy next to him, a small, fiercely malodorous man who said he was from Kelowna showed him how.

"Thanks, friend. Name's David Hirsch," he said, extending his hand.

"Pleased to meet you," said the man but declined to give his name, and David knew better than to press it. Men on the road were allowed to keep whatever secrets they chose.

The sun beat down unmercifully and their flesh burned through their shirts and the rags they wrapped around their heads. The little guy next to him must have had three layers of clothes on, and David couldn't understand how he didn't pass out from the heat. David himself burned so bad he had blisters from his shoulders to his waist.

He hated the fat white slugs that curled up at the base of the leaves. You couldn't help but crush them and they left a sticky slime all over your hands that itched like hell. Maybe it was being so hungry, or maybe it was the infernal angle at which they had to hold their arms, but it was harder than he remembered work on the family's own farm had ever been. Still, it had been work, and any work was all right and he felt let down and lost when it ended. It had been the first work he'd had in a year.

He leans back on the rock and chews a stalk of dry grass while he tries to figure out where to go now. Most likely back out west for no other reason than there isn't anywhere better to go. Maybe he'll hit Montreal for a few weeks and then skip back to Vancouver for the winter. It isn't so cold out there. He scratches his groin. Shit. He's probably picked up crabs in the tobacco camp. He'll have to get some kerosene.

"You're fucking crazy!" says Pete, a hulking guy with a scraggly red beard.

"I'm fucking crazy? You're the one who's fucking crazy!" says the little guy who'd worked next to David in the fields.

Somebody has got hold of a couple of bottles of wine and they've been passing them back and forth among the other six men. Voices get louder with every round. David is eighteen now. He is taller and stronger than when he left home. No matter how strong he is, though, he doesn't want to get mixed up in a fight over something as stupid as this. He watches from the shadows, keeping an eye on Pete, who gets up, swaying a little. The bottle hangs from his right hand.

"I'm telling ya, ya jackass, that it's Teddy who's president," says Pete.

"And I'm telling you that you're fucking wrong. Franklin D. is president. Don't you read the goddamn papers?"

"You calling me ignorant?"

"Sit down, Pete," says another man. "Have another drink and then pass that bottle along, why don't ya?"

"You probably don't even know who the prime minister is, do ya?" says the little guy.

"You calling me ignorant?" repeats Pete. He passes the bottle but stays on his feet, takes a step closer to the little guy.

The little guy stands up, too, and David wishes he wouldn't, wishes he would sit back down. The little guy's head barely reaches Pete's shoulder.

"You know about as much as a dog knows about its grandmother," he says.

Pete grabs him and throws him like a sack of rags. It happens very quickly. David hadn't thought Pete could move that fast, drunk as he is. The little guy's head hits the rocks surrounding the fire with a thick crack. He kicks his legs out a couple of times and makes a noise like he's being strangled, then he lays very still.

For five, perhaps six, seconds, no one moves, until a sharp pop from a piece of burning wood breaks the terrible enchantment. One of the men gets up and touches the little guy's neck, feeling for a pulse. He pulls his hand away and it is covered in blood.

"Shit, you bastard, Pete."

"It was a fucking accident! He fell. You all saw that!" says Pete. "It was a fucking accident."

The men stand and look down at the inert form. David stands, too, but doesn't approach the circle. Silently, Pete picks up the body and carries it down the tracks. After a few minutes he comes back, sits down and snatches the wine away from the man to his right. He drinks it all down, until the bottle is empty, and he throws it into the wood, where they hear it land with a thud. He glowers at the men, daring them to say something. After a while they hear a train coming down the line.

The next day there'll be talk about a drunk who fell asleep with his head on the rail. Who's to say? It happens all the time.

David picks up his pack and walks into the night. He feels his throat tighten and sharp prickling behind his eyes. He thinks about the little guy and how scared he'd been all the time, wearing his three jackets and two pairs of pants, no matter how hot the weather, so no one would steal them before winter. Only the booze had made him fearless, and look what that moment of courage had got him. Didn't matter a damn that the little guy'd been right. Right didn't matter much out here.

11

As Rory walked he worried his knuckles until they cracked and popped, and by the time he arrived at the shop he'd gone over what he wanted to say to his brother-in-law. The little bell over the door rang as he strode in.

What he saw surprised him. When he had last seen the place, it had been a run-of-the-mill little pharmacy. Shelves of creams and oils and hairpins and salves. An appropriately gleaming counter behind which Douglas stood dispensing pills. A rack of magazines. Nothing ostentatious, but a proud little shop.

It had changed.

To the right of the entrance was a long counter and eight chrome stools with red leather seats. On the wall behind were the shiny-loud trappings of a soda fountain. A cooler for ice cream. Large arced taps for the soda. A big mirror reflecting glasses and bowls and spoons. There were three small black metal tables, each with two chairs, in the centre of the room. The place looked deserted, though.

Toward the back of the room was a second counter, smaller, as though huddled shamefully in the shadows. On it stood a large cash register and a small sign: Prescriptions Filled. Rory was relieved to see that against the wall, shelves displayed the sorts of things he expected to see in a drug store: toothbrushes, hair-brushes, packages of bandages, smelling salts, soaps, eucalyptus inhalations, and packages of powders for making spruce and ginger beer.

Rory's brow furrowed as he examined the mirror behind the soda fountain; it was speckled with spots and smears. The wooden floor was dusty, and none of the bottles and tins of health supplies had the ship-shape-shiny look Rory remembered. The windows were dim with grime, and dead flies lay on the sill.

To think he used to laugh at his brother-in-law for being so meticulous, almost prissy.

Douglas was nowhere to be seen. Rory looked at the clock on the wall. Four-thirty on a Saturday afternoon. Surely if this was supposed to be a hangout for kids, it wasn't working. It didn't look as though anybody had been eating ice cream at those tables in days.

"Doug!" Rory called out. "It's Rory. You in the back?"

"Just a minute. Be right with you."

Rory heard scuffling from the storeroom and rustling papers, then Douglas stepped through the curtain. He was sweaty and flushed. His eyes were bloodshot, and he looked far older than when Rory had last seen him. His features were loose and soft and battered. Rory knew that no matter how crazy she might be, about this one thing Margaret sure was right.

"Well, I'll be damned," said Douglas. "Look what the cat dragged in." He came around the counter, his hand extended. As Rory took it, the familiar odour reached him. The smell of men long-gone was always the same. It seeped out of their pores, sickly sweet and sour at the same time. The smell of a body trying unsuccessfully to cleanse itself of a poisoning.

"It's been a long time. A long time," Douglas said, his voice blustery with good humour.

"Too long, I think. How are you, Doug?"

"Oh, can't complain. Times are hard but you soldier on. Make the best of a bad situation, eh?" He scratched the back of his head, and little white flakes of dandruff fell on his knitted vest. "You'll come and see the girls, of course. They'll be mighty glad to see you. Mighty glad."

"I've been up to the house already."

"Oh, yes? Well, then, that's good. Good. Bet Margaret was pleased. So tell me, what do you think of the place? You want a soda? You can see I've made some improvements. A real brainstorm." He gestured toward the soda fountain. "Or maybe something a little more grown-up? A little more fortifying?" He winked at Rory and rubbed his hands together.

"Not for me, thanks all the same."

"What, no celebratory drink? Well, I'm certainly going to celebrate," he said defiantly, as though Rory had told him he should not. "Don't you go away." He disappeared into the back of the shop and returned carrying a half-full bottle of whisky and two small glasses. He motioned for Rory to sit at a table, took a seat himself and filled both glasses to the rim.

"Go on, man! A toast to homecomings!" He held out the glass. Rory took it and sipped. Douglas took a large gulp from his and then shook his head. "Strong stuff that! Wowzer! Puts hair on your chest. Drink up!"

The change that had come over Douglas seemed nearly impossible to Rory. When he'd first met Douglas all those years ago, hovering around his sister, timid and awkwardly proud, hoping for an introduction, Rory had thought him too stuffy, too obsessed with social constraints. A bit old-womanish. Douglas wasn't a man who would have suited the word *wowzer*, a foolish word used, in Rory's opinion, by foolish people trying to be more sophisticated than they could ever hope to be. Now it suited him all too well.

"Doug, I want to talk about Margaret. She doesn't seem well to me."

"Not well? Oh, now, don't you worry yourself about Margaret. She's a nervous little thing."

"I'd say it's gone a sight past nerves. She tells me she won't go out because the neighbours are spying."

"Nonsense—and tomorrow she'll say something different." Douglas poured himself another drink. He didn't bother to ask Rory, whose glass remained virtually untouched, if he wanted more.

"Does it seem normal that your wife thinks the neighbours are spying on her?"

"She's moody."

"I think it's more than that."

"You've decided this, have you? After a few hours in my house—*my* house, mind—after years of absence?"

Rory was both impressed and appalled at how Douglas resisted admitting his wife was ill. He didn't want to betray Irene's confidence, and suspected he would get little support for her cause from Douglas at any rate. And when all was said and done, Margaret might be his sister, but she was Douglas's wife. He could interfere only so far.

"She says she hasn't been out of the house in months."

"She exaggerates." Douglas drank from his glass, which was nearly empty again. He crossed his arms and leaned back in his chair, scowling.

"Look, Doug, I don't think I'm getting through here. I'm saying I think Margaret's sick. She needs someone to look at her. A doctor."

"Nonsense. I don't know who you think you are, quite frankly. May I suggest you tread lightly, Rory, tread lightly." He toyed with his empty glass. "Have a drink with me. Let's have no more of this talk."

Rory covered his glass with his hand.

"Suit yourself." Douglas put his own empty glass down with a sour look. "But I'm telling you once and for all, there are no problems in my house, Rory, and I would tell you to look to your own, if you had one, which I suspect you do not."

"Then, explain to me why Margaret tells me you're drinking yourself to death and drinking this place into the ground."

Douglas stood up from the table. He walked behind the counter and began to polish the top with a grimy-looking cloth. "I told you, Rory. There is no problem that requires the assistance of outsiders."

Rory watched Douglas's eyes roam back to the whisky bottle, and noted the look of hunger. Rory rolled his own glass between his hands, his elbows on the table. He stared into the amber liquid and said quietly, "So what are you doing drinking like this in the middle of the day? I'll bet my last nickel you've been going at it pretty good since, what, noon?"

Douglas slammed the top of the counter with his open palm.

"I will not be spoken to like that. Not by you or anyone, see.

Not anyone! And particularly not some road dog hopeful for a ... Yes, I might just as well say it—for a handout and a free ride." Douglas wiped sweat off his neck with a grey handkerchief and blew his nose. He looked at Rory with his chin stuck out as though daring him to take a swing.

Rory studied Douglas, the pouting and yet slightly loose lower lip, the indignant eye, the bright flame of alcohol-induced rage. He fought down the impulse to give Douglas a pop in the snout and then shake him until ... That was the problem. Rory wasn't sure he'd know when to stop.

"And what about Irene? Even you must see she's unhappy!"

"Must I?" Douglas bristled. "You seem to have a great number of opinions, my man, for someone with no family of his own." His eyes strayed back to the shining bottle, to the empty glass, but he stayed where he was. He was shaking, but whether with rage or the desire for a drink, Rory couldn't tell.

"Look, Douglas, ending up in a brawl isn't going to help either one of us. Hell, I'm awfully fond of my sister, and Irene. Truth be told, Douglas, I'm even kinda partial to you." Rory smiled, cocked his head and raised his eyebrows, looking a bit of a fool on purpose. He had learned it was sometimes easier to disarm rage if he let the other man think himself superior.

"I've got no job for you here, if that's what you're thinking."

"Never occurred to me. I've gotta go back on the road soon. No two ways about that. There's a bit of work I've got to see to out Nova Scotia way."

This was true. Rory knew, no matter what disaster he found here, there were other, larger causes to which he had committed himself. He would soon be on his way again, and what he could do for his sister was limited. That's my escape route, he thought, and the thought didn't make him proud.

"Nothing down there but fish and coal mines," said Douglas.

"Not an easy life, that's true. The miners have it harder than most."

"Don't tell me you're going to take up mining? Listen, did I ever tell you about that fella I knew, thought he'd make it big mining for gold in South America?" Douglas's mood had shifted again, in the mercurial way of drunks, and he began to tell a long, twisted tale Rory suspected was only half true. Douglas poured himself another drink and when he had finished that he poured another, and they sat together for more than two hours, because as distressing as it was watching Douglas in the condition he was in, it was better than dealing with Margaret. The two men stayed until the street grew quiet as one store after another closed for the day, but no customer ever entered the shop.

It was nearly noon the next day and Rory was in the vestibule getting his pack ready to leave, stuffing in his still-dirty clothes with short hard thrusts. A shirt, a pair of socks, an undershirt and extra shorts, an unmailed letter to a girl in Saskatoon whose face had now faded into his memory in a blur of sun-rose skin and wind-tangled hair, a blanket, a map of Canada and a dog-eared copy of Upton Sinclair's *The Jungle*.

"Don't tell me you're on your way already," Douglas said.

"'Fraid so."

"Well, if you must go there's not much we can do to hold you, is there?" He kept his hands in his pockets. "Got the road fever, eh?"

"You bet," said Rory. He left Douglas to his hangover and went upstairs to Irene's room.

"What ya doing, Doodles?"

"Reading." She sat at her desk again, her back to the door, her ankles latched around the chair legs.

"What are you reading?"

"A book." The flat answer told him he was unforgiven, and he didn't blame her.

He walked to her, stood next to the desk, looked out into unkempt backyard. He turned to face her, a simple movement more difficult than he had expected.

"You mad at me?"

She closed the book, which he suspected she had not really been reading. Seeing the look on her face told him that yes, she was angry. He knew she was trying to be brave and hoping for some miracle of diplomacy or heroism.

"No. I'm not angry."

"You just got to remember that you won't be in this house forever."

Her eyes looked so intently into his that it was all he could do to keep from turning away. "I'm afraid I'm going to disappear," she said.

"You won't disappear. You can have anything you want in a couple of years. Things will get better. I promise." They both knew he was probably lying, that it would not get better and that no help would come.

He wanted to be a different man just at that moment, but there were some burdens, he shamefully admitted, that he did not have the moral strength to shoulder. He was fine at a short storm of fists and boots and sticks, fine for a strike, a march, a rally, a speech and the cinematic sorrows of strangers. He was no good at the long haul, no good at the intimate struggles of family, no good, it seemed, at fulfilling the contract of love.

He put his arms around her and she was the one who pulled away first. He went downstairs into the kitchen, where he found Margaret but not Douglas, which was just as well.

"I'm going now," he said to his sister, who sat playing solitaire. She put down the last three cards and sighed, finding nothing useful there.

"I wish you'd stay," she said, and he had no idea if she meant it or not.

"I've got to get back to work."

"That work," she said. "You'll get yourself killed."

"Not me. I'm too tough for that."

"People get killed all the time, tough or weak, makes no difference to God." Her voice was gummy and flat as molasses on a gritty floor. He kissed her on the top of her head as she began to shuffle her cards again.

"Margaret," he said. "You've got to pull yourself together, sister."

She dealt another row of cards.

Margaret remained where she was in the kitchen, and Irene stayed where she was in her room. Only Douglas moved to the window to watch Rory walk down the street. Lucky bastard, he thought. He pressed his lips between his teeth and stuffed his slightly trembling hands into his pants pockets, where they tightened into fists. His life had become a tangled and unmanageable mess. He had seen the look on Rory's face whenever he took a drink, the disapproving look, the judging look. But some days he was sure that if he could just find his way to the bottom of a perfect bottle, the answer would be there waiting for him, clear and sweet and simple. Some days it was all that kept him from getting a gun and shooting them all.

Irene sat on her bed and pretended, in case her mother came in, to be reading. The late-afternoon light slanted across the floor onto the bed. She stretched out her legs and warmed her toes. From the kitchen came the sound of chopping, the knife's *thud* on the wooden cutting board. She could smell onions frying, and the smell comforted her. Her mother making dinner was always a good sign.

Her father was in the living room now, reading the paper and occasionally sneaking off to the closet under the stairs for sips from the bottle he kept hidden in his old croquet bag. Why he'd thought no one would find it there, she couldn't understand. She'd snuck into the closet one day nearly a year before, and if *she'd* figured it out she suspected her mother had as well. Irene found the bottle in the canvas croquet bag, nestled like a hard brown beetle within the folds of an old green towel. She'd taken it and poured it out. Right down the drain and turned the water on full force to wash the smell away. She put the bottle back, hoping her father would find it and understand that she'd got rid of it and left the empty husk as a silent plea. Three days later a new bottle had replaced the old.

Irene shut the book and rubbed her eyes. Uncle Rory had come for a day. What good was a day? Irene hadn't realized until she'd seen him standing in the doorway, his face wind-marked, his shoulders so broad, that somewhere in the back of her mind she'd been waiting for him to come and set things right again. He was their only relative, really. Daddy's parents had gone back to Scotland. If it hadn't been for the photograph standing on the mantel, Irene knew that there would come a day when she wouldn't be able to remember what they looked like. Her mother's parents were dead, of course, buried on a hill somewhere, her mother said, although Irene had never seen the graves. Her mother kept a small picture album, but never took it out, nor did she want their photos "cluttering up the furniture," as she put it. Then there was Aunt Janet, but she didn't count.

Her mother didn't like Aunt Janet, and neither she nor Daddy liked Uncle Oscar, whom her father referred to as the Mouse. They saw them once a year when they were invited over to their big airy house for lunch in the garden, as Aunt Janet insisted on calling their yard. Her cousins, Brad and Earl, were noisy ten- and eleven-year-old boys who produced frogs and dead mice and sad-looking turtles from every pocket. They were never, in turn, invited to visit the house on Homewood, and her mother said, "Don't they get the hint?" Apparently they didn't, even though for two years now Margaret had refused to accompany her husband and daughter.

So that was the extent of their family. Irene tried to picture them all together, but found nothing in her head but blank spots, like photos with shadows where the faces should be, as though they'd moved at just the moment when the photographer snapped the shutter.

Her father tuned the radio to the Canadian National Railway hour of music. The announcer introduced Ernest Seitz, the boy prodigy who created such a sensation when he appeared with the famous soprano Madame Albani some years before. Irene wondered what it must be like to be a prodigy, feted and flung before the world like that. She had seen a photograph of Ernest Seitz once in the *Evening Telegram*: an overly serious young man with dark hair and just the sort of intense, deep-set eyes and slightly pouting mouth you would expect in a genius. He hadn't looked very happy, but perhaps that was only the expression he adopted for publicity photos. Surely he must be happy to be travelling around the country, maybe even around the world, with all those people making such a fuss of him. He probably flew in planes. And stayed in hotel rooms all by himself and rode in his own automobile. And wouldn't that be heaven?

"Dinner's on. Come and get it, or I'll throw it to the dogs!"

Irene knew the sound of that voice, knew the threat contained even in a remark meant to be amusing. Uncle Rory's coming and going had rattled them all and it was just like her mother to respond the way no one else did, by suddenly becoming full of vigour. She braced herself.

"Coming." She put her book away and smoothed her hair.

As she came down the stairs she met her father. He folded his copy of the *Mail and Empire* and placed it on his desk, carefully centring it and aligning a pencil along the top edge. He patted the pockets of his pants and then his vest.

"Coming, Dad?"

"Yes, yes, coming right along."

He turned his back to her, opened the drawer of his desk and then closed it, without taking anything out. He put something in his mouth and then turned back to Irene. "Doesn't that smell good!" he said, his words buoyed up with the scent of peppermint and whisky. For a moment Irene thought he meant his breath.

"It's getting cold," her mother called.

"Oh, yes. Smells great," Irene said as she and her father went in to dinner. A piano concerto accompanied them down the hall.

Margaret stood proudly at the stove, spooning carrots and peas into a dark blue bowl.

"Irene, get the butter, will you, dear?"

Irene got the butter dish from the cupboard and took her place between her mother and father at the table. Her mother hummed along with the radio. "That's nice music," she said. "Mozart, isn't it? I like it. Who's that playing?"

"It's that Jew, I think. The young one." Douglas sat down at the table and put his napkin on his lap.

Margaret put the bowl of steaming vegetables down next to the platter of pork chops. It was a feast tonight, a real treat. Margaret had opened one of her jars of applesauce to go with the chops. She even put a bottle of beer out for Douglas.

"I wish you wouldn't say it like that," Margaret said, taking her seat. She picked up her fork and looked at it closely, checking for watermarks or bits of old food.

"Say what?"

"That *Jew*. Like that." Margaret polished her fork.

"How should I say it? That's what he is, isn't he?" Her father's half-smile told Irene he considered it a foolish remark.

"This is really good, Mum. Really good."

"You say it like it's a dirty word," said her mother to her father.

"They're a dirty people."

"They're not allowed to sit at the bus stop on Carlton," said Irene, who knew she should keep her mouth shut. "Someone put a sign up—Gentiles Only."

"People can be so disgusting." Margaret cut her meat into tiny pieces.

"Yes, I saw it, with that Nazi symbol," said Douglas. "Well, that may be a bit extreme, but you can't blame people. These immigrants, they infringe, you see. And they are devious. You give them an inch and they'll take a mile."

"Douglas! I'm surprised at you. Honestly."

"May I have the applesauce, please?" said Irene. Her mother passed it to her without paying attention. "What's the difference between us and the Jews, Daddy?"

"Suffice it to say, my dear," said her father, passing her a bowl of mashed potatoes, "that they are not like us. They live differently, have strange habits. They do not believe in Jesus Christ."

"And since when have you considered yourself a devout Christian, Douglas?"

"I don't have to be a churchgoer to know that Jews are not to be trusted. Look at the way they live, for crying out loud, all jumbled together over in Kensington. Chickens and pickle barrels everywhere. Women in those dreadful wigs, men with those ridiculous beards and hats. They are an ugly people, and not clean in their habits. We shouldn't be letting so many of them in the country. I am somewhat inclined to believe Prime Minister Bennett when he says they are at the root of the economic problems."

"Are you saying all Jews are Communists?"

Margaret had stopped eating, which Irene knew was a bad sign. Irene thought she might be disagreeing just for the sake of it, but she couldn't be sure. In fact, Irene found the entire conversation confusing. Her mother and father seemed to have reversed roles: her mother sounded reasonable and kind, her father sounded angry and mean-spirited.

"Who said anything about Communists?" said her father loudly. "Why are you always bringing up Communists?"

"Me? Good God, Douglas. It seems I can't mention that word without you becoming incensed these days. Methinks you doth protest too much!" Margaret picked up her fork and looked pleased she had got a rise out of him. "Perhaps I should denounce you to Police Chief Draper's Red Squad, like they're doing in Germany these days."

"Don't be absurd. Me, a Communist! You say very foolish things, Margaret. Very foolish, indeed. This argumentative streak is not attractive." He scowled while he chewed furiously. He swallowed and took a swig of beer from the bottle, not bothering with the glass set out for him.

"You're one to talk about attractive, my man. Wipe your face."

Irene tried to think of some way to diffuse the growing tension, to return them to the nice meal, a meal like other families were eating in other houses all over the city.

"Do we know any Jews?" she said, because maybe if they knew

one and her parents agreed on how they felt about that person, then they might not argue.

"Of course not," said her father.

"Why would we know Jews?" said her mother.

Nothing was said after that. Her father finished his plate, drank his beer, pushed himself away from the table and went back to the living room to listen to the news. Her mother pushed her peas and carrots around the plate for a few moments, and then put her fork down.

"Irene, why do you think your uncle Rory left?" she said.

"He had to go to work," said Irene.

"He has no work."

"He said he had work in the Maritimes."

"And you believe him."

Irene didn't answer. Yes or no would be equally dangerous.

"You don't think he left because of something else?" Her mother looked at her out of the corner of her eye. Irene knew her mother was digging to see if Uncle Rory had left because of something her mother had said or done. This would fill her with shame, and the shame would twist around to annoyance, and then to anger.

"No. He only left because he had to. He wanted to stay, he said so."

"I know you talked to him." What her mother meant was: *I know you talked about me.*

"He told me about riding on a train."

"You told him things."

"Just about school and stuff."

"What stuff?"

"Like what I'm reading. Books and things."

"You think I'm stupid?"

"No," Irene said, bracing herself.

"Yes, you do, you both do, you and your father. You think worse than that."

Margaret picked her plate up, opened the refrigerator and put it in with a clatter. Irene quickly tried to finish her supper.

"I had peach preserves and biscuits," said Margaret, shifting moods again, now sad and pathetic, a child whose birthday party has been ruined.

"I can get you some," said Irene. "Do you want some? I'll have some with you."

"I don't want any," her mother said and walked out of the kitchen, past her husband, who was reaching for something in the back of the hall closet, and climbed the stairs.

Irene heard her feet in the hallway and then heard her close the door. She heard the springs groan as her mother lay on the bed. Her mother would sleep in her clothes tonight. Soon there was nothing but the sound of her father, back in the living room now, trying to dial in *Amos 'n' Andy* on the wireless.

Irene cleared the table and began to wash the dishes, her stomach heavy with the clay-like lumps of pork chops and potatoes.

Upstairs, Margaret pulled the pillow over her head and wept. She had made an effort, hadn't she made an effort? Too little too late, perhaps, but an effort. She reached her hand across the empty space in the bed next to her, wishing it could stay empty.

12

In the nearly a year and a half since Rory had last been to town, Joe Fleischman hadn't changed much. He was still a big raw-boned man. Maybe his shock of wavy hair was starting to thin, and maybe he looked a little unhappier than at their last meeting, but Joe had never been a smiling sort of man. His jacket was patched, as were his pants, and his shirt looked threadbare, but that was the uniform of the working man these days. Joe and Rory often joked about how the poor looked worse but the rich looked better during these hard years—domestic work was so cheap they could afford to hire twelve maids for the wages they used to have to pay two.

The Blue Tulip Restaurant hadn't changed much either. There was still too much smoke in the air and the coffee was still bad. The same mysterious men came and went out of the back room, where, when the door opened, you caught a glimpse of a blackboard and some desks, a number of phones and a couple of glowering faces with cigars stuck in their chops.

Rory and Joe met once every few days to talk about how the work was going. Rory was helping Joe organize the men at the various shantytowns and flophouses to hold a march protesting unemployment levels and the lack of government response. Most of the talk today, however, centred around the recent fascist activity in the city. Here in Kensington Market, the Jewish neighbourhood, people were scared, but mostly they were angry. There was a core of hard young men in the pool rooms and the bookmakers in the area who didn't take kindly to what had been going on in the city since Hitler had been voted into power in Germany, from where came stories of beatings, torture, confiscation, book burnings and, recently, the outlawing of all political parties, except Hitler's own Nazi Party. The conversation inevitably swung back to Toronto and recent events at the Balmy Beach Canoe Club.

"They call themselves 'civic-minded young men,' keeping the beach free of 'undesirables,'" said Joe.

"It true they've been wearing swastikas?" said Rory.

"Yup. Wearing buttons on their shirts, painting it on the goddamn trees!" Joe's spoon clattered as it hit the tabletop, and he rotated his wrists until the joints popped. "I went out to the Beach, you know. I saw what they're doing. I saw the signs. Swastikas up and down the boardwalk, all over the canoe club, on the porches. 'No Jews' scrawled on a bench. I sat my Jewish ass down, I can tell ya. Guys who don't even know what the hell Hitler stands for are walking around with a swazi in one hand and a stiff-arm salute on the other. They've been showing up at baseball games."

Rory pressed his palms together as though warming up for something. He felt the adrenaline start to flow, sluicing a pathway through his veins, clearing out the anger he felt at Douglas and

Margaret and the whole damn mess. It had been three days ago, but he couldn't get it out of his head and it was making him edgy.

"There might be more trouble," he said.

There were five softball games being played that night, and the crowd of spectators numbered in the thousands. Rory and Joe sat on the small hill that made up the periphery of Christie Pits Park. It was the game between the Harbord Playground team, which was mostly Jewish boys from the neighbourhood, and the team from St. Peter's church at Bathurst and Bloor, on which Rory and Joe focused most of their attention. Shouts of "Heil Hitler" were heard now and then, and other voices called, "Get out of the country, go to Germany if ya like Hitler so much!"

"Fascists!" Joe bellowed and stood up so everyone could see him.

People jeered each other back and forth.

"Kike!" someone yelled.

Rory scanned the crowd. He knew a number of guys by sight. The Christie Pit gang was out in full force, young guys with their shirtsleeves rolled high to show off their muscles. Rory could see them on the south hill, drinking beer and cheering every time the Catholic boys made a run. He thought somebody must have put a call out to the pool halls and the bookmakers around College and Spadina because some of the local Jewish toughs from Euclid Avenue were there, and the Spadina Avenue Gang, too. Mostly these young men kept their jackets on, and Rory wondered what they might be carrying beneath them.

Now and then the Pit Gang partly unfurled a banner with what looked like a swastika on it. Skirmishes across the park stopped as quickly as they started. In the second inning a fight broke out. A guy behind Joe leaned over and told him in a low voice that a gentile had been hit with a lead pipe and two young Jews had been chased from the park. The game resumed after ten minutes. Rumours spread that the Pit Gang was drinking pretty heavily.

St. Peter's won the game, five to four.

"Look," Joe said and elbowed Rory in the ribs. "Those guys are the Willowdale Swastika Supporters." On the small hill near the south of the park, the knot of Pit Gang-ers was joined by nearly thirty others. Two of them stepped to the front and held up a white blanket emblazoned with a swastika.

"Heil Hitler," they yelled, and the words echoed across the park.

Rory saw two red-faced players from the Harbord Playground team start to rush forward, and then they were pulled back by their friends. The flag and its emblem was held high. For a moment nothing happened, and Rory felt the tension thicken as, one by one, people began to point and mutter. He saw a boy hit the earth with his bat, small clouds of dirt flying up from the force of his rage. A skinny kid wearing a yarmulke who'd been playing second base threw down his catcher's mitt and kicked it.

Fury ran through the Jews like a giant sheet flapped over their heads, snapped at the end with a great *crack*. All heads turned toward the southern end of the park, toward the gently rippling swastika. Then one kid picked up a bat. As though it were a signal, the rest of the team began picking up anything they could find—bats, sticks, rocks. They, and their supporters, surged across the diamond toward the small hill. For a few seconds it looked like the men on the hilltop with the flag might stand their ground. With every step the crowd of Jews grew in number, and the Nazi supporters scattered throughout the crowd hesitated. Then they ran around the Jews but failed to gain the lead. The Jewish boys closed the gap between them and the flag bearers. The Pit Gang scrambled down the southern slope onto Bloor Street, banner in hand, the Jews in pursuit. The rest of the Nazi supporters began swinging their fists, picking up bats and rocks and wading in to fight in earnest.

"Well, all right, then," said Joe, and he rushed forward.

Rory followed right behind him, both men pulling lengths of pipe from under their jackets.

The police, who had been hanging around anticipating trouble, were powerless in the face of so many people. They struggled to bring one knot of brawlers under control, only to have another hundred go unchecked. A sea of bodies, hurling stones and slugging each other with bats and fists and trash can lids and anything else that came to hand, rolled in wave after wave along the street. A man with a tire iron used it as a stave to block off the blows of a man with a crowbar.

The riot spread along Bloor Street. Reinforcements from the Pit Gang poured in. Truckloads of Jews from down at Spadina and College began to arrive, carrying pool cues, chains, pickaxes and bricks. They yelled to whomever they passed on the street, "Gevalt, me shlugt yidn!" Help! They're beating Jews!

The surging mass moved along Bloor to Montrose Avenue. The air was a massive confusion of grunts and screams. Rory found himself next to a bearded rabbi with a broom in his hand. The man looked at Rory for a moment, unsure which side he was on, then, when Rory punched a man wearing a swastika button, smiled and said, "Shalom."

"Shalom," replied Rory and spun around to knock the legs out from under a thug coming at him with a broken bottle.

The next morning all of Toronto was in a state of shock, and Margaret was among those most disturbed. She didn't know that Rory was across town in a shanty tent nursing badly bruised ribs, a black eye and a knot on his head the size of an orange. No one had been killed, but scores were in hospital, mostly with head injuries, and who knew how many more were being treated in the privacy of their own homes. Even with horses and motorcycles, the police hadn't been able to stop the violence until nearly midnight. Thousands of people had been involved in what was being called a race riot. The mayor had agreed to take swift steps against Nazis and called on Police Chief Draper to account for himself. All league baseball games were cancelled for the duration, although for the duration of what was unclear.

Margaret finished reading, having twice gone over both the *Telegram*, which insisted a Jewish Communist conspiracy was to blame, and the *Star*, which said it was the fault of the Swastika Clubs. She folded the papers carefully and put them in the ever-growing pile in a corner of the kitchen.

"You will stay home today, Irene. And probably for the rest of the week. The city is coming apart," she said, and Irene nearly burst out laughing, for when was the last time her mother had let her out of her sight?

Three nights later, Rory and the other bindlestiffs sat in a circle around the fires. Many of the men drank canned heat. They scooped the pink jelly from a can of Sterno into a sock, strained it and mixed the highly potent cocktail with soda pop and water. When they passed the cup to Rory, he said a quiet no thank you, which the old-timers respected, and the cup passed on. Talk of the riot hadn't lasted long here, for the men had all seen violence before and didn't find it surprising. They swapped stories about their travels across the drought-plagued prairies, up into the Gaspé, the lumber and railway camps, over the Rockies and through the big cities, from Halifax to Victoria. They told tales about the town clown-cops and the city harness-bulls who were famous for either their brutality or their compassion. They told of meals handed out and women who had sympathy for them, and if the number of silken thighs and dimpled smiles were exaggerated in the interests of keeping morale as high as possible, such lies were overlooked.

Rory paid little attention. The banter and the bluster soothed him. He felt he was back in a world he understood. He wished things had turned out differently at his sister's; he wished he'd never gone to visit in the first place. He knew he'd failed some kind of test there and he wasn't proud of himself.

1933

He has spent the night in the railway station waiting room, surrounded by others of what he's come to think of as his tribe. More women sleep in the stations than out in the street, which makes it safer, because the men try not to scare them, try to behave like protective males, especially if the women have children with them. However, it also makes it more danger-ous. It is not unheard of that the sicker among them troll the stations looking for girls. This night, though, has passed without incident, and even over the crying of a baby, he's been able to get a couple of hours of shut-eye.

At six-thirty he rouses himself, washes in the public toilets for a nickel and heads to the employment office. It is lonely and dark on the street and the buildings stand soldier-stiff with No Help Wanted signs hanging like tarnished medals in the windows. Nearly sixty men are lined up ahead of him, and the office doesn't open until nine. His stomach feels like it's pushing up against his spine but he dares not eat the little food he has left. He makes a fist and presses it into his belly. Everywhere he looks men clap their hands and swing their arms, partly because the air is cold, but mostly because it's something to do. He shoves his hands in his pockets.

At eight-thirty the line is around the block so far he can't see the end. A man tries to edge in somewhere, but hoots and curses drive him to the back, his pleas about the sick wife falling on tragedy-deafened ears. At nine o'clock when the door opens as many shuffle in as can fit, and the guard closes the doors behind them, with some pushing and shoving because no one wants to be the last one who just couldn't squeeze in. They stand waiting for the phones to ring. Behind a low separation office workers move about, largely ignoring the crowd. What is there to say until the phones ring?

At last one does, and when the clerk hangs up he turns to the expectant mass and says, "Dishwasher. Dollar and a half a day. One day's work. Desk number three." Men dash to the counter and plead their case. There are babies at home. They are hungry. They have worked in a restaurant all their lives. The clerk selects two men and sends them on their way. Two men so the employer can choose the best between them. The rest, dejected, turn to wait again. After an hour, the group is turned out, forced to go to the back of the line, and the next group is herded in. Of the first group, five have found work, none for more than three days.

He is not among the chosen.

He spends the rest of the day in the public library, trying not to fall asleep, for if he does, they will turn him out. It is hard, with his eyelids like stones and every muscle weighted and wooden. He tries to concentrate on Ovid, on Rousseau, on Victor Hugo. Hunger makes him drowsy. Once his head falls back and he wakes himself up with a snort. He looks around with his heart beating hard, sure someone has heard and will make him go. Go where? Just away. Go away. Move on. Can't stay here.

The library closes and he heads west, picking newspapers off the street and from trash cans along the way. He hasn't had his boots off in more than seventy-three hours and his feet are a mass of blisters. He limps badly. He has a third of a roll of sausage in his pack and the heel of a day-old loaf, paid for with the last of the window-washing money, so he doesn't have to line up outside the relief house. He's had enough of lining up for one day.

When he gets to the park he picks a bench far away from the street and the fountain, but with a view of the paths so he can see if anyone tries to creep up on him. He hasn't counted on how tired he was. He eats the bread and sausage, trying to save some for the next day but unable to make himself stop chewing. The food hits his system like a drug and the last of his resistance against sleep gives way. As soon as he's settled under the thin layer of newspapers, his head on his pack, he falls into a deep slumber.

The patrolman swings his nightstick with all the force in his arm. The blow lands on the soles of his blistered feet and sends a jolt of searing pain to the top of his skull. He thinks his heart will stop and before he knows what he's doing, he jumps up and raises his hands to defend himself.

The cop takes him away in handcuffs, down to the city lockup on a thirty-day vagrancy ticket, and tells him he should be glad it isn't more, that he could have him up on charges of attacking a police officer, resisting arrest, and if the jails weren't already so full he'd do just that. As he's hustled along the street a woman nudges the man she's with and *they stare at him, shaking their heads. He isn't even ashamed, not very much. All he can think of is that he'll be eating regular for the next month at least.*

13

December 1933

For Irene, school was both a blessing and a curse. It was her only escape from home, where for the better part of a day she was absolved of her mother's nest of bitter sorrow and her father's abdication into alcoholism. However, school was also a daily reminder that the MacNeils were not like other families, that she was not like other girls, and if she found relief from the stranglehold of her own home, she must also cope with the chilly hinterland of not belonging.

Today Irene approached Jarvis Collegiate dawdling, as she did every day, no matter the weather. She walked past the tidy houses along Maitland. Some had angels in their windows and wreaths hung on their doors in anticipation of Christmas.

Uncle Rory had been gone for more than a month, and the holidays were nearing. Irene found the prospect of Christmas exhausting. Every year her mother made a miraculous effort. Every doorway, every nook and cranny was decorated. Cookies were baked from morning until night, even if they were made without raisins, without real butter, without candied cherries—all too expensive these days—and were mostly oatmeal and flour. Somehow money would be found for a small turkey and sweet potatoes and cranberries.

It was as though her mother wanted the holidays to be perfect in order to make up for the rest of the year. It was always a bittersweet time, for while Irene marvelled at how her mother managed to pull it together and to seem so happy and gay, she also knew that January would be a month of drooping exhaustion and bleak moods. Still, for a few days at least, they'd be the perfect little family.

Not *exactly* like other families, for they will not have friends over. They will not go to parties. Irene will not go door to door singing carols, nor will she go to skating parties or hayrides. The three of them will stay indoors and listen to the King's address on the radio, eat the food and open the presents. Her father will drink only so much and no more. His knuckles will be white on the arms of his dining-room chair, but he will manage, for he too will keep sacred the miracle of Margaret's Christmas.

It was like those ceasefires you heard about in the trenches in France during the war, where on Christmas Eve the Germans and the British had crawled from behind their sandbags and met in no man's land, sharing tea and brandy for one night only, and then resuming the shelling the next day. It was an undefended time, which only made Irene realize how hard it was the rest of the year and made it worse when the moment passed.

Irene climbed the steep school stairs.

Life was more complicated for her than for other fourteen-year-old girls. For example, there were now rules involved with how she should get through her school day. She must not approach anyone who did not approach her first. She must neither make eye contact nor seem to avoid it. She must not be seen to hesitate before entering a room, not be seen to be gathering her courage. She could enter into a conversation if invited to do so by being asked a question, but should not initiate. If she had to go to the girls' room she should use the toilet quickly, wash her hands and then, rather than running out of the washroom like a scared rabbit, she should take a moment to comb her hair, smooth her eyebrows or pinch a little colour into her cheeks, just like the other girls. She should answer questions in class if called upon or raise her hand occasionally if she absolutely knew the answer, but not so often as to make it seem she were trying to be teacher's pet or a know-it-all. Most of all, she should always have a book with her. A book gave her a reason to sit in a chair or at a table by herself, it gave her something to do instead of waiting to be spoken to, to be noticed, to be included.

Mrs. Duff's class was Irene's most favourite and at the same time least favourite class. On one hand she loved Mrs. Duff, loved the way she bumbled around, her breath smelling of the humbugs she always sucked. On the other, she feared the relaxed structure of the class, the way the girls paired up to practise their sewing. Violet made no secret of avoiding Irene, and Angela McMurphy had rolled her eyes last week and refused to let Irene use the scissors. Irene heard her whisper to Vera Carver about not letting people who had lunacy in their families near sharp things. Vera hadn't even had the good grace to look ashamed when she saw Irene had overheard them. Ebbie had said, "Oh, for heaven's sake, don't be absurd!" but even Ebbie kept her distance.

Today Irene planned to finish a pair of pyjamas for her father's Christmas present. The other girls would be making similar gifts. No one had money for store-bought presents. Last month she had made a pretty frilly apron for her mother, which she knew was a silly gift even as she made it. When would her mother ever wear such a thing, intended as it was for cocktail parties and afternoon teas? Still, it was pretty enough, and she was proud of the little Scottie dogs she'd embroidered around the edge.

"Take your seats, girls," said Mrs. Duff, in her high-pitched, reedy voice. "We've much to do today! Only three more classes before Christmas!" She clapped her plump hands while girls scattered to gather cloth from the cubbyholes at the back of the room.

Girls fluttered around, laying out material and onion-skin patterns, squabbling over who got to use the sewing machines first, who took whose box of pins, and did anyone find a red tin thimble. Irene went to a table at the end of the room. She'd finished the shirt, which was the most difficult part of the pyjamas. She had the bottom half already started, having laid out the pattern last week. Now all she had to do was cut the fabric, run up the side seams, put elastic in the waistband and then hem them at home. She smoothed the material. It was a nice pattern, a tartan. Her father would like it. She picked up the scissors.

"Can I help, dear?" Mrs. Duff smiled down at her. You could see where the red dye in her hair was growing out, and the pale hair, mostly grey, ran like a swath of cotton along her centre part. Mrs. Duff was the only woman Irene knew who dyed her hair. Her mother said it was evidence that Mrs. Duff was cheap.

"I'm okay, I can do it." Mrs. Duff sometimes made mistakes, and Irene couldn't afford any more material if something went wrong.

"Well, I'll just help you cut it out, dear. It'll go faster with both of us working on it." She pulled out her own pair of scissors. She kept smiling at Irene with her mouth full of small teeth. Irene knew she was trying to make her feel better because none of the other girls were working with her.

"Really, Mrs. Duff. I'd like to do it myself. It's okay." Irene fought the urge to pull the pattern away, to hug it to her chest.

"Nonsense, Irene. Many hands make light work." She began to cut into the fabric. Irene began on her side, trying not to pull the fabric askew. It seemed such a silly thing to try to do, both working on one small piece of cloth. The transparency of the effort humiliated Irene and made her angry. She snipped away, the scissors clicking.

"Mrs. Duff, I can't catch the thread in this smocking," Violet called out.

"Just a minute, dear. I'm just finishing up here."

"You can go ahead, Mrs. Duff. I can do this."

"Almost done," she said cheerily. "Almost done." Irene and her teacher seemed in a race now, first one to the inseam. "Got it!" Mrs. Duff cried. "All done! There, now, didn't we do that in record time! You get it pinned up and I'll see a machine frees up for you, dear."

Irene held up the pyjamas. Did the legs look uneven? Did one look too narrow at the bottom? Was it the one she'd cut or the one Mrs. Duff had? Was it ruined? No, please God, it couldn't be ruined.

A few minutes of pinning and measuring did nothing to allay her fears. One leg was definitely narrower than the other. But maybe it wasn't too bad. Maybe it wouldn't show when it was done. When her turn came at the machine she hurried through the job, hoping that speed would help her meet success at the finish line before failure caught up with her.

She held up the nearly finished pyjamas. She had only to hem the bottoms and put the elastic in the waistband now. It didn't look too bad. A little crooked, maybe, but not too bad.

Janet MacKenzie pointed and laughed. "Gee, Irene, you making those for somebody with a peg-leg?"

Irene's face flamed and she snapped the material back down on the table before anyone else noticed. What was she thinking? Tears sprang to her eyes as she looked down at the ruined pants. One of the legs tapered so much toward the ankle that only someone footless could ever get their leg into it.

Violet Clark arched her eyebrow. "Can't anyone in your family cut a straight line, or should I say *walk* a straight line?" Janet laughed, and so did Sue-Anne.

"That's enough, Miss Clark!" said Mrs. Duff, who rushed over to see how bad the damage was. "Oh dear," she said, holding them up again, which Irene wished she would not do. "Oh dear."

Everyone in the room stared at her and the ruined pyjamas. Irene thought how everyone was probably thinking how useless she was and how maybe they were right not to trust her with scissors and she was probably just as crazy as the rest of her family. But she wasn't. And she didn't do this, anyway, she didn't make this mess, and she was tired of having to cover up for everybody else. She glared at Mrs. Duff, who was trying to stretch the material and wouldn't look back at her.

Irene looked around at the girls, some sniggering behind their hands, some openly laughing at her, and some, like Ebbie over there in the corner, looking sorry for her, and she was suddenly tired of that too. And all the things that she couldn't say and wasn't allowed to say. Who were these girls, some of whom were on relief, for crying out loud, and depended on vouchers for food and hand-me-down dresses and came to school with nothing but bread and ketchup for lunch? Some of these girls had fathers who didn't work, fathers who'd run off and left them destitute, mothers who had "friends" that paid the rent. Who were they to make fun of her?

"Perhaps we could make shorty pyjamas," said Mrs. Duff, once again ready to help by cutting Irene's material.

Violet Clark laughed again, and without knowing really why, except that it was the only thing to do if she wasn't going to start crying right then and there, Irene laughed along.

"You know what?" she found herself saying. "By the time he opens his presents, Dad'll have so much whisky in him that they'll probably look even. He'll be, as they say, legless." And then, since her family was not the only one with problems, she said, "Hey, Sue-Anne, maybe you want me to make a pair for your brother Bill?" For who here did not know that Bill Richmond could be found most every Friday and Saturday night weaving out of Rupert's Tavern with a red-mouthed woman on his arm and all his pockets empty?

There was nothing but silence. Then there was a loud snort, and all eyes turned to Ebbie.

"Good one, 'Reen. Good one," she said as her eyes met Irene's.

"Irene, I'm surprised at you," said Mrs. Duff, although the slight upturn at the corner of her mouth told Irene it was not an entirely unpleasant surprise.

"I'll take that, thanks, Mrs. Duff," Irene said, and with one decisive snip she turned the pyjamas into knee-length shorts.

On Christmas morning her father said the pyjamas were quite splendid and her mother agreed and wore her apron all that day and the next before wrapping it in tissue paper and putting it away in a drawer. At dinner Margaret brought out the turkey, glazed to lacquered perfection, and they applauded and it made Irene want to cry, her mother looked so proud and happy. On New Year's Eve her father went out and didn't come back, her mother locked herself back in her room with a chair under the doorknob, and Irene made a resolution that this year, this very year, she would begin to say what was on her mind, now and again, and perhaps once in a while she would go out if her mother was sleeping, sit in the Allen Gardens with a book, even if her mother didn't want her to. This year she would try, and things would be better.

1934

The two of them sit on stumps outside the mess hall, away from the stink of the open trench toilets. David whittles aimlessly at a small branch while the union man talks. The government provides nothing in the way of entertainment, no radios, no cards, no baseball, no books, so the talk is welcome, more so because the man speaking is passionate and intelligent. He is a labour organizer, so most of the men haven't paid him much attention. Who cares about saving the world? they say. We ain't got no world left to save. But now, after being in the relief camp for a couple of months, David is starting to think this guy has something. The union man calls himself Bob. Organizers are blacklisted and use an alias when they move from one camp to another. The man has smuggled in a copy of the union paper, "Relief Camp Worker." David has taken a look at it. It makes some sense. Organize, it says. Don't let them treat you like dogs.

"I only came up here 'cause I was tired of getting kicked around in Vancouver," David says. "They said we'd get fed and all."

The union man pushes his hair back from a high widow's peak and smiles. "So, you'd rather get kicked around up here, working for twenty cents a day laying rail? Why, do you know that men are hired from outside the camps and they're making twenty-five cents an hour for the same work?"

"Guess the government figures these fine accommodations are worth something."

"This place is worse than jail. Christ, we're even dressed like convicts. Tarpaper shacks. Two men to a bunk. Mud floors in the wash shed. Food you wouldn't feed a dog, and fourteen-hour days clearing land, breaking rocks and laying rail. It ain't so much of a deal."

"I've maybe had about enough of that guy McIntock," David says. McIntock has an unpopular way of calling the men to work: "Okay, slaves, off your asses. We're cutting trail today."

"Most men here don't have too much spirit left in 'em, but I'm thinking you do." Bob looks at him closely. "Maybe we should both get out of here. You might be interested in doing a little organizing with me."

"We're a long way from nowhere to be talking about leaving."

Like all the relief camps, this one is set back about twenty miles from the nearest railway line and a hundred miles from the nearest town.

"We could maybe hitch a lift to the rail yard with one of the supply trucks. Or walk. Either way, best to go before the weather turns."

The next day they appear before the sergeant-major in charge, a fat man with a mole the size of a nickel on his cheek.

"Time for us to be leaving," says Bob.

The sergeant-major doesn't look up from his desk. *"Nowhere for you to go, pal."*

"We'll take our chances."

"Bad idea. Go report for work before I lose my good mood."

Bob says, *"Just here to pick up our pay for the week. Five days. One dollar apiece. I'll take mine in dimes if it's all the same to you."*

David can't help but smile.

"What're you grinning at, asshole?" says the sergeant-major.

"So, I think I'll take mine in quarters," he says, because he feels brave. There is something about the union guy that makes him want to be better than he is. Proud again. A man.

"Ya think so, do you?"

"If it's no trouble." He can say this smiling, and not smugly, either, but just smiling because it doesn't matter to him one way or the other what this man thinks of him, and this is a good feeling. It doesn't matter, even, if he agrees to pay him what he is owed or not. Suddenly it is easy to stand tall, and he realizes only then how low his head had been hanging.

"Have to deduct your room and board, and those clothes you're wearing. Seems to me we break even."

"Seems to me I can break your neck," says Bob, leaning over the desk.

"Riley, get your ass in here!" the sergeant-major calls.

The door opens and Big Riley comes in, slapping a nightstick against his leg.

"Trouble?"

"Naw. Get these two assholes fifty cents apiece. And the papers. They're leaving."

"You owe us a dollar each, Mac," says Bob as Big Riley leaves.

"I owe you lazy Communist bastards nothing." The sergeant-major stands up and goes nose to nose with Bob. "If I wanted to I could have Riley here throw you in lockup until you rot."

"You're not in the fucking army now, pal," says Bob. "This isn't a fascist state yet."

Riley comes back and tosses four quarters on the table. Then he puts a sheet of paper in front of them each to sign.

"This here says that by leaving, you agree you'll never apply for residence in a camp again, or for any kind of public assistance. Stay or starve. You got that?"

"Oh, yeah. Been getting it all along," says Bob, snatching up the money.

"It's your funeral, friend."

"Surprised you don't make us sign a request for voluntary deportation like you do the immigrant guys."

"Get the fuck out of my camp."

The supply trucks refuse to pick them up. They walk the twenty miles and then wait eighteen hours for a train going slow enough to come by.

"I sure am hungry," David says when they've climbed onto the roof of a south-bound freight.

"Yeah," says the man who calls himself Bob, handing him a slice of stale bread and a couple of slices of bologna. "Well, we'll be a lot hungrier unless somebody gets on this car with some food and a sharing mind."

No one does. It takes them two days to get to Vancouver. All along the ride, the man who calls himself Bob tells him about the labour struggle and the new world they're trying to build, where a guy can get a fair deal. By they time they reach the city outskirts, he knows the man's real name and considers him a friend. The first friend he's had in a long, long time.

Part III

14

April 1936

It was Saturday, April 18. Douglas stood behind the soda counter, absently polishing the chrome seltzer dispenser and listening to the radio accounts of the attempted rescue of D. E. Robertson, Herman Magill and Alfred Scadding from a collapsed gold mine in Moose River, Nova Scotia. Robertson was the chief surgeon at Toronto's Hospital for Sick Children. The men had been inspecting the abandoned mine to determine whether it could be reopened when they were trapped at the 141-foot level by a catastrophic rock slide. They had been down there, in the rising water and the pitch black, for a week. Draegermen, the local miners specially trained for hazardous rescues, worked around the clock to free the men, and all Toronto stayed glued to their radio sets, listening to the CBC's J. Frank Willis's frequent bulletins.

"Faint voices can now be heard coming from the drill hole these courageous draegermen have managed to sink into the mine shaft. We do not know how many of the three men trapped below are alive, but for the moment at least, hope shines brightly here. Cocoa and brandy have just been lowered into the shaft, providing the men with their first nourishment in seven days."

Douglas shuddered. To be trapped below the earth in the dark, entombed. It was horrifying, yet neither he nor the rest of Toronto could tear themselves away from their radios.

The bell over the door rang and startled Douglas. The woman's hair, a most improbable shade of blond, was a dull, teased-out nest. Her cabbage-coloured dress was so snug across her bony hips that a seam had given way and revealed a tongue of greyish slip beneath.

"Do you sell medicine?" She looked around the shop dubiously.

He thought she might be twenty-two or thirty-two. Her skin was pallid and her eyes were bright from either fever or drugs.

"The sign says Druggist, doesn't it?"

"I wasn't sure ... "

"Do you need something?" He snapped off the radio and popped a mint in his mouth.

"The doctor gave me a prescription."

"Yes, yes. Let me see it." Douglas crossed the room to the druggist's desk. He filled so few prescriptions these days, he wondered if he would have what she needed in stock. He fancied she might be seeking mercury treatment. He suspected a venereal disease, perhaps a hazard of her profession. He held his hand out while she rummaged in her purse.

"I have it here," she said and then began to cough. The sound was deep and rasping in her thin chest, a bark, a honk more than a cough. Instinctively he covered his mouth and nose with a handkerchief, fearing tuberculosis. She had one hand, with pipe-cleaner-thin fingers, over her mouth, holding a soiled scrap of rag, the other flat against her chest as though pressing back the pain. *Was that blood on the cloth?*

"Do you want a glass of water?"

She nodded.

At the sink behind the soda counter he poured her water and then poured himself a shot of whisky from the can marked Beckman's Strawberry Syrup. He quickly downed the whisky and brought her the glass of water. Her fit had subsided somewhat and she leaned against the desk, her face covered in a sheen of perspiration.

"Here." He held out the glass and noticed that the edge was chipped. He thought of taking it back and getting her another one, but then berated himself. *For someone like her? What difference would it make?*

"Thank you." She sipped daintily.

"Are you all right now?" He wasn't sure if he should offer her a seat.

"Yes, much better. It comes on so quickly. But it passes." She smiled, and he was surprised by how good her teeth were, strong and white. He had expected decay and stains.

"Do you have the prescription?" he asked.

She put the glass down and reached into her bag again. "I know it's here ..." She pulled up a crumpled piece of paper and handed it to him. Cough syrup. A strong one, with laudanum in it. Menthol vapours. Sulfapyridine. So, a bacterial infection of the lungs. He suspected more. The date on the scrip was nearly three weeks old.

"You should have filled this before now. You've probably become worse since it was written. I'll fill it, but you should go back to your doctor. You may have pneumonia."

She did not reply, and he went to prepare the medication. At the same time, he helped himself to a sip or two of his own remedy, for the woman rattled him. When he returned she was sitting at one of the small tables and he could not help but notice that her skirt was hiked up above her knee. It was a very fetching calf, if a bit thin. Her left hand rested on her thigh. Her eyes met his directly, and the look in them, together with the parted lips, was a flame going through him.

"All done," he said.

Again she did not reply, but looked at him and breathed through her open mouth, her frail chest rising and falling beneath the thin cloth.

"Will there be anything else?"

"I don't think so," she said. She stood, wobbled a little on her heels, and came toward him. He found himself wanting to take a step back, which was ridiculous, because at the same time he wanted also to go toward her. He turned to the cash register and rang up the sale.

"That will be, let's see, five fifty-seven." He looked up from the register tape to find her standing closer to him than he had expected. "Five fifty-seven," he repeated.

"I only have two dollars," she said. "That's all what I have in the world."

He had known that, of course. A woman like this, in this condition, would not have been able to make any money for some time. He understood then how she had dragged herself from her bed in some cheap room nearby, dressed as well as she was able, hoping to make the right impression, and he understood what an effort like that must have cost her, the putting on of stockings and garters and a slip and such, all the soft and complicated things women wore under their clothes.

"This is more than that," he said.

"I thought that maybe, it's just that, people said ... I heard around that you was a kind man, a man that would maybe help a girl." She began to cough again, and he feared a repeat of the previous bout, but she managed to choke it back.

"I'd like to be able to help, miss, but where would I be if I just gave away all my stock? If I gave in to every sad story that came along? It isn't fair to ask. I have a family to feed myself."

"There must be some way."

Douglas was repulsed by her, and at the same time he was aroused. She was completely at his mercy and they both knew it. It was a feeling of power he was horrified to find excited him.

"I don't know what you mean," he said.

She came around the desk, as he knew she would. She put her hand on his arm. She had a ring on her right hand, with a little blue stone in the middle. He looked at her hand there, touching him, and his skin became hot even from so light a caress.

"Is there no way I can persuade you? No appeal I can make?" The words sounded rehearsed. Her face was close to his and her breath smelled of something overripe, too sweet, milky. He did not want to kiss that mouth. He looked around him, as though unsure of where he was, and saw the scene as an observer might: this little shop with its dusty shelves of medicines and fly-sprin-kled windows; this woman with her heartbreaking need, her Woolworth's finery. And of course, Douglas himself, a whisky-bloated fool of a man with an erection.

"You should stand back. This is a public place. Someone could come in." He looked at the glass door, at the large glass windows, where people passed by.

"We could discuss it in private. I'd be so grateful."

He felt her fingers farther down now, on his thigh. His penis pressed against his trousers. It had been so long since a woman had touched him. Since anyone had touched him, for that matter. There was nothing right about this, nothing he recognized as coming from the man he supposed himself to be. A good man would give her the medicine, and he was a good man. He had given medicine to people before for nothing, old rheumatic men and anxious women with wheezing children in their arms. A smart man would tell her to go to the House of Industry on Elm Street, to the Salvation Army, anywhere but here. The fingers floated over the front of his pants, lingering over the buttons, and his penis jerked painfully. He thought of Margaret. He touched the girl's throat and felt the warm pulse there. His hand began a slow descent to her breast. He grunted. He pushed her aside roughly and walked to the door. He turned the sign to read Closed, and slouched back to her, grabbed her arm and wanted to bruise her.

"Go in the back. Now." He hardly recognized his own voice. She looked afraid, and this aroused him further.

As they stepped behind the curtain she opened her mouth as though to kiss him or to speak, but he pushed her face away. He didn't want her lips on his, the threat of contagion. He reached up to the shelf over his head and grabbed the whisky bottle. He drank deeply, put the bottle up to the girl's mouth, forcing her to drink while she choked and a coughing fit came on her again. The whisky spilled down her dress and he rubbed it into her skin, not caring that she was coughing. He put his hand on her throat again and pushed her back against the stock cabinets. With his other hand he pulled up her skirt, grabbed her soft inner thigh above her stockings and squeezed hard until she cried out. Quickly, he grabbed a handkerchief out of his back pocket and pressed it over her mouth. With the other hand he tore aside her panties and stuck his fingers inside her, smiling when he saw her wince.

He reached down and freed himself from his pants. He turned her around and bent her over. He flipped up her skirt and exposed her thin buttocks. He entered her violently, making her moan. He stabbed himself into her, the feeling rising up from the soles of his feet. It lasted only a few moments and then he grabbed her hips and thrust her back, impaled against him while he came in great spasms that made him grit his teeth and dig his fingers into her hips.

He came back to himself slowly and knew that the sound he heard was the girl crying. The bloody passion of a moment before was replaced with self-loathing. Hurriedly, he rearranged himself and helped her to stand, leaning her up against the cabinets. She was gasping for air, choking, gagging.

"I'm sorry," he said, "I'm sorry, so sorry." He mopped at her face with the soiled handkerchief. She began to slide down to the floor.

"No! No! Wait!" Gesturing with his hand, as though through will alone he could force her upright, he raced into the shop and grabbed a chair. As he passed the counter he snatched the bag that contained her medicine. When he returned she was leaning on the cabinet, her arms extended, her lungs heaving, her mouth open in an effort to get air. Each laboured breath ended in a long, uneven rattle. He noticed a trickle of fluid on the inside of her calf and tasted bile in his mouth.

He sat her down and slapped her gently on the back until she could catch her breath, then opened the bottle of cough syrup and handed it to her.

"Drink some. Drink. It will make you feel better."

She tilted the bottle and drank, bowed her head and pressed her hand to her chest. "It hurts," she whispered.

"Yes, yes. I'm sorry," he said again, unsure whether it was her cough or what he had just done to her that was causing the pain.

She ran her hand along her forehead, which had broken out in a sweat. "I want to go home," she said. "I want to lie down."

"Of course," he said. "Take the medicine. You don't have to pay for it."

The look of contempt on her face made him lower his eyes.

"If you need more, come back," he said, and then knowing how that must sound, added, "I won't want anything, nothing at all, you understand. But if you need more medicine, I'll see you get it." He pulled a five-dollar bill from his pocket and held it out to her. She hesitated, but then silently took it and slipped it in her brassiere.

"I want to go," she said again. He saw that he was standing in her way, but he didn't want her to go out the front door. Did not want to have to walk with her, with her face looking like that, to the front door, and unlock it, and let her out. If someone was passing ...

"Go out this way," he said and pointed to the door behind her that led to the alley. As soon as he spoke he was again ashamed of himself—was there no depth to which he would not sink? Once again she stared at him, but this time her frown and slightly open mouth, the slight shake of her head, showed that he'd amazed her with his recurrent cruelty.

She took the bag of medicine and without another word opened the back door and left. She didn't bother to close the door behind her.

Douglas stared after her for a few moments and then closed the door, sliding the bolt in place. He put his hand up to his mouth, noticed with some surprise that he was crying. The tears wetting his hands might have been blood. The bottle of whisky lay on the shelf. He picked it up, but instead of putting it directly to his mouth, he began to sob. When he threw the bottle at the back door it shattered with a satisfying crash. The fumes rose up and hit him hard enough that his eyes would have watered had he not already been weeping.

He collapsed in the chair and put his head in his hands. *What had he done? What had he done?* Taken advantage of that pathetic creature in a way he had never imagined possible. He knew, of course he knew, what liquor did to him; knew he was a drunk. That was the root of all his problems. If he could just stop drinking. He *would* stop drinking. He'd turn over a new leaf. Clean the shop. See Margaret through this bad time. He'd be better. A better husband, a better father, a better man.

If only he could be forgiven what he had done.

Douglas poured all the booze he could find down the sink.

Bottles behind books, in the back of drawers, under old long-unused cleaning rags, whisky stashed in syrup tins, in seltzer canisters. When he was done he closed the shop early, needing to be absent from the scene of his crime. He came home, his mouth dry and his head full of the memory of the afternoon's depravity. He found Margaret sitting in the late-afternoon sun, her face buried in a year-old *Chatelaine* magazine. The radio was still tuned to the CBC, where reports came in from the Nova Scotia mine. Douglas kissed his wife on the top of her head, and she looked up from her magazine with surprise, but said nothing. Irene came out of the kitchen to see what he was doing home so much earlier than usual. He knew from the look on her face that she expected the worst, and he hugged his daughter, trying to reassure her. Irene patted him absently on the back as though she were the parent, not he, as though she knew it was he who needed reassurance, but her interest, and her patience with his problems was worn thin.

Every nerve in his body wanted a drink, sizzled near the edge of his skin with that need. But he was committed. Feeling sick and exhausted, he went to bed, but release evaded him, and he tossed and turned, haunted by images of vile, debased acts and the face of the woman condemning him for his lack of mercy.

Margaret and Irene climbed the stairs some hours later. Margaret settled herself in bed, as far from him as she could, nearly leaning over the edge of the bed, her hand trailing on the floor as though out of a boat. For the first time in many months Douglas longed to put his arms around her, to hold her, to tell her he understood how dreadful life could be. He felt he was to blame for everything just now, most certainly at the core of his family's floundering, and he was sorry, so sorry. But he neither touched her nor spoke to her, fearing she would push him away, or worse. He lay as still as he could in his itchy skin so as not to disturb her. He felt it was the least he could do. It was a place he could begin.

Douglas gave in to wakefulness. It was before dawn on Sunday, and although his stomach felt filled with writhing worms and he trembled so badly he fumbled with the buttons of his pants, he clung to the remorse-born moment of clarity he'd found. He went down to the kitchen and put on a pot of coffee. He was sweating and ill, but he knew this would pass, knew it was a rite of passage to a better life. He sat at the table, watched the day arrive over the back fence, and embraced it all, even the sensations of his body trying to cleanse itself—the shivers and the nausea and the spike he felt being driven into his head. An end to all their suffering was in sight. He had lost his way, was all. The terrible events of yesterday had been a wake-up call and he would heed it. He felt a sense of redemption and as he watched the sun rise and waited for his family to waken, he made lists in his head of things he would do.

Later that morning he watched Irene eyeing him skeptically over her own morning cup of tea. This was not the first time he had made a stab at putting down the bottle, and he knew he would have to prove himself, but his mind was made up. Starting today, things would be different.

He looked at his daughter and noticed what had happened to her over the past few years. *Where had he been?* She was a young lady now. She sat with legs crossed at the ankles, her back slightly arched. She wore a dress she'd sewn herself, well made, with a little lace around the neck salvaged from an old outfit of her mother's. She had a quiet dignity about her, a determination, that gave her an air of mystery. She was seventeen now and would graduate from school this year. She might go to college next fall. He would have to talk to her about that. Although girls were marrying later and later, she might still be married in two or three years. He hoped she would marry early and settle down to a life of her own. Children. A future. Of course, she'd never marry if she didn't get out of this house, didn't meet young people and learn to sparkle a bit.

"What are you doing today?"

"Nothing special. I thought I might go to the eleven-o'clock service. I'll be back in time to get lunch on." That was something she had begun to do in the past year. Her mother couldn't very well refuse her permission to go to church, although she made her displeasure known every Sunday by coming down with one of her "bilious" attacks, or a sick headache, or a sudden over-whelming premonition that Irene would be hit by a streetcar. Still, Irene held her ground more often than not, and Douglas was proud of her.

"Why not go out this afternoon?"

Irene looked at him with undisguised suspicion. "Why do you want me gone all of a sudden?"

"What do you mean, why?" He wanted her to stop looking at him like that. She should have more respect. No matter what had happened, he was still her father and a girl should have respect. "You need a more rounded life, Irene. I know you've been a great help to your mother, you're a good girl. Still, there is a limit. You can't stay under her skirts forever, you know."

"Stay under her skirts? I wouldn't call it that, Daddy."

"Never mind what you'd call it. I'm trying to tell you that things are going to be different around here now. You may not believe that, and perhaps I can sympathize with your doubt, yes, sympa-thize. However, I am telling you now that I have decided to take a more active role in caring for your mother. A far more active role."

"I see." She looked so tired sitting there, as though she were holding herself together by willpower that might at any moment fail her.

He could see that action was required.

"Wait here," he said. He went to the hall closet and returned carrying the bottle that had lain for so long in its dubious secrecy. He had her attention now. He went to the sink and poured the contents down the drain. The smell of the liquor rose up and made his stomach churn. For a moment he was afraid he might vomit.

"There, I thought you should see that." It was, he thought, a grand gesture.

"Oh, Daddy, what's the point?" Irene put her elbows on the table and rested her forehead on her fingers, her thumbs along the side of her face. "I know you mean to stop, but — "

"But nothing. It's going to be different this time. I promise you."

"All right, Dad, all right." She pushed herself up from the table and smiled at him. "It's good, Dad. Really. I'm just going to go up and make sure Mum's all right before I leave, okay?"

Even after yesterday's hard rain the neighbourhood looked as if it could use a good wash. The air smelled of worms and spring-thaw garbage. It was that unpleasant season when the trees had not yet begun to bud and cast their veil of hopeful green. The yards, newly clear of snow, revealed the debris of a harsh winter— sodden paper, scrappy brown grass, dead mushy leaves. Only the mild wind held an undercurrent of scented promise, and Irene breathed deeply when a whiff of lake breeze passed her. Just to be out of the house was such a relief.

As she walked to the Sherbourne Street United Church she tried to quell her annoyance at her father. She wanted to believe him, of course she did, but how could she? How many times had he vowed he'd had his last drink? What worried her was the motiva-tion behind it. The first time he'd decided to quit was after he'd given Mr. Casselman the wrong medicine. If the man hadn't been suspicious about the dosage and asked to reread the prescription, he might have died. Then there was the time he'd "misplaced" the grocery money and they'd had to eat bread, beans and ketchup for a week. Once he'd fallen down the stairs and broken his wrist. It was always some near-calamity that she was convinced would one day go too far. She was getting as bad as her mother, fearing that every knock on the door would be the police. She wondered what had induced him to pour his precious whisky down the sink this time.

Stay under her skirts! Didn't he know that it was all she could do to stop from running down the street and never coming back? But she had nowhere to go, and she couldn't support herself even if she did. Then, too, she was a little afraid of her mother, and fear was an authoritative warden. But it wasn't as simple as that either, for no matter what, she loved her mother, even loved her sorry excuse for a father. When her mother was "better" she was so repentant, so full of shame. Her mother was sick, and you simply didn't leave a sick mother. Or maybe some people did, but Irene couldn't.

She still had a few minutes until church began and wondered if she had time to sit in the Allen Gardens for a moment, but feeling restless she decided to take a walk around the block. She walked down Seaton Street, and just before she turned the corner at Gerrard she spotted Ebbie Watkins and Sue-Anne Richmond walking directly toward her. They were with a young man Irene didn't recognize. He was tall and had a rolling gait, the long stride of his legs making Sue-Anne take two mincing steps to his one, while Ebbie loped along with ease. His wavy blond hair was slicked back from his forehead, and Irene thought he looked ever so much like Leslie Howard in the poster she had seen for *The Scarlet Pimpernel*. Ebbie linked her wrist through one of his arms and Sue-Anne hugged the other. It struck Irene that they might at any moment begin a tug of war with him, although he didn't seem to mind a bit. In fact he looked perfectly pleased, a big smile on his face and a cigarette dangling between his lips.

Irene started to cross the street.

"Irene, hey there! Where are you off to?"

"Hi, Ebbie. Hello, Sue-Anne." Irene never knew what to say to Ebbie, who was never unfriendly but wasn't exactly a friend anymore either. The same was not true of Sue-Anne, who would never, ever, start up a conversation on the street, who would just walk past like she'd never laid eyes on Irene before. Irene preferred it that way, in fact. It was simpler all round and solved the problem they now faced: the quandary of what to say after hello.

"So, where are you going?" asked Ebbie. "On your way home?"

"No. I was going to church, actually."

"Church, huh?" said the young man. "Part of the angelic choir, then? Haven't seen one of those in a while."

Irene blushed.

"Oh, pay him no mind." Ebbie elbowed him in the ribs and gave him a look of mock disgust. "He is a degenerate. Nothing wrong with going to church, Harry. In fact, it might improve some people."

Sue-Anne giggled and smiled up at Harry, ignoring Irene completely.

"Where are my manners, for heaven's sake? Irene MacNeil, may I present Harry Madison, my thoroughly unredeemable cousin. Harry, this is Irene MacNeil, an old friend."

"So, why have I not had the pleasure before, old friend?"

"Irene has to stay home with her mother, don't you, dear?" said Sue-Anne.

"My mother's not well. Hasn't been well for some time." *Now, why did she say that?* Sue-Anne giggled again and Irene wanted to pinch her. "Dear," indeed.

"Sorry to hear that," said Harry.

"It's nothing new." *Why couldn't she stop talking?*

"That makes it worse, not better," he said, which was true.

"Come on," said Sue-Anne, pulling at his arm. "I don't want to waste my day standing here."

"Don't suppose you can come with us, can you?" said Ebbie. "We're going up to Riverdale Zoo."

"No, I don't think so." Which was exactly the answer they all expected. "I'm going to be late. Nice to meet you. 'Bye, Ebbie."

"Okay, then, 'bye," said Ebbie.

"See you around," said Harry.

Sue-Anne of course said nothing, but tugged again at Harry's sleeve.

Irene trotted a few paces along the street and vowed she would absolutely not turn back and look at them. Five steps later she couldn't help herself and glanced over her shoulder, but of course they were not looking back, they were just walking along, three friends going on a lovely outing.

She hurried along the road to Sherbourne Street and opened the door just as the organist struck the first chord in the opening hymn. The door squealed loudly on its unoiled hinge and several people turned to stare at the latecomer. She edged into a pew at the back of the church, thankful it was empty. As the congregation began to sing "Come into His Presence," she tried to clear her mind and put the unpleasant encounter behind her.

Irene had begun going to church merely as a way to get out of the house for an hour or two. However, she had come to look forward to the hour of ritual and contemplation as an oasis of calm and solace. She didn't know what she had in mind when she said the word *God*, but she couldn't deny that she sometimes felt, as the hymn suggested, in the presence of something, and that was enough for her. Her prayers were not so much requests for divine favours as they were moments of openness, of stillness, of just being, and not of being needed. It was not her custom to ask for specific boons, but she decided it might not hurt to send up a wee prayer that her father's resolve not fail him and that whatever powers-that-be there were, see that he stay sober once and for all. Maybe, she chuckled to herself, she should become Catholic. Didn't they have St. Jude, the patron saint of lost causes?

When Irene returned home after church she found, somewhat to her surprise, that Douglas was as good as his word. She felt a stab of elation, but still, it wouldn't do to become too optimistic. He had made lunch, and if she was annoyed to find he had used up both tomatoes in the salad and the cheese that was to last them until the end of the week, Irene held her tongue. At three o'clock he prepared a plate of jam-filled cookies and a pot of tea and brought it in to the two women in the living room, proud as a child who'd baked his first cake. He poured Margaret's tea and added milk and two sugar cubes. He stirred the cup and as he held it out to his wife, she turned to him quickly, as if startled, pointed her finger, the nail with its dark crescent of dirt, and said, "I see you. I hope you're proud of yourself."

Silently, his mouth set in a rigid line, he put her cup down on top of the radio and went back to the kitchen, where he tried to concentrate first on a crossword puzzle and then on the comics and then came back to the living room and listened to the radio. He fussed and fidgeted through the afternoon, and Irene kept expecting him to suddenly jump up and disappear from the house.

At five o'clock Margaret said she was tired and returned to her room and her nest of blankets.

"Why don't you go out again?" said her father when they heard Margaret's bedsprings creak.

"Where would I go?" She didn't trust the invitation. She was afraid he would ferret out some last-chance mickey stashed in the potato bin, perhaps, or in the rag box.

"I don't know. Where do the other kids go? Go to the Gardens. Go to the beach."

"No, I don't think so." After years of keeping her in the cage he now opened the door and expected her to bound happily away into the wide, wide world.

"Why ever not? I'm telling you. Go out."

"She'll need me."

"I'll take care of her, for Christ's sake!"

"You don't know how, Dad."

"What do you mean by that? Of course I know how. She's my wife, isn't she? I can certainly take care of my own wife. I can certainly do that."

Irene glimpsed the push and pull he too must be feeling, trying to be a father and a caregiver when there was so little to recommend him. She saw his weakness and its intimacy embarrassed her.

She should go. Should be able to go without a backward glance, just into the day, down a street, like normal people did.

"Well, I don't know." It was so tempting, the possibility of a park bench, of an hour or two free of accusation, free of the clutch of duty.

"Go on, Irene. Really, Pet. It's okay." *Pet.* He hadn't called her that in a long time. Wouldn't it be a gift to both of them, a gift of trust and maybe even conspiracy, the two of them together?

"All right, I will, then," she said, as though testing his sincerity.

"Go on." He smiled at her, and it was the smile of a man she hadn't seen in a long time, half remembered from childhood. Yes, she would go. A girl going out for a couple of hours on a Sunday afternoon. Simple as that.

She took her coat and gloves and opened the door like a sleep walker. Such an uncomplicated motion, one foot in front of the other, down the porch, to the sidewalk, turn left, keep going with the spring-sprung breeze and the sound of sparrows busily going about sparrow business.

She walked through the glass house in the Allen Gardens and admired the banana trees and the orchids. She smelled the honey and musk-rich scent of the lilacs. She found a wrought-iron seat near a small fountain and sat there with her eyes closed, just breathing, in and out, the scent of the garden and the enchantment of time, all her own, with no one in the world wanting anything of her.

Margaret had been downstairs waiting for her when she came back from her walk, complaining that she was sick with pains in her stomach, her voice thick with accusation. Irene had persuaded her to eat some toast and sausage, and she finally went back to bed, letting Irene know all the while that she was not pleased to have been left alone with Douglas.

Now Irene and her father sat side by side and listened to the CBC. They drank weak tea, and her father smoked one cigarette after another. He gulped his tea and tapped his nails on the rim. Irene tried not to glare at him. She grit her teeth so she wouldn't snap "Quit it, just quit it!" She knew that any excuse would be enough to send him back to the bottle.

The CBC announcer read another report about the three men in the Moose River mine. The danger of more rock slides forced rescuers to sift through the soil with their bare hands, so fearful were they of what a pick and shovel would cause. They worked by lamplight in shifts, vowing not to quit until the men were freed.

"It's a shame, a terrible, terrible shame," said Douglas.

"Must be horrible, down in a pit like that," said Irene.

"I'm sure they'll get them out. They have to get them out."

"I don't know what makes you think so. Bad things happen all the time. Even I know that." Irene collected her teacup and the empty pot and took them to the chipped kitchen sink. She stood staring out the window but saw nothing except for her own night-distorted reflection staring back at her. She wondered, as she often did, where Uncle Rory was. It had been almost a year since he'd last written and that was just a hurried postcard from Kenora saying he was on his way out west and would write more later. Irene wondered if maybe he'd found a girl, married and settled down somewhere far away where the sky never ended and it was miles between you and your neighbours. She fantasized about him from time to time, picturing him in a farmhouse with a pretty lady and a fat pink baby.

On Monday, April 20, Alfred Scadding, one of the men trapped in the mine, shouted up the drill hole with bad news. Herman Magill had died. The water was rising. Scadding said it was only a matter of hours before he and Dr. Robertson would also die. The rescuers redoubled their efforts, acutely aware that haste might trigger another slide and caution might make them too late. In Toronto it seemed that half the city waited, holding their breath and tilting their heads toward their wireless sets. All over the city the talk centred around the plight of the men.

A tightly corseted lady hobbled into the shop and asked Douglas for something to take the ache out of her knees.

"Used to be I hired an Irish girl to come in once a week and do the heavy cleaning, but these days I'm down on my knees myself, and me with the rheumatism. Some mornings I can't hardly straighten my legs out."

Douglas recommended some aspirin and an ointment to rub in to her inflamed joints.

"Listening to those poor men trapped in the mine, are you?" she asked as she paid for her medicine.

"Yes. Terrible thing."

"No hope for them, as I see it," she said with finality. "They're in their graves already."

"I pray you're wrong," Douglas said.

"It'd take a miracle. They're just hanging on," she said as she left.

Douglas felt as though he were just hanging on himself. He would gladly cut off his left leg for a small shot of rye. He began to polish the countertops, shine the taps, clean out the ice cream bins. He would keep busy and he wouldn't drink. He'd get a new sign painted. Why, things were even picking up today. How many customers had he served? Seven, eight? More people so far today than he'd served over the past three days. It was as though word was getting round already that he was a changed man. He scooped up a spatter of dead insects from the windowsill and brushed them with distaste into a rubbish bin. He put his hands on his hips and looked around. How had he let the place get so run down?

On Tuesday, Dr. Robertson called up from the mine in a weak voice and requested a fountain pen. He wished to draw up his last will and testament. Three hundred rescuers and draegermen worked in a frenzy of perilous activity, trying to bore through from an old shaft near the one in which the men were trapped.

It was Douglas's third day without a drink and he was feeling good, proud of himself, puffed up with self-congratulations. He had woken that morning without a churning, acid-rattled gut, and the ghastly feeling that a cheese grater had been used on his skin was receding. The shop was a model of cleanliness, every surface shining and bright. The shelves had been rearranged, the dust swept out. He had called Borden's Dairy and waited for a fresh supply of ice cream. He left the door open all day, as though signalling passersby that this was now a good and pleasing establishment to enter, and it seemed to be working. The trickle was slow, to be sure, and people were not making expensive purchases, but even with only these few hours of upright industry behind him, he could see that things could be turned around.

On Wednesday afternoon, it appeared the prayers of a million people were about to be answered. The exhausted Nova Scotian miners were nearing the trapped men, who by some fluke, some incredible gossamer thread of stamina, continued to breathe, one gasp after another, hour after hour.

Although the men were not yet above ground, the atmosphere

was so optimistic that the evening newspapers hollered "RESCUED" on their front pages.

As Douglas closed the shop for the day his spirits soared along with everyone else's. Things were going to be all right; people in the street smiled at each other, exchanged glad tidings and hurried home to sit next to their radios, intent on being right there when the men were brought out.

At 10:44 p.m., Toronto time, Dr. Robertson was at last brought up to the surface, followed an hour later by Scadding. The Salvation Army, who had stood by the mouth of the mine with sandwiches and coffee throughout the long ordeal, and the bone-weary miners doffed their hats and sang "Praise God from Whom All Blessings Flow." The men were pulled from the earth blind and weak as newborn moles, and the people of Toronto poured out into the streets laughing and crying. The bells at city hall pealed out a joyful noise. All across the city, spontaneous celebrations burst forth.

Margaret clapped her hands and began to softly cry. Irene danced around the living room like a dervish, her hands outstretched and her head tilted back, and if Margaret was afraid her daughter would knock something over and break it, in the spirit of the moment she said nothing.

1935

They start in Vancouver. There are fourteen hundred of them. People stand in the dark and wave flashlights. They throw sandwiches up to waiting hands, and David leans out and catches one. They cling to the tops of the cars, bracing themselves as the trains swing around the bends. When they get to Coquitlam, the cops open the boxcar door for them.

David looks at his friend. "You wanna go inside?"

"We can't all get in. You think you can make it, staying on top?"

"Figure so. Won't be easy."

"Good man."

In the town of Golden they get down off the trains. A woman has been sent a telegram they were coming and she and some other women have set out food on trestle tables. Stew for all of them. Fifteen hundred by then.

"We believe in what you boys are doing," a hard-looking woman says, handing him a bowl. "You get to Ottawa, you tell that Mr. Bennett he can't treat you boys this way. You're mothers' sons, every one of you."

"I'm grateful, ma'am. Thank you."

The woman kisses his cheek and he blushes, making his friend laugh.

They get back on the freights after they've filled their bellies, and for some of them it is the first full belly they've had in some time. David and his friend choose to ride on top again. They are going into the spiral tunnels. They are dark legend. Men have passed out because they couldn't breathe. They have fallen off the trains.

"You got that wet handkerchief like I told ya?" his friend says.

"Right here."

"Well, tie it on, then."

They tie them over their faces. His friend slaps him on the shoulder, tips his hat down low and butts his forehead against the roof of the boxcar. David follows his friend's example. His heart pounds time with the steel wheels. There are miles and miles of ink black ahead of them, and the tunnels are low. If you sit up, you'll get decapitated on the rocks. They have to stay low, their faces in the throw-back from the engines. Cinder and smoke and ash and the shrieking, hammering noise.

After about half an hour, David thinks he'll go crazy with panic. He can't breathe for the smoke. He clings to the boards and begins to pray. His mouth feels like it's filling up with coal dust, and he can't spit without lowering the rag. His eyes are glued shut, full of grit, burning like hell. He starts to cry, calling himself a fool for not taking the opportunity to ride inside when he had the chance. The train's screeching and moaning so loud his screams can't be heard and so he doesn't try to hold them back anymore.

He doesn't know how long he's been in the tunnels. Time doesn't move in any normal way. It could have been three hours or two days. Could have been always and forever, in a long chain of torment behind and *before him. He knows he is going to die and he wants so badly to live.*

Suddenly they come out into the thin clear air of the Rockies and he is blind with light. He raises his head and tries to get his eyes all the way open, but they are so full of black dust and tears that the world is a scatter of wet shattered brightness. It is a miracle. David looks over at his pal and starts to laugh. He looks like a vaudeville minstrel, with his face all black, except that his eyes are as red as burning coals. His friend laughs back at him, pointing and slapping him on the shoulder. They are silly with relief. Then he throws up. He is ashamed, until he sees he isn't the only one.

When they cross the border into Alberta, a small crowd of B.C. cops wave and cheer them on. It makes him feel like something, after so long of being nothing.

"See that? Do ya see that?" says his friend. "We're gonna make it! We're gonna make something happen, I tell ya!"

"Ottawa, here we come!" David yells, and he whoops and hollers and his heart is swollen with possibility.

15

The next day the festive air held. All across Toronto people smiled at strangers, repeating bits of news they'd heard about the Moose River rescue. Men slapped one another on the back and women brushed tears from their eyes. After all the years of bad news, wasn't it wonderful to have something like this happen, to have your faith restored? Sometimes an awful tragedy brought out the best in the people, didn't it? So sad about that Mr. Magill, though, wasn't it? Such a shame they couldn't all have been saved. Still, it was wonderful news. Wonderful news.

Douglas left the door of his shop wide open, delighting in the sound of neighbours walking by, the sound of their chatter mingling with the music from the radio. He was surprised to find, in the clear thinking of sobriety, that he greatly enjoyed the company of others. He missed the friends he and Margaret had before she became ill. Perhaps that would change now.

He decided the shop still needed a bit of elbow grease and turned his attention to re-sorting the stock in the back room. It was deplorable the way he'd let things slide. He'd have to reorder a number of medicines, get his stock up to date again. Then he saw it. A bottle of bootleg booze behind a stack of liniment tins. He'd so completely forgotten it that for a moment he couldn't think where it had come from or how long he'd had it.

He wasn't prepared for the jolt of compulsion. He could picture himself pulling the cork, tilting it to his mouth. He could almost feel the friendly fire of it through his arms and legs, warming his belly. For a full ten seconds he stood with the bottle in his hand. It occurred to him that he could keep it, *should* keep it, use it in some preparation or other. Rubbing alcohol, perhaps, or herbal tinctures. Then, frightened, he wondered about pouring it down the sink, but didn't trust himself to open it, to smell the fumes. Then he drew a deep breath and walked to the dustbin, raised the lid and tossed the bottle in. He immediately put the bin out into the alley, came back in and bolted the back door as though he were afraid the spirits in the bottle would be loosed and come knocking.

He laughed a little and mopped at his brow. It was a test, that was all, nothing more. He was fine. He had all the willpower in the world. Nothing to worry about. It wasn't as though he was one of those gin-soaked wretches lying about in a gutter. He'd simply let a bad habit get out of hand under the pressures of the past few years. But he was not an alcoholic, certainly not. He had proved that, hadn't he, quitting just like that? No dipsomaniac was capable of such self-will. He was a man of medicine himself, after all, and knew about such things. In fact, it was perfectly within reason to assume that after a period of some abstinence he would be able, once again, to drink like a gentleman.

The Borden's truck pulled up out front and a man hopped out of the cab.

"Delivery," he called.

"Yes, yes!" Douglas hurried out to meet him.

The shop had never looked better. The ice cream containers were all filled, and he had even served three sodas and a root-beer float to four boys coming home from Jarvis Collegiate. They were a little loud, and normally Douglas would have been annoyed by their raucous behaviour, but today nothing bothered him. The noise of the boys had attracted a group of girls passing by, who had come in and ordered sodas themselves, making a point of ignoring the boys. Shortly after, a man wanted hair tonic and another needed bicarbonate of soda. By the end of the day, Douglas had earned more than in the previous two weeks.

As he closed the shop he noticed Richard Rhodes, the butcher from across the street, coming toward him.

"MacNeil, say, you've been doing a bit of work 'round the place I see."

"It was time for a spring cleaning," said Douglas, pleased that his efforts had been noticed.

"Looks good, man. I've been meaning to come over and tell you." Rhodes shook his hand vigorously. He was a large man who suited his voice. He must have been athletic in his youth, but his girth had slipped into prosperous middle-age. He was bald, with a sparse but well-groomed ring of grey hair. "Thought for a while there you might go under. Glad to see things are turning round. Flurry of activity over there the past couple of days." He winked.

Douglas's mouth was dry. He did not like the idea that Rhodes had been watching his shop. Had he seen that girl enter his shop and not leave? Was Rhodes laughing at him? "Yes, well, I believe things are finally turning 'round, don't you?"

"Certainly hope you're right, Douglas. I see little outward evidence of it, though. This is a neighbourhood in jeopardy, I fear. Should we lose any more ground, I can't say what will become of this place. People are fools, MacNeil, fools. Whole damn country's going to hell in a handbasket and do people wake up to the truth? No. Here's what they do: they get rid of that idiot Bungling Bennett and put Cowardly King back in the prime minister's seat. I say we have to stick together, don't we? That's the foundation for rebuilding this country, is it not? Men of sound judgment, responsible men like us?"

"I'm not so sure about that, Rhodes," said Douglas. "Don't know whether I agree with you about King. I say there may be some hope for the future. I believe we may have turned a corner."

The two men stood side by side, surveying the street. Shops were closing for the evening. Normally Douglas found this time of day a bit dismal, faced only with the failure of his day and the unavoidable return to the dark, claustrophobic atmosphere of his family. But now he was filled with a combination of pride over his freshly laundered-and-pressed shop, Rhodes's attention, and the festive air that lingered all over town.

"I've got to admit that King's got one thing right. We must watch the Jews. Communists, most of them, and too powerful by far."

"I can agree with you there," said Douglas, although he had not read that the prime minister had said this. "They've gained far too much control of the financial picture. Too much control entirely."

Rhodes put his arm around Douglas and clapped him on the chest with his other hand. It took Douglas off guard and he struggled a little.

"Yid bastards!" Rhodes hissed in his ear before letting him go. "MacNeil, I think you and I should have a drink together."

Douglas studied Rhodes's face, and there was nothing in the man's expression to indicate he was being mocked, but Douglas knew very well that Rhodes was aware of his problems with drink. The whole street knew it—the whole neighbourhood, for that matter.

"Yessir, we'll celebrate the unearthing of Scadding and Robertson from their entombment," the butcher continued. "What say we head to the Winchester? I'm off to meet a friend there, a great guy. We often meet for a short one at the end of the day."

Rhodes had only the slightest smile on his lips, and Douglas couldn't tell whether the smile was cruel.

"No, no. I couldn't," Douglas said.

"Of course you can," said Rhodes, still smiling that unreadable smile.

He looked up at Richard Rhodes, who had become both saviour and executioner. Water rushed into Douglas's mouth and he fancied he could smell the heather-rich, peat-infused smoke of good whisky. He started to say that he could not go to the Winchester Bar, could not join his fellow businessman in a gentleman's drink. He took a breath and his lips parted to say these things.

"Just one, then. Just one couldn't do a man harm at the end of a day's good work, now, could it?" And with those words it seemed like the most natural thing in the world. To have a drink at the end of the day like other men did. What could be the harm in that?

"Wife and kiddies waiting at home for you, eh?" said Rhodes, nudging Douglas in the ribs. "Need to get permission?"

Douglas felt the crust of something cruel beneath the surface of the words. He felt it very clearly, and he knew he should simply say he'd changed his mind and walk away from this man, who he suspected was not his friend at all.

"Certainly not. My wife doesn't run my life."

Rhodes held up his hands. "Just joking. Never occurred to me that a man such as yourself wouldn't rule the roost. No offence, eh?"

There it was again, that tone, light as silk and lethal as venom.

"None taken."

"Right, then, off we go."

As they walked, Richard Rhodes began a short lecture on what was needed to effect the salvation of Canada and how a firm hand was required when dealing with the undesirables flooding onto Canadian shores. He spoke of the abolition of the provincial system in favour of one central government. Douglas listened with half an ear and wondered if Rhodes could possibly be a member of some fascist group, possibly the Christian Front. He agreed that the Jews were a blemish on the Canadian landscape, but the Christian Front were little more than thinly disguised Nazis.

Douglas wanted to form an opinion, but found he could not keep his mind on the conversation. With every step closer to the bar at the Winchester his entire being focused on one thing only: the lure, the song, the enchantment of whisky. It was all he could do to nod, to mutter the occasional grunt of agreement, to keep pace with Rhodes and not break into a headlong run.

They arrived at the red-bricked old hotel, passed the dining room and the ice cream parlour and entered the room at the back of the lobby. The walls were smoke-stained and the red-and-yellow paisley carpet was threadbare. The radio near the bar was on and Cab Calloway sang something about a moocher named Minnie. Rhodes frowned.

"Mickey, for God's sake, can't you change the station?" he called out to the manager, who stood talking to a bellhop in the doorway.

"Customers like jazz, Mr. Rhodes, and to be honest, I do too, see," said Mickey, and turned back to his conversation. Rhodes snorted.

"Ah, there he is. Jack!" called Rhodes, and he waved to a man at a corner table smoking a cigar and reading a paper. Douglas immediately noticed the bottle of whisky that stood in the centre of the table.

"I've brought a fellow to meet you. Douglas MacNeil, may I present Jack Tower."

"Glad to meet you," he said.

"A pleasure," said Douglas as he tore his eyes away from the bottle and smiled.

"MacNeil owns the drug store across from my shop. Been doing some improvements to the place. A man with vision. You put in a soda fountain, didn't you, MacNeil?"

"I did, yes, but that was some time ago." *A man with vision.* He could be that, would be that.

"Oh yes, I believe Rhodes has mentioned you. Pull up a seat," said Tower, who leaned back in his chair and regarded Douglas coolly. His eyes were the palest shade of blue, so pale they were nearly white, and their gaze made Douglas uncomfortable. *What had Rhodes said about him?*

Douglas looked at Tower's demeanour, his good suit, his gold watch, and felt that all his own dilapidated insides were seeping out, like stuffing showing through a shoddy chesterfield. He wanted to fit in, to be approved of.

But most of all, he craved the taste of whisky in his mouth.

Rhodes spoke, as though reading his mind. "Wanted to bring MacNeil here along to help us celebrate. Mickey! Another glass here, man!"

The proprietor sent over a girl with two more glasses, a pitcher of water and a bowl of stale pretzels. As she minced away, Douglas noticed that Rhodes's eyes followed her swaying rear.

"Whisky all right, MacNeil?" Tower held the bottle poised teasingly over the glass. He looked Douglas in the eye.

Many things went through Douglas's mind. The faces of Irene and Margaret appeared, and he thought of his polished chrome soda fountain and newly filled ice cream tubs. The innocent purity of the pale green pistachio, the rosy cheerful strawberry, the pale sweet vanilla. He could see quite clearly the perverse pleasure these men, who were not his friends, were taking in his pain. *Why are they doing this?* And then he knew. They were doing it because they could and for no other reason. It was sport. And in the fit of his addiction, his anger twisted round on itself. *Fuck you,* he thought. *I'll have the goddamn drink. Fuck you.* And it made no sense, and it made no difference that it made no sense.

"Yes, thank you," he said, and he tried not to sound too eager, not to sound as though he wanted this drink more than he wanted his next breath. He watched the drink being poured, the way it settled silkily in the glass, the golden sheen of it as a ray of late-afternoon sun glinted through it like a blessing. Douglas heard a voice in his head, a calm and rational voice, telling him there was no reason in the world not to have this drink, which would ease his nerves. He would have the one, which would not turn into many, and then he would go home. What could be more normal?

"Here's to the men of the mine," said Rhodes, holding his glass high. "To the heroic efforts of the rescue crew and a better future for us all."

"To the men in the mine," said Tower.

"To a bright future," said Douglas.

Ah, the sweet indescribable moment as the lover approaches the beloved. Every sense heightened, blocking out all other memories, all other faces, all other promises, all other desires. The smell of the Scottish moors rising from the cool, smooth glass. The colour of the whisky: honeyed ambrosia. The saliva in the mouth, the tremor in the fingertips. Douglas opened his lips, closed his eyes as though for a kiss.

The face of a girl with the bones of a lark rattling like a skeleton under the force of her cough and a terrible condemnation in her eyes rose up in front of him. He toasted her, downed the liquid and watched her fade away like a ghost.

Douglas didn't guzzle the next drink but sipped the good bonnie barley bree like a gentleman, and it filled his limbs with its warm sweet smoke. Rhodes and Tower chatted along about the news of the day, the miners, of course, and less encouraging events. Tower worked at a bank, as a loans officer, although Douglas suspected the chances of anyone getting a loan from this lean, shark-eyed man were unlikely indeed.

"I quite agree with the action taken by Quebec," Tower was saying, his thumbs hooked into the pockets of his vest. "Ontario should follow suit, scrap the dole completely. That would teach the immigrants not to expect a free ride in this country."

"People must be made to work for what they receive," Douglas concurred, finishing his drink. He looked at the glass forlornly.

"Yes, but I understand that King's thinking about closing the relief camps." Rhodes refilled the three glasses.

"There is no decent leadership in this country," said Tower.

Douglas saw that Rhodes was the follower here, merely parroting the opinions of his betters. Pleased with his insight, he poured another drink and offered the bottle to the other two. They refused, and Douglas saw a glance pass between them but he did not care, not at all. He would prove to them that he was not a common drunk. He would be both informed and intelligent, and he said that he was not at all sure he agreed with Tower on some of the more extreme aspects of his theory. With every drink he felt himself grow both more relaxed and more confident. His vision became loftier, his perspective more erudite. And then he reached that blessed place where he no longer saw any reason to share his opinions, cosseted as he was in his balmy, boozy bath.

He realized with some surprise that two hours had passed. Eight o'clock already and dark outside. He should go home. But why? The company here was far more convivial. It was good for a man to have stimulating conversation, good for the mind, for the soul, even. They were the community leaders, the merchants of standing, the literate, head and shoulders above the unwashed masses, who spilled like so much flotsam on Canada's great shores. Douglas smiled, poured himself another glass and tried to keep his mind on the conversation.

"You must look at Hitler in the context of the situation," Towers was now saying. "Conditions were pressed upon Germany after the Great War which were intended for one thing and one thing only: the humiliation of a people."

Douglas put two fingers up under his nose and extended his right arm. "Sieg Heil," he said and laughed, rather too loudly.

Neither Rhodes nor Tower joined him in this little joke.

"I hardly find Chancellor Hitler an object of ridicule," said Tower, with his oily silver eyes.

"Oh, come on, Tower," said Douglas. "Lighten up, pal, lighten up. Just a little joke."

Rhodes cleared his throat and looked at his watch. "Perhaps it's time to call it a night. I suppose I should be on my way. No use solving all the world's problems in one night, eh?"

"You may be right, Richard," said Tower. "I've an early meeting and some paperwork to do tonight."

"Oh, don't tell me you big shots are going to cash in your chips already? It's early yet, shank of the evening. Come on, have another drink, on me." Douglas picked up the bottle to pour another round.

"Not for me, thanks," said Rhodes.

"Nor me. I know my limit," said Tower, smiling that smile again, the one that Douglas would like to smear right off his face.

"One for the road," insisted Douglas.

Rhodes laughed and slapped Douglas on the back. "Think maybe you've had enough already, MacNeil. Good fellow. Time to go." He pushed back his chair and stood, as did Tower. Douglas felt he had no choice but to follow their example, but he didn't like the implication, didn't like it one bit. Stuck-up two-bit philosophers. Who did they think they were?

Tower pulled some bills out of his pocket, picked up the half-empty bottle and handed it and the money to the passing bar girl. "If you'll allow me, gentlemen. Drinks on me tonight."

"I can pay my share," said Douglas, digging in his pockets. He swayed a little and put a hand on the table for balance.

"No need, MacNeil. Honour of the first meeting and all that. You can return the favour. Buy a round next time, eh?"

Where did they get off implying he couldn't afford to pull his own weight? Well, fine then, let them pay if they were so hell-bent on being big men.

"Good night, MacNeil," said Rhodes, extending his hand. "Delighted you could join us."

"Been a great pleasure meeting you, MacNeil. I'm sure we'll have more invigorating discussions in the future."

Douglas shook their hands sullenly, told them he would say good night here, as he had to use the men's room. He walked with dignity, he thought, to the back of the bar.

Standing at the urinal, Douglas told himself he was happy they were gone. The world was right again, all things had fallen back into their natural order. He was freed from the anxieties of the past few days, which now seemed like nothing more than a vague mirage. He washed his hands and ran his wet fingers over the thin rim of hair above each ear. Why, this was a nice place. There was no reason to rush home. If he wanted another drink, one for the road, why not have one? The past few days in the shop had been rather good. He'd treat himself. Yes, that's what he'd do.

He went back and stood at the bar, ordered a double and started a conversation with a man named Howachuk, a Pole who'd been laid off from the Kingwell Glassworks three years ago. He was altogether a fine, fine fellow, and Douglas bought him a drink.

"To better times," he said, raising his glass.

"Yeah, sure," said the Pole, and downed his drink in one gulp.

When the bar closed, Douglas wobbled out into the street, happy as a dog with two tails. A light rain had begun to fall and the streets were shiny and the sidewalks glittered and the whole world looked like diamonds dancing in the lamplight. Douglas felt a song in his heart. In fact, he felt like doing a little of that old soft-shoe. He stepped off the curb, began to hum and did a little shuffle. He tipped a little, stumbled and, laughing, righted himself. Right foot and a little hop, arms outstretched, he sang:

Pack up all my care and woe, here I go, singing low,
Bye-bye, blackbird.

He turned, did a little pirouette, saw the lights of a car approaching, and as nimbly as his rubbery legs would allow, he capered to the sidewalk and bowed as the vehicle passed. "Toro!" he called.

Back out into the street, he stamped into a puddle. He threw back his head and let loose, singing like Al Jolson, his hand over his heart.

No one here can love or understand me
Oh, what hard-luck stories they all hand me
Make my bed, and light the light, I'll arrive late tonight
Blackbird, bye-bye.

The driver had come south from Sioux Lookout the day before in search of work. He looked down to consult the map on his lap, holding a lighter to read by. He looked away from the road for only a second. He couldn't be blamed, everyone said later, it really wasn't his fault, after all the man was clearly drunk as a Davey's sow and raving in the middle of the slippery road. One minute there was the man's face in his window and then his body all twisted there on the street, his blood flowing out of him in an astonishingly vast river, red to pink in the rainfall, and pink to nothing at all as it ran down the drain into the sewer.

Part IV

16

The day of the funeral was damp and dull. Irene sat at the kitchen table, wrapped in her tartan housecoat with her feet in a pair of her father's old socks. She had given up on sleep hours before. She rested her elbows on the slightly sticky tabletop and her forehead on the heels of her palms. More than anything else this grief was exhausting. Since the news, Irene moved through the house as though through a pool of viscid liquid. To lift a kettle, to fold a towel, to butter a piece of bread—all these things had to be thought out in advance, had to be navigated and achieved with the weights of mourning tied to her wrists. She wanted only to lie in bed, to sleep, to forget. But muzzy with the desire to sleep as she was, she could not quiet her mind enough to actually rest, and so more often than not she found herself sitting at this table, with a cooling pot of weak tea in front of her.

The last time she'd seen her father, he had given her a kiss and squeezed her arm. "It's going to be all right, Pet, I promise." This as he left the house for work on Thursday. *And it was Monday, now. How did it get to be Monday?* He had whistled as he sauntered down the street that day, whistled *Happy days are here again, the skies above are clear again.* The face of the policeman, early Friday morning. He was so solemn, so ashamed looking, as though he himself had run her father down like a rabid terrier in the street. Her mother screaming and smashing about, flinging herself like a demonic rag doll, so that finally the policeman called a doctor and she had been sedated and had remained so all that day and the next night.

And her father on the slab in the morgue. *I'm sorry, miss. This will be hard, but we need to be sure. Can I get you something, a glass of water?* She had looked at the man in astonishment. What good would water do to wash away the memory of his face, his head, the appalling shape of his head, all wrong, his mouth with the lower lip torn away …

She put her hands over her eyes.

You'd think the house would feel empty, but it felt more cramped than usual, with the rock of sorrow so large in the centre of everything, and the ghost of her father appearing before her as she entered every room.

This was the hardest part. Irene could hardly bear to look at his things, not because they reminded her of him; she wanted to be reminded. It helped erase the terrible image of the morgue. But there was, in this most final of equations, so little of him, so little to tip the balance in favour of his life. A few clothes, hung tidily in a closet. A pair of brown shoes. A pair of black shoes. An old hat in need of blocking. A corner of the living room for his desk and his papers. And that was all, really. The rest of the house was filled with her mother's presence, her sharp acrid scent, her preferences for deep colour and cluttered surfaces.

How could someone spend nearly fifty years on the planet and have so little to show for it? It was like the house was no more than a hotel to him, a place where you brought only what you would need for a brief stay. Her mother muttered about him having other women, and although Irene didn't believe he had a woman stashed away anywhere (for how could he have afforded it?), she almost hoped it was true. It was a comfort, somehow, to think that somewhere out there he had a fuller life, a life that was not so glaringly unfulfilled. Surely he could not have tread so lightly on the crust of the earth that he didn't leave any imprint at all.

It broke her heart to think how little she had known about her own father. They had never had a conversation about what he hoped for in life, what he regretted, what he believed. She didn't know whether he believed in God, in an afterlife, in anything.

She had found a shoebox of old photos in the back of the closet. There was a picture of her father and mother standing in front of the house where her mother had been raised. She had taken the photo out of the box and slipped it into her pocket. She took it out now and studied it. Her father wore an ill-fitting, light-coloured tweed suit and a dark tie that was slightly twisted around and puffed out from the top of his vest. He held a cigarette in his left hand, while his right arm tightly clutched her tiny, dark-haired mother, who stood nearly on tiptoe, her body hitched up with the force of his grasp. Her mother wore a funny checked coat and impossibly small black shoes. Her father had hair then. He smiled, looking pleased with himself and his girl. He looked so self-contained and proud, with his narrow chest stuck out and an eyebrow raised. Irene put the photo back in the pocket of her robe and pressed her fingers to her lips.

Although she thought she was done with weeping, her eyes already red and swollen, she wept again.

Where was Uncle Rory? She wanted him here so badly. But there was nowhere to write to. That last postcard from Kenora hadn't even had a return address on it. It had read: "The wind's blown me back out west. Conditions in the mines in Nova Scotia enough to break your heart. We're not giving up, though. We'll make them listen yet. Keep your head up, Doodles. And keep studying. You're a smart girl and can be anything you want. Never take a factory job! I'll write more from where I land. Love to your mum and dad, and to you, Rory X X X."

She was unclear who the "we" referred to, and didn't really believe it was the Communists, as her mother said. Not that she cared. She just wanted him here. Wanted not to be left alone.

From upstairs came the creak of bedsprings, and she heard her mother shuffling to the bathroom. Irene closed her eyes and turned her face up to heaven. *Please, God, just a few minutes more alone. Let her go back to bed.* But heavy footsteps on the stairs made it clear God's deafness was to continue today as it had yesterday and the day before that. Her mother moved as if afraid she might fall.

Irene stood up and filled the kettle again. Tea, more tea, always tea. She added a few more leaves to the pot. Her mother announced her presence by blowing her nose.

"I'd kill him myself, if he were here," her mother said, not for the first time.

"Tea?" Irene kept her face turned to the window.

"These pills the doctor gave me, they're not helping. They just make me dizzy. I can't think straight. What are we supposed to do now? What's going to happen to me?"

"We'll be all right."

"How can you say that? How the hell are we supposed to be all right?"

"I told you. I'll quit school, I'll take over the shop."

"What the hell does a kid like you know about running a shop?" Margaret snorted.

"I'm seventeen. I'm not a kid anymore. Lots of young people work, younger than me. If they can find work, that is. And I'll hire someone to help."

"Hire someone? That's a laugh. And where's that money going to come from?"

Irene had told her mother about the unexpected gift she'd found among her father's papers.

"I doubt that fool even kept up the premiums."

"I told you, Mum. I called Great-West Life. They'll be here tomorrow with the cheque. Two thousand five hundred dollars, Mum. We're going to be all right."

"Oh, *you'll* be fine. After all, you're the beneficiary. Not me. Not his wife."

They had been over all this before and Irene didn't believe that telling her mother again that she'd always take care of her would do any good.

"With the mortgage on the house and the store, we won't be fine at all," her mother continued. "You're not a druggist! What are you going to sell? And I'm not well enough to help, you know. Not with my headaches and now this. It'll kill me. You'll be burying us both."

"Drink your tea, Mum, you'll feel better."

"A soda fountain. What the hell was he thinking? He's ruined us, you know that, don't you? The second he gave Mr. Casselman that poison!"

"He made a mistake, that's all. He didn't poison anyone."

"That's not what the neighbours are saying, you know that, don't you?"

Irene rubbed the space between her eyes with her middle finger, willing herself not to turn around and scream at her mother.

"Your father was a drunk and a fool, Irene. And everyone knows it. They whisper about it. I know that and you know that. Why, I can't even leave the house."

"I don't know what *everyone* is saying, and neither do you! Can't you leave it alone, just for today, Mum? Can't you please? We're burying Dad today, for God's sake."

"Oh, so it's going to be like that, is it? Very well, Irene. Very well. You're a cruel girl. My husband's just died and you won't even let me talk about it. That's just like you. You're upset and that's all that counts. Your father wasn't the man you think he was. He wanted more children, you know. Wanted a son. That was his big regret. Not having a son."

Irene wanted to scream that Margaret was probably the reason her father had been a drunk, that living with her would drive anyone to drink. She wanted to scream that it would serve her mother right if she just walked out the door this very minute and took the insurance money with her.

But she knew what fury that would unleash. Hadn't she learned that as a little girl? It didn't matter that she was as tall as her mother now. In her mind she was still small. She felt like a prisoner brainwashed to believe the bars of the jail were there, even if they weren't anymore.

So she kept her mouth shut, although the pressure of the words blowing tornado-like against the inside of her head was so great it made tears spring to her eyes.

Seeing those tears, Margaret thought her remark concerning Douglas's disappointment at not having a son had struck the mark. She picked up her teacup and took a sip. She was ashamed of herself. She said these things and she knew she shouldn't, the hurtful words kept slipping out and she couldn't stop them. She wanted to throw herself in her daughter's arms, asking forgiveness. Maybe everything would be better if she did. She opened her mouth to speak.

"This is bitter," she said and put the cup back on the saucer carelessly, slopping tea onto the table. She left it there, wrapped her housecoat around her and left the kitchen.

"Take a bath, Mum," Irene called after her. "The service starts at ten. They'll be here in a couple of hours."

"I'm not going," her mother called back.

Irene followed her and stood at the bottom of the stairs. Margaret made a great display of struggling up each step, one hand on her heart, one foot quiveringly raised, the other hand gripping the banister.

"What do you mean, you're not going?"

"Just what I said." She kept her face averted. "I have no intention of making a spectacle of myself. In front of all those gawking eyes. I couldn't stand it."

"You have to go."

Margaret turned. "I don't have to do anything. I told you I thought this funeral was a waste of money and in bad taste, too, given the state your father was in when he died. The only people who'll come are the neighbourhood snoops wanting a show."

"Aunt Janet will be there, and Uncle Oscar."

"Just coming around to see what they can get."

"Don't be ridiculous."

"Ridiculous, am I? Fine. Do what you want. What I'm going through doesn't matter."

"Mum, please ... "

"No, *no*! I won't! I won't go!" Margaret slapped her hand on the railing. "I won't fall apart in front of strangers. I *won't*!"

"All right, Mum, you don't have to go. It's all right. Go back to bed." And she smiled at her mother. If she worked herself up into hysteria, neither of them would be able to go.

"I don't want you to go either. I need you here. Don't leave me, Kitten." She reached out her hand.

As clearly as if her mother had spoken aloud, Irene saw how Margaret thought they'd live together, the two of them, locked up in this house, sharing everything until they melded into one single entity. *Where do you end and I begin?* She looked at her mother's hand, the bird-like scrapping hardness of the fingers and slightly yellowed nails. Afraid, she involuntarily put her own hands behind her back.

"I'm going, Mum. You don't have to, but I'm definitely going."

"You don't have to, you know. It won't matter, dear. Why put yourself through it?" said Margaret, wheedling. "We don't need to parade our grief. It should be private. We can comfort each other."

"Go to bed if you want, Mother. Or come with me. It's your choice. But I'm going." Irene turned back to the kitchen.

"Selfish!" her mother called after her. "Selfish like your father! I might just as well take all those pills the doctor left. I might just as well!"

Irene cut herself a slice of bread. She heard her mother upstairs pacing and muttering. She poured herself a glass of milk and heard something shatter. A glass, a bottle of pills, maybe. Or a photograph. Irene forced herself to eat.

When she went upstairs her mother's door was shut, but it was quiet inside. Irene went straight to her room and closed her door.

She had laid out her dark dress on the back of the chair with her stockings and slip. She took off her robe. She slipped her clothes on and looked at herself in the mirror as she buttoned up the collar. A serious girl looked back at her. Pale and wan, but with dark brown eyes in which Irene thought she detected a trace of her uncle Rory. A capable person. A person who could do anything she wanted. Arrange a father's funeral, say, or run a store, be an employer, or tread water for as long as necessary, even when her mother would like to pull her down among the reeds and fishes and drown them both.

Irene picked up her purse, checked to see she had her gloves and headed to the door without saying goodbye. She plucked an umbrella from the stand and as she opened the front door she brushed against the black wreath hanging there. This had been another expense her mother said was showy and unnecessary but that Irene had insisted on, hoping it would attract some of the neighbours to call. She was disappointed that they had not, but didn't hold it against them, understanding all too well the difficulties her family presented.

The driver from the funeral home had not arrived yet, but Irene decided to wait outside on the porch. She felt she had let her father down. They should have buried him from home. That's what people did when they couldn't afford a grand viewing at the mortician's, but of course her mother wouldn't hear of it. Irene wanted at least to have the hearse come to the house, but she'd been shouted down on that as well. She hated to think of her father lying all alone on the cold mortician's slab, travelling all alone to his final resting place.

She took a deep breath of the mild air and thought, if you had to pick one, that April was a good month for funerals. The earth was soft enough to dig in but cold enough still not to be rude with bursting life. And then there was the bleak bone-grey sky, the coat-soaking drizzle, and the trees caught between the promise of life to come and the skeletal fingers of leafless March.

The black car arrived and the surprisingly young black-suited man came around and opened the door for her.

"All alone, miss?" he said.

Without looking back at the house to see if her mother was peeking out the window, she replied that yes, she was alone. "The rest ... will meet us at the cemetery."

"Yes, miss. Sorry for your loss."

"Thank you," she said, and they drove the rest of the way in silence.

The hearse, Mr. Carrick the mortician, Reverend Dillard and the mortician's assistant were waiting for her. The coffin was already placed at the graveside. Irene blushed and twisted her gloves in her hands. She felt exposed out here under the roofless sky. Perhaps it would have been better to have had a service at the church after all. At least she could have sat and made herself small, could have taken some comfort from being enclosed, if not by the support of friends and family, then at least by walls. But she had to admit that few people would likely come, even with a notice posted, and the idea of sitting alone, or nearly so, in a place made for many made her shudder.

Mr. Carrick opened the door for her and took her hand.

"My condolences, Miss MacNeil. Deepest sympathy," he murmured.

"Thank you."

As she stepped out of the car she saw worms wriggling by the side of the roadway, washed out of the earth by last night's rain. Two gravediggers stood under a nearby tree, their hats pulled low and their collars turned up against the drizzle. The minister came toward her, carrying a big black umbrella. Irene realized she must have forgotten her umbrella on the porch. She was doing that a lot the past few days—losing a train of thought, a hairbrush, walking into rooms and then forgetting why she was there.

"Good morning, Irene. I'm so sorry for your loss. How's your mother?" he asked.

"She's not doing so well, Reverend. She couldn't face it."

"We'll take it one thing at a time, then, shall we?" He didn't insist on visiting as he might with another sort of family.

A car pulled up behind the hearse, and Aunt Janet and Uncle Oscar climbed out. Their sons had not come. Aunt Janet, narrow in the chest like her brother but making up for it in her broad soft hips and thighs, waddled toward Irene, her knees turned in, making her look like a fussy hen dressed up in a raven's clothes. Her husband trailed behind, blinking myopically behind his glasses, his head turning this way and that on his turtle-like neck.

"Irene, oh my dear," said Janet, taking her in her arms, tilting her ruffle-rimmed umbrella in the process and sending an icy rivulet down the back of Irene's neck. "You poor thing. Sweet, gentle Douglas. I can't quite get my mind around it. I can't make sense of it. How could such a thing happen? We all loved him so much. Good morning, Reverend. I'm Janet Reade, Douglas's sister. This is my husband, Oscar." She looked around. "Where's your mother, dear?"

"She's not feeling well enough to come," said Irene, disentangling herself. "But she sends her love."

"Not coming? But it's her husband's funeral," she said.

"Janet, dear, don't work yourself up. Irene's not to blame for her mother."

"Someone has to say something, Oscar. In fact, it's a darn sight overdue is my feeling. We should have taken things in hand long before now."

Oh, the conversations they must have had, snug in their pretty, carpet-muffled house, about the sad, mad MacNeils.

"I think," said Aunt Janet, "that I should go and get your mother. Oscar can drive me. I think that's the right thing to do. She really must be here." She dabbed at her eyes with a pale blue hanky.

"Mrs. Reade—it is Reade, isn't it?" said Reverend Dillard. "I understand your concerns, and there'll be time enough to talk later. But right now I think we should get on with the service. Mrs. MacNeil is here in spirit, if not in body." He gestured with his hand toward the grave. "Shall we proceed?"

"Yes, let's start, " Irene said, and she took the arm the minister offered her.

"Irene, you're too young to understand. Reverend, you'll just have to delay the service. We'll go alone. Margaret will see the benefit later. Oscar, get in the car."

"Aunt Janet, please, don't do this." Irene's hand was tight on the minister's arm.

Mr. Carrick looked stricken. "Madam, I'm dreadfully sorry and I certainly understand your point of view, but this isn't possible. I have, sadly, other commitments, and if this service is delayed, well then, there are other bereaved ... waiting ..." He looked from one of them to the other. "I have to honour my schedule. Forgive me, but we can't delay."

"That, sir, is not my problem. It's yours. This is not a pleasant situation for any of us," said Janet, dabbing once more at her tears. "She's a selfish woman. I don't mean to be harsh, dear, but honestly. I simply must insist. It's a question of respect. The entire family should be here."

"The entire family? Where are Brad and Earl?" said Irene. "Riding their bikes over, are they?"

"Irene, they're just young boys. It's not the same."

Irene gritted her teeth. She was one year older than Brad. "Well, lucky them," she said, and was about to say more when she saw another car pulling up. It was a beautiful black Packard, shiny and new. She couldn't imagine who would be in a car like that. When the doors opened and Ebbie Watkins got out of the passenger seat and her mother out of the back, Irene was speechless. And getting out of the driver's seat, unfolding like an elegant, loose-limbed hound, was the boy with the Leslie Howard hair.

Ebbie put her hands on Irene's arms, not quite hugging her. "Irene, I'm so sorry."

"How are you, dear?" said Mrs. Watkins.

"God, you must be frayed, you poor thing," Ebbie went on.

Irene blinked quickly. "It's nice of you to come."

"How's your poor mother holding up?" said Mrs. Watkins.

"About as you'd expect."

Aunt Janet bustled forward and introduced herself, and Uncle Oscar said, "We were just deciding how best to handle the situation."

"No, we weren't," said Irene. "We were starting. Everything has already been decided." Her voice had a slightly frantic edge to it that she had not intended.

"I think we should begin," agreed Reverend Dillard.

"Yes, we should begin," repeated Mr. Carrick, jingling the coins in his pocket.

"Now, Reverend, I think this is a family matter." Oscar Reade's voice was nasal and timid. "No offence, you understand, but I believe it is best handled along familial lines. I'm sure you can see … understanding that family must be of one mind … a unified, uh, unit, yes …"

"Oh, shut up, Oscar," said his wife. "Irene, come along with us, dear."

"No, Aunt Janet. You can't do this. It's out of the question." Irene folded her arms. She wanted to be a lady, not to burst out crying, not to stamp her foot and not to slap her aunt.

"But surely you understand, Reverend. Douglas was her husband," said Aunt Janet, her voice shrill. She pointed at Irene. "Make her see reason."

"Wasn't it Eliot who talked about a stubborn season?" said Harry Madison, who leaned against his polished automobile with his arms folded and his long legs crossed at the ankles. They turned to him in surprise. He pushed himself up from his lazy posture. "I'm sorry. I'm barging in where I don't belong, aren't I?"

"Harry, for heaven's sake," said Ebbie. "He was kind enough to drive us, Irene, and promised he'd behave."

Harry opened the car door and retrieved two large umbrellas. He handed one to Ebbie and her mother and then opened the other and held it over Irene's head. "Of course it's none of my business, but I understood the doctors had ordered Mrs. MacNeil to stay in bed, heavily sedated. That was the case, wasn't it, Irene?" He stood next to her, facing her aunt and uncle. "Of course, Irene didn't want to burden you, I'm sure, with the sight of her mother so stricken. You have your own grief to contend with, naturally. However, I'm sure we can all have compassion for a mourning so profound."

"Are you a friend of the family?" said Aunt Janet, her hanky-clutching hand at her throat. "I don't believe we've met."

"Harry Madison," he said, smiling. He extended his manicured hand, the gold wristwatch bright in the sombre light, and she had no choice but to take it. "It's a difficult time, and so hard to know what to do."

Janet Reade stepped back.

"I knew you'd understand, Mrs. Reade. Irene?" Harry held out his arm and she found herself taking it.

"I don't know," said Aunt Janet, but no one was listening to her any longer. She began snuffling into her hanky, and she and her husband joined the small procession to the graveside.

With every step they took closer to the grave, and to her father's plain cheap casket waiting next to it, Irene was more and more terrified she would begin to wail, to scream. But becoming hysterical was her mother's domain, not hers.

Grief came in spasms. Under normal circumstances she would never have been brave enough to take Harry's arm, but under the sodden weight of loss, she became numb. She moved like a hollow thing, barely aware of what she was doing, while at the same time her skin tingled with the warmth of Harry Madison's fingers resting reassuringly on the top of her gloved hand. The heel of her shoe sunk in the softening earth, tilting her, and she was afraid for a moment that she might faint. Only Harry Madison's arm kept her rooted.

One of the gravediggers smoked a cigarette, and the scent wafted across the open grave. Irene looked at the man, although she didn't give a damn if he smoked or not, and he crushed the butt out under his heel.

She removed her hand from Harry's arm and took a small step sideways. She needed to stand alone in this place, with the heels of her one good pair of shoes sinking in the muddy, partly thawed ground.

The Reverend was saying something now and she realized the service was over. It had been so short. How could she not have noticed it going on around her? She wanted to tell them they would have to begin again for she hadn't really been here, had been somewhere else altogether. The gravediggers stepped forward and took the straps that lay under the casket, looped them over their shoulders. They wrestled it over the waiting bed of earth and lowered it jerkily down.

Watching this made Irene's chest lurch. Aunt Janet sobbed and buried her face in her husband's shoulder. Norma Watkins dabbed at her eyes with a hanky. Reverend Dillard patted Aunt Janet on the back and whispered something to Uncle Oscar, who nodded and led his wife away. Irene heard the engine start up, heard the crunching gravel beneath their tires.

She didn't know what to do now. She couldn't leave. She felt she should say something, but what? And to whom? Ebbie and her mother stood quietly on her right side. Harry stood on her left. She felt hemmed in, conflicted with feelings of gratitude that they had come and shame that they should witness this pathetic little performance. She opened her mouth to speak, and then closed it.

Mrs. Watkins put her arm across her shoulders. "Would you like to come back to our house, dear? Have a bite to eat? And you too, of course, Reverend." Gently the woman turned Irene from the grave. Irene heard a wet clod of earth hitting wood.

"Yes, Irene, come back with us, for just a little while, even." Ebbie took both her hands and rubbed them back and forth, the way one rubs a child's hands to warm them.

Irene shook her head. The tears were there again, behind her eyes in sharp prickling drops. She could defend herself against the outrage and condescending disapproval of her aunt and uncle, but not against Ebbie. She wanted to hand all the hurt and the fear over to her. She wanted to throw herself in her friend's arms.

"I can't. I have to get back. It's kind. Really."

The unaccustomed compassion made her feel naked and unprotected; and yet to go home, back to what would surely be coiled and waiting for her ... In her mind she spun in circles, looking frantically for a place to land, like a bird trapped in a house, hands grasping for it. There was no open window through which she could escape, no leaf-sheltered limb on which she could perch. She closed her eyes.

"The driver's waiting. I need to go. Thank you for coming." She hugged Mrs. Watkins, smelled the powder-fresh scent of her. Then she turned to Ebbie and buried her face in the soft white halo of her hair.

"Mr. Madison." She held out her hand and was relieved to see it did not tremble. "Thank you again."

He ignored her hand and took her by the elbow. "I'll walk you to the car," he said, and she did not protest. The rest followed in a small parade and left the gravediggers to their task.

They reached the side of the car and he opened the door for her.

"Will you be all right at home?"

"Why wouldn't I be?"

"No need to be alone, you know."

"I'm not alone."

"Yes," he said. "Well, goodbye, then."

1936

David has to get out of the country. After what happened, the nightmares don't leave him. Every time he closes his eyes he sees things he doesn't want to see, can't get his mind to stop trying to rewrite what happened. There is a terrible sorrow at the centre of his chest, hollow enough that the wind seems to blow right through him. The sorrow is personal, the disillusionment with his country is political, so he crosses over to the great American promised land, hoping to find things are a little better there. Or if not better, then at least different.

In New York, no further away from starvation, no closer to a job and still unable to outrun his sorrow, he finds himself in a Hoover Hotel as they are called, even though Hoover isn't president anymore. The Municipal Lodging House is run by the Department of Public Welfare, on 25th near the East River. Only the most derelict end up there, and he guesses he belongs. Since Regina, David hasn't been able to sort himself out, hasn't been able to get a footing on his life. He'd had it there, he believes, for a while, travelling and working with the man he called a friend, but of course, that's over now. So he takes his place in another line that snakes around the block, holding the lapels of his thin coat together, trying to keep warm. When he gets inside he eats his bowl of mutton stew and drinks his coffee, not looking to the right or left of him, for what's the point of getting to know anyone? Then he hands in his clothes to have them fumigated and takes a shower, leaning for as long as they will let him with his hands against the tiles and his head under the scalding water. He sees the doctor for the mandatory physical, a quick examination wherein he is declared fit to receive their charity, and he is given a white nightshirt and a cot in a room with hundreds of other men and is so tired the noise doesn't wake him.

In the morning he asks if he can work at cleaning, or fixing something, or serving the breakfast, in order to pay for his stay, for he still wants to be proud, as his friend had drilled into him. "Stand tall. Be a man, no matter how far down you find yourself." The friend who had reminded him, in some ways, of his proud old man. But they say no thanks, it is a charity place, and his humiliation feels complete. New York does him no good, and he wanders west.

In Chicago he can't find room even in the shelters, and it gets colder every night. The wind is a knife-wielding witch. He goes all along the streets, to restaurants and bars asking if he can do anything, mop up, clean the toilets, in return for a meal and a place to stay. The answer is always the same.

'Round midnight he goes into a dingy grill joint.

"We already got a boy," says the owner and gestures with his knife to a man coming out of the bathroom carrying a mop and bucket.

"I don't see any boy," he says, but the man looks at him without understanding.

As he steps out onto the sidewalk, the man with the bucket follows him.

"Hard to keep your head up, ain't it?" he says. "Sure hard."

"Not easy, but I guess you know more'n most," David replies.

"Yessir. Guess I do."

"Least ways you're working," he says.

"Up north here, they might give a Negro a job, but they won't pay him. I reckon if they had any money for pay, there'd be a white man standing in front of you now."

The look on David's face shows his confusion.

"I don't get no pay, see. Get scraps to take home, is all. From the kitchen at the end of the night."

"That's not right, friend," says David.

"Ain't much that is these days. Could be worse. Down Mississippi, where I come from, the Klan are shooting Negro coal men right off the trains so they can give the job to a white man."

They introduce themselves.

"Tell you what," says Walker, "my wife and me, we rent out the bathtub if we can. Know it don't sound like much and it ain't, but put a plank over it and a pillow for your head and I bet you've done some worse."

"Sounds good to me, but all I've got in my pockets is a hole."

"Yeah, that's just about the going rate when it's this late and the tub's empty. You're welcome to wait around till I finish up and come on back with me, take your chances she ain't found nobody. Vera'll make you work it off, just to keep you happy."

Walker and his wife live in a rickety tenement on the south side. The foundation is shifting, the building near collapse and wedged up with concrete blocks under one corner and along the porch in front. The heat and water and lights have long been turned off and the building should have been condemned, but the city knows the people who squat here have nowhere else to go. The stench from the backed-up toilets in little closets at the end of the halls thickens the air. The top floor of the four-storey building has been gutted by fire and the smell of smoke mixes with that of human waste. He learns that two people died in that blaze, which was started when someone tried to cook over an open flame on some bricks in the middle of the floor. Thin, timid children play in the dim hallways and broken staircases. Walker was once a Pullman car porter. His wife had taught school. Prostitutes accost David as he and Walker make their way along the hall. "Ooooh, looky here, pretty chicken meat. Look at this little baby needs a momma to take care of hisself." The rooms are inhabited by junkies and preachers and gangsters and former cooks and domestics and labourers and pimps and war veterans.

He sleeps on a board over the bathtub and wakes up every few minutes to kick at rats. He wonders at the noises coming from the other rooms, the shouts and curses and cries of babies and moans and groans, all impossible to separate. The next day he does what he has said he would never do: he goes into the financial district far across town and he puts his cap on the ground. At the end of the day he has a dollar twenty-five, and he gives *it all to Vera, a silent woman with arthritic hands and knees from years of scrubbing white people's floors. She insists he stay for another night. He does.*

The next day he heads back to Canada.

17

As soon as the car door shut and Irene drove away to the funeral, Margaret knew she'd made a mistake. A sinister amber of silence filled the house.

"I can't stand it! What'll I do now?" she cried, as she raked her fingers through her hair, tearing at it. In the centre of her chest a fire burned and she knew it was her heart consuming itself. She hadn't known losing Douglas would feel so horrible, because for so long she had believed she didn't love him. But now, with his absence taking up so vast a space in her future, an avalanche of grief buried her.

She feared she would die, too. She *wanted* to die. She went downstairs to the living room and sank onto her knees, driven down by the weight of grief. The carpet scratched against the skin of her thin shins. As her robe opened in disarray her own scent rose toward her nostrils and filled her with shame. Even the robe itself was sour and stained. She should wash herself, scrub everywhere and get the filth out.

"Douglas," she said, and the sound of his name brought tears to her eyes again. It would be a relief to die, and if she did, it would be of heart failure. Her failed heart.

She punched herself in the chest. *Stop. Stop. Stop beating!*

What would become of her? Widow woman. The widow MacNeil. *I am too young. Too young to be a widow. Black-weed widow woman.*

If the street had conspired to laugh at her before, now it would be a mob of pointing fingers and whispers. She would never again be able to set foot outside her door.

Even now, with the excuse of her husband's funeral carving a clear path for her straight out the door, she was paralyzed between wanting to do the right thing and her untameable anger, her bitter discontent. If she could fully give herself to either one, then she would, she believed, find relief. Let her quench her thirst for love and loving, let her be a woman kind as apples, calm as butter. Or else let her release all grip on hope and fling herself toward the Other One. The Other Margaret. Let her become wind bred and lightning born. Fierce as rabies, unforgiving as a sharpened and thirsty sword.

Misery stabbed at her when she remembered how cruel she had been to Douglas, how she had turned away from him in bed, telling him he disgusted her. How she had failed at being a wife. Hadn't she tried, though, hadn't she tried? And wasn't he an impossible husband, after all? A drunkard. A philanderer. A fool.

She had had such dreams, once. Even when she knew he would not be the great passion of her life, she had held the hope that they might be gentle with each other, might be kind, might bring out the best in each other. She had dreamed they might grow old and fat and prosperous together. She had dreamed they might laugh. Why did she never laugh? Wasn't she filled with laughter somewhere deep inside? Hadn't she once been the Laughing Girl?

Margaret sat on her heels in the middle of her darkened bedroom and wailed. She doubled over so her forehead nearly rested on the floor, her arms wrapped across her aching chest. She could not go to the funeral, but having stayed behind, she could not forgive herself for it, nor forgive her daughter for not either pulling her along or staying with her.

She had never minded being alone in the house when she knew someone would soon be home, but now being alone took on new meaning. She had taken it for granted that when Irene grew up and left home, Douglas, no matter how inadequate, would still be there. But now, if Irene went, there would be no one. No one to care for her, no one to distract her from the tug of the Other Margaret. She listened to the noisy silence, the house empty as a dry husk. Haunted by whispers in the walls, in the pipes, in the floorboards. There was just her. And Her.

She would be left to scratch out her days like marks on a jail cell wall and no one would care or hear her screaming. Sound rose in her mouth, pushed at her teeth and lips. She moaned, but then clamped her hand over her mouth. What if she couldn't stop screaming? They would take her away then, wouldn't they? To somewhere filled with drooling women strapped to beds. She'd heard about such places. Needles in the skull. Puddles of urine on the floor. Straightjackets. Baths in icy water. Packed and tied in wet blankets.

Margaret began to dash about the living room. She overturned the brass crookneck lamp on Douglas's desk. It fell to the floor with a clatter and the bulb shattered. She ran upstairs to her room. She had to think. She had to plan. She didn't want to die alone. Terror crouched, waiting to pounce. She slammed the door behind her. Pushed a chair under the handle and began to pace. She had to think of a way. She must not be left alone.

It was nearly dark when Irene woke. For a moment she couldn't tell if it was morning or evening. She went down the hall. She listened at her mother's door but heard nothing. Perhaps she was sleeping too, but it seemed to Irene her mother was too quiet. Had she taken sleeping pills? She'd done it before, several times before, standing in a good light, making sure she was seen. Head tipped back, pills going in. Irene didn't think her mother was suicidal. *But how could you ever be sure this time wasn't different?*

Irene decided she'd make some scrambled eggs and toast and bring them up to her. Food was a symbol for her mother; it meant care and concern, and often worked to soothe her when no words would.

As Irene came downstairs something in the living room caught her eye. Glass on the floor. The lamp overturned. Oh God. Why hadn't she checked on her mother as soon as she got home?

She knew full well that if she rushed headlong up the stairs, panicked herself, it would only make things worse. Her mother fed off the emotions of others. A placid, unruffled surface was best. They both might know it was an act, but since so much acting took place on their small stage of a house, it was a long-accepted deception.

She filled the kettle and banged it down on the stove. Had her father cared so little about her that he would leave her here alone to deal with her mother?

A clunk from upstairs and a small scrape. The chair being removed from under the door handle. And so Irene was expected.

She poured water in the pot, swirled it around to heat it, emptied it, spooned the leaves in and added more hot water. She placed her hands around the warm pot. Small rituals were comforting. Wash the dishes. Polish the silver. Shell the peas. Letting her hands do their tasks while her mind stilled was one of the weapons she used in the war not to become her mother, not to let her mother slice open a flap in her skin and crawl under, inhabiting her, taking her over. She watched her face in the mirror for signs of similar expressions: the frown, the pulled-down mouth, the suspiciously squinting eyes. If she caught herself scratching the back of her hands, she panicked and shook her fingers as though to scatter any taint. She celebrated any variance. She was taller than her mother and more solidly built. The difference in their hair colour, in the kind of clothes they preferred. Irene loved earth tones while Margaret loved her blood-red kitchen, her bright pink comforters.

Teacup on a tray. Milk jug. Sugar. A small silver spoon with a carved high-masted boat on the handle. Her mother loved that spoon. Teapot. Yellow crocheted cozy on top of that. And up the stairs we go, *one-two-three*, every step echoing in the narrow canyon of the house.

She tapped on the door. "Mum? Are you sleeping? I've brought you some tea."

Silence.

Irene turned the handle and opened the door. Her mother wasn't in bed, as she had expected, but was sitting at the window in the chair that had so recently been blocking the door. Her head hung down, framed against the long rays of late-day light.

Oh, very dramatic, thought Irene. "Come on, Mum. Have some tea. You'll feel better." She set the tray down on the bed and poured. Milk and sugar. A brisk stir. She held the cup out. Her mother didn't take it. She sat with her hands in her lap, plucking at a thread. Irene put the tea down on the sill beside her. She considered just walking out of the room without saying a word, leaving her mother to sip or sit as she wished. But the broken lamp was hard to ignore. Something must be said about a broken lamp and jagged glass left on the floor, for if she didn't know what had happened, how could she stop it from happening again? This was an old dance between the two of them, Irene knew, but she was compelled to try to fix things, to make them better, to reassure, to console.

"You might as well talk, Mum. You might as well tell me what you're thinking."

"My husband's dead, what do you think I'm thinking?"

And my father's dead, what about that? thought Irene. Does that count for nothing? Why was nothing ever normal in their house? Not even grief. Where they should comfort each other they only clawed at the raw wounds. Irene sighed, loud enough to be heard.

"I know, Mum. I know how hard it is."

"You don't know. You haven't had your heart broken, not yet. You don't know what it is to be betrayed." That was not what Margaret intended. She pursed her lips, shook her head. "It hurts," she said, which was closer to what she wanted to say.

Irene went over to her mother, wanting things to be different between them; there was always that, always the hope that somehow she would find a word, a phrase, the perfect speech, that would reach her mother, that would find its way into the labyrinth of suspicion and misery and pull her back into the world.

She moved the teacup aside and leaned against the sill. She took her mother's hand.

"I suppose you'll leave," said Margaret.

Looking at her mother's face was like looking into the face of a sickly child trapped in the flesh of an older woman. Irene wanted to shake her, shake her until the child disappeared and the mother took her place, took her responsibility, took the burdens back.

"You'll go and leave me here now, won't you. I know you will," Margaret said again. Her eyes sparkled with tears.

"Why would you think that? Where would I go? This is my home." And Irene wanted it to be a home, wanted it to feel like a home, a place where the heart rested, where defences could be left with your boots at the door. It was part of what kept her there, the opium of this possibility.

"He should have left it to me, not you."

"The insurance money?"

Margaret nodded.

"Yes, he should have, you're right." She handed her mother the tea and was relieved when she took it. "But it's just a piece of paper, isn't it? We're still a family. We'll be all right."

"You think you can manage it, do you? Because I can't work in that store. I can't. I just couldn't stand to be there."

"I know."

"You'll have to quit school."

"We talked about that. I said I would. It was my idea."

"If your father hadn't been such a fool, you could have gone to university. I know how much you wanted that. And you could have done it too, if your father had been a better man." Margaret wanted to push the needle of resentment through both their skins, sew them up together.

"I don't mind," said Irene, and she couldn't help but avert her face as she said it. She had had dreams of going to the University of Toronto, studying English, maybe, or of becoming a teacher or a nurse. They had never talked about what she would do. All it had ever been was a vague destination, but still, until now at least the possibility had existed.

Sensing the nerve touched, Margaret eyed Irene. "He was no good, that man, no good at all," she said.

"He tried his best, don't you think?" Irene said.

"His best? Useless, that's what he was. A drunk."

"I feel sorry for him. Don't you? What did he have, what did he do? I don't think he ever got what he wanted. I don't even think he knew what that was. I think he just went on, day to day, trying to get through, trying to make it to the end, and look at how little there was to show for it." She was speaking to herself more than to her mother now. "Look at how small his life was. No mark at all."

"He left his mark on me, I'll tell you that, my girl."

"We'll be all right, Mum. I promise."

Margaret patted Irene's knee. "You're a good girl, Irene. You won't leave me, will you?"

"No, I won't leave you. There's no reason for you to worry. Do you understand?"

Margaret studied her daughter's face and then, seeing the quiet sincerity, she relaxed. Perhaps they could love each other.

"You mustn't mind what I say sometimes. I can't help it, you know. I get so depressed." And she smiled, for it was good to be able to open your mouth and have the words you wanted to say come out.

"I know, Mum. It's okay." She pushed herself up from the window ledge. "Tell you what. I'll make some eggs. Some scrambled eggs."

"I don't know if I can eat."

"We'll try, shall we? We'll try and eat something."

"I suppose," said Margaret and she rose. "I'll be right down."

She went into the bathroom and splashed water on her face. Perhaps she'd bake something this week, something just for Irene.

Have dinner ready for her when she got home from the store. Irene hadn't had a cake this past birthday and she should have one. Margaret would bake a cake for her daughter, a fluffy white cake with pink icing.

18

June 1936

The new sign on the gleaming front window said simply "MacNeil's" and underneath in smaller letters, "Notions and dry goods. Ice cream parlour." Irene, with Ebbie's help, had thrown herself into transforming the store. Chrome glistened, glass sparkled, even the wooden floor shone brightly. The pharmaceutical supplies were gone, as Irene didn't have enough money to hire a pharmacist. But to the left side of the shop, where the druggist's counter had once stood, new shelves were bursting with all manner of household goods. Brooms and mops and buckets, pots, pans and enamel cookware, buttons, bobby pins, mothballs and mousetraps. She even had hair ribbons and sewing supplies. Next to that, a modest supply of nonprescription goods: Gold's Anti-Itch Powder, bandages, corn plasters, California Fig-Syrup Children's Laxative, Zam-Buk salve, various hair tonics and one or two ladies' face creams, shaving supplies. To the right was the ice cream parlour, a veritable shrine to confection: candied cherries, walnuts, and chocolate shavings rested coolly in covered glass dishes ready to be sprinkled on sundaes and floats. Tubs of ice cream beckoned temptingly, tilted just slightly toward the customers. Fresh strawberry, rich luscious chocolate and creamy vanilla. A radio sat on the back counter and Rudy Vallee sang "You Are the Girl of My Dreams."

Three girls, perhaps thirteen or fourteen, sat at the counter sipping milkshakes through straws. Their legs were hooked around the stem of their stools.

"I think I like Rudy Vallee best," said one.

"He's a dreamboat," said the one in the middle, "but Bing Crosby, he's divine."

The third girl merely sighed and sipped on.

Irene stood behind the cash counter across from the entrance. She held out a jar of skin cream, assuring the woman that it would fade freckles completely and in no time at all. The bell rang over the door, and she smiled at Harry. He had taken to dropping in on her now and again, just, he said, to see how she was getting along.

As soon as her customer left, Irene came around the counter, and as she did Harry plucked a sprig of lilacs from his lapel and handed it to her with a small bow and a click of his heels.

"For the first day of summer."

"Why, thank you, kind sir," she said and held the flowers to her nose.

"Looks like things are coming along here nicely."

"Well, I'm trying. I'm not overwhelmed with business, but it's picking up. School ends this week, but I don't know if that'll mean more business for the ice cream counter or less. Most kids will have to work for the summer. They've got to find something, anything to help out." She looked around. "I have to find a way to get more cash coming in."

"It takes time, surely. Especially after a place, well ... "

"Yes, I know—after a place has gone downhill." She blushed a little and picked at a roll of string.

"Did you hear about what happened in Etobicoke yesterday?" said Harry.

"No, what?"

"Seems a crowd protesting relief cuts imprisoned the reeve in his own office. Had him trapped in there for hours. Stripped him naked, apparently." Harry laughed.

"They didn't!"

"That sort of thing doesn't surprise me anymore. What surprises me is that there isn't more of it. The way things are going. Of course, my father says I'm in danger of becoming a radical. There are more and more homeless on the streets, have you noticed? No one in Rosedale seems to, but they're everywhere. Passed a man on the street on the way over here wearing a sign that said 'Will Work for Food.'"

"I've been thinking," said Irene. "There are two perfectly good rooms upstairs. They're filled with junk, but I think I could fix them up. My grandparents lived up there when they first opened the business. They only left and got a house after Dad was born. I don't know why he never did anything about them."

She was just about to tell him that she was planning to rent out the rooms when the door opened and a trio of dusty, rough-looking boys headed for the ice cream counter. "I'll be right with you," she called to them. "Do you know what you want?"

"Root-beer float!" one called out.

"Chocolate sundae," said the other. "And come on, baby, hop to it. I ain't got all day." He snapped his fingers and elbowed the third boy, who snorted. The one who'd spoken had a cap pulled low on his forehead. He stared at Irene openly.

"I beg your pardon?" said Harry, turning to the boy.

"Do you?" said the boy, wiping his nose loudly with the back of his sleeve.

"Never mind, Harry," said Irene. "It's all right."

"Yeah, never mind, Haaaarry," said the boy.

"I don't think I like your attitude," said Harry.

"I don't think I give a fuck," said the boy, stepping away from the counter toward Harry, who took his hands out of his pockets. The other two boys took their hands out of their pockets. Harry's face went red.

"All right, all of you, that's enough," Irene said. She looked at the boy. Scruffy, torn shirt, dirty hands. He was a working boy already, with no prospects for the future. Just a neighbourhood kid with a well-earned chip on his shoulder. "You've been here before." She searched for a name. "Your name's George, isn't it?"

"What if it is?"

Irene couldn't let anything jeopardize the store and everything she'd worked so hard for over the past few weeks. She would treat this boy George as she treated her mother when she became unreasonable. The way you'd treat a dog with its hackles up. You show no fear. "If you'll give me half a minute, I'll be right with you, and if you're very nice, I'll give you extra sprinkles."

"I'd rather have a cherry," he said, and his friends giggled.

Irene hesitated, but then she took Harry by the elbow and nudged him toward the door. "I can handle these boys," she said, although she wasn't exactly sure this was true.

"You should not permit them to speak to you like that." Harry looked severe, and she felt as though she'd done something wrong, that she had failed somehow. "Perhaps you shouldn't be here alone. You should hire someone. A man."

"They don't mean any harm. Do you want a soda?" she said, because she couldn't think of anything else to say.

"What time are you closing?"

She looked at him to see what he meant, why he wanted to know, but she couldn't tell. "I don't know. About six, I guess."

"Why don't I come back then? We can go for a coffee somewhere."

"I'd love to, but … " He would lecture her on how to behave. She'd hate that. Another person to explain her shortcomings to her. Or could he be asking her out?

"But what? Have another date?" He drew back in mock jealously.

"No, no. Of course not." She did not date, and they both knew it.

"Irene!" wailed the boys. George grabbed his throat and made a noise as though he were dying of thirst, just a boy again, a harmless boy. "Heeeellp us!"

Irene laughed. "I'm sorry, Harry, I've got to go. I wish I could go for that coffee, but I can't. You understand."

"You are a successful businesswoman, my dear. You have obligations." He hesitated and then said, "Sunday, Irene. I'll call for you at eleven o'clock."

"Sunday?"

"Yes. The day after Saturday. The shop is closed and the proprietress will have earned some diversion. I'll get the car and we'll go out. Kew Beach. Hanlan's Point. We'll go out to the country. Have a picnic."

"I'm not sure, Harry. I wanted to tackle those rooms upstairs."

"Work in the morning, then, and come with me in the afternoon."

"I don't know, Harry. I'd like to but ..."

"Well, perhaps it's for the best. I have an engagement myself for part of the day."

"Oh," she said. "Yes, of course."

"I'll tell you what. Why don't I just come by the store about one? You can make lunch. I'll walk you home and we can have a picnic at the Allen Gardens. Would you like that?" He shifted from one foot to the other. He glanced over at the boys, who seemed to have turned their interest to the girls at the other end of the counter. George was expertly rolling a cigarette.

"I'd like that very much, Harry."

"Excellent. I'll see you then."

"'Bye," she called as he shut the door.

"Irene's got a boyfriend." George grinned as he licked the cigarette paper with a sharp little tongue.

"I do not!" She turned to them, hands on her hips, blushing furiously, and then, realizing that she sounded just like a schoolgirl denying a crush, she hurried behind the counter and began rattling spoons and ice-cream dishes. "Come on, now, let's have it," she said to the boys. "What'll it be?"

Irene walked in the front door and was confronted with the conflicting smells of fish and baking. Margaret poked her head around the kitchen door and waved.

"I've made poached haddock for dinner, and potatoes and green beans," she said. "And a cobbler for afters."

"That's great, Mum."

Margaret's resurrection had begun twelve days after the funeral, when she'd arisen early one day—which wasn't that unusual for she often complained of not sleeping—but didn't go back to bed. The next day had been the same. And then she had begun making the coffee in the morning. A week later she took a bath, washed her hair and was waiting for Irene when she came home, proud as a little girl who'd just brought home an A on her report card. Now she was up with Irene every day at six, brewing coffee and making toast. She sent her off to the store with a thick sandwich wrapped in wax paper, carrot sticks and sometimes even a slice of homemade pie. She cleaned the house. She still wasn't going out, but her hair was combed back into a soft bun and her nails were clean. She chattered on like a five-year-old. "Look, Irene, look at this dress in the catalogue, isn't it nice? Do you want more pie? Have more pie. Where are you going? When are you coming back? Would you like an aspic for lunch on Sunday?" She talked so much that there were times when Irene almost longed for the old days of sulking and silent scorn.

Irene knew her mother's improved condition could evaporate just as quickly as it had appeared. And there was something not wholly healthy, Irene felt, in the sudden enthusiasm Margaret displayed for becoming a model mother. Or was it mother? Sometimes Irene felt as though Margaret was behaving more like a wife. Having dinner on the table when she got home, asking her about her day, commenting on her clothes and hair, asking too-intimate questions about her monthly cycle, her feelings about men.

"Irene, are you coming, dear?"

"On my way," she called. She heard the radio's crackle and squeak as her mother tuned in her favourite music show, The Black and Gold Room Orchestra.

Her mother had doubtless been shocked out of her entropy, was all. Maybe the death of a husband was like an emotional slap in the face, the sort you give someone who's hysterical. It was to be expected that she'd continue to behave a little oddly.

Irene thought maybe one day Margaret would be able to take care of herself and she could finally have a life of her own. It wasn't so much to ask. Perhaps she could begin with something small. She would like very much to go out on Sunday with Harry.

It was a normal thing to do, for a girl her age to go out with a boy. So why did she feel so uncomfortable about broaching the subject with her mother? It was more than simply feeling guilty about leaving her alone; it felt like she was cheating on her.

Where do you end and I begin?

Irene hurried downstairs and took her place at the table. Her mother brought her a plate heaped with fish in a thin white sauce and potatoes and green beans. Although Irene didn't really like poached fish, it was one of her mother's favourite dishes and one she rarely made when Douglas was alive because he refused to eat it. Irene smiled and said it looked delicious.

She said, "Guess who came into the store today?"

"Who?"

"Mrs. Hatton, the barber's wife, you know the shop a few doors up from us? Her daughter's getting married this summer to some man from Baltimore. They're going to set up house here, though, and she bought all sorts of housecleaning things and pots and such to get her started. She said my prices are better than the hardware store and that I've got a better eye for what a woman wants. Isn't that great?"

"She gave you cash?"

"Of course."

"Don't give out credit. Your father gave out credit, you know. We'll never see that money again."

"The ice cream's doing well. I must have had a dozen kids in there today."

"Not much money in that. It cost too much to put in."

"Oh, I don't know, Mum. It brings people in, the hot weather's coming, people will want a local place. There's nothing else like it on the street. I actually think Dad had a pretty good idea there."

"We'll see."

"Someone else came in today, too."

"Oh?"

"Do you remember me telling you about Harry Madison, Ebbie's cousin? Or second cousin, I guess—the rich one who lives up in Rosedale?"

Her mother put down her fork and regarded Irene with a focused gaze.

"His father owns Madison Carpets and Fine Furnishings, down on King Street."

"King Street's a long way from Parliament and Gerrard. What did he want?"

"He just stopped in to say hello, I guess. He does that now and again, on his way up to see his cousins."

"Just pops in, does he?"

"Yes." Irene squirmed.

"Is he the one you said looks like Leslie Howard?"

"Yes, I guess so. Well, his hair is like Leslie Howard's. And he's tall."

"So, you think he's good looking?"

"Well ... yes. I do think he's sort of handsome."

"Sex. You watch out, my girl. He's only sniffing around for one thing." Margaret shovelled dripping fish into her mouth and pointed her fork at Irene's breasts. "Those things and what's between your legs are what he wants. They're all the same."

Irene kept her eyes on her plate. "For goodness' sake, he's just a nice boy. You should see how refined he is. Such wonderful manners, and he knows all about poetry. He's been in England, you see, in Oxford, studying literature. But then his father called him back to learn the business."

"Did he buy something?"

"No, he didn't buy anything."

"Irene, listen to me, you're a smart girl, I've always said that. But let's face it, dear, you're not exactly the sort of girl a man from Rosedale is likely to take seriously. He's not about to take a shop girl home to Mater and Pater. You're pleasant enough to look at, I'm not saying you're not, but Rosedale's a different world. Lots of glamour and shine up there. And we're just scrabble-by people. Maybe we could have been more. I thought when I married your father he might have amounted to something, but you can see how wrong I was. Don't get your hopes up and make a fool of yourself. Keep your mind on the shop and forget about men. Time enough for that later. And for God's sake, don't let him take advantage of you. If you got yourself in trouble it would be the end of us, do you hear me?"

"Mother, for crying out loud! A nice boy just came by the store, is all. And I think you're wrong. I think he likes me, and why shouldn't he? He's asked me if he can come and walk me through the Allen Gardens on Sunday, and you know what? I said yes. I'm going to work on the rooms upstairs at the store, see if I can get them in shape for a renter, then I'm going for a stroll with Harry Madison. I'm going to make some sandwiches and we're going to sit on a bench in the Gardens and have a nice visit."

"You keep your legs closed. It'll end in tears, my girl, you mark my words."

"It doesn't have to end in anything, Mum. I'm not even going steady with him, I'm just having a walk with him on a Sunday afternoon. What could possibly be more innocent than that?"

"You're going to bring him home, introduce him to your mother?"

Irene had not considered this possibility, given that her mother had for so long refused to see anyone. "If you'd like to meet him, I'm sure he'd be delighted. He's asked about you, but I didn't think you'd be feeling up to it yet."

"Oh, I think I'm up to it. Why don't I make the sandwiches? You can bring him here to pick them up before you go to the Gardens. I'll make you some iced tea."

Irene pushed the white fish around on her plate. "You'll like him, Mum," she said. "Really you will."

Ebbie came into the shop on Thursday. She was just days away from high school graduation. Next year she'd be entering the University of Toronto in the chemistry department. She was going to be a researcher, she said, mixing up potions and studying reactions in beakers and tumblers.

She came through the door nearly staggering under the weight of a black satchel filled with library books. She wanted, she said, to get a head start on next year's studies.

"Irene, quick, something wet and sweet, for heaven's sake, or I won't make it home!"

"One float coming up!"

Several of the tables were already occupied by groups of girls and boys sipping drinks through straws and spooning up ice cream. The shop was filled with the sound of voices and the occasional giggle as one table took stock of another.

"Haven't seen you all week. How did exams go?" said Irene.

"I think I did okay." Irene knew this was a modest understatement. If Ebbie never opened a book to study she'd get straight A's anyway.

"Of course you did. How was Mr. McGrath's math test?"

"Well, let's put it this way. Sue-Anne put down her pencil after half an hour and sat chewing the ends of her hair, and I do believe Fred Rollins uttered a rather foul word."

"Bad, eh?"

"Not easy, that's for sure. Mrs. Duff asks about you. Said to come by and see her anytime."

Irene gave Ebbie her drink and wiped her hands on her apron. There wasn't much else to say about school. It was still a tender little wound on the skin of her new life.

"Any more trouble with the McCauley gang?" said Ebbie. This was the name they had given to the crew of unruly boys headed up by George McCauley. They came into the shop at least once a week.

"That whole family's tough as nails. The father and two older brothers are all in jail for robbery, from what I hear 'round the streets. Usual story. No work, no food. I think George and his bunch are mostly talk, but I have to admit I'll be more comfortable when I get the upstairs rented out. Being alone in here, especially at closing time with the day's money in my pocket—that can be worrying."

"Don't suppose you could afford to hire a kid for the summer?"

"No, not likely. Maybe in a few months if things pick up and I get some rental income. We'll see. I like having this great big space of time during the day when I can do as I please, with no one looking over my shoulder. It's up to me, you know, whether things go well or not. I'm not dependent on anybody else. It's not a bad feeling."

"Good for you."

Mr. Badali, the man who ran the fruit and vegetable market a few doors up, came in.

"Irene, I need a new mop. You got one for me?"

"Sure, Mr. Badali, right with you."

When Irene finished with her neighbour she came back and stood next to Ebbie, her elbows resting on the counter.

"You look like the cat that swallowed the canary," said Ebbie.

"Has Harry been up to see you lately?"

"No, not for a while. At least, I haven't seen him. Maybe Mum has. Why?"

"Well, he came in on Monday."

"Did he? What did he want?"

"He asked me out." Irene grinned.

"Harry's taking you out?"

"Well, I'm not sure it's really 'out' like that. We're just going to take a walk in the Gardens." How she loved saying "we."

"Oh."

"What's that look for?"

"Nothing, 'Reen. Really. It's just that ... " Ebbie stretched her neck from side to side as though to work out a knotted muscle. "Nothing. It's nice."

"You don't look like you think it's nice at all. It's just that what?"

"I love my cousin, for heaven's sake. Love him to death. It's just that he's, he's such a boy."

"What does that mean?"

"Pay no attention to me. He's swell, really he is. He just isn't very serious, that's all."

"Who needs serious these days? Isn't there enough serious to go around?"

Ebbie took a sip of her float and banged her scuffed heel against the leg of her chair.

Irene said, "He didn't tell you he was coming by on Sunday?"

"Like I said, I haven't seen him. But with Harry you never know what he's going to do next."

"You make it sound like it's a shocking thing, him asking me out."

"Oh, don't pout. I didn't mean it like that." Ebbie laughed, the sound from her throat so big, so round, it startled the girls at the table behind her. "For heaven's sake, if anything, I'm just thrilled he's finally showing such good taste."

Irene knew that there was some message behind the words, for she'd grown up listening as much to what was not said as to what was. But she held her happiness like a fragile, prism-hued soap bubble, shielding it from every lethal breeze.

1936

She smells of cinnamon and roses and soap. Her skin is the colour of the terra-cotta hills in the north of Italy where her people come from. Her name is Maria and she has invited David into the barn, into the hay, into her arms, and he has fallen there, as though from the top of a great cliff. He has fallen into grace.

Her young son sleeps in the house nearby, and the dog sleeps on the porch and the cows chew their cud and the pig sleeps in the sty and the chickens have tucked their heads beneath their wings.

For three days he has worked next to her, repairing the well where the wall collapsed and must be fixed, for without water, in this hot, searing decade of unforgiving dryness, the animals will die and the woman and her son will be forced to leave their home or perish. And he felt it was good fortune, to find a well fallen just as he rounded the bend and two seasons after the woman's husband had driven the tractor into town to be repaired and not returned.

He has worked hard and has eaten well and slept well in the soft bed of her hospitality in the corner of this barn, and all the while he has watched the woman who has watched him from the corners of her almond eyes.

He has never touched a woman in this way before and he is unsure of himself and briefly, as she sees this, a sad shadow falls upon her face, and then she takes his face between her hands, which are strong hands and long-fingered, and with nails broken and torn and she turns his face to hers and she kisses his lips, her tongue parting his lips and moving inside his mouth. She puts his hands on her breasts, which are heavy and a miracle to him in all their softness and he buries his face between them and she moans and presses herself against him.

She takes off her dress and underthings and when he sees her naked he is shy again, for she is beautiful and it is clear her body is full of knowledge he does not have. Her skin is hot and her arms are brown but her breasts and stomach and thighs are fairer, the colour of toffee, and he wants to put his tongue on her thighs to taste her. There are small webs of blue veins on her breasts and white lines on her belly and he traces one with his finger and she misunderstands and begins to turn away.

"You are lovely," he says, "so lovely."

And she does not turn away but lies down in the hay and pulls him to her and runs her hands under his shirt along his stomach and chest and he begins to disappear from the wasteland where he has been wandering. Everything around him in the barn slides out of its disguise and reveals itself to be a thing of wonder. The bit for the horse, the shovel, the lantern hanging from a nail. The cat in the corner with her kittens mewling for milk. All are numinous, glowing and flawless. He is afraid he will cry, for he has been lonely a long time and haunted and with her breath and tongue and fingertips this woman washes off the crust he has baked around his skin. He is newborn next to her.

And when they are finished they are smiling at each other and then they are laughing and then they are crying, for both of them have held their emotions tight beneath a weighted lid for many a sleepless night.

They talk then, of their losses and their wounds and their anger, and then they touch to soothe and swim again in the sea of each other's skin. And finally they sleep and wake believing they might go on another little while and perhaps the world is not so hard a place, not completely hard, after all.

And she does not ask him to stay, and he does not ask her either, for he is a Jew and she is a Catholic and a Jew is good enough to stand on a plank just above the waterline in a broken well and trust the woman to keep the line from the block and tackle taut in case the plank gives way, and a Jew is good enough to seal the stones in the well so the water is sweet, and this Jew, this one man, is more than good enough, is perfect in her arms, but a Jew cannot stay and live in this place with a woman named Maria.

19

June 1936

Irene kept seeing Harry's face, hearing his voice, the slow music of his speech. The image of his fine hands, his fingers interlaced, or straightening the rim of his hat, or handing her a sprig of lilac, his nails polished, his fingers long. Thinking of his hands, his fingers, sent a thrill of warmth right through her.

There were only two small shadows on the day. One was her mother. Would she behave herself on Sunday? Margaret had grilled her every day since Irene had told her Harry was coming. "Have you let him kiss you yet? I'll bet you want him to kiss you, don't you? That's how it starts. Letting them paw you. You be careful you don't end up on the streets." And then she would suddenly talk about baking cakes and having Harry in for tea, perhaps even asking his family. Irene would like to trust her mother, would like to sit at the kitchen table and pour out her heart and her worries, but her mother could turn in an instant, nodding encouragement one minute, accusing her of being a tramp the next. There was no telling what she'd be like on Sunday.

The other dark spot was Ebbie's inferred warning. Maybe, she thought, both women were just jealous.

She'd gone to the library and found a book of poems by that man Harry was forever quoting, T. S. Eliot. Irene wasn't sure she understood it all, in fact, she was quite certain she did not, and yet there was a music to the words that settled inside her and did not require full comprehension. She had studied poetry in school, Tennyson and Byron and Shelley. They hadn't meant anything to her then, dry and twisted in the mouth of Miss Sargeant, who read while waving a perfumed hanky about like a flag of surrender. But these poems touched Irene. Mr. Eliot, she decided, understood despair, and understood being trapped. He wrote about being drowned in odours, and roots that clutched at a person. The idea that she was sharing such emotions with someone who was at that very moment alive, breathing, walking about out there in the world and expressing these very emotions on paper was the most extraordinary feeling. It was like having a stranger walk up to you on the street, look directly into your eyes and say "You are not alone. We are the same, you and I." It made her want to cry and laugh all at the same time.

Her mother asked what she was reading one night when they were sitting across from each other in the living room, each under her own yellow pool of lamplight, but she'd said, "Oh, nothing. Just some silly old poems. They're not very good."

She read *The Waste Land* and in it found a voice that could be her mother's own, a voice full of circular sentences and impossible-to-meet demands. There was a world out there, and in it were people like her who had to live with people like her mother, had to find a way to protect themselves, to let out the hot stale air of someone else's craziness. She had looked over the top of the book at Margaret. Irene read on and for a while floated on a benevolent sea of words, drifting away from the sound of her mother's voice ("Are you listening to me? What is that noise? Don't you agree?") coming from what seemed like an ever-receding shore. Irene smiled. She was falling in love with poetry and she wanted to talk to Harry about this. Wanted to thank him. She thought she would never be able to wait until Sunday, that most blessed of all days.

It was just dawn, but the sky looked clear as sea-glass. Irene was puzzling over what to wear. None of her clothes were as pretty as she would have liked; the one good skirt she had, blue and slimming, with a side opening and three covered buttons on the hip, she couldn't wear to clean in, so she put it into a satchel with a sheer white blouse and a pair of shoes. They were not the delicate summer shoes she wished they were. They were black and a little too solid to be pretty, but they did make her ankle and calf look tidy, she thought. She slipped on her old flowered work dress and hurried out the door just as her mother was getting up.

"Don't forget to come back here and get these sandwiches," Margaret called from the top of the stairs. "Irene?"

"I won't, Mum. Thanks very much."

"Don't be disappointed if he doesn't show up, now, will you, dear?"

"'Bye, Mum."

She hurried to the shop, anxious to get a good bit of work done before lunch. The activity would keep her mind off worrying about exactly what her mother had said, because of course it had occurred to her: what if he didn't show up?

Loaded with an arsenal of cleaning products, Irene took stock of the place: two good rooms. A tub in the kitchen. A toilet in a little closet. Why, she could get any number of tenants. The first thing was to see what was really in the place. The hall closet held nothing more than some old paper bags and newspapers. She picked up one yellowed and fragile sheet and read from a page dated February 1912. The British secretary of state had visited Berlin to offer the Germans support for their colonial ambitions in return for an end to the naval arms race. The compromise had been soundly rejected and further German aggression was feared.

It seemed they were playing the same old game all over again. She shook her head and tossed the paper into the bin. She would not think of such things today.

The kitchen table was all right and there was a solid wooden chair. Heaps of old magazines and empty boxes. *What was her father saving them for?* There was an old bedspring in the sitting room, but the mattress was beyond help. She crinkled her nose and wrestled it down the stairs to the alley. The kitchen she tackled with bleach and vinegar, and found two whisky bottles tucked in the back of a cupboard. She threw them in a box to be taken out to the garbage.

Irene had hoped that somewhere in these two small rooms she would find some evidence that her father had lived a larger life than she had imagined. But no clues were forthcoming. It seemed he might have used these rooms as a sort of nest from time to time. She could picture him sleeping off too much whisky, lying on the stained mattress, his face turned to the wall, his hand between his knees. She swept the picture into the dustbin along with the cinders and the scraps.

Before she knew it, it was twelve-thirty. Irene thought she'd made amazing progress and soon she'd be able to show the room. Perhaps a coat of paint wouldn't hurt; she wanted good, respectable people living here. Most of the people in the neighbourhood who could afford the better rooms were prostitutes, and while she had nothing against them personally, almost considered them part of the working class, she didn't think it would be a good idea to have one living above her newly respectable store. Irene wanted someone who would make her feel more secure, working by herself down below, but single men could be risky too. They might be all right, or they might bring their friends to live with them, as had happened over Mr. Han's laundry. The little man had had an awful time with them, their drunken brawls and parties, and finally had to ask the police to evict them. But someone would come along who was right. Of that she was sure.

She had to hurry—what if Harry was early?

She went into the kitchen and quickly washed and changed. She peered at herself in the broken bit of mirror on the back of the cupboard door and ran a comb through her hair, smoothed her eyebrows, noting with irritation, as she always did, that the left one had a perfect arch while the right one lay stick-flat above her eye. She dabbed colour onto her lips. *Painted hussy!* Irene could practically hear her mother's voice. She took a tissue and wiped most of it off. She pulled out her precious bottle of gardenia water and splashed a little under her arms and behind her ears.

It was nearly one o'clock. Surely he'd arrive at any moment. She stifled a nervous giggle. Her first real date was about to begin.

As she entered the shop she was filled with a rush of pride, as she was each time she saw it. If only her mother would come down and see what she had done—but then, what would it mean to her, since she hadn't seen the way it had deteriorated? In fact, her mother hadn't been in the shop for almost four years now.

Irene sat at one of the tables. But then she thought this might look too eager and she didn't want Harry finding her like some spaniel poised to pounce on him the minute he walked through the door. She glanced at the clock. Two minutes past one. She got up and stood behind the ice-cream counter, but unless she started cleaning the already glossy surfaces, there was no real reason to be there. Attempting to look busy, she took the order book from below the shelf and ran her finger over the dates when she'd last ordered goods from her various suppliers. Her finger stopped and she stood there, gazing down at the page without seeing it.

The clock said nearly 1:10.

He had said "about one," hadn't he? Not "exactly one." When did "about one" begin and end? "About one" could be as early as a quarter to one, couldn't it? A person could definitely say "about one," arrive at a quarter to one, and not be considered too early. Which meant that if someone arrived at one-fifteen, they could still be considered on time.

What if her mother was right? Irene turned the pages of the order book but didn't get very far; as the book was new, only the first page had writing on it. If he didn't show up, she'd say he had. The thought of facing her mother was unbearable. She could go up the street to the lunch counter, but no, that wouldn't be open on a

Sunday. The museum would be open. She could spend the afternoon looking at the fossils.

She began to make deadlines. *By the time I count to one hundred he'll be here, but not before I get to fifty. One, two, three ... no, too fast. Start again. One ... two ... three ...* When she hit seventy-five she looked out the window. *One hundred.*

One hundred and twenty-five.

Oh, let him come, please let him come.

She went into the stockroom and looked at the shelves, neatly stocked, alphabetically arranged. She decided she would begin a projection of expected earnings based on the past weeks' receipts. That sounded very official and just the sort of thing the proprietress of a business would be doing. As she took the heavy leatherbound book off the shelf she thought, Maybe I should have gone to church. Maybe I'm being punished. But she hadn't wanted to go to church. In fact, since her father's funeral she hadn't wanted to set foot in a church at all. She was carrying the book out into the shop, a frown on her face, just as the bell over the door rang and Harry walked in.

Harry, so beautiful in a crisp white shirt with the sleeves rolled back and a tobacco-brown blazer slung carelessly over his shoulder, the crease in his linen trousers sharp. Harry with an easy grin on his face. Harry, who, even now in the earliest of summer days, looked sun-kissed and healthy. Harry of the golden hair. Harry who could have any girl he wanted, she supposed. Harry who was here to walk with her, just her.

"Not still working?" he said, smiling. "Thought you'd be waiting for me. Did you think I wasn't coming? Got my wires crossed, I guess."

Irene didn't understand until he held out a basket with a familiar woven pattern and leather strap: her mother's basket.

"I must have misunderstood. Thought I was to meet you at your house."

"But how did you know where I lived?"

"Called Ebbie. She told me. I should have got the address when I saw you, of course, but it slipped my mind."

"You saw my mother?" she asked.

"Sure."

"What did she say?"

"Nothing much. Surprised to see me without you. But I think I managed to charm her. In fact, I think she was rather taken with me. Took me a while to convince her I was your friend, but then ..." He chuckled. "Well, I would have been here sooner, except she insisted I come in and taste her pie. She said, by the way, that you're not much of a cook, young lady." He wagged an admonishing finger.

Irene stood blinking at him. The news of her mother inviting a strange man into the house and offering him food, never mind being "taken" with him, was more shocking to her than if he'd said Margaret had run him off with a rolling pin.

"A pie?" she said, because just at the moment she could think of nothing intelligent to say. She was worried only about what he thought of her mother and their tattered house, the eaves in need of cleaning, the porch with a list, the ghastly red paint in the kitchen, the smell of something musty about the place, like unwashed feet.

"Your mother has made a strawberry pie."

"Yes, I know, I bought her strawberries yesterday."

"Well, there you are, then."

"Was she ... my mother ... she didn't ... " How could she ask Harry what she wanted to ask. *Did she look crazy? Was she dressed? Did she say anything embarrassing?* But Harry was here, wasn't he? And her mother, no matter what had happened, had not scared him off. That was enough. Irene's shoulders dropped from their perch around her ears. "Oh, never mind," she said.

"Are you ready, then? Shall we be off?"

"I'll just get my things." She went into the back and picked up her purse and gloves. When she came back Harry was standing with his back to her, framed in the bright light of the day. He filled up so much space, his broad back and shoulders, the wide stance of his legs. She was shy of him then, the breadth of him, the maleness and assurance of his way in the world. Sensing that a man such as Harry Madison would be bored by little-girl bashfulness, she desired to be sophisticated and at ease.

"All set," she said and ran the fingers of her right hand along the fingers of her left, settling the cotton of the gloves into place.

They set off up the quiet Sunday street. The shops were closed, and across the street, people sat on their front steps and two boys hunkered on the sidewalk playing jacks.

They crossed to the north side of Gerrard Street, and passed houses that once must have been quite respectable but had taken on the shabby dust of the times and were, for the most part, broken up into boarding houses. The voice of a woman yelling at a crying child fell like splinters from the open window of a house with torn curtains that moved listlessly in the warm air. A ginger cat with a shredded ear sat smugly on the sill.

Irene felt tongue-tied. She wished Harry would lead the conversation, but he was reserved and contained, as though he were walking along the street without her.

"I went to the library and got a book by T. S. Eliot," she said.

"Did you? Which one?"

"*The Waste Land.*"

"That's a rather heavy-going introduction. What did you think of it?"

"I think it's the most powerful thing I've ever read."

"Not many would use the word *powerful* to describe poetry. Interesting."

"I wanted to thank you for telling me about it."

"You're welcome. Poetry is the bread of life, or at least, if not the bread, certainly the gooseberry jam."

"I'd like you to teach me more about it," she said.

"I'll give you the names of some more poets, shall I? Hart Crane and Rilke and Whitman, of course—you must know Whitman." He transferred the basket to his other hand and offered her his arm to take as they crossed Sherbourne Street and then the park, to the grand entrance of the conservatory.

"Shall we take a stroll through the Palm House first and lunch after?" he said.

He steered her into the close warm wash of air in the circular, light-spilled glass room of the Palm House. The air was rich with the smell of wet earth and humidity. An older couple passed them, stiff and proper in corsets and waistcoat. The man tipped his hat at Irene. She nodded. The smiles the older couple gave them showed they were considered a couple, a young couple in love. Irene held her head a little higher.

They walked first around the perimeter of the room and then along the path leading under the dome where the largest of the palms grew. Irene bent to read a plaque.

"'Chinese Fan Palm, *Livistona chinensis*, from the sub-tropical woodlands of Ryukyu,'"—she hesitated over the unfamiliar word—"'and Bonin Islands, the Volcano Islands and Islands off Kyushu, Japan.' Imagine! All the way from there." She gazed up at the tips of the tall palms, the watery light dripping through them. "Do you ever want to travel to faraway places like that, Harry?"

"I have no doubt I will, and in the not-too-distant future, too, I should imagine."

"Really? Where?" No one she had ever known had travelled farther than her uncle Rory, whom she considered an impossibly exotic creature just for having ridden the rails from coast to coast.

"Buying trips. My father's off in China at the moment, buying carpets. He goes once a year, sometimes twice. It'll be my turn next, I hope, if the old man will agree to it. He's rather protective of his solitary travels, but he's getting on and has come back completely wrung out the past few years. He'll have to hand over the reins soon."

She looked at him as though he'd grown wings between his shoulder blades. "But that's amazing, Harry! Why, I'd give twenty years off my life just to see China!" Then, thinking it might sound as though she were asking to be included in his travels, she added, "I'll go one day, too, I will."

"Of course you'll travel. Every person must. Maybe we'll even see the world together, eh?" He smiled and steered her past the wood-and-iron benches toward the thicket of golden bamboo.

"Don't you love the smoothness of the stalks?" He ran his

fingers up and down the closest one, ignoring the signs that admonished visitors against such behaviour. He took her hand, peeled off her glove and turned her knuckles against the plant. "Here, feel."

She felt a sudden intensity in that area of her skin, as though every nerve ending in her body had rushed to the very spot where his flesh met hers.

"Feel how almost cool it is," he said.

"Yes," she said, for her lips would form no other syllables just at the moment. A small girl with blue ribbons in her hair ran past them, squealing shrilly.

Harry dropped her hand and stepped away to look at a small palm with a bulbous root and leaves like uncombed hair, and another with branches like tubers, and then to the *Leguminosae calliandra haematocephala*, the powder puff tree from southern Brazil. Irene followed him like a somnambulist. The air inside the conservatory was soft as she breathed in, and she felt the effects of this nearly liquid oxygen insinuating itself further inside her, to her lungs, her belly and beyond. Around her the ferns and palms unfurled like a verdant veil. Near them was a plant with leaves spread so far and so muscularly it looked like a large sculpted mushroom. Irene had the impression that the world around them had grown to enormous size, or that they had shrunk down to the height of elves, and that at any moment goblins might appear from some hidden marketplace, like in the poem by Christina Rossetti.

She tried to focus on a plant whose leaves were hung with small red berries, like pomegranate seeds within pale, translucent pods.

"Aren't they pretty?" she said, although *pretty* was not exactly what she meant. She meant *succulent*. She meant *sensual*.

"They look edible, don't they? But I suspect they're probably poisonous. The red colour, you know. It's a warning in most things, plants and toads and insects and so forth." Harry cupped the berries in his hand. "Come on," he said and led her through a door into the next greenhouse, which was the Cool Temperate House. Water dripped and gurgled musically all around them. Harry pointed up, and Irene saw, running along a pipe, a squirrel, which froze in its tracks when it saw them. They followed the meandering path lined with Greek myrtle and genista from the Canary Islands.

"Through here," said Harry and opened yet another door.

The air was warmer here, rich and ripe and pulsing. The room was alive with thick green plants sprouting up to the pearlized light. Irene felt damp; her slip clung to her body and her skin felt plumped and silky with the air's moisture. In a special glass booth, orchids clung to the sides of trees like undersea creatures.

The atmosphere was like a perfumed piece of moss held beneath her nose, infused not only with the scent of flowers but with something else: the smell of Harry, spicier and dark as cloves. Overhead hung a golden trumpet plant, its pulpy yellow flowers dangling near her mouth like forbidden fruit.

"*Apocynaceae allamanda cathartica*," read Harry, and it sounded like an incantation to a deep magic spell. He moved on, leaving her standing where she was, hypnotized by the blossoms hanging overhead.

"Passion flower! Come here, Irene. Do you know these?"

She stepped up beside him, aware of his hand on her arm, above her elbow, near her breast. She looked where he indicated, at a not very impressive group of leaves.

"*Passiflora coccinea*. Red passion flower. It was a religious symbol, you know, for early Christians. You see—pity they don't have at least a drawing of the flower, because it's quite amazing— but the construction, it's all in the way it's constructed. They say the ten petals symbolize the apostles of the crucifixion, the five anthers are the five wounds, the three stigmas are the nails, do you see? And there's this extraordinary corolla, all purple, which is the crown of thorns. Quite amazing."

"I'd love to see one," said Irene, who actually wanted nothing more than to continue to stand close to Harry and to hear his voice.

"A tall order, I'm afraid. The flowers last just one day and then close forever as night falls."

"That's sad, but somehow beautiful too, isn't it?"

"I suppose. Nature. Such a showoff, eh?" He laughed, and he looked at her. For a moment they didn't speak, but simply stood near each other, the pulse in Irene's throat clearly visible. It was just then that her stomach growled. She clamped one hand over her belly and the other over her mouth as she giggled.

"Oh, I'm so sorry! Listen to that. It's all the work I did this morning. I haven't eaten since, I don't know, sixish, I guess."

Harry looked slightly disappointed, but also relieved.

"Lunchtime, young lady. I'm famished myself."

He steered her outside and she breathed more easily here in this passive place where the lines between skin and leaf, between leg and root were more clearly drawn.

They chose a bench with dappled shade beneath a tree. Harry leaned back, spread his arms along the width of the bench and stretched his legs in front of him. He tilted his head to look through the branches, and Irene's eyes ran along the bow of his throat. A trio of sparrows twittered mindlessly above them.

"So, you're enjoying Eliot, are you?"

Irene handed him a chicken-salad sandwich. "Yes, but I'm sure I don't understand it. I'm not that clever, I'm afraid."

"Don't sell yourself short, Irene. You have a good brain."

"Iced tea?"

"Don't be evasive. Or coy. It doesn't suit you." He took the glass she poured. "Nothing wrong with recognizing you're bright. In fact, it's quite attractive."

"That's not what my mother says." Irene drew back her shoulders, pursed her lips and spoke in a hard-edged imitation of her mother. "Don't lord it over boys, Irene, if you're smarter than they are. Men are like skittish workhorses, you keep the blinders on 'em, keep them focused on what you want them to see and don't let them get distracted by things that'll only frighten them."

"Your mother," said Harry, "is wrong."

"I suspected she might be. About any number of things." She looked away, spread a napkin over her lap and bit into her sandwich.

"Like what else?"

"She has some funny ideas, is all."

"Tell me. I'm curious."

"Oh, I don't know. She's so bitter about everything. She has her ... I don't know, her demons, I guess. She's not very strong."

"Everyone reacts differently to grief." He gazed up through the tree branches as he said this. Then he finished his sandwich and wiped the crumbs away from his mouth. "Any chance of another one of those?" he said.

"There's egg salad, or devilled ham. Looks like Mum made enough for an army."

Irene tried to think of something to say that would bring his attention back to her. A blond girl with a handsome young man walked past them and Harry's eyes followed. Irene envied the girl's ripe curves and easy air.

"Tell me about Oxford," she said. "You must have had some lovely times there. I've seen such marvellous photographs of England."

"There's no place like it in the world, that's for sure."

"Do you miss it very much?"

"Yes, I admit I do. On a day like this we'd be in punts on the Thames or maybe at Lolly Spencer's for afternoon tea. She had fox hunts during the season. Beautiful horses." And Harry went on to describe his life abroad. His speech became languid and his eyes half-closed as though dreaming. Irene studied his face, the clean planes of it, the hollow of his cheek and the front tooth ever so slightly crooked.

When he had spoken for some minutes he said he'd like to sit on the grass, that the bench was a step removed from the real pleasure of earth. She said they had no blanket, but he said never mind, the grass was dry, but she spread out a napkin and sat on that, fearing a wet mark on the back of her skirt. Harry ate a large piece of pie and drank another iced tea. Then he settled himself, lying down with his hands behind his head, his legs crossed at the ankle, and began to recite:

"'Loafe with me on the grass, loose the stop from your throat, Not words, not music or rhyme I want, not custom or lecture, not even the best, Only the lull I like, the hum of your valved voice.'"

For the next hour or so they talked about Walt Whitman and his *Song of Myself.* Or rather Harry lectured and Irene listened. Harry spoke of the bodily delights and how Whitman's genius was in accepting himself as a natural man. Irene didn't notice the passing of time, except to sense that her world was spinning ever so slowly on a particular axis, centred directly on Harry's face and Harry's hands and Harry's lips.

She hardly registered what he was saying. She was mesmerized by the cadence of his voice. Then suddenly he said he must be off and would walk her home. It was mid-afternoon and far earlier than she'd hoped, but he said he had to run, for he had family engagements. When they reached her house (such a small distance, it wasn't fair, she wished she lived in Outer Mongolia so she could walk next to him for years and years) he did not kiss her mouth but did give her a kiss on the cheek. Better, she decided, on the cheek than on the mouth, because on the mouth would mean, if he kissed her out on the street, that he didn't respect her and she would surely have become unrespectable for she would-n't have been able to resist him, no matter that the neighbours were watching or her mother was peeking from behind the curtains, and Harry knew it and winked and waved as off he walked.

Her mother pounced on her the moment she floated through the door.

"I saw you out there on the street. All the neighbours could see you. You're turning into quite the little chippy, aren't you?"

"Oh, Mum, don't start."

"What did he try? What did you let him do? Men can smell it, you know."

Irene had no idea what it was precisely that men could smell, and she wasn't going to ask. She merely smiled and said it was a lovely day and thank you for the picnic. She went upstairs, undressed and took a long bath, with the door locked so her mother couldn't come in, although she did knock three times, making sure, she said, that Irene hadn't slipped down the drain. Irene ran her hands over her breasts and her stomach and her thighs and her throat and let Whitman's words, rolled in the memory of Harry's tongue and teeth and lips, slide over her and under her and buoy her body up and away to somewhere thoroughly splendid.

Margaret sat in the living room, listening to Irene's gentle splashing in the bath above. She slapped herself lightly on either side of the face. *Stupid, stupid, to leap on the girl that way.* Margaret had been trying hard in the past few weeks and was proud of herself. It had been the fear, of course, of what would happen to her if Irene left that had propelled her to pull herself together. Sometimes she still felt the old madness creeping back, and she would lock herself away then, back in her room where the Mad Margaret could be contained, quieted again.

She'd read somewhere that if you think you're crazy it doesn't mean you're sane, it just means you're far more intelligent than most people. If that was true, and she liked to think it was, then she had decided she could teach herself many things. Like how to hide, how to arrange herself so that it was not so noticeable that she was from time to time taken over by Mad Margaret.

There was even the small hope that she might teach herself not to be crazy at all. In fact, since she had been experimenting with this new line of thought, she was taken over by the Other Margaret less and less. And that was important, because only two things would happen if she didn't learn a new way of presenting herself to the world. Either Irene would leave or Margaret would be sent to the bug-house. Terror kept Margaret trying, if not to be normal, then to feign normalcy.

It had begun with small things. Washing her face, her hair, her body. That made a person look quite normal. And no one had to know that while you were washing you had to grit your teeth, because the touch of your own skin was so repulsive. Skin of any kind was revolting. Particularly the fleshy sort of skin that young girls had. All that bursting sex everywhere. The breasts, the hips, the thighs, the lips. Irene's type of skin. It wasn't her fault, of course, all girls had to go through it, Margaret supposed. Still, she was trying to warn Irene not to trust such flesh, for it would lead you to despair.

It would not do to jump on Irene the way she did. She tried not to, but when the longing came over her, to speak, to tell, to be heard, she couldn't control it. Margaret looked down at her hands and noticed one was scratching at the other. She slapped the offending hand. *No. Bad hand.* Things were going so much better. She must keep at it. She longed to climb the stairs again and whisper through the door. *Did he touch your breasts? Your cunt? Did he touch your cunt?* She clapped a hand over her mouth, afraid the filthy word might have come out. Where had she even learned a word like that? She gripped the sides of the chair and willed herself to stay put, to speak no more. She would practise being still, being quiet, being normal, until bedtime.

She turned on the radio. It crackled and hummed as the tubes warmed up, and then the sound of people speaking, of the audience's laughter, soothed her.

20

July 1936

One Friday, the last day in July, Harry dropped by the store and invited Irene to the picture show. She hadn't seen him in ten days, although he'd called once to say his father had returned from the Orient in a pitiful state and he'd be stuck at the office double time, since the old man wasn't really capable of much just now. She agreed at once, but said she'd have to pop in on her mother first, to make sure she didn't mind.

"Aren't you a tad too old to have to ask permission? If she says she does mind, what then? You won't go?"

"No, of course not," she replied, stung. "I'd go anywhere with you."

"Fine, then," he said, adjusting the hanky in his jacket pocket. "You can't spend your whole life running back to her, you know. You'll have your own life one day soon, a husband, children of your own. You'd better start cutting the umbilical cord now."

"You have to understand, Harry. She goes to so much trouble, trying to make the house nice. She has dinner ready every night. I don't want to do anything to upset her."

"She certainly has you well trained. You're beginning to sound like a hen-pecked husband." Harry agreed to stop by the house, but they'd have to hurry. It would be too late to see *Mr. Deeds Goes to Town* with Gary Cooper, and he'd rather had his heart set on that. He supposed they'd have to settle for that Robert Young movie.

"*Three Wise Guys?*" said Irene. "The one by Damon Runyon?"

"Well, based on his *work*, his stories, yes."

"I'd love to see that. Although it doesn't much matter, as long as I'm with you," she said.

"Oh, all right," said Harry. "Sounds rather foolish, but I need something light and foolish. All this talk of the war in Spain is enough to depress anyone. Besides, Rebecca Palmer saw it and she said it wasn't half bad."

"Who's Rebecca Palmer?" she asked.

"Just a girl I know."

"Oh."

"Are you ready? We really need to hurry."

On the way to her house Harry stopped in to a fruit market to buy a bag of cashews—an unheard of extravagance these days and her mother's favourite.

"That should keep her happy," he said, and although Irene didn't like the inference that her mother could be so easily bought, it seemed he was right, for Margaret was delighted with the offering and told them she didn't mind being left home.

"But I must say, young man, you should have the common courtesy to give a girl a bit of notice when you ask her out on a date, don't you think?"

"It's just a show I wanted to see, Mrs. MacNeil. Thought Irene might enjoy it."

"You took a risk. After all, Irene could very well have had other plans."

"Is that right?" said Harry, grinning.

"Yes, it is," she said, looking at him with a sharp eye.

"Guess I would have been out of luck, then, wouldn't I?"

"Oh, come on," said Irene. "We'll miss the newsreel."

"Have a good time, you two."

"I won't be late."

"Good night, Mrs. MacNeil," said Harry, who clicked his heels, took the older woman's hand and bent to kiss it.

She slapped his hand away and blushed. "Don't be a fool! Go on, out with you both," she said and closed the door. Going to the window, she rubbed the feeling of his lips off the back of her hand. Margaret watched as Irene leaned toward Harry and repeatedly glanced up at him. She noted, too, the way Harry slouched along, his hands in his pockets, his gaze looking every which way but at Irene.

"He's a rascal, that one," she said aloud. He was just the kind of boy she'd have fallen for herself in her youth. They were two of a kind, she and her daughter—same sad and sorry taste in men. Why, they were just like those Siamese twins from China, what were their names? Eng and Chang. And hadn't they married sisters? Imagine what must go on in their house when the lights were turned down low! But the similarity between them didn't mean Irene had to make the same mistakes her mother had, not if she could help it.

Margaret felt a great separation from the rest of the world, and never more exquisitely than now, as she watched Irene walk away from her with a man. It was only with Irene, flesh of her flesh, that she could feel the flow of one into the other, one person becoming two through the small exchanges in daily life. Irene would get her heart broken, no doubt about that, but it didn't mean she had to fall into a bad marriage as a faulty cure, the way Margaret had.

Perhaps if Irene was hurt it would make her more receptive to the peace that could be found in a world populated by just the two of them. Serenity was Margaret's shining goal. Who needed love? If she could not have it, then companionship, calm, security would do. For that she would keep up the fight against Mad Margaret. Make the dinners, sweep the floor, brush her teeth.

Irene would have to learn the hard way, of course, because she was stubborn, just like her mother. But with Margaret's guiding hand she could be spared much misery. They had to stick together. It was best that way. After all, look what happened to those Chinese fellows, one dying just three hours after the other. Just couldn't live apart. Simple as that.

Irene and Harry sat in the dark theatre, their shoulders touching now and then. Harry smoked a cigarette, Irene munched on wine gums (she would have preferred licorice, but she didn't want black bits in her teeth) and watched the newsreels. The Spanish Civil War had begun a few weeks earlier when General Francisco Franco led an uprising of army troops based in Spanish North Africa. German Minister of Propaganda Joseph Goebbels was shown at a rally of thousands, proclaiming Max Schmeling's victory over Joe Louis a triumph for Germany and Hitlerism. "Schmeling's victory," the announcer translated Goebbels's words, "was not only sport. It was a question of prestige for our race." People in the theatre booed, and Harry threw a wine gum at the screen. Next was the dedication of the Vimy Memorial by King Edward VIII and pictures of athletes training for the Berlin Olympics and Miss Amelia Earhart preparing to be the first woman to fly nonstop across the United States later that summer.

Then the stories turned to local news. The relief camps had been closed, although many of the men had been reassigned to temporary seasonal work. The screen then filled with the words "MAD GUNMEN HUNTED." Two Toronto boys, Marion Faggio and

Sam Brown, had escaped from the Penetang Mental Institution, a brief vacation that ended in their being shot dead on a concession road after a high-speed chase.

"They're not giving you half the story," said Harry. "The two had been sent to Penetang after they'd gone crazy up in the Kingston pen, the conditions are so appalling. They met at the mental institution. And all for what? Less than twenty-five dollars in Faggio's case and some liquor and cigarettes in Brown's, which he'd been hoping to sell so he'd have money to buy food."

"How do you know all that?"

"I read the papers, my dear. I make it a point to stay informed."

If there was a rebuke in this, Irene decided to ignore it. She had been to the movies only twice in her life and she thought that sitting on the velvet chairs watching the smoke drift up into the beam of light was as close to heaven as she was going to get this week. She left her hand dangling on the armrest between them, in case Harry should want to hold it, but when he wasn't smoking he kept his hands folded across his chest or leaned both elbows on the armrest and interlaced his fingers. Irene was aware of every movement of his body and willed him to put his arm around her or take her hand in his, but he did not. Several rows behind them a couple loudly kissed and giggled, and Irene was relieved when someone hissed at them.

When the film ended she cried and Harry laughed at her and called her a very silly girl indeed, but he was smiling when he said it and let her use his hanky. They left the theatre and walked along Yonge Street. She sighed now and then, content to just be there, walking with him on this lovely night. She chattered on about the movie and how beautiful she thought it was.

"I didn't know Runyon was such a sentimentalist," said Harry. "Bit disappointing, actually."

"Do you think so? I thought it was swell."

"Well, you girls are soft about these things."

They walked along in silence. Harry didn't take her hand or put his arm around her shoulders. Irene tried to hold on to the joy of a few moments before, but it began to slither and slip away and she couldn't catch it. She wanted to share emotion with Harry, who was so smart and who, loving poetry the way he did, could be so moved by words. Perhaps by weeping over a silly movie she was showing that she was unsophisticated, uneducated.

"Oh, look," he said, "there's an ice cream vendor. Do you want one?"

"I can't face any more ice cream."

"I forgot, you're around it all day. I think I'll have one, though. Have an ice, at least. Strawberry?"

And so she agreed, as she did to everything Harry suggested.

Before going home in the evenings, if Harry wasn't coming by, Irene would take a quick run up to the library and pick out a book of poetry by Rilke or Auden or Beaudelaire or Blake. After her mother went to bed she sat in the window seat in the living room memorizing snippets that particularly moved her. She was happy to find that, although she had first turned to poetry as a way of feeling nearer to Harry, she returned time and time again for no other reason than that it pleased her so. She found herself lost for hours in the words, and it was a great comfort to her. It made the walls of the house seem wider, the air less stifling, and herself less isolated.

One day Ebbie insisted she put her poets back on the shelf and come with her to the Canadian National Exhibition. The CNE was attracting record crowds that year, as most people couldn't afford to go away on vacations and were looking for a little diversion amidst the horses and the garden shows and the wonderful Automotive Building. After much pleading one Friday evening, Margaret finally agreed to be alone for a few hours. Irene and Ebbie took the streetcar to the Princes' Gates and walked along the fairgrounds. They ate cotton candy and hot dogs. Ebbie tried her hand at the pitch and toss and lost twenty-five cents before she quit. They watched a strongman with a handlebar moustache and a striped leotard pick up four giggling girls sitting two each on the ends of a pole slung over his shoulders. Then they wandered over to the dressage event in the Horse Pavilion.

"Our own local Olympics," said Ebbie. "Without the swastikas and the Heil Hitlers."

"Wasn't Jesse Owens amazing?" said Irene.

"And then Hitler refusing to acknowledge his victory because he's a Negro! I tell you, I don't know where it's going to end. Dad says we're going to war for sure."

"It can't be as bad as that, can it?"

"Come on, let's go to the freak show," said Ebbie, dragging Irene along.

They paid their nickel to the fat lady at the tent door and went in. Every few feet the tent was partitioned into little alcoves where the freaks sat on stools displaying themselves. They saw the Pillow Man, whose body and head were the size of a small oblong cushion, the Bearded Lady, the two-headed calf and the deformed babies in jars. Ebbie would have stayed to see the man who could hammer nails into the side of his head, but Irene said she couldn't stomach any more and insisted they leave.

Irene wanted to talk about Harry. If anyone knew what was going on with Harry, it was Ebbie.

"So, how's Mike?" she said.

"Fabulous. I met his parents last weekend. Darling people. Of course, you know what that means!" Ebbie waggled her pale eyebrows at Irene and grinned.

"Do you think he's going to ask you? Really?"

"Maybe not right away, but he'll get around to it. If he can ever get his nerve up. I may have to do the asking, for heaven's sake."

"I wish Harry would take me home to meet his family soon."

"What do you want to meet that bunch for? Dry as twigs."

"Harry says his mother's very refined. She does all sorts of charity work, doesn't she? And anyway, well, I'll have to meet them eventually."

"Do you want to go on the Ferris wheel?" said Ebbie.

"Harry says when I meet them I'll have to call his father sir. He says even he calls him sir. Do you call him uncle, or what?"

"Harry said that? *When* you meet him?"

"Yes. But what do you call him? And her? Do you call her ma'am?"

"I don't see them very often. Don't even see Harry that much, to be honest. Now, come on, let's go on the Ferris wheel. Pleeeease? Pretty please?"

"Oh, all right," said Irene. And she laughed at her friend, although she wished Ebbie wouldn't sidestep her questions about Harry. She and Ebbie might very well all be family one day, after all.

"So, did you have a good time last night?" Margaret asked, the following Wednesday morning. She spread marmalade thickly on her toast.

"I had a wonderful time."

Irene wanted to remember the bright sparkle of the night and not how it had ended. "You should have seen the floorshow. The singer was marvellous, she was all the way from New York, and we danced. Oh, it was grand."

"Tuesday night seems an odd night for going clubbing to me."

"It's very modern, Mother, we're not locked into all your generation's old rules about things. We're different."

"If you're talking about courtesy and respect, I'll agree with you there. It just seems to me that Harry might take you out on a Saturday night like a regular person. Don't you ever wonder what he's up to when he's not with you?"

"He's busy, what with the business and everything. He's going to take over for his father completely one day very soon and he has to be ready. And his father's very demanding. Things will be different when he's his own boss. And I expect that day won't be long off. After all, everyone says the Depression's nearly over."

"So why do you look like Chief Thundercloud? I know it's about that boy. A mother can sense these things. I'm on your side, Irene. I don't make a fuss when you leave me alone to go out with him, do I? I don't complain. Have you had a fight? I'll bet you have. I'm sure it's nothing—after all, every couple has little spats."

"We didn't have a fight."

"A disagreement, then."

Margaret felt pleased. She was growing closer to her daughter, saying the right things and seeing things clearly. She'd given a lot of thought to Irene and Harry while she was alone the evening before. That was her least favourite time of the day, as night approached. She always felt nervous then, but along with the anxiety sometimes came flashes of insight. Small prisms of clarity, where she could peer right down into the heart, the truth of things.

"Look, Irene. Sometimes boys get nervous when they really like a girl."

"Do you think so?" said Irene in a small voice, and she looked so hungry, so hopeful, so vulnerable. And so it has begun already, thought Margaret. Oh, my poor daughter, and she doesn't even yet know the way a pain can burn like acid, never stopping until it reaches bone and then not stopping yet but going clean through a person like a tunnel where a cold wind blows and you are never really warm again. I would spare her this if I could, I truly would.

Margaret took a bite from her toast, savouring the thick sticky sweetness of the marmalade, rolling it around on her tongue before swallowing. Let it be, she said to herself, let it be. She put her hands under the table and squeezed them together. She made herself concentrate on the taste of burnt oranges and sugar until the Other Margaret hushed herself. *Good girl. Good girl.*

"Yes," she said. "I think so."

As Irene walked to work she tried to come to a decision. So much hinged on the right strategy. She tried to concentrate on the dilemma, but her mother's words haunted her. How had she intuited that something had gone wrong last night? Why was she suggesting Harry might be seeing other girls? His father expected him to accompany him on business dinners at their men's club on Saturday evenings. That seemed reasonable.

"But I get so lonely without you." She knew she'd sounded sulky. It was just the sort of thing her mother would say, but she couldn't seem to stop her lips from moving.

"My dear girl, you mustn't wait about moping, you know. It's not attractive. Don't go all wan and droopy on me now." And he had chucked her under the chin, just the way she didn't like at all. "There you go! Look at the flash in those eyes. A fellow likes a girl with spark."

He leaned over and ran his hand along her thigh. She wore a bias-cut burgundy satin dress, made over from one of her mother's old dresses. She let his hand stay there, and instantly she was all liquid and boneless. They sat in a booth with a back like a scalloped shell, a round table in front of them draped in a fine white cloth. His hand was hidden from view and he began to inch her skirt up little by little, smiling at her all the while as though nothing at all were going on beneath the table.

His hand was on her knee. His fingers twirled gently. It had been so unreal, his hand on her there, the waiters milling about, a girl with a gardenia in her hair on the stage singing about lost love. Her entire world had been pinpointed at the end of his fingertips.

It had been all she could do to refuse him at the end of the evening, when he had tried to persuade her to get a room with him. He was becoming more and more persistent about sex and it was becoming harder and harder to say no. She knew what became of girls who gave in to desire before they were safely tucked up in the marriage bed. But still, wouldn't a man like Harry, worldly and sophisticated, expect the woman in his life to be just as modern, just as devoid of what he called "petty-bourgeois" morality?

And more to the point, she'd been on the verge of surrendering to him, and would have if only he hadn't spoken just then. They had been out in his warm dark car, and his hand slipped under her coat, cupped her breast and she had pushed him away and then let him come close again, sighing out the last of her resistance, when he said, "'A little still she strove, and much repented, and whispering 'I will ne'er consent'—consented.'" He had said these words with his lips up against her own open mouth and then had added, "Byron, the *Don Juan* poem."

She pushed back and glared at him. "Thank you for the lesson, professor, but don't you think your timing's a bit off? I'd rather not have bloody Lord Byron in the car with us just at the moment, if you don't mind."

His face had gone cold then. She'd never spoken to anyone like that before.

"I'm sorry, Harry," she'd said. "Please don't be mad. Please don't be."

"Why would I be angry? You're quite right to say the moment for poetry is lost. And the word is *angry*, dear, not *mad*. I'm not mad. Mad is what your mother is."

"That's a mean thing to say, Harry, a very cruel thing. Sometimes I don't know why I even like you so much." She'd begun to cry.

"I can't imagine," said Harry, lighting a cigarette and blowing the smoke out through his nose.

"I just want you to respect me. I want to be something special to you. But if it's that important to you ... " She would have gone with him then, she would have, but Harry said he'd better drive her home, and he had, without another word.

When they pulled up in front of her door she found she couldn't stop crying and she didn't want to leave him but at the same time she wanted to get out of the car and slam the door and run up the street and keep on running.

"Please, Harry ..." she hiccupped at him, "please, Harry."

"Irene, stop crying. Don't carry on so. It's not the end of the world. Everything's fine. I'm not angry, see? I'm not."

He put his arm around her and drew her against his chest where she snuffled, careful not to muss his coat.

"I don't ever want you to be cross at me, Harry, I can't bear it."

"I know you can't. I know. And I'm not cross. A fellow just gets all worked up, that's all. It's not good for the system, if you know what I mean."

"I want it to be special, Harry. I want to wait until the time is right, you know what I mean."

"Listen, Irene. You're a sweet girl, a pretty girl. You can't blame a man for wanting you. But run along now. You have to get up early, don't you? I know I do."

"I don't want to leave angry."

"No one's angry. Give us a kiss." He'd turned her face toward his and kissed her tear-wet cheeks, first the right and then the left and then he'd kissed her mouth, and it was a long, lovely kiss.

"I love you, Harry," she'd sighed into his breath.

"Sleep well, Irene. I'll call you."

Of course she had not slept well, with her mind racing on what had gone wrong and what she could do to make it right. Her mother couldn't be right. She was Harry's girl. She had to find some way to prove it.

Irene now passed a man slumped in a doorway. She'd seen him before, one of the many homeless, jobless men down on their luck and letting themselves fall asleep in the last place their tired feet had led them. She pulled the sandwich her mother had made for her out of the brown paper bag and put it down next to him. The man jumped and looked at her, wild-eyed.

"It's just a sandwich," she said.

"Oh. Thanks, thanks a lot," the man said and began to eat it right away, bits of wax paper clinging to his lower lip.

We all live so close to that line, she thought. I can't let myself get caught. What if the store fails? So many have.

A life with Harry would be a life free of worry. A life with Harry would be one long, elegant, gracious dream. She couldn't lose Harry. Why did her mother have to ask her awful questions? *"Who does he see when he's not with you? You don't think he has other girls?"* There were decisions to be made. Harry would call. And by the time he did, she would have made her decision.

1936

David has been told to look for smoke coming out of the chimney of a garage on the outskirts of Winnipeg. The garage has the words FREE FOOD painted on the side. The smoke is clear in the frigid morning air. He and Emil pick up the pace. It is so cold their breath forms little crystals that fall on their chests. Emil's gloves are full of holes and he keeps his hands under his armpits.

"I don't care she only got old boots and dishwater in the pot, eh? Me, I'm gonna lick my plate clean." Emil is only sixteen. David tries to look out for the kid. After what happened in Regina, he feels it is the least he can do. He's learned the terrible things that could happen to a friend when you aren't there to watch his back.

"Hope there'll be some left," says David. He can see a number of men waiting by the door.

"What that smell?" says Emil as they get nearer.

"Food," David says. "Cooking."

They nod to men as they stand in line, most of them like him and Emil, too hungry for conversation. The line moves pretty quickly and soon they are in the garage. A young skinny boy with jug ears hands them each a tin bowl and a spoon. There is a big black Majestic wood cookstove by the wall and a pile of wood next to that. It is warm in the garage, from the bodies and the stove. Steam rises off some of the men, and with it the smell of unwashed, road-cured flesh. The only good thing about the bone-cracking cold is that it keeps them from smelling each other too much.

Emil nudges him and points with his chin over to the corner. A girl sits there, holding her bowl up to her face and shovelling in the food. Her hair is matted and her face smudged and dirty. She senses their eyes on her and glares at them until they turn away. He hasn't seen many girls on the road, and the few who travel on the rails are hard as hellfire, usually running away from something even worse than life in the hobo jungles.

He and Emil hold their bowls out and a smiling woman with red cheeks fills them up with porridge mixed with peas and beans and *raisins. It looks like crap and doesn't smell much better and he could eat a dozen bowls. They get cups of tea laced with sugar and a slice of stale bread and sit on the makeshift benches to eat.*

"Don't eat so fast, kid," he says when Emil begins wolfing it down. "You'll give yourself cramps."

"I tell my hand go slow but my stomach makes the rules," says Emil between gulps.

When he's finished, David approaches the woman.

"You want some more, son? I can let you have a little more," she says.

"You save it for the next guy, ma'am. Just wanted to know if there's anything I can do to repay you. Maybe you need some wood split or something?"

"Why, aren't you a sweet thing? That'd be a great help. Jimmy," she calls to the boy, "can you show this nice young man to the wood pile? He's gonna split some kindling for us."

The boy takes him around the back of the garage and he gets to work.

"You'd be surprised," the boy says. "Don't nobody ever offer to help. I guess they're mostly down so far they just ain't looking up no more."

"Well, that far gone I'm not. Yet," he says.

When he's done he goes back into the garage and gets another cup of tea. The woman has made the leftover tacky porridge into patties, fried them up in grease and is handing them out.

"Here, son. You have one. You earned it. And take this too. Write your mama. I know she's worrying about you." The woman hands him a piece of paper, a pencil stub and an envelope with a stamp already on it.

"I'm grateful," David says. He sits down next to Emil, who is scribbling out a letter of his own, back to his family in Shawinigan.

"She give them to us all, eh?" says Emil. "Nice lady, that one."

David sits on a bench and pulls a tattered notebook out of his pack. He thumbs through it, wondering what he can say to send back home. The notebook has one blank page left, which means it's nearly time. David has a ritual. When a notebook is finished he burns it. He can't go hauling around a sack full of heavy books with him. And he can't send the books home with his letters when he gets the chance to write them, because some of the things he writes down he doesn't want his father reading.

And some things he can't bear to write down at all. Like the Regina riot. At least not yet. Maybe never.

But the pages are filled with words and thoughts and those secrets that he's able to face, knowing they are safe, knowing they'll be consecrated in fire. Then he burns them and sends them up to the sky, like the Cree back home who burn tobacco to take their prayers to K'itchi Manitou.

He picks up the pencil and begins to write in his journal. He writes about Emil and the porridge and the girl in the corner with the fury in her face. He writes about not knowing where he's going next, and how he's travelling away from things, not toward them. In writing that, it occurs to him that maybe he'll go to Toronto. Maybe he'll stop in and see the family his friend talked about so much.

He closes the notebook, takes it over to the wood stove and drops it in. Then he goes back to the bench and writes a letter home.

21

October 1936

It was a fine night, cool and crisp as fresh-washed linen, and who cared about anything except that it was clear and starry and night and Saturday. Harry had called for Irene and she had put on her new yellow dress that made her brown eyes look hazel. He had taken her first to the Casino Burlesque at Queen and Bay. They had seen "Twinkle Toes" Yvette in her famous and original muff dance and Gertie Beck and Lorrie La Mont, who came all the way from Paris, and it was grand and exciting.

Harry had been in such a good mood then that he had decided they must go to the Club Esquire, where they watched Mademoiselle. Corrine, billed as the famous daughter of Eve, perform the exotic apple dance, and they had drunk gin and tonic with lime slices.

"No more for me," said Irene when Harry ordered a third round.

"Oh, come on, don't be a party pooper."

And so she had a third drink and a fourth, even though she had vowed, after what had happened to her father, never to have more than one drink in an evening, ever. But tonight was different. Wasn't it different?

They were celebrating. Harry's father had just announced that the next buying trip would be taken by Harry alone. He told her about the trip to Afghanistan and all the things he'd see: the souks and carpet merchants, the date trees and wild dogs, the high craggy mountains and outlaw bands who always wore great knives tucked in their sashes and knew the best weavers, for a price. He talked about what this meant for his future, and there were so many questions Irene wanted to ask.

"I'm going to take over the business soon. And you know what that means," Harry said, squeezing her hand. "I'm finally going to prove to the old man I can handle responsibility and settle down. He's never respected me, I know that. Thought I was wasting my time in England. But he'll see. This trip will show him what I can do."

It was nearly midnight when they left the club, trying to decide where to go next. Down the street several men huddled around a fire burning in an old oil drum. Their clothes were thin and torn, and one had newspaper tied around his shoeless feet with string. As the men passed a bottle back and forth, Irene thought about the money Harry had spent that night and how half of it would probably have paid their rent for a month. Their lean and hungry faces made her feel spoiled, but Harry ignored them completely. He leaned up against a lamppost and pulled Irene to him and she fell into him like there was nothing in the world to keep them apart. Her head was full of bubbles from the gin and tonics and maybe she had drunk too many of them but she didn't care. Nothing mattered except Harry and his hands holding hers, pressing down at the sides of their bodies so she had no choice but to be pressed up against him and feel him underneath the sophisticated twill suit, hard and demanding.

When they were together and Harry was happy like this, nothing could shake her confidence, but when he was gone there were so many doubts. Which she would not think about now, she wouldn't, and why couldn't she keep her mother's voice out of her head, not let it slither in at unwanted times like this? *"Who does he think he is, Mr. High and Mighty? Coming and going when it suits him. Don't be a fool, Irene. Don't be a fool, a fool, a fool ... "*

Only one way to block out her mother's voice. Irene wanted Harry to kiss her, right now, here on the street and she didn't care how it looked or who saw. She didn't care about the homeless men looking on, so silent and dark down the street. Her face was turned to his and the lamplight shone on it. She thought of movie scenes, of Loretta Young with her face lit from above as if by a holy light. She tilted her head without opening her eyes, and it felt as though the world was tilting too, but she wouldn't open her eyes. She opened her lips instead, and her tongue darted out to wet her lips.

"You look tired, Irene."

"Oh, but I'm not tired. I feel like I could stay out all night long and would too, for half a reason." She giggled, for her words might be a little slurred, but wasn't that what a sophisticated man like Harry wanted? Not the syrupy Loretta Young but Carole Lombard, who knew how to take a joke and could hold her liquor and her man.

"Maybe I should take you home," he said. He looked over her shoulder down the street, then glanced at his watch.

"I could stay out all night with you, Harry," she said and pressed herself up against him with no thought at all for her reputation.

"A most tempting suggestion, I must say." His lips on hers, but so quickly gone, just a peck when she wanted a bushel.

"But you don't want to go, do you? You don't want me to go?" What was he looking at behind her? She twisted round and saw a man she'd seen in the club, that friend of Harry's, the one from England, the one with the foolish name, Gee Whiz. But his name couldn't be Gee Whiz. No, wait, his name was Warwick Gee.

"Isn't that your friend?" she said. She hadn't liked him, that man who came by their table with a giggling fool of a girl in a dress that looked like she'd been dipped in raspberry sauce and lipstick smeared on her front teeth.

"What friend? Where?"

"There, Harry. Yikes."

The man waved and started toward them. The girl hung on his arm. As they wove past the group of homeless men, one of them put his hand out, asking for money, but Warwick Gee was oblivious and the man spat at his feet.

"Oh, yes. That's Warry, all right. I wonder what he wants." Harry took his hands from her and put them in his pockets.

The laughter from the other couple could be heard up and down the street as the girl wobbled and tripped and Warry Gee hauled her back to her feet, both of them braying like drunken donkeys. Irene would never laugh like that or stumble because she was drunk; the happy bright gin and tonic bubbles began to burst in her head and she found her mood shifting to sullenness.

"What on earth are you pouting for, Irene? You're not going to spoil tonight, are you? I don't know why this happens with you so often, I really don't. You have this extraordinary propensity for going all drab at the end of an evening. Do you know that? Makes me wonder sometimes, I must say."

Harry waved back at Warry Gee, and then gestured to them to wait.

"Harry, I don't want to stay out here on the street. Can't we go somewhere?"

"Perhaps it's best if I just get you a cab home," he said, looking bored. People came out of the club now, bejewelled women in beautiful clothes and perfectly marcelled curls. Irene reached up and patted her bangs, making sure they lay flat.

There was some secret she must learn, some word, some spell that if said just right would keep him with her, would make him love her. No, not love her, but love her *more* (didn't he put his arm around her in the restaurant and say she was his favourite girl, that there was nowhere else he wanted to be in all the world than right there by her side?).

She stepped back and looked at him coyly. "Fine, Harry, put me

in a cab. Pity, though. I thought tonight might be the night."
What brazen girl had possessed her?

Harry's cigarette dangled from his lip, just like Clark Gable's,
and his eye squinted against the smoke.

"Now, Irene, what sort of night were you thinking this might
be?"

"You said you want us to be real lovers. You want that, don't
you?"

"Come here," he said, and she went to him, with her chin out
defiantly. He raised a hand and stroked the side of her face, sending
a shiver down to her toes. He chuckled and ran his thumb over her
lower lip. She opened her mouth and let her tongue touch the
fleshy pad. "And what's brought this on, all of a sudden?"

"I've given it a lot of thought. What with you going away and
all ... Won't you miss me?"

"Sure. Sure I will. 'Course I will." And she saw that his face was
flushed and his words slurred a little too, so that she didn't feel so
bad about having drunk just a smidgen too much.

"Come here," he said again, his voice hoarse, and he held his
arms tight around her, one hand straying down to her buttock. At
that moment Irene didn't care about her mother, or about the
men watching from down the block. His tongue was in her
mouth, just the way she liked it, demanding. This time she was
giving in, giving over, giving anything he wanted.

He pushed her back with a strange look in his face.

"Harry?"

"Get in the car," he said.

He had her by the elbow and steered her to his Packard. Once
she was inside he leaned over and kissed her again, his hand on her
breast.

"I'll be right back," he said and closed the door.

Inside the car everything was still and quiet. Irene watched him
walk down the street toward Warwick Gee and that distasteful
girl. She watched him lean toward Warwick Gee and say something to him and watched Warwick Gee grin and look at the car
and punch Harry in the shoulder.

What am I doing? Irene thought What in the name of God am I doing? And she felt a little sick to her stomach and part of her wanted to get out of the car and run away home to her bed with its clean white sheets. But she couldn't do that, not now, not after she'd said what she'd said. There was a name for girls who behaved like that and it was one thing to be a sophisticated worldly girl who was not afraid to make love to the man she loved, but another thing entirely to promise a man something and then run home to mother.

Harry walked past her, holding up a finger to her as he did. "Be right back. Don't you move," he said and he disappeared back inside the club.

You've made your bed now, my girl. She wanted to cry and began to shiver.

Just as she thought she'd lose her nerve, Harry reappeared carrying a bag under his arm. He looked up and down the street and then he got in the car and with him came the smell of cigarettes and gin and the sticky scent of that dreadful girl's musky perfume.

He leaned across the seat and kissed her. He looked so beautiful and young and she smiled back and felt safe again, safe with him.

"Hold this," he said, handing her the bag. "Thought we should make this a real celebration."

And she could feel it was a bottle and thought it might be champagne, but no, it was a bottle of gin, and she guessed that was all right too.

"Where are we going?" And she hoped he'd say the new Park Plaza up on Bloor Street, or maybe even the King Edward, where she fancied the beds were big and soft and covered in satin sheets and the bathroom taps were made of real brass and the walls were covered in damask silk.

"Oh, there's a little place I know," he said and winked at her.

The Excelsior was a discreet establishment, pleasant enough, but low key, with nothing about its façade or lobby to draw attention to itself.

They signed in at the desk (large and high and dark, as Irene imagined the desk in a police station to be) as Mr. and Mrs. Carter, and Irene kept her gloves on. The desk clerk looked as though they had woken him and was none too pleased, his greyish mouth pulled down at the corners. She was sure they weren't fooling him for one single minute, this old man with a cataract in one eye, which Irene suspected did nothing to hamper his vision.

"No baggage?" he said.

"It's in the car. We'll bring it up later," said Harry.

"I see," said the man, and Irene was sure he did. The only thing she was grateful for was that if he had seen Harry before, he made no sign.

As they walked across the clean but worn blue carpet Irene took Harry's arm and he reached down and patted her hand. They pressed the button for the elevator and stood watching the arrow move from the sixth floor to the fifth to the fourth. Irene wanted to be laughing and listening to Harry say pretty things to her.

When the elevator came Harry said, "Sixth floor, please" to the antiquity in a uniform operating the controls.

"Yes, sir," replied the man, and the machine cranked and wheezed its way upward.

They rode in silence, although he put his arm around her. She felt the weight of him against her as he balanced.

He unlocked the door of the room and held it open for her. Shouldn't he be carrying her? No, that was stupid. They were not married.

There was a double bed with an iron headboard. There was a white cover on the bed and in the middle a heart-shaped pillow with pink embroidered flowers. To the right of the bed stood a nightstand with an ice bucket and two glasses wrapped in paper, and a black telephone. Over the small chest of drawers was an oval mirror in an imitation gold frame. The wallpaper must have been pretty once, with cabbage roses, faded now to greyish pink. This was not the room she had dreamed of, but she had known it wouldn't be from the second he had said "a little place I know." It didn't seem to matter how much she steeled herself against disappointment, though, for there it was like a small brown toad that had hopped up onto the windowsill.

Harry went to the nightstand before taking off his coat, unwrapped the glasses and poured them both a shot of gin. She didn't like straight gin, thought that only the worst kind of people drank straight gin, without even an olive to make it think it was a martini, but still, she took the glass from him and raised it to her lips.

"I propose a toast," he said.

"Fine, then, a toast." She held her breath.

"To you, my dear, lovely Irene, to you."

She wished he'd said "to us."

Harry drank his glass down to the bottom. He came behind her and slipped her coat from her shoulders. He hung it on the hook near the door and then took his own coat off and his jacket and tie and hung them next to hers. He sat on the edge of the bed and patted the space beside him.

"Come here," he said, and she came to him. He took the glass away from her and put it down on the bedside table.

"Are you frightened?" he said.

"Yes, a little," she said, and she might have said more, but his lips were on hers then and his hands were on her breasts and she felt herself go stiff and still.

"Are you sure about this, my dear?"

"Yes, completely sure."

"I don't want you saying later that I seduced you."

"I've never wanted anything more." She looked at him directly, for she was a grown woman now, or soon would be. There was no reason to be shy or coy, not with Harry, because Harry knew everything there was to know. And he was the only man she would ever want, would ever love, and so what difference would it make, now, or in a few months when they were married, for surely he meant to marry her?

He kissed her again, his juniper-sweet tongue rolling around inside her mouth. Then he pulled away, panting slightly.

"Do you want to freshen up a bit?"

She hesitated, and he said, "I have protection. You needn't worry on that front."

"Oh. Good," she said. "Yes, I'll be right back."

She went into the small bathroom and closed the door behind her. She had no idea how to freshen up with no toothbrush, no toothpaste. There on the side of the sink was, just as she had expected, a small bar of soap, and on the rack a thin towel. Not knowing what else to do, she ran the bath, and while the water was running she used the toilet and flushed, embarrassed at the sound. She stripped off her clothes, folding them carefully, stepped into the bath, which was hot but not deep, and washed herself. Then she towelled off with the thin towel and, using her finger, scrubbed along the inside of her mouth with a bit of soap, gagging on the taste. She held her hand beneath the faucet and scooped water into her mouth, rinsing until she was sure the taste of soap was gone.

She fluffed her hair and combed her fingers through it, avoiding her own glance in the mirror. She wished she had perfume.

How long had she been in the bathroom? Was she supposed to come out naked? She had always imagined that she would be wearing a beautiful peignoir, something frothy and pink. She slipped her cream-coloured slip back on and hoped that she was pretty.

It was true that a man, a gentleman like Harry, must marry a girl he deflowered. A gentleman would have no other recourse and would only embark on such a course of action knowing its inevitable outcome. Her mother's voice: *Why buy the cow when you can get the milk for free?*

She opened the door. Harry was waiting for her, already under the covers. He had turned the lights out so that only the glow of his cigarette and the light from the street lit the room. His chest and shoulders were naked and the flesh shone with a pale silvery tinge. His arms looked thin.

"Here, Irene, have another drink," he said, pulling her by the arm down onto the bed and putting the glass in her hand. She noticed the bottle by the bedside was a third gone already. How long had she been in the bathroom?

"Drink up," he said. "You're stiff as a board."

And so Irene did as she was told. He pulled the slip over her head. She drank up and lay back on the bed in Harry's arms. The room spun slowly around her.

"You're beautiful, Irene," he said, with his mouth on her nipple. "Good girl."

He explored her body. He turned her and twisted her this way and that, his fingers, his lips everywhere until Irene was nothing more than sensation, hot and filled with hollowness. She reached for him, ran her hands along his back, the long muscles there, across his shoulders, his arms. Under the influence of his touch she had lost all shyness, but every time her fingers sought out his penis he gently pushed her hand away.

"Not yet, love, not yet," he mumbled, and she took this to mean his passion for her was too great.

They went on like this for a long time, or so it felt to Irene. She didn't know how things were supposed to proceed, but she wanted to touch him the way that he was touching her, wanted to please him. She twisted her arm around beneath her and reached down his belly. She was surprised to find him limp as a soft sleeping mouse. Was she not desirable? Was she doing something wrong?

"I said not yet." He sounded annoyed.

"I want to make you feel good," she said.

"Stroke it, then," he said, "gently."

She moved her hand back and forth, trying to arouse him, wanting him to want her as much as she wanted him. He grew harder, lengthened as she raked her fingernails gently across his skin. He pushed her away and lay on his back with his hands under the covers. He was putting on the rubber, she guessed, and she looked away. It seemed so ungraceful a motion, and so intimate, she didn't think she should be watching him. He turned and raised himself above her, parting her legs with his knees.

"It might hurt a bit," he said.

"I don't mind," she said.

Harry strained against her, trying to force his way in. He

fumbled between their bodies, grunting and sweating above her. Irene felt her arousal dwindle away. His breath stank of gin and cigarettes. Their bodies were sweaty and sticky. He finally rolled away.

"Seems the gin's got the better of me," he said, with his face turned away from her. He lit a cigarette. "We can try again in a little while." He did not touch her.

"Is it me?" she said in a whisper.

"No. I told you. It's just the bloody booze. I drank too much, that's all." He crushed out his cigarette. "I'm going to take a wee nap. We'll try again."

"I think I want to go home." Tears were dripping into her ears.

"For crying out loud, Irene. You're not going to start carrying on like a schoolgirl, are you?"

"I'm sorry," she said, but could not stop crying.

"God save me from virgins."

"Don't you love me, Harry?"

"Irene, what do you want me to say? That I love you? Will that make everything all right, then?" He was pouring himself another drink. "Oh, for the love of God, stop that snivelling!"

Irene tried, but it just wasn't possible. She got out of bed, scooped her slip up from its puddle on the floor and dashed into the bathroom, clutching it across her breasts.

When she came out again, Harry was rolled over onto his side. His back was pale and cold in the false moonlight coming in from the streetlamp.

"Harry?"

There was no response. Irene stood looking down at the bed, where the imprint of her body could still be seen, a hollow next to Harry's form. Without touching him, without actually making an effort to rouse him, there was no way of knowing whether he was really sleeping or just pretending. She did not want to touch him. She felt shame like a cramp down deep inside her.

She opened the door and stepped out into the hallway. The lights were dim and the hallway looked far longer leaving than it had when she and Harry had arrived. As she waited for the elevator, she was afraid Harry would follow her. When the doors opened, she looked back, hoping to see him. The elevator operator took her down to the lobby without even a glance. All the way down she prayed the desk clerk would be asleep behind his desk, but there he sat, talking into the phone and smoking a cigarette. He smirked, telling Irene all she needed to know about what sort of woman he judged her to be.

"I need a taxi. Would you get one for me, please?"

"Not spending the night with your husband, *miss*?"

"Are you capable of getting me a taxi or not?" She was dangerously close to tears again.

"I'll call you back, Mabel," he said into the phone and hung up. "Are you all right, miss?"

"I'm fine. I just need a taxi. Please."

"'Course. May take a few minutes, this time of night and all, but we'll get you one. Billy!" he called, and a young man in a bellman's cap appeared. "Lady needs a cab. Get her one."

"This time of night? Might take a while. "

"Yeah, yeah, just do it!" He turned back to Irene as the boy moped off through the lobby. "Why not take a seat."

"Thank you, but I think I'll wait outside. I could use the fresh air."

"Suit yourself," he said and picked up the phone again.

22

When Irene came home, she sat at the kitchen table and the tears poured down her face, making dark stains on her pretty yellow evening dress. Margaret made her daughter cocoa, with tiny marshmallows floating on the top, and sat beside her stroking her hair and encouraging her to talk. But Irene would only say that it was over, all over, and that she had been a cheap and stupid fool.

"Irene, tell me you haven't gone to bed with that boy!" Margaret said. "That's all I need, an illegitimate grandchild."

Irene turned to her and said, "No fear of that, Mum, you needn't worry," with such bitterness that Margaret didn't know what to think.

"I should hope so. I can just imagine what the neighbours would say if that were to happen. *Lord.*"

"For God's sake, Mum!" Irene wailed, and worked herself up into such a state that Margaret had to put her to bed, tucking the sheets under her chin.

"You're Mother's little kitten, you know." She kissed Irene's hot, dry forehead. "Yes, you are. Mother's little kitten."

Irene did not come out of her room at all the next day, and wouldn't talk, no matter how Margaret tried to draw her out. She wouldn't eat. On Monday she didn't even bother to go to the store. She called Mr. Badali and asked him to hang a sign on the door: Closed Due To Illness. Margaret tiptoed around all day, trying to give the girl some room.

Oh, she felt sorry for her. She knew what that pain felt like and she could feel it radiating off her daughter in hot waves. The poor wee thing. And couldn't Margaret just remember how awful it was, not wanting anyone near you, because even the air hurt. It was like all your skin had been peeled away and even the slightest breeze would set you to screaming again. She remembered. It brought the two of them closer, this shared pain. Peas in a pod they were, two peas in a pod.

On Tuesday morning Irene ate some toast and tea and went to work, although she came home at the end of the day looking like she'd fought the battle of Culloden all over again and lost.

Margaret discovered she was very good at taking care of her daughter. She made her milkshakes with a raw egg whipped up in them to give her strength. She brought her toast and honey, or cinnamon toast, or sometimes soup. Yes, nice thick soups with chunky vegetables and bits of beef.

Which was what she was doing this Saturday evening, exactly two weeks since Irene had come home so distraught—preparing a nice thick soup for her daughter, who sat listlessly in the living room, wrapped in her old tartan housecoat. She listened to the evening's broadcast from the CBC, and the words floated into the kitchen. "On Saturday night, the tenth anniversary of the passing of Harry Houdini, Mrs. Houdini staged a final séance on the roof of a Hollywood hotel in what she said was a last effort to communicate with him. 'He has not come,' she said. 'I have abandoned hope.' And so, the light that has burned for the past decade above a photograph of the great magician in his widow's home was at last darkened."

Margaret chopped the onions, the carrots, the celery. She fried the flour-dredged hunks of flank steak in the skillet before adding them to the broth already in the pot. The store was doing so much better these days that they could afford flank steak. Salt and pepper, a pinch of rosemary. She stirred the deep cast-iron kettle and held her face over the fragrant steam, breathing deeply. There is nothing, she thought, more soothing than the smell of a pot of soup on the stove.

"Is that about Mussolini?" Margaret called. Il Duce had declared that conflict between Great Britain and Italy would lead to a general European war. Apparently he was now offering to exchange pledges to respect each nation's rights and proclaimed an "armed peace" rather than the "illusions" of disarmament and collective security.

Margaret could see through the bully's words. It was one of the compensations for living with the Other Margaret. She had swift, sudden flashes of insight that the Real Margaret never had. She knew what the Italian Fascist was up to, knew that he had his own form of madness, as did Hitler. Bug-house candidates, both of them. They were like kin, almost. It was odd, really, how crazies like that could manage not only to function in a way she could not, but to wangle themselves a place on the world stage. She could see from the newspaper photos that there was something in their eyes, something that no one should have to look upon. The reports she read said Hitler's eyes were blue. She paid attention to the colour of eyes.

Blue-eye, beauty, do your mammy's duty,
Black-eye, pick a pie, Run around and tell a lie;
Grey-eye, greedy-gut, Eat all the blue world up.

No matter what colour, their eyes glinted. She shuddered, knowing that when Mad Margaret was in residence a similar dark spark might be found in her own eyes.

"Irene, did you hear me?"

"Yes, Mum. It's about him."

"Anything about King Edward?"

"Not yet."

"He's a fool, that man, trying to escape his duties. And all for a bit of skirt."

Irene looked out the window to the dark skeleton trees. Yes, a fool indeed. What was he thinking? What was anyone thinking when they tried to leave behind where they were? Your destiny always caught up with you, didn't it? And this was, Irene now saw, her destiny. To be sitting in this house, night after night, with her mother, growing older, growing more eccentric, until they were just two crazy old ladies, maybe keeping cats, hundreds of cats, and collecting newspapers, until the house caved in around them and everyone said what a shame it was.

"Hungry?" her mother called.

"No."

"Oh, sure you are. You must be. I bet you haven't eaten all day. You have to keep your strength up, you know."

What was there to say to this? Her strength must be kept up so that she could keep going. You breathe in, you breathe out; you do the work and keep up appearances and fulfill your obligations. When all the while the only thing you really want is to sit in a chair and not speak. It was what her life would be about, now.

Now that Harry was gone.

She had hoped Harry would call. Hoped he had seen the error of his ways, that he now knew what he was losing, that it was all a terrible mistake, that he would never hurt her again, that he was here to beg her forgiveness and ask her to marry him, to marry him right away ... and get her out of this terrible padded-cell house.

Yes, she had hoped that. Foolish and cheap girl.

The announcer droned on about the King and country, duty and honour. Her mother was right. The King must be the King, and all the desire in the world wouldn't make a bit of difference.

"My goodness, Irene, can't you at least turn a light on in here? You shouldn't sit in the dark, dear. I can barely see to walk. It'll ruin your eyes. And you don't want to have to start wearing glasses, now, do you? Hide those pretty eyes?" Her mother carried a tray with a steaming bowl of soup and a cup of tea. Invalid food.

She pulled out a small folding table from behind the chesterfield and set the tray down.

"Fine, then, I'll put on the light myself." She reached under the pink floral shade of the floor lamp and the room became softly lit. Irene looked small huddled inside the big housecoat, her feet in thick socks. Margaret held a napkin out. "That's better. Now, sit up straight, dear, and try and eat something. I know it's hard to eat when you feel so blue, but you must try. Just a few mouthfuls. That's a good girl, just a sip. Now, isn't that good?"

Margaret dunked the bread into the soup bowl.

"You know, dear, I know how you feel. Like you're way down at the bottom of a great dark well, and you can see the light, way up there above you, but can't imagine ever being able to make your way up to it again."

Yes, Irene thought, it feels just like that.

"I know it feels like the world is ending just now, but try and look at it this way: you've learned a very important lesson early. You'll be the better for it." Irene was crying again. "Oh, dear. Oh, you poor thing."

Margaret went and put her arms around Irene's shoulders, bending her head so that her mouth was close to Irene's ear. "There, there," she said over and over. "There, there. It's going to be all right. It's going to be fine."

She could feel her daughter's bones under the heavy housecoat. She could see the pulse in the soft skin on her neck. *Blood of my blood, bones of my bones. We are made of the same flesh.* For the first time in a very long time, Margaret felt as though they were practically the same person. It was so reassuring to have someone in the world with whom you were bonded in this way. And hadn't she been good over the past while? Hadn't she said all the right things and none of the bad things that had swirled around inside her head? She had almost called Harry Madison a cocksucker, but she hadn't. She hadn't laughed, which was sometimes a difficult thing to control. As long as the pain was in Irene, it wasn't so much in her. They were sharing things. Making each other better.

"I'm here, dear, Mum's here. Don't you worry. I'll never leave you."

She hugged her daughter tightly, but the poor thing just kept on crying and crying and crying. She'd probably spend the whole day in bed tomorrow, and Margaret knew just what she'd make for her. Scones with homemade strawberry jam. Just the thing to tempt a finicky palate. Just the very thing.

Part V

23

It was Friday, December 4, and Margaret was in a frenzy of cookie baking. There was holly on the mantelpiece, and mistletoe hung from every doorway. The tree, a riot of brightly coloured baubles and bells and tinsel, stood in the corner of the living room with a new pink and white angel on top, her wings gold-coloured satin. There was a wreath on the front door and another in the front window. Red ribbons entwined the banister, and every surface was covered with candles in the shapes of Santa Claus or snowmen or evergreens.

Margaret wore the pretty apron Irene had made her years ago and hummed as she took another sheet of shortbread from the oven. She'd made two fruitcakes, orange cookies, rum balls, cookies in the shape of stars, in the shape of wreaths, in the shape of angels. She had made chocolate macaroons and almond cookies. She might just finish by day's end.

This being their first Christmas without Douglas, Margaret knew she should be dreading the day without him, and she was sad, at least at times. Sometimes she'd walk past his chair and out of the corner of her eye she'd swear she saw him there. Or there would be the creak of a floorboard somewhere in the house when she was the only one home and for a second, just a second, she'd think he was upstairs, in another room, just down the hall. But she never longed for his return.

She slid the cookies onto the rack to cool. She loved the smell of sugar and almond that filled the kitchen. The bright light reflected from the snow outside made the red kitchen look clean and crisp and warm. Christmas carols played on the radio. A cardinal pecked at a lump of suet Irene had hung from the tree in the backyard. Margaret sighed. It was good, this peace that had come upon her. *Hush, hush.*

Life could be so sad and so hard, but weren't she and Irene better off now? Wasn't the house ordered and regulated, calm and predictable? And there was more money now. Not just the insurance money—she had to thank Douglas for that, even if it still rubbed her nerves raw to think he'd made Irene the beneficiary—but the store was doing well. She had to hand it to Irene. She was a smart one. Margaret had always said so.

Irene didn't talk about Harry anymore, never even mentioned his name. He would have hurt her in the end, no matter what, for didn't they all, and it was better to pull the bandage off quickly and let the wound heal in the air.

They'd be all right, the two of them. The two of them together.

She heard footsteps on the porch and checked the wall clock. It was just past four and certainly couldn't be Irene coming home. Margaret cocked her head and listened. Then the bell rang. She wiped her hands on the cloth slung over her shoulder and started down the hall. She had no intention of opening the door, but she wanted to know who was out there.

She parted the curtain on the living-room window and peeked out. Standing on the porch was a dark-haired young man, shabbily dressed, with a pack over his shoulder. Looking for a handout, she thought, and has some nerve too, coming right to the front door, instead of around the back like he should. His face, from what she could see at this angle, had the tanned, wind-burned complexion of a man who'd been out of doors a long time.

He knocked on the door again and peered in the little window, trying to see through the sheer curtain that covered it. He shifted the pack on his back and stamped his feet a time or two. The snow that had drifted on the porch last night squeaked under the man's heels. He must be cold. Well, he'd move on.

He knocked one last time, then stepped back and looked up at the house as though checking the number, and she pulled herself quickly away from the window to avoid being seen. She heard him take a step or two. She waited, expecting to hear his feet going back down the stairs, but the sound didn't come. After a moment she couldn't resist and looked out the window again.

Margaret was surprised to see the man sitting on the front step, rolling himself a cigarette, calm as you please.

Who on earth does he think he is?

As though he could sense he was being stared at, he turned toward her. Margaret jumped back, but not quickly enough. She pressed herself against the wall. His footsteps on the porch were loud. A shadow fell over the window and Margaret's heart began to pound. She scratched at the back of her hands, digging deep.

"Hello, is anyone there?"

She stayed very quiet.

"Hello?" He tapped lightly on the window.

Margaret bit her lip to keep the Other Margaret from screaming out something obscene. She heard footsteps going to the door and a light tapping again.

"I'm not selling anything. I don't want anything."

"Go away, then," she yelled. "Go away!"

"I don't mean to scare anybody. Maybe I got the wrong house. Can you just tell me if I've got the wrong house?"

"Yes. You have the wrong house. Go away!"

"Is this the MacNeil house? Are you Margaret?"

Her hand went to her throat. "What do you want?"

"My name's David. I was a friend of your brother's," he said. "A friend of Rory's. I'm just passing through and thought I might stop by and say hello. Rory spoke about you many times."

"You're a friend of Rory's?"

"Yes, ma'am."

"Stay there." She had to think. She needed Irene to come home.

"Yes, ma'am."

"Where is he?" she said, finally stepping toward the door. She could see him through the thin gauze. "Is he coming home?"

There was a moment's silence.

"Well now, ma'am. I guess I don't know. So, is your husband home, ma'am? Maybe I could just say hello to Mr. MacNeil."

He's lying about something.

"My husband is dead."

"Oh, shit! Oh, sorry, ma'am! Uh ... I'm sorry to hear that, sorry to hear that, very sorry. Uh ... Look, you think you could maybe open the door?"

"No." Her voice was high, the voice of the Other Margaret, poised and ready to pounce.

"Okay, then, okay."

"How do you know my brother?" There was something here, flicking its angry tail around the edges of her mind. She did not want to look at it.

"We met in a relief camp some time back. We did some organizing I guess you'd call it. He said if I was ever in Toronto I should come by and see his sister and her family." She could hear him shuffling out there in the cold. "So, are you alone, Mrs. MacNeil? Is your daughter here? Irene's her name, isn't it? Maybe she's home? I'd sure like to say hello if she's there."

Why did he keep wanting to know if she was alone? He didn't sound dangerous, but Margaret sensed there was much to be afraid of around him. The air was so cold, with the sun just a sliver of steely light on the horizon.

"What did you say your name was?"

"David, ma'am."

"Don't you move, David. I'm going to call my daughter."

Irene had planned to keep the shop open a little later that night. She was doing that more often these days. There seemed no reason not to. Other than seeing Ebbie now and again, since she and Harry had broken up she no longer had any social life. She'd brought in some Christmas decorations that were selling well, as were the little bottles of cheap perfume that children could buy for their mothers with pride, decorated with gaudy ribbons and imitation-gold caps, little wooden boxes with surprise toys inside, hand puppets, small bags of jawbreakers and gumballs that made, she assured her customers, excellent stocking stuffers. Better to have a stocking filled to the brim with lots of little things, for wasn't it a time of frivolity, and forget the bikes and train sets and roller skates that so few could afford anyway.

The phone rang, and her mother told her she'd better come home.

"Why? What's wrong?"

"I don't know."

Irene closed her eyes. "What's that supposed to mean? Is something wrong or isn't it?"

"There's a fellow here. Young fellow."

Harry! Could it be Harry, after all this time?

"He says he's a friend of your uncle Rory's."

"Oh my God! Is Uncle Rory coming?" Irene's breath caught in her throat.

"I don't know. Come home, Irene. I can't make head nor tail of this person. You need to come home now."

"Is he in the *house?*"

"He's on the porch."

"I'll be right there."

She shooed out two boys giggling at the magazine rack and locked up the shop.

Irene could see the man on the porch. He was sitting on the top step, smoking a cigarette. As she approached he stood and threw the cigarette away. A movement at the window caught her eye. It was cold, and the man's breaths came in short foggy puffs.

"I'm Irene MacNeil," she said.

"David," he said, holding out his gloveless red hand. Even through her wool gloves she could feel how cold he was. "Look, I'm sorry. I think maybe I scared your mother."

"What can we do for you?" He wore only a thin wool jacket. He must be frozen.

"Rory said I should stop by if I was around. I didn't know about your father. I'm real sorry."

"Thank you."

"So, could you and I maybe have a talk?" He looked uneasily at the front door, which snapped open as if on cue.

"What does he want?" said Margaret. Irene could see the fear graven in furrows on her mother's forehead. The backs of her hands were scratched red.

"I don't know. I think he should come in."

"Maybe I shouldn't," he said.

"Nonsense, it's freezing out here."

"Irene ..."

"It's all right, Mum. You can go upstairs if you want." She stepped into the house and her mother moved back. She gestured for the man to come in. He looked pleasant enough, but so uncomfortable. There was a strange charge in the air, an electrical crackle, like before a storm is about to break. Irene was suddenly afraid of what had stepped in the door with this man. He entered and twisted his cap in his hand, then reached up and pulled on his earlobe.

"I want to stay," said Margaret, and she clutched at Irene. If she was alone the Other Margaret would take over, she knew that. Even now it was all she could do to keep her words in check, to not rave at the man, tell him to get the fuck out and your bad luck with you! For she could see the evil all around him like shadows.

"Fine, Mother, but let go, you're hurting me." Margaret relaxed her grip a little. "Let me get out of my coat. Why don't you go put the kettle on?"

"No."

"Fine. Then come with us. Come through, please," she said to the man, and she led the way down the hall to the kitchen. She put Margaret in a chair and hung her coat on the back of another. She got the kettle and turned to fill it at the sink. The man was standing in the doorway.

"Please, David, please sit down."

"Thanks very much," he said and sat at the chair nearest the door. "You've grown up some since your uncle last saw you, I guess … I'm very sorry to hear of your father's death. Very sorry. Rory, he spoke highly of him."

"Thank you," said Irene, filling the kettle. She doubted very much that her uncle had said nice things about her father, given the condition he'd been in when Rory saw him last. Still, it was a kind thing to say.

"Where's Rory?" said Margaret.

"Last I saw him was in Regina, ma'am."

"When was that?" said Irene. "You'll forgive me, but we haven't heard from him in some time, and quite frankly we've been worried."

"It was July, miss, of 1935."

"That long! But you've heard from him since?"

"You haven't heard anything?" he said. "Nothing? Either of you?"

They shook their heads.

"I'm sorry, miss. I don't know what to do here. Maybe you and I should go for a walk?" He pulled his earlobe again.

"What is he saying?" said Margaret, looking from one to the other.

"I don't mean to be dancin' around here, it's just that I thought it might be better to wait until you got home, miss, to explain everything. And I'm sorry to mention it, but I know your mother has been … well, your uncle mentioned … Oh, God damn!" He tossed his hat on the table and punched a fist into his palm. "I'm no good at this. So, you're telling me you've heard nothing?"

"Just come out and say it, please."

"Irene?" Her mother whimpered and began chewing at her knuckle.

"It's all right, Mum," she said, but of course she had known it wasn't going to be all right, known it for the longest time, for Uncle Rory wouldn't have gone all this time without a word, a card. She looked away from this man's face and from his eyes, because they burned her. Her mother started to cry and reached out for her hand.

David ran his hand through his dark hair. "I guess there's no good way to say a thing like this, is there?"

"My uncle's dead, isn't he?"

"No! Irene, you mustn't say such a thing!" Her mother's hand was a sharp clutch on her own.

"Yeah. He is. Yeah."

Her mother began to wail, her hands in her hair. Irene put her arms around her, but she arched backwards in the chair, like a child who would not be restrained. Margaret's eyes were wide, locked onto Irene's, and she let out a long, low moan.

"Breathe, Mum, just breathe. We're all right. We're all right."

"Is there anything I can do?" said this stranger in their house.

"Upstairs, in the bathroom, in the medicine cabinet. There is a prescription bottle. Pills. Could you get it, please?" He scrambled out of the room. "It's all right, Mum, it's all right. I'm here," she said, when all she wanted to do was to break down and cry herself and she couldn't or else who would tell her mother to breathe, just keep breathing.

David stood before her. "Is this it?" He looked frightened, and held a small bottle in front of him.

"Yes. Water, please."

Margaret began shrieking and pointing at David.

Irene took the water glass and tried to get Margaret to drink, but she knocked the glass out of Irene's hand. It fell to the floor but didn't break. Irene grabbed at her mother's flailing wrists while David got more water.

"Open up, Mum," she said. "You've got to take the pills."

Margaret opened her mouth as though to scream again and Irene tossed the pills in, being careful not to get bitten in the process. She poured water into her mother's mouth, most of it spilling down her front.

"You'll feel better, Mum, you'll be all right. Just relax."

David stood pressed up against the kitchen counter and watched during the long minutes it took the girl to wrestle her mother into stillness.

• • •

Finally Margaret fell into a drugged sleep, her fists gripping the bedclothes. Irene sat in the living room with David, and she tried not to hate him, knowing it was irrational, knowing it was unfair, knowing it wouldn't bring back her uncle.

"So, she's going to be all right?" said David.

"I don't know."

"Is there anything I can do? I feel terrible, being the one to bring the news this way. I was sure ... People were supposed to have told you."

Irene began to cry.

"Look, I'm really sorry."

She wished he would stop saying that.

"I should go, maybe," he said, as though reading her mind.

"Yes. I think that would be best." She wanted to know what had happened, but not now.

He took a pencil stub out of his pocket and wrote on the torn scrap of an envelope. "This is where I'm staying. In the market. So, if you want to talk or anything. If there's anything I can do." He kept pulling at his ear and brushing the curls off his forehead.

Irene took the piece of paper and put it in her pocket.

The next day, when Irene had left her all alone in the house with her ghosts, Margaret decided that corners were good places, and so she sat in the small dining room, on a high-backed walnut chair with a black leather seat, facing out into the room so that nothing could sneak up on her. *Can you not spare me even this?* The words repeated over and over in her head. She thought of Catholics and the easy comfort of their rhythmic phrases. *Hail Mary, full of grace, the Lord is with thee, blessed art thou among women and blessed is the fruit of thy womb, Jesus. Pray for us sinners, now and at the hour of our death. Amen.* Yes, let her talk to Mary, who brought life into the world and was there to see it gone again. Bloody at birth and bloody in death. *Can you not spare me even this?*

Maybe it wasn't her fault. Maybe God hid his true face there behind the blue skirts of an angel-raped woman.

Cunning. But Mad Margaret would not be fooled.

Margaret decided she had been wrong all these years. The danger did not come from being crazy. The danger was being unprepared, not paying attention to the messages Mad Margaret sent her. The clues had been there all along. A crow on the lawn. One crow sorrow, two crows joy. Never two crows. A shattered mirror last week. A cake that had fallen in the oven on a Tuesday. Yes. It was clearer now. Random acts? She thought not. God was never random with His terrible, swift sword. The danger came from one place, one omnipresent Face. The danger lay in the lap of God Himself, who lies and is cruel. God who shows no mercy or is indifferent. God who turns women into pillars of salt, who stones them at the gate in payment for the crimes of men, God who giveth and then always, always, taketh away. Mad Margaret understood then. Mad Margaret was at war with God. She saw that now, and would be on guard in the future. No one would sneak up on her again. She would leave nothing to chance.

She walked into the living room and stood before the Christmas tree. She reached out and took an ornament, a green and silver glass bell that had been her mother's, and she plucked it off the branch like an offending eye. She closed her fist around it until it shattered, and the slip of blood on her palm pleased her. She reached up and took another, a little bird on a spring. This she ground beneath her foot. She threw a gold ball over her shoulder, tossed another in the fire grate, and so on, until only the angel on the top remained. She had to tip the tree over to get at this last one. The tree fell, scattering needles and filling the room with the crisp scent of pine. She picked the angel up and tore its dress off, then its wings and finally its head, which she crushed beneath her heel.

She looked around, satisfied. She would tear down the ribbons and the mistletoe next.

24

Irene's eyes snapped open to find her mother's face hovering over hers, her lips nearly on top of her own. She looked like a feral cat trying to suck the breath out of a baby. Irene's heart thumped.

"Slain. Sacrificed," Margaret hissed. "He was murdered by God for his sins. He was nailed to a cross and left for the crows to pick out his eyes. Crows are filthy."

"No, Mum, I'm sure that's not it," Irene said, struggling for words, struggling to decipher what her mother was talking about, for, although frightened, she was still soggy with sleep. Cautiously, she slipped out from underneath her mother's face. She tried to speak normally. "Come and get some breakfast."

"I'm all right," said her mother.

"Yes. Of course you are."

"I don't have to go to the bug-house." Margaret tugged at the sleeve of Irene's nightgown with her bandaged hands.

"No, of course not." She disentangled herself and put her robe on while her mother stood watching her. "Why don't you go downstairs, Mum. I have to go to the bathroom."

"I'll wait for you."

Irene went into the bathroom and ran the water so her mother, standing just on the other side of the door, would not listen to her urinating. She flushed, splashed water on her face and rinsed her mouth. *I can't take much more of this.* She opened the door. Her mother stood there, arms wrapped around herself as though she were cold.

"Where's your robe, Mum? Get your robe."

Margaret dutifully walked back into her room and picked up her robe from where it lay crumpled on the floor. She put on her slippers. "I'm hungry," she said.

"Yes, good. We'll go have breakfast, shall we?" Irene went downstairs and the older woman followed like a beaten dog.

Irene was heartened that her mother was talking now, even if she had scared the bejesus out of her. Margaret had been a passive zombie ever since the doctor had been by that night Irene came home to find the house near-wrecked and her mother huddled in a corner of the dining room, muttering "God is a bastard" and bleeding from her torn palms.

The doctor had prescribed phenobarbital. "An effective treatment of anxiety. A teaspoon as necessary. But not too often. It can be addictive. We'll see how she is in a week or so, shall we? And then, if there's not much improvement, I think you may have to consider other options."

Irene had stayed home from the shop since then, for she didn't trust her mother alone.

"I heard the doctor," Margaret said, looking up at Irene.

"What did you hear?"

"I heard him say I'd go to the bug-house."

"He didn't say that."

"He said that."

"I won't let that happen."

"I won't go there."

"No, of course not. You'll be fine. You're just tired, is all."

"Yes. I'm just tired." Margaret put her elbows on the table and rested her head in her hands. "My head hurts. It's so hard. The fighting all the time."

"We're not fighting."

"I'm fighting. I have to fight. I won't go there. They'll put needles in my head and I'll die screaming. God's crows will eat my flesh."

Irene shivered. "Oh, Mum, you won't. It'll be all right."

"Give me time, Irene. I'll make her go away. I can make the dinners again."

Make who go away? "You can make dinner whenever you want."

"Don't go away, Irene. Tell me you won't go away."

Irene slammed the cupboard door harder than she meant to. Then she opened it and slammed it again. Again. It was a good, sharp, clean noise. "*Goddamn* it, Mum!" she shouted. "Stop it for just a minute, can't you! Can't you, please? For the love of God! Just stop asking me for every goddamn thing! I can't take much more of this! Leave me alone!"

Her hands were in fists. She swung around to look at her mother. Margaret's bandaged hands were drawn up to her chest and her mouth and eyes were wide.

"Aw, Mum. I'm sorry." She went over, knelt down and took her mother's hand. "I didn't mean it. Don't look like that. It's all right."

"Why did he have to die? Why do they all go away? Everyone goes away." Margaret's eyes filled with tears again, just plain old ordinary grief and not the jagged edges of raving.

"I don't know, Mum. Look, I won't leave you, but I have to get back to the store or we won't have any money." She stood up and pressed her fingers into her temples, trying to massage out the tension. "I have to get back to work."

"Yes. But stay with me today."

"I'll stay today. Tomorrow, though ..."

"I can win soon. If you come home. Will you come home?"

"Yes, Mum. I'll come home."

"I think I need some medicine," said Margaret, scratching the back of her hands.

She spent most of the day in the living room, watching every move Irene made. Late in the afternoon she went up to her room and closed the door.

Irene heard the chair being put under the handle.

"Are you all right, Mum?" she called.

"Yes. I need to be here. I'm all right."

Irene went back downstairs and tried to lose herself in a book, but found she couldn't concentrate with her mother in the room overhead, crying and speaking as though bullying someone. She crept back upstairs, but before she reached the door her mother called out to her.

"Irene, you're not going to go out!"

"No, Mum. I just want to make sure you're all right." Irene made an effort to sound cheerful.

"Don't leave the house. Stay in the house." She sounded breathless.

"I'm right here, Mum. Do you want to open the door?"

"No. I'll take my medicine. I'll go to sleep."

Irene heard her mother getting into bed then, heard her taking her medicine, and then no more. She stood there until she heard her mother's soft snoring and felt her own shoulders relax.

On Wednesday, Margaret sat quietly. Irene hated to look at her face, it was so full of fear. Once when she wondered aloud what had happened to Uncle Rory, her mother yelled, "No, no! I don't want to hear his name. Don't say that name."

By Thursday, Margaret was well enough that Irene could go back to work. The next day she had taken a bath and put on clean clothes. She changed her clothes again today. She took less and less of the pink medicine, "the friendly sleep," as she called it. Irene could see the effort it cost her, could see how every small step was hard won against the urge to slip back down the slope.

Everything was going wrong, Irene thought. Harry first, of course, but she would not let herself think about that. Then the renters she had found for the upstairs rooms, a man and a woman and their two-year-old boy, nice people, she'd thought, until they did a midnight runner and took two of her kitchen chairs with them. And now this. Her mother so much worse again. Uncle Rory's death. Irene had cried herself to sleep for three nights.

She just had to know what had happened to him, although part of her was afraid of what she might find out. The mystery was a fish hook pulling at her skin. She took the scrap of paper out of her pocket. She made up her mind. As soon as her mother could stand being on her own a little longer, she would go and find him, if he was still there.

25

Irene had never been to Kensington. Of course, she was aware it existed, everyone knew of the Jewish market in Kensington, and it was just a mile or so from her own house, but it could have been on another continent completely. It wasn't until she arrived nearer the neighbourhood and found herself with Jewish people right and left and all around her that she realized why David hadn't told her his last name. *Did he think she'd treat him differently if she knew? And would she have?*

She walked along College Street to the intersection of Spadina. A woman walked toward her, pulling two heavily bundled-up boys along behind her. Her boys had little skullcaps on their heads and long curls on each side of their face.

"Excuse me," she said.

The woman looked her up and down. "Yeah?"

"I'm looking for the market area, for Baldwin Street, near Shoichet."

"Near what?"

"Shoichet Street."

The woman laughed. "So now the chicken killer's got his own street, heh? That's a good one. But you ain't looking for no *shoichet*, I'm thinking. I bet I know what you're looking for, sure."

"I'm looking for a house owned by the Gutkind family."

"What you're looking for I shouldn't send you to, bad for you but good for business, yes? Fine. Your funeral. You go this way"— she pointed south—"three blocks, then you turn in, see? Then go one block. It's in the lane, see, behind like. You ask, they'll tell."

"Thank you."

"Don't thank me, darling. Don't thank me."

Irene pulled her coat around her more tightly. It was getting dark quickly, and although the wind had died down, it was very cold. She walked in the direction the woman had indicated, but felt less sure of herself with every step.

Soon she was in the midst of the market area. It was a narrow, labyrinthine network of streets and alleys. Even in the cold air, the smells were so strong she could taste them on her tongue. Chickens and rabbits and pigeons in cages, fish and rotting garbage, cooking cabbage and meat. The little tilting houses were pushed right up to the sidewalk, which was covered with pickle barrels and half-frozen rotting lettuce leaves and a steaming pile of what might have been chicken guts and newspapers written in an odd squiggly script. Children ran every which way, and junk dealers and vegetable sellers pushing carts hawked their wares in loud voices with words Irene didn't understand. People looked at her and tried to get her to come into their shops. Mothers yelled at their children and children cried and old women stood in gaggles, laughing loudly, covering their mouths with their hands. Everywhere she looked there were bearded men in long dark coats and women with scarves on their heads and young boys with those long strange curls and bits of yarn hanging down from their jackets.

Irene felt a little dizzy and tried to get her bearings. A boy stood near the entrance to an alley, stamping his feet and warming his hands. She held out the paper with the directions on it.

He winked at her and pointed up the narrow lane. "What you want is up there."

"Up there? There's a house there?"

The boy gestured for her to hurry in.

Her breathing was shallow and her heart pounded as she walked into the alley. It was a cul-de-sac, fenced in on three sides by the backs of the buildings. It was dark and dirty and smelled foul. Behind one small building two women stood talking, dead chickens dangling from their baskets.

Irene felt sure the chicken house couldn't be where David was staying. It must be the bigger house next door. She went up, but before she could knock, a stout woman with dark hair streaked grey opened the door.

"Come on, get in out of the cold, darling," she said.

"I'm looking for—"

"Yeah, yeah, we know, we know."

Irene found herself in a small, warm kitchen. At the table sat two men, with glasses in their hands and a bottle on the table. Three small children sat on the soiled wooden floor near the stove, playing with some string and several jacks. A little girl put a jack in her mouth. Her brother slapped her arm and made her spit it out, and she began to cry.

"What's it gonna be?" said the woman.

"I don't think I'm in the right place," said Irene. The men at the table were, if not drunk, certainly well on their way.

"You want something to warm you up? I got something good. Real stuff, not bathtub stuff."

"I'm in the wrong place. I'm terribly sorry."

"You no want a drink?" said the woman, standing firmly in her path.

"No, no, I thought I knew someone here. I'm awfully sorry. I won't say anything. I promise!"

"Who you know, sweetheart?"

"David."

"David Hirsch?"

"I don't know, maybe, yes, probably."

"David upstairs."

"He's here?"

"Sure, sure, he and some of the boys they stay upstairs. Rent a nice clean place to sleep, heh? You want to see him, you go up. Go on, darling." She pointed to a narrow flight of stairs.

"Could you call him for me?"

"Go on up, won't kill you." The woman turned back to the men at the table and demanded money from them before another drink would be poured. Irene climbed the rickety stairs.

At the top were two doors; one was open, showing an untidy room with three beds and a washstand. None of the beds was made and the sheets were grey with wear and old dirt. It was nearly as cold up here as it was outside. On the floor lay a child's porcelain doll with the legs broken off.

She knocked on the other door.

"Yeah? What?"

"David? It's Irene MacNeil."

She heard a sudden movement and the door swung open. David wore his jacket and held a newspaper in his hand.

"Irene! What are you doing here?"

"You gave me your address. I thought I'd come. I wanted ..." She wrapped her arms around herself. She didn't want to touch anything. "I shouldn't have come."

"No, it's all right. I gave you the address? What the hell was I thinking? You want to come in, maybe?"

The room behind him was in a dreadful state. Irene could see several dirty mattresses on the floor and one iron bed, on which a fat man lay with his back to them. There was a bucket in the corner with a lid on it. The walls were stained and the old paper peeled.

"No, of course you don't want to come in. What's the matter with me? Come on, we'll get out of here." He folded the paper and stuck it in his jacket, then stepped out into the hallway and closed the door behind him. "Come on," he said again, heading down the stairs.

"Mrs. Gutkind, I'll be back, yeah? Don't give my bed away."

"I would do such a thing? You paid for it, you got it," the woman said, not turning to look at either of them.

They walked down the alley without saying anything. As soon as they got back on Baldwin Street, Irene said, "I came because I want to know about my uncle."

"Yeah, I figured."

"Where are we going?" She caught his sleeve and he stopped walking.

"I don't know." He looked up and down the teeming, noisy street. "I don't know a place around here where we can go. So, maybe you want to go to your house?"

"No, we can't go there. My mother ..."

"Yeah, how's she doing?"

"All right. I guess. I don't know. It changes day to day."

"Yeah," he said.

"We could go to my shop."

"You've got a shop? Nice."

"Didn't my uncle tell you?"

"I don't remember."

"It used to be a drug store, but it's not anymore. We could go there."

"Fine. Anywhere you want." He sounded a little angry.

They walked for a time without saying anything.

"Look," he said at last. "I'm no bootlegger, okay? I just flop there because I'm broke and it's a cheap place."

"You don't have to explain to me."

"Not that I've got anything against a little honest bootlegging. People have mouths to feed. I don't see much wrong with it. It's a lousy place, I know that, but I don't have any options just now, you understand?"

"You don't have anything to be ashamed of."

"I'm not ashamed," he said.

At the shop, Irene turned on the hot plate she kept in the back and made them some coffee. When it was ready she took a seat across from him at one of the small round tables.

How could she explain that she wanted this death to have some reason to it, some message attached? So many bad things had happened, so quickly, that she needed to believe it wasn't just all random disaster in the world.

"Okay," he said. "Okay."

She knew if she cried, and he was able to comfort her, it would make it easier on him, but she didn't want it to be easy. She wanted someone else to have a chest full of jagged things. The only light came from the storeroom, and he sat in the chair near the window, and the light from the street lamp fell on him alone, and it was in this way, in the shrouded comfort of grey shadow, that she was able to listen.

He talked about how he'd first met Rory, up in a relief camp in northern British Columbia.

"He called himself Bob then, because he'd been ratted out as an organizer for the Workers' Unity League in another camp and couldn't use his own name anymore." He shrugged. "Lots of guys went from camp to camp that way, either because they were union men or they were looking for a camp better than the last. Course, there were no better camps."

He told her about clandestine meetings where things like strike dates were decided by men with names like Slim Evans and Big Bill Haywood. She heard about the Relief Camp Workers Union, *work and wages, work and wages,* the words kept repeating themselves as David squirmed and told his story. He told her what they wanted, these men who lived in the camps: fifty cents an hour for unskilled labour, a thirty-hour week, first-aid equipment in the camps, the end of military control.

"That wasn't so much to ask, was it?" he said.

David told of the small army of men who'd gone to Vancouver in dribs and drabs and then in a great torrent, massing over train cars like ants. All had come from relief camp walk-outs that had been staged throughout the west. They stayed in the port city for the best part of two months, until it was clear they'd have to go to Ottawa and confront the prime minister himself.

"I never was a real Communist, not like Rory," said David, who seemed now to be speaking mostly to himself. "He believed in it all. Me, I just couldn't stomach those camps anymore. Some things you have to take a stand on. I never thought we'd make it, not all the way to Ottawa, not to see the prime minister. But I thought: so, we'll make something happen.

"When we got to Calgary we were feeling pretty proud of ourselves. We had ourselves a tag day, even though the mayor said we couldn't, and we raised over a thousand dollars, too. Some of the boys got cocky, went into the city relief office and held the chairman of the Alberta Relief Commission prisoner for a couple of hours. He said we were a 'dangerous revolutionary army.'" David laughed bitterly. "I only heard about that, wasn't in on that part. But I sort of liked the name. More men joined on after that. We heard more wanted to come, from Winnipeg and

Toronto, even. Why, there were even women who wanted to come along, to provide 'solace,' you know? Oh ... sorry."

"Go on," said Irene. She was caught up in the rhythm of the trains and the travel and the hope, even knowing how it was going to end.

"We kept going. Medicine Hat. Swift Current. Moose Jaw. Then we got word the government wasn't gonna let us get past Regina. They called us a menace. We weren't doing any harm. People were kind to us. They waited at the trains, fed us, gave us blankets. It was the government that was afraid of us. Bennett was afraid.

"Don't know how he did it, but Old Bennett, he got the railroad owners to say they needed protection all of a sudden, that we were a threat, maybe, and that we were trespassing. One day the railroads are doing everything they can to help us, the next day we're a menace. Does that make any sense, any sense at all?"

Irene shook her head from the shadows. Nothing made any sense.

"We were on the road for eleven days. There were maybe two thousand of us now, and on June 14, we arrived in Regina. The province agreed we could bed down in the Exhibition Grounds and they gave us two meal tickets each a day. The people were coming out again, too, bringing us food." David shook his head. How could he explain their dreams, the fragile blue flame of belief? How could he explain Rory's face, the way it almost glowed, believing they were finally going to change something?

"We had picnics. Rallies. Then Bennett tried to stall us. He took all the power away from the province, whether they liked it or not, and sent in his negotiators. Slim Evans, he gave them our demands, which everybody knew about, you understand. They'd been in the papers for months. The government negotiators said they'd never heard about them and said it with a straight face. Said Evans should head a delegation to Ottawa to see the great man himself and the men could wait there in Regina, be fed and paid twenty cents a day.

"So, what could Slim do? He'd been asking for just such a meeting for months. Eight thousand people stood outside that night while the negotiators sorted the details. Rory and I, of course, we weren't in the delegation, we stayed behind while they went to Ottawa, riding on the cushions, so to speak, travelling first class. They left on June 18, and four days later they came back. 'Course, we'd heard by then. Bennett had just laughed and yelled and laughed some more. They planned to put us in a temporary camp in Lumsden.

"Slim was a disappointed man when he got back. We all were. He called for folks to come out and drive us to Ottawa, form a convoy, but we all knew that wouldn't happen. The roads were shit, and besides, Ottawa wasn't going to let us move east under any means. And people were afraid to help us by then. They'd been told maybe they'd be arrested if they did.

"But we weren't going to be shoved back into another one of their camps. Not in Lumsden, not anywhere. Slim Evans, he was trying hard by that time to find any way out, you understand. Any way for some honour to be saved.

"Rumours were circulating. They were coming to arrest Slim and the other leaders. Slim went to the government, trying to get amnesty for everybody but himself, trying to get them to let us disband and just go on back where we came from, to whatever homes we might have someplace, to, well ... anywhere but there."

David's voice trickled off to a near whisper. He hung his head and rested his arms on his knees, his fingers interlaced.

"Go on," Irene said.

He lifted his face to her shadowed one again. "So, we were in Market Square, having a fundraising rally, a last-ditch attempt. Rory and I were there, in the square. You need to understand this, though, 'cause it's important to see how stupid it all was. There were lots of people in the square, that's true, but only about four hundred of our boys. The rest, over a thousand others, they were just people, just ordinary people, kids and families and citizens, just curious citizens come to see us. Most of the trekkers were over watching a baseball game, see. It was Dominion Day. It was a holiday."

There had been the smell of cotton candy in the air, he remembered that.

"Folks were sitting in rows of chairs, listening to the speeches. Then a note was passed up to the stage, to Slim, saying that the square's surrounded by Mounties. There were three wagons. It was so hot they'd left the doors open so they could breathe, I guess, and we could see them, the yellow stripes on their legs. It all happened so fast. A whistle blew and then out of nowhere came the city police, swinging clubs and heading for the stage. They got to Slim Evans and hit him down and the same with George Black, and they hauled them into a wagon and off they drove. I guess they were looking for all seven leaders, but they only got two for all their trouble."

He remembered the look on Rory's face, the awful pallor that had come over it, and he guessed he'd looked about the same. Their eyes had met. "We'll stick together," Rory had said.

"Then out swarmed the Mounties, wearing those steel helmets they wear when they're bringing trouble with them. It took less than a minute, maybe. Rory and I got separated."

David twisted and turned in the sea of bodies, trying to catch sight of his friend, feeling as if he was drowning, looking for a lifeline. He glimpsed Rory's head, farther away with every minute, and his hand rose and then disappeared as David was swept along and he almost began to cry, and felt ashamed for it.

"The people in the square, see, they didn't know what was happening. They just saw these Mounties coming at them with their batons raised and they panicked. Started to run, pushing and shoving. God, the noise was terrible, like an earthquake. People went crazy, and who could blame them? They had their wives to protect, some had their children. I'll never forget their faces. I'm telling you, they didn't look human, they looked like animals—panicked wild animals.

"The police, maybe they went crazy too. They flailed away at anything that moved, and it's a terrible thing to say, but true, they hit people who were down. Women fell and were trampled. Baby carriages were knocked over."

There was this sound, he still heard it sometimes in his nightmares, a woman screaming and the sound of a body falling and the feel of flesh underfoot and no way to stop stepping down ...

"And there was no way to get out. Why didn't they let those people out? What the hell did they think they'd do? A man has to protect himself, his family. They picked up stones, bricks, pieces of wood, chairs, anything they could find and starting flinging it at the cops. 'Course the cops came back with clubs and batons. Folks started tearing off chunks of concrete from the sidewalk and lobbing them.

"The cops threw tear gas. Some of them were caught and tossed right back at them. But there were fellows down all over and the cops were just pummelling the hell out of them. A guy'd go down and then two or three cops'd stand over him, swinging those bats like he was a rat they'd cornered. People were yelling 'Murderers! Murderers! Why don't you just shoot him and be done with it?' The crowd beat any cop unlucky enough to find himself isolated. I don't say I blame people, but it wasn't any better to see the beating on one side than the other. And I did my share. I had a piece of wood, torn off a bench. I swung it a time or two."

David looked up and saw that Irene had covered her mouth with her hand.

That sound, that sound of wood against skull, against bone, the sickening crunch of it, and the face of the man who fell, that puzzled, wide-eyed look just before the eyes rolled up and the knees gave out ...

"It went on for a long time," he said. "I caught sight of Rory now and then, and he had blood on him, but so what? Everyone did."

Rory's face twisted with rage, his teeth bared, his face red with blood pumping and blood spilled. He stopped and smiled and waved at David as though it was all a game and came toward him and then got hit with a billy club across the shoulder and he turned and grabbed the stick and David was hit and when he looked again there was no sight of Rory.

"The square was clear by nine o'clock and the riot spread over to Tenth and Eleventh avenues. The Mounties moved in with horses. We kept throwing rocks and concrete and anything we could get our hands on. The cops swung clubs. Windows were smashed. Guys shimmied up poles trying to get out of the way, up onto rooftops.

"The crowd was crazy-gone now too, and they looked for things to tear up. They were so mad, see, so scared about it all, and we'd been on the road, cooped up in camps, for so long. But no excuses." He clenched his fists until the knuckles cracked. "I'm not making excuses for anyone. The cops made it happen, but I don't excuse us either.

"So, it was a riot, a full-fledged riot by ten o'clock. Cars dragged into the intersection at Eleventh and Cornwall, tear gas everywhere, windows smashed. Then somebody yelled, 'They've got the guns out!' The cops were outnumbered, but hell, we didn't have any guns. They shot into the crowd and people started falling. Horses were screaming. This guy, I saw him get shot and crawl under a streetcar, but the cops dragged him out. Another guy was gut-shot and screaming like hell."

A horse fell on the street and struggled to get up but its leg was broken and a cop stopped as though he was going to shoot it in the head and then didn't and David wished he had because the sound of a screaming horse is an awful demon-bred sound. And the sound of the horse mingled with the sound of the man who'd been shot ... David felt urine run down his leg then, warm as blood. He knew what terror was and how you only felt it when you understood how paper-thin was the membrane of skin that covered you.

"By the time it was over, seventeen people were shot, five of them just plain citizens. The cops had gone in trying to arrest seven men and ended up with more than a hundred in jail and one plainclothes cop beaten to death.

"We were pushed back into the Exhibition Grounds and it was then, as we moved back, that I found Rory. Your uncle was sitting in an alley off Scarth. I nearly missed him. Just happened to glance over and there he was, looking like he was resting, leaning up against the wall. I called him but he didn't answer. I went over, afraid then, for I could see the blood all over him and I thought he'd been shot. But it was weird. I walked up to him and called out, and he just looked over at me and said, 'Hey.' Like nothing at all was wrong, see?"

How to describe the look on Rory's face, puzzled and sad and something more than sad, as if he'd just seen the truth of things and the truth meant something hopeless, something loved and lost.

"His face was swollen and his nose looked busted. I said maybe he should go to a hospital, but he said there was no need. I asked him if he was dizzy, and he said no, but he sort of stumbled as I helped him up and he leaned on me. The cops pushed us back into the Exhibition Grounds and kept the place sealed off, so we couldn't get in or out.

"Rory curled himself up in his bedroll, saying he had a powerful headache but it wasn't anything that a little sleep wouldn't sort out. I let him sleep." *If only he could take that back now. Go back and do more than just put a blanket under his head.* "Lots of guys nursed wounds, and those of us who weren't badly hurt were trying to keep things as calm as possible. We figured they were going to try and starve us out, maybe, and force us to the camp at Lumsden.

"I guess the premier, Jimmy Gardiner, was pretty mad by then, what with Bennett pushing his weight around and taking his power away, and he blamed Ottawa for causing the riot. He finally convinced Bennett that he could get us to disperse peacefully and demanded the government throw out their ideas about sending us to the Lumsden camp. Imagine that. The same thing Slim Evans had been saying how long back? I guess if I saw Bennett on the street, I'd ... well, I don't know what I'd do and that's the truth.

"So, we got some food, no thanks to Bennett, and we started working on getting everybody out of the city in an orderly manner. People were frightened that maybe another riot would break out. I didn't think there was much real chance of that. We were plain tuckered out by then, and hungry and hurt. We were all in a state of shock, maybe. We knew we couldn't trust the government. But still, you don't expect a thing like that, them using guns. There's no way to prepare for it.

"I'm getting tangled up here. I've never told this story before. Not all of it. Sorry."

He met her eyes, shrugged, and then looked down again. It was the only way he could continue making what felt like a confession, and it made him feel like a coward.

"Your uncle ate a little that night. I saw him. I asked him how he was doing, and he said he was all right. Just tired, he said. I think, looking back on it, that something was maybe wrong with his hand then. He had his plate balanced on his knee and was eating with his fork in his left hand, his right hand in his lap. I must have noticed it at the time, but I didn't pay much attention."

The look on Rory's face a kind of peace, a kind of hopeless peace.

"The next morning he was sick to his stomach. Said he couldn't see right. I said we needed a doctor, and he finally agreed that maybe that was a good idea, but his speech was funny, he couldn't move one side of his mouth.

"He was lying on the ground and I tried to get him to sit up because he'd been sick." David looked up at Irene suddenly, as though he'd just remembered she was there. "Do you want to hear this? Maybe I should skip over this part."

"I want to hear it all," said Irene. "I want you to tell me everything."

He didn't have to tell her everything. Rory vomiting blood, his eyes rolled up in his head. Rory's body stiff in a seizure. Rory biting the end off his own tongue. She didn't need to know.

"All right, then. So, I got him sitting up. But I could see maybe he couldn't walk. Big Jim Walburn and Steve Welch stayed with him while I ran to get a doctor. Those cops, they didn't want to let me out of the Exhibition Grounds, but they said they'd send for somebody, and I said how serious it was, that we needed an ambulance quick. I didn't trust them at first, but I guess they were all right, because a doctor came not long after. But it was too late. There wasn't nothing they could do. Maybe if he'd been treated right when he got hit, maybe he would have been all right. But it was just too late. The doctor took one look at him and called for an ambulance right away, and I could see how mad he was, the doctor, and he yelled some pretty foul things. And the ambulance came and they wrapped Rory up in blankets, even though the day was so hot, and they put him on a stretcher. I wanted to go to the hospital with him but they wouldn't let me. They pushed me back.

"They wouldn't let us out to go see him and we thought, maybe, you know, maybe when they got him to the hospital and operated, or gave him medication or something, that maybe he'd be all right.

"The doctor came back the next day. He told us Rory had passed. He said the blow to the head caused bleeding inside the brain. There was nothing he could do. And he said he had your family's name and a photo, even, said he'd write your mother and tell her. He said they'd probably ship the body back to you. I remember that clearly. I would have done it myself. I should have." He pressed his thumbs into the hollow above his eyes. "He was my friend."

"You had no way of knowing."

"They shipped us out the next day. Back on the trains the way we came. Going west again. And we marched in good order, because we felt like we were soldiers in a way, see. Guess maybe that sounds foolish. But it's how we felt. I ended up back in Vancouver for a couple of weeks and then crossed the border, going east. Drifted. No one place seemed any better than any other. But that doesn't matter. I'm rambling again."

"What would have happened to his body, do you think?"

"I'm not sure. I guess maybe the city buried him."

"In a pauper's grave." And she found that hurt as much as anything, that he would lie unnamed and untended when he had been so well loved. "How did he get hurt?" she said. "Do you know?"

"Yeah. Jim Walburn told me he saw it. There was a fellow, a civilian, mind you, just some guy who happened to be around, maybe he lived nearby. I guess he and his wife lost their baby carriage in the commotion. The guy was running around frantic, yelling and screaming had anyone seen his baby, because they were using tear gas then, and he was yelling there was poison in the air, going to kill his baby. Maybe he was from the war and thought it was the mustard gas. I guess they found the carriage overturned and the wife went crazy, thinking the baby had been trampled. The guy grabbed a cop by the lapels, not going to hurt him, just trying to get him to help, you know, like folks think a cop will help them when something bad happens.

"Maybe the cop thought the guy was attacking him, but he started beating on him with his baton, and the guy fell. Rory saw what was going on and came up behind the cop and grabbed the baton away from him. He pushed the cop away and went to help the guy up. That's when it happened. The Mounties saw Rory push the cop. Saw the baton in his hand and misunderstood, maybe."

"And the baby? Did they find the baby?" That was important, it made the difference somehow.

"Yeah. Somebody'd seen the parents get pushed away from the carriage and scooped the baby out before the carriage was overturned. The father had some broken ribs, but he was all right."

They were both tired, and quiet. Irene kept looking at David, who could now meet her gaze.

"Thank you for telling me," she said. She felt hollow and numb, but clean inside too, as though she'd been washed out with icy water. "I know it was hard. You must be pleased the camps are all closed now."

"It doesn't feel much like winning."

"It never does, does it? Things are just over, nothing more. It's so hard to believe I'll never see him again."

There was silence between them. This young man, this stranger really, didn't feel strange anymore. It felt companionable, familial, to have him there, as though he had been adopted through Uncle Rory.

"Where are your people, David?"

"Oh, my mother died some years back, but my father and three brothers are still back home. They're all older than me. Married with kids of their own. We've got a farm in Saskatchewan, a little town called Sonnenfeld. Don't know how much longer the place'll be there, though. Not after these past few years. Last letter from my brother said they were talking about maybe moving to the city."

"Have you thought of going back there?"

"Not much for me there, and they've got enough people to take care of as it is. I'll go back one day, though. I want to see my father again." He shrugged.

"So what are your plans?"

"I'm not sure. I thought I'd go down to Flint, Michigan, maybe. There's a big strike coming down there at General Motors and I thought maybe I could lend a hand."

"Haven't you had enough of that sort of thing?"

"Enough to last a fucking lifetime. Sorry," he said, but she shook her head. "What the hell else am I going to do? Drifting around, picking up a day's work here and there, well, it's not much to sustain a man. So, at least if I'm organizing I feel like I'm maybe doing something worthwhile."

"Yes, I can see that. But if you're ready to stay in one place for a while, I could use your help in the shop. I have a room over the store. It's a good room. Clean. I could offer you room and board, a few dollars a week." She had had no idea she was going to say this. She had not thought about it in advance, but it would serve many ends if he would stay. If her mother took a turn again, she could stay home without losing business. She'd have a man around in case the neighbourhood toughs gave her a hard time. And the only other person in the world she knew who had known her uncle wouldn't just disappear the way everyone else did. "Does that sound like something you'd be interested in?"

He scowled. "I don't want to be a charity case."

"You'd be doing me a favour. The store is a lot for me to handle alone. As you may have guessed, my mother isn't able to help. Maybe one day, but not yet. I could use someone in the store I trust."

"You don't even know me."

"I'm trusting my instincts."

"Not many Jews on this side of Spadina."

"It's no problem."

"Not for you, maybe, but what about your customers?"

She shrugged. "Not any customers I care about keeping."

Finally he said, "I guess that'd be a pretty good deal. I'd be stupid to turn it down." His mouth was dry. She couldn't possibly know what such an offer meant to him, after where he'd been.

"Good," said Irene. She slapped her hands on her knees. "I'm very tired, David, and I've been away from my mother a lot longer than I'd planned. Do you want to stay here tonight? You're welcome to. There's a bed upstairs."

"I think maybe I can manage to survive without having to sleep with five other guys tonight."

"Then, you'll stay."

"So, I'll stay. First I'll walk you home, then I'll go back to Ma Gutkind's and pick up my pack."

David lay on his back on the thin mattress, his hands behind his head. It was hard to believe he was here. Hard to believe he could shut his eyes and wake up in the same place tomorrow and not have to move on. When he'd first come into the room he'd run his hands over the walls, over the top of the table. He'd turned on first one tap and then another, let the water flow over his fingers. He'd filled the bath up to the rim and lay down in it, sinking under the water, letting his ears fill with the silence. He'd stayed in the water until he was wrinkled and waterlogged and almost fell asleep and drowned himself.

He couldn't stop grinning, and yet he didn't want to keep grinning for he was afraid it wouldn't last. What if she changed her mind after a few days, or a week? He vowed to be the perfect worker, the perfect tenant. He'd do whatever it took to be able to keep this room, with a toilet of his very own.

26

January 1937

David sat in his room on New Year's Day morning, drinking a coffee and reading the *Globe and Mail*. The front-page headline said fascists and Nazis were flowing into Spain. Below that was news that Toronto had just spent its merriest New Year's in a decade, the nightclubs full to overflowing. There was a cartoon saying that Old Man Depression's goose was cooked. David thought that if that was true, it was only because war was coming. Things getting better only so they could get worse, he grumbled to himself.

While the rest of the city had apparently been out dancing and drinking and buying gardenias for pretty girls at a buck fifty apiece, he'd been sitting right where he was. But what right did he have, he thought, to be feeling low when life had taken this miraculous turn? Only a month ago he'd been homeless and near destitute.

It had been only two weeks since he'd moved in and started working. There were nights when he woke up, his heart racing after some dream-demon, panicked, sure it would all prove to be a figment of his imagination. He'd reach out and touch the wall, the bed, the floor, until reassured by their solidity. The tension of the past years was lessening with each day, and he was slowly learning to trust that Irene was as good as her word. He put his edginess to good advantage, pouring the energy into work. He liked working in the store, liked waiting on the customers, filling up brown bags with small purchases, tidying the stockroom, joking with the boys who hung around.

David took care of the ice cream counter while Irene dealt with customers on the other side of the store. He handled the heavy work of the stockroom. He did the cleaning and let her go home at the end of the day without worrying about that, at least. He liked making her life easier and he liked the steady rhythm of his days.

He even got a kick out of the look on some of the customers' faces when they saw him. "And where's your family from?" they'd say. And he'd say, "Saskatchewan." And they'd say, "The prairies?" and he could see them thinking, But he can't be Jewish then, can he—do they have Jews in the prairies? He'd wink at Irene and say, "Just call me Dave, ma'am," and leave them puzzling.

The little apartment above the store felt like home, which was a feeling he hadn't had since he'd left Sonnenfeld. The place was as clean as a sun-bleached sheet. He'd become a fanatic for cleanliness, sometimes taking two baths a day and never letting a dish sit dirty in the sink. There were curtains on the window that Irene had made herself. Three white plates in the cupboard and two white cups. A pot, a pan. A chair to read in and a good lamp behind for the evenings. He liked the watery winter light on the walls and thought he might like to get a picture or two to put up. There was a desk, there was a chair.

On the shelf he'd put up above the desk, next to second-hand paperback copies of Jack London's *Iron Heel* and Edward Bellamy's *Looking Backward,* stood a filled-up notebook. Saved from the fire for the time being, at least. Lying on the middle of the desk itself was a brand-new fifteen-cent hardcover book with all but the first few pages blank and the rest as full of empty space and possibility as a cloudless dawn.

He'd thought he might not have much to write about, a family-owned notions store, a room, no great labour battles to fight. However, he was finding the pages were filled with different sorts of observations, about kids and their crushes on each other played out over the ice cream counter, about the rhythms of the street and the fruit vendors who came at dawn to unload their fresh produce. About the grey fatigue of middle-aged women looking for a little escape in cheap novels and the promises of face powder.

He picked up the journal now and scanned his entry for December 25. *A Jew at the feast of Jesus,* he read, *maybe I should have brought a bar-mitzvah gift.* He'd been surprised to be included in the invitation the Watkinses had extended to Irene and her mother, being both a stranger and a Jew, but Ebbie Watkins had insisted, and who was he to pass up a free meal? Mrs. MacNeil had refused to go, but Irene had managed to gain her mother's permission for an hour after dinner.

The house was a baffling and boisterous chorus of chaos. Isabel and Lisa Watkins, Ebbie's sisters, had five kids between them, and this tribe was involved in a complicated made-up game that involved dashing about the rooms and grabbing handfuls of nuts or candies while at the same time avoiding the good-natured swats of their parents. Isabel and Lisa stood by the piano, singing a loud and magnificently off-key rendition of "God Rest Ye, Merry Gentlemen," accompanied by their mother, who flailed at the keys as though flapping dust. Their respective husbands lazed in the afterglow of too much turkey, the top button of their pants undone, and took turns beating each other at checkers. Ebbie chased the children and seemed like an overgrown kid herself. David and Irene and Mike Hughian, Ebbie's red-haired beau, stood in a corner trying to talk over the din.

Just after nine o'clock the front door opened and, along with an icy blast of air, in came a tall man in a baggy Santa Claus suit, lugging a pillowcase full of gifts. He smelled of gin.

David heard Irene's gasp as she spilled her ginger ale.

"Sorry, Irene," said Mike. "We didn't know Harry'd turn up."

"Ho, ho, ho," said the man.

"Merry Christmas! Merry Christmas!" yelled the children, circling round him like mice around a block of smelly cheese.

"I'm going to go," said Irene.

"Don't go," said Ebbie, who had appeared at her elbow and was dabbing at her skirt with a cloth.

Madison excused himself, going up the stairs, no doubt to the toilet to have another toot, thought David. When he came back down he'd removed the Santa suit and cleaned himself up a bit. He cut an undeniably dashing figure, the cloth of his suit expensive, his tie silk.

David felt shabby then, and the feeling made him angry. Even looking at the thick black hair on his forearms made him feel less civilised than this smooth pale man. Harry was not that much taller than David, and yet David felt squat around him. The rag picker's son. The fruit man with his cart and horse.

"It's getting late," Irene said. "It's been wonderful, really. Tell your mother thank you for me." She turned toward the kitchen. The coats and boots had been left in the back porch.

"I'll walk you home," said David.

"No, I'm fine. Really. I'll just slip out this way."

"I'm so sorry, 'Reen. I didn't know, honestly. There's no telling with Harry," said Ebbie.

"Yes, I found that out," said Irene and she disappeared out the door.

27

February 1937

"I'll bet young David's glad he stuck around here where it's safe and didn't head down to Michigan," said Margaret with her nose in the morning paper.

"Why, what does it say?"

"They're going to use machine guns and bayonets if the strikers don't vacate."

"That's awful! I mean, a quarter of the people in that town— Flint, isn't it?—they work at the plant, don't they? The police are their neighbours. How can they turn guns on their neighbours?"

"That David's a smart one. Found himself a soft place to land. But then, they're all smart, aren't they?"

"Oh, Mother, don't generalize."

"Well, then, Jews. They're a smart people. Everyone knows that. They're tricky."

"Tricky? Now why would you think David's tricky?" Her mother had never been anti-Semitic. In fact, it had been Margaret who had defended the Jews when her father spoke ill of them.

"You make it sound like I'm saying a bad thing. I'm not. I'm just remarking that the Jewish people have an ability to survive, they're a little slippery."

"What nonsense! There's nothing slippery about David. He's the most forthright person I know."

Margaret got up to pour more coffee. *Quiet. Quiet. Keep your mouth shut.* She knew he had cast some dark Jewish spell on Irene, some malevolent charm. How else could he have persuaded Irene to give him a place to live, and practically for free? The problem had to be approached by a circuitous route. She leaned against the counter and watched her daughter.

"I want to make Yorkshire pudding for dinner on Sunday, and roast beef. I need you to go to the butcher's."

"Fine."

"Did you hear? They say the Germans are going to invade Czechoslovakia."

"Yes, I heard that," said Irene, sipping her coffee and leafing through the paper her mother had left. "It's here. Front page."

"We should be prepared. Those *bastards!*" Margaret shook her fists near her temples. "Someone should kill them all! War will come!"

"We can hope for the best, can't we?" Irene tried to keep her voice level.

"I can see things you can't. Bastards! So much evil! You don't know where it will come from next!"

Irene said nothing. Her mother had made significant progress, and the doctor had agreed that she probably didn't need to be institutionalized. She hadn't regained the ground she'd lost but could at least be left alone during the day, although she became fretful as evening fell. She kept herself clean and cooked meals. But she was still paranoid, and the paranoia had taken on this angry edge.

"Bastards!" she said again, but quietly, baring her teeth, and then, "You still think it was a good idea, having a Jewish clerk in the store?"

Irene hated it when her mother circled back again and again like a little mosquito.

"I think having David in the store is one of the best ideas I've ever had. You know, he's got a great head for business."

"Well, they all do, those people."

"Mother, stop it, really. You should hear the way you talk sometimes."

"I talk the way other people talk, and don't go calling me anti-Semitic either, young lady. I don't like what's happening to Jews in Germany. I believe in live and let live. I just think it's better that people stick to their own kind. That's the way they want it too, you know. Jews live together over in Kensington, running their little kosher markets and whatnot. Why, when I was a girl, there was a rag picker, a tinker who went door to door selling things. My mother always gave him lemonade in the summer. He loved to gossip. He was a nice old fellow with a long beard and those funny ringlets. We were glad to see him, but he lived somewhere else, with his own kind. That's the way they want it. They have their own ways. They're not like us." She looked at Irene. "Which makes you ask yourself, what's young Hirsch doing up on this side of the table?"

"I think David's very nice."

"None of the good stores will hire Jews, you know. There's a reason for that. People don't like to be served by Jews—not me, mind you, so don't look at me that way, but other people. You've read those sermons in the *Telegram*, the ones from Knox Presbyterian. 'Invidious Jews,' they call them. What does *invidious* mean, anyway?"

"Unpleasant."

"I thought it meant odious."

"Close enough."

"I'm just saying, Irene."

"Mum, I have to go." Irene put her cup in the sink without rinsing it, which she knew would irritate her mother.

Margaret slathered another piece of toast with marmalade. She picked a chunk of orange rind from the jelly and ate it like candy. *Careful. Careful. Things must be arranged just so. One had to be cautious to avoid the nasty traps God sent one's way.*

It never stopped, the constant natter, natter, natter, pick, pick, pick. Ever since she'd woken up that morning and found her mother hovering over her, she'd been a little afraid of her. It wasn't that her mother would ever hurt her intentionally—*would she?*—but sometimes the things she did and said were so, so ... crazy. Irene was perplexed by the dislike for Jewish people that had grown in her mother since David arrived. She wondered if, because David had been the one to bring the bad news, and because David was Jewish, Margaret had, in her faulty way, concluded that all Jews were to blame.

As she walked into the shop, David's head popped up from behind the ice cream counter.

"Morning. Thought maybe you decided to take the day off," he said.

"Can't I be a few minutes late if I want to? It is my shop, after all."

David held his hands up in front of him as though to ward her off. "Yes, *ma'am.*"

David glanced at her as he cleaned the spigots on the soda fountain. She had hung her coat in the back and was tying the white apron she always wore around her waist. There were circles under her eyes and a rigid tremor in the way she held herself, as though she were afraid she'd crumple up if she let go.

"So, I got a pot of coffee upstairs," he said. "I could get you a cup if you want."

"Okay," she said, without looking at him. "Yes, thanks. I could use one."

David went up the narrow tilting steps to his room and came back down with two mugs of steaming coffee, hers thick and caramel-coloured with cream.

"Here," he said. She leaned up against the counter and closed her hands around the heavy crockery, shut her eyes and breathed in the scent. She opened her eyes and looked at David, who stood near her sipping his own coffee.

"You all right?"

"I'm fine."

"You don't look so fine."

"Thanks very much." She pursed her lips.

"I don't mean you don't look good. You always look good." He tugged his earlobe. "I just mean you look like you're inside too much. Spend too much time indoors."

"You think I'm too pale?"

"Not too pale. A little pale. We farmers, you know, we've got an obsession with fresh air." He winked at her, at least she thought it was a wink. "So, how's your mother doing?"

"Mum's dandy," she said. "Just dandy."

"Then, the problem is clearly one of fresh air. You got skates?"

"Skates? Ice skates?"

"No, I'm thinking the weather is good for roller-skating, maybe. Yes, of course ice skates."

"I think I had some when I was six, so even if I found them I doubt they'd fit. Why?"

"Doesn't matter, we'll rent some. I think it's a good idea. You and me, we're going to go skating tonight after work."

"I don't want to go skating."

"You don't want to?"

"No, David, I don't want to go ice-skating."

"So who asked you if you wanted to go?" He looked at her with such mock severity that she was forced to grin at him. "I think we'll work it out this way: you get to be boss in the store, but me, I get to be boss of the skating rink."

"Oh, you do, do you?"

"Yeah, I think maybe that's a good plan. Now here's what we'll do." He counted off the points on the tips of his big fingers. "You call your mother, tell her not to make supper for you. Since she is so dandy she won't mind. We close up the store at the regular time. I feed you a big bowl of my chicken stew, famous in hobo jungles throughout the continent. We go to the Riverdale Park. We skate until you lose that prison pallor. At this time I buy you hot chocolate. I then see you home, a new and revived young woman."

"I don't know, David."

"Irene, you gotta have a life."

"I have a life."

"Yeah. But I'm not so sure the life you have is your own."

David laced the skates on her feet. He drew her up onto the ice, holding her hands. The night was cold. Irene wobbled and gripped David tighter.

"Relax," he said. "Just relax."

"You can really skate," she said, seeing how easy he was on the slippery surface, which threatened to toss her off her feet at any second.

"Not much to do in Sonnenfeld in the winter. We were big hockey fans. We all thought we'd grow up to be King Clancy. Never mind he's Irish. Never mind he's as Catholic as the Pope's pointed hat."

"I guess there aren't any Jews in the professional teams, are there?" she said, watching her feet carefully.

"Not yet. But you wait."

Her foot shot out and he made a grab for her waist and arm, steadying her.

"And you call yourself a Canuck," he teased. "Nobody'd believe it."

They circled the rink once and then twice. She had her hand tucked up in his arm and she began to trust the feeling. Their breath formed small white clouds around their faces.

"I used to come skating with my mum and dad," she said, "when I was really little."

David took her hand and spun out in front so he was facing her. "Close your eyes," he said.

"Why?"

"Go on. Close 'em. Let me lead you. Trust me, I won't let you fall."

And so she did, and she held his hands and he skated backwards and drew her around the ice. She tipped her head back and let the cold wind hit her face and the darkness invade her body completely. She felt as if she were flying like a night bird over the clouds. She felt the subtle shift from foot to foot, the roll and dance of this movement, the sturdy heaviness of his hands beneath her weight. He pulled her in a circle, and the noise of the other skaters faded into the background. She kept her eyes closed and it felt as though what was inside was bigger than what was outside, like a crust of something thin and silvery, crisp with cold, covered a vast landscape of star-filled dark inside her. The only thing that connected her to the ground was the slim blade under her feet and the solid flesh at the point where she ended and David began.

David watched her face intently, felt her muscles relax under his touch. He let go of the breath he'd been holding when he saw the frown disappear from her forehead and the smile come to her lips. He smiled himself then, and knew that he had taught her the wonder of letting go. For just a moment he gave her the gift of unburdened lightness.

When Irene got home her nose and her fingers tingled with cold and her ears felt like frozen metal had been held against them. She stamped the snow off her feet and gently rubbed her ears to get the blood flowing. She had stayed out far longer than she'd planned.

Her mother stood at the top of the stairs with a bowl in her hands.

"I thought that would be you," Margaret said. She had pincurls all over her head, the metal bobby pins sticking out this way and that.

"You're up late."

"You know I can't sleep until I know you're safely home.

287

Anything can happen to a girl these days. The streets are full of criminals."

"I wasn't alone."

"Two girls! That's not safe. You shouldn't go out at night anymore."

"I was with David." Irene felt bold and reckless after her wonderful evening.

"David! You said you were going out with Ebbie!"

"She couldn't come."

"So you went out with this David?" *Hush! Hush! You knew it would happen. I can still control this. Weed out this thistle in our midst.*

"Yes. What's in the bowl?"

"Oatmeal. It's good for the complexion."

Irene could feel her mother's eyes on her, so hungry, so reddened by craving, but for what? More of me, Irene thought. Margaret blocked her way up the stairs and into the dubious refuge of her room.

"I'm going to get a cup of warm milk. Do you want one?" she said, turning away.

The hackles rose on her back as she heard her mother's footsteps on the stairs.

"Here, Mum, I'll take that. Did you want milk?" She reached out to take the green glass bowl. Her mother had a dollop of grey sticky oatmeal clinging to her jaw, another by her ear, as though she'd been eating from the bowl like a dog. *Where were these thoughts coming from?* This was her mother. Irene mustn't think like that.

"It's all right. I'll come with you. Come on, let's go," she said, shooing at Irene. "So, did you have a good time?"

"Yes, actually, it was fun."

"Just David and you," Margaret said. She handed the milk to Irene, who poured some into a chipped white enamel pot and gave the rest back to her mother.

"Uh-huh." Irene scattered a pinch of nutmeg in the milk.

"Irene, you can't think that's wise."

"Here's your milk, Mum. I'm exhausted. I'm going to bed."

Irene kissed her mother on the cheek and felt a dab of oatmeal stick to her lip. She brushed it off with distaste.

"I'd just hate to see you get hurt, dear." Margaret's voice followed her down the hall. "I can't imagine what any nice boy would think of you if he knew you were out gallivanting with a Jew."

"Good night, Mum."

"You never would listen to good advice. Don't come crying to me later, then. You'll see! You'll see." She stuck her knuckles in her mouth to stop the words.

"Good *night*, Mum." As she closed the door to the bathroom she heard her mother slam a cupboard door.

Next to the sink an oatmeal-covered washcloth lay in a soggy heap. Irene rinsed it off and hung it over the towel rack to dry.

She looked at the large tub with the friendly lion's feet and thought about running a bath. It would warm her up and give her a pool in which to wash away the confusion from her thoughts. *Her life. Her mother's life. Was David right? Did it have to be one or the other?* But a bath would mean she wasn't sleeping and her mother might well be waiting for her when she got out. She filled up the red rubber hot-water bottle with water so hot it scalded when it splashed on her fingers. She went into her bedroom and closed the door as quietly as possible behind her, leaning against it for a moment. She looked at the wooden chair across the room in front of her desk and considered putting it against the door. *She gets to do it, so why can't I?*

Irene changed into her pyjamas and put thick socks on her ice-block feet. She slipped between the sheets and held the hot-water bottle to her stomach. Slowly the warmth spread throughout her body, sending goose bumps along her arms and legs.

She heard her mother clump up the stairs and settle into her own bed. Irene rolled onto her side. She folded the sheet over and smoothed the surface, then tucked the edge of the bedclothes up to her chin. This felt right. Some nights it felt right to have her ears under the covers. It was a question of sensing the energies of the night. As a tiny child she'd lain in bed and then decided covers up or covers down. The right choice made the difference as to whether her dreams would be good or bad. Superstitious, she knew, but wasn't there more out in the world than she was able to make sense of? Look at tonight, for example.

Cold. Wind. Dark. Movement. David's hands.

Irene found herself considering his hands. They were large hands, and work worn even though he was so young. They were not beautiful, tapered, well-tended hands such as Harry had. She had been surprised to find them so gentle, so deliberate in their actions, as though David knew the strength that lay behind them could crush or crack or mangle, and was careful.

28

July 1937

"They say this is the hottest summer in Canadian history," said Margaret, reading the paper. She and Irene sat in the kitchen with both the back and front doors open, hoping to catch some sort of a breeze. "It's 105.1 today."

"Uh-huh," said Irene. She fanned herself with a magazine.

"It says here thirty men were arrested for indecent exposure at the city beaches for wearing bathing suits that failed to cover their chests. Imagine that! And people are dying. The newspaper's publishing lists, like the dead were war casualties."

I know, I know. Do we have to keep talking about it? It was all anyone talked about all over the city and her customers spoke of nothing else. Even David, usually so energetic, was a melting mass of irritability and exhaustion. Every night he joined the thousands who left their sweat-box houses and apartments to sleep on the grass along the lakeshore at Sunnyside Beach or the grounds of the Canadian National Exhibition. You couldn't buy a fan anywhere in the city. Dogs tied out in the yard during the day died from lack of water by the time their owners returned. Three children roasted alive after they had climbed, just for fun, into the family DeSoto and almost immediately fell into a heat-induced stupor.

The crime rate soared, not with crimes that took a lot of planning (for it was too hot to think) or much effort (too hot to scale a wall, or dig a tunnel underneath a bank, or even run from a robbery) but with crimes of dubious passion. The stabbing to the heart that might, in cooler, less nerve-grating weather, have been nothing more than a few broken plates. Neighbours fought over things that had been tolerated for decades. Women slapped their children for misdemeanours that a month before would have been overlooked with a loving eye. Men stood in the middle of the street and threw their hats to the ground and then their fists into the noses of other men, along with a torrent of curse words, and all for the sake of a bumped shoulder or a sideways glance.

Irene and Margaret were too exhausted by the weather to be anything more than irritable. They lay about in torpid heaps sipping cool water and lemon, fanning the fat sluggish flies away and mopping at their sweating necks and arms and chests.

Irene wished she could shut down the shop until it was all over. Shopkeepers stood in their doorways, hoping to catch a whiff of a breeze, and complained that sales were down. Some people fainted over factory belts and machinery, and accidents were plentiful. The hospitals were the busiest places in town, between the damage caused to limbs from these mishaps and cases of heat stroke and heart attack and dehydration. Irene decided the one blessing from the heat wave was an increased demand for ice cream.

For once, their house looked the same as every other house on the street, as people tried to keep the sun at bay by pulling every blind and curtain. Margaret huddled in the darkened recesses.

"You're not listening," she said.

"I'm sorry," Irene said. "It's just been a long, hot day."

"Well, it's not a picnic being trapped in this oven alone all day either, I'll tell you."

"You don't have to be trapped here, Mum."

There was silence, and Irene knew she shouldn't have said this. Then her mother said something, but so low Irene couldn't hear it.

"Pardon?"

"I have tried, Irene."

"I know, Mum."

Margaret sat with her skirt hiked up, and folded a piece of newspaper into a fan. Irene took a sip of the sweating glass of lemonade in her hand.

"I would have liked a cottage," said her mother. "A place to look out over the lake. My mother and father used to have a little place they rented every summer on Beaver Lake, did I ever tell you?" And of course she had, but Irene said nothing. "The kids were like little fishes, never out of the water. We picked blueberries and played badminton. Mum and Daddy played whist and cribbage in the evenings."

"Must have been nice."

"It was. Everyone was doing so well then. We thought it would go on forever. And then the war came and changed everything, everyone. Did you read the number of dead? As of this morning's paper there were 458 dead in Ontario, 220 in Toronto alone. We could die in our beds, cooked. Roasted alive. Imagine what it must be like to live like some of the poor, in rooms with no windows, even. Poor little children. I heard a man on the radio today talking about children lying in wet mud under a porch to get cool, like little dogs."

"We'll never get any sleep in the house tonight," Irene agreed, somewhat surprised by her mother's empathy for children she didn't know. "Lots of people are going down to the beach to sleep. Thousands, in fact. What do you say we join them? At least there might be a cool breeze down by the water."

"That's not possible."

"Anything's possible, Mum. You just have to believe it." But not even Irene did.

"I couldn't."

"You could if you wanted to."

"What do you know?"

"All right, Mum. Forget it."

They sat in silence for some minutes, and Irene was halfway into a heat-induced doze when she heard her mother's voice.

"I'm not sleeping with a bunch of strangers."

"Nobody's a stranger in this heat. It's too hot for strangers."

"It's too far."

"Well, what say we go down to the Gardens, then?" It was important to keep her voice calm. "I passed Mr. Steedman on the street yesterday and he said he takes his family down there to sleep now, like camping out. He said it's fun."

"Mr. Steedman does that?" Her mother held Mr. Steedman up as the pinnacle of propriety, had done ever since that night so long ago when he had brought her dad home in a state best not discussed.

"Yes. We'd see him there."

"I don't know."

"Oh, please, Mum. Just for a half an hour, even, we'll see how it goes. It's only down the street and if it's not proper, in any small way, even, we can come right back. I'll bring down the mattress from the lawn chair for you. It'll be better than sweltering to death here, you have to admit."

"If we leave the house, robbers might come. This is the perfect time for them. They know people aren't at home."

"What do we have? What would anyone want to steal?"

Margaret looked around the kitchen as though she hadn't seen it in a long time. "We don't have much, do we."

"It would be all right, Mum. We could do this."

Margaret put her fingers over her lips. "All right, then. I could try. Irene? Yes, I think I'll try."

It came as a shock to both of them.

For the first time in five years, Margaret MacNeil walked down the front porch of her house, along the path to the sidewalk and kept on going. And although she had a frown of concentration on her brow, there was a slight smile on her lips. Neither of them commented on the novelty. They walked quietly, Margaret carrying a pair of pillows and two light sheets, and Irene lugging a blanket for herself and the lawn-chair mattress for her mother.

They set their pallet on the grass a respectable distance from the other relief-seekers. They saw the Steedmans not far away, their two boys long-legged teenagers now. Irene waved and Mrs. Steedman waved back and put a hand on her husband's arm, smiling. Mr. Steedman smiled as well and touched his forefinger to his temple in salute. Margaret nodded to them, shy. All around, people quietly settled in for the night, a lumpy carpet of bodies across the lawns. Babies cried and were hushed. Occasional laughter was heard, for it was almost festive here. Children, excited by the strange carnival atmosphere of sleeping under the stars with so many strangers, wanted to run and play, but were so exhausted by the effort of getting through the sizzling day that even they floated toward sleep without protest.

Irene lay on the sheet, with a portion folded over her legs for modesty's sake. Her mother was silent, and Irene didn't care why. It only mattered that her mother, with surprisingly little protest, had come out in the world. It was a miracle. Irene gazed up at the dome of stars and offered thanks to whomever might be listening. Margaret sat, stiffly leaning against a tree trunk, her hands clasped in her lap, her feet straight out in front of her. Her eyes roamed over the park, as though she were a sentinel on her watch. Irene reached over and gave her mother's birdlike hand a reassuring squeeze. Her mother patted her hand and smiled at her.

"Go to sleep, Kitten," she said. "Go to sleep." Just like any mother to her child. Just like any mother at all.

Irene tucked her hand beneath her cheek and closed her eyes and was asleep before she could think one more puzzled thought.

For some time Margaret sat and watched the sweep of bodies all around her. She listened to the swell and release of breath from so many sets of lungs, not unlike the whisper of ocean waves. Why did it seem so easy to be here, when it ought to be so hard? She lay her palm flat on the grass beside her, ruffled it as if it were hair. It felt brittle and sharp after so long a dry spell. A waft of tobacco smoke floated past her nose and she glanced to see where it came from. A man about her age sat not far away, his legs bent and his arms resting on his knees. A handmade cigarette dangled from between his fingers and his head was bowed low. He looked thoroughly beaten, thought Margaret. The seam of his shirt was torn at the shoulder. He was in need of a haircut and a shave. *Poor man. He needs someone to take care of him.*

I am in a crowd of people. I am floating in a sea of people. The words kept surfacing from the pool of her consciousness like her own reflected face. *I am outside, outside, outside ...* Why had she stayed inside for so long? It made no sense to her now. These people were not a threat to her. *But couldn't they be? Couldn't they turn and begin to slather and snap at you at any moment? Aren't they just waiting for you to let down your guard?* Margaret closed her eyes and rubbed her ears. *Go away. I am trying to be better. I am smart and can learn.*

She looked at Irene. Had she said that aloud? The girl didn't move, slept on with her mouth open slightly and a frown on her forehead. She always seemed to have that small crouched frown, thought Margaret.

Look at me. Look at me. Here I am under a starry sky.

Margaret didn't want to sleep. She was filled with a delicious sensation of belonging. A woman, just a woman sitting with her back up against a tree. With other people.

It wasn't so complicated. As long as we are together, as long as Irene is at my side, I will be all right, thought Margaret as she drifted off. I will be all right.

29

"Listen to what I'm telling you," said Mike. "Nazi planes raid the Basque town of Guernica. It's an appalling massacre. The *Ciudad de Barcelona*, on its way from Marseille to Barcelona, is torpedoed by an Italian submarine. The ship's carrying volunteers to fight in

Spain, among them, I might add, a number of Canadians. You have to consider that an act of war."

"I'm just saying that I think there's a place for diplomacy," said Ebbie. "For heaven's sake, you men are always so ready to go off and shoot at something."

"An ambassador is an honest man sent to lie abroad for the good of his country," said Mike. "Henry Wooton, 1604."

"Walk softly and carry a big stick. Teddy Roosevelt," said David. "Some time more recent."

Ebbie, Mike, David and Irene sat in a booth at Murray's Restaurant, finishing up the last of their coffee and apple pie. The heat wave had evaporated into a sweet, warm summer, and when Ebbie and Mike had come by the shop at closing time and invited her to join them for a walk, she hadn't been able to resist. Her mother had been better, Irene thought, since the night they had slept out in the park, but still, Margaret was none too pleased when she'd called. "Fine, then, do as you please. You always do." Her mother would not go back to the park, no matter how much Irene pleaded, although she did say Irene could go without her. Irene had stayed with her mother, though, as they both knew she would. But still, there had been improvements. Her mother had accompanied her to the market once, and once she had walked with her to the end of the street and back. She sometimes even sat out alone in the garden, or on the porch.

And David had come too. He was going to see a boxing match later, between Sammy Luftspring and Frankie Genovese, and had some time to kill.

"Fascist bastards," he now said, "sinking a volunteer ship. They were sitting ducks."

"I read they were in the water for hours, drowning. They sang that song, what is it, the Communist song?" said Irene.

"The *Internationale*," said David. "And our prime minister, dear old Mackenzie King, goes to meet with Hitler and says he was 'charmed.' *Charmed!* Can you believe that? Both him and Chamberlain—Jew haters."

"Bad time for Jews in Germany," said Mike. "And getting worse in the rest of Europe, too."

"So, you think this is new? This isn't new. Let me tell you. The Cossacks with their boots to the head, the door bashed in, the raped women. The Russians. The Poles. The Germans. Can't buy land, can't live in this town, can't live in that. My great-uncle was shot to death in front of his wife, and her two babies bayoneted right after him. My uncle, my father's own brother, just a baby, was tossed down a well and drowned!"

"We're all lucky to live in Canada, no matter how hard it is at the moment," said Mike into silence after David's speech.

"You think it's so different here? Can't work behind a counter at Eaton's. Can't buy a cottage in the Muskokas." David slapped the table with each new *can't*. "Can't be a doctor in a hospital. Can't study law at the University of Toronto. You've seen the signs on the park benches, at the Sunnybrook Pool—'No Jews or Dogs'? Yeah. It's bad for Jews, all right. Worse if you're Negro. And if you're an Indian? Forget about it!"

People turned to look.

"What're you looking at? Jews not allowed in here either?"

A woman tut-tutted.

"People are only looking at you because you're shouting," said Irene, although she wasn't sure, now that she said it, whether this was true or not.

"So maybe I have good reason to shout."

"Yes, maybe you do. But why are you shouting at us?"

"Because I'm pissed off, is why!"

"Sorry, David. Didn't mean to say anything to offend you," said Mike, looking downcast.

"Usually it's me who says the wrong thing," said Ebbie.

"It's early yet," said Mike, and she punched him.

David said, "No, it's me. You didn't say anything wrong. I'm sorry. Maybe I'm not used to being with all you heathens." He laughed softly. "It's hard to sit by and do nothing when I know what's going on over there. Could be my relatives, see? And I know it's going to get worse. I don't know how much longer I'm going to be able to stay out of it."

Things would get worse. David was right. And maybe he would leave. And then what would Irene do? It hadn't been long, but she'd come to depend on him. She wasn't sure she liked that. When people took care of you, they wanted a great deal in return, and then it was hard to tell just who was taking care of whom. She didn't want any more of that.

But was it so simple? There were moments, watching him as he joked with the customers, or the way he tugged his ear when he was nervous, that her feelings for David were confusing. Sometimes it was his face that formed in her dreams, and his laughter, and his hands, and she woke, as she did now from her reverie, to the sound of his voice.

"Listen, folks, why don't you come to the fight with me?" said David. Maybe being the minority in a crowd would do them some good. The place was bound to be filled with Jews and Italians.

"I've got to get back," said Irene.

"I think I might like to see the match," said Mike. He pushed his glasses up on his nose and looked at Ebbie. "What do you think, honey?"

"Sounds exciting. I'm game." Ebbie grinned and clapped her hands. "Oh, Irene, it'll be fun. Come on."

She blushed and said nothing. She hated that her cheeks went red.

David watched her. "I know your mum was upset when you called earlier, but if she's mad already … Besides, she's a bit better these days, right? This is a great fight, two great fighters. And Sammy, he's a kinda hero. Him and Baby Yak could've gone to the Olympics in Berlin, but they didn't go on account of Hitler. They wrote a letter to the papers and said so. I got a copy of it. Sammy would've won a gold medal, but he wouldn't go to a country that was, like he said, 'treating his brothers and sisters worse than dogs.' You have to see this guy. He's going to flatten Genovese. Come on. Think of it as an educational experience."

"I'd like to." It was a little dangerous, and felt exciting. She'd never done anything like this.

Ebbie put a hand on hers. "Your mother will be all right, Irene. She has to get used to being on her own. I mean, you can't be with her forever, now, can you? She might surprise you by being tougher than you think."

"I don't know ... Yes, all right! I'll come."

"There you go!" said Ebbie.

"Good for you!" said Mike.

"So, let's go. We got to get tickets," said David.

As they approached Maple Leaf Gardens they could see the crowd milling about. Thousands of people, mostly Jewish and Italian, yelling good-natured taunts at each other and making side bets.

"Geez," said David, scanning the crowd. "I knew it was going to be big."

"It's sooo exciting!" squealed Ebbie.

The arena was crowded and noisy with men yelling and talking and smoking cigarettes and big cigars. The smoke was already thick in the air, even though the match wouldn't start for another twenty minutes. As they walked in, David greeted a man here, a man there, shaking hands and slapping guys on the back.

"Irene, Mike, Ebbie, I want you to meet my pals. This is Lenny, Ben and Simon."

"Nice ta meet ya," said Lenny, with a toothpick in his mouth.

"How you doing?" said Simon.

"Some crowd, eh?" said Ben.

"He's gonna kill him," said Lenny.

"Genovese doesn't stand a chance," said David.

"Genovese's a bum," said Ben.

"Hey, you watch who you call a bum!" said a man standing behind them. "Frankie's the Italian Bomber. He gonna cream you guy."

"Yeah, yeah, words, words," said Lenny and he spit on the floor without removing his toothpick.

David checked the tickets and led them to their seats. Irene thought that if the ceiling had been any lower they would have choked to death from the smoke. Below them was the brightly lit boxing ring. Men milled around it, talking to each other and taking notes. A table ran along one side, where four men sat, one with a round bell in front of him.

Irene looked around. The men had their hats off or tilted back on their heads, their faces shiny in the warm air. Coats were off, ties were undone. A few women punctuated the mostly male crowd, and they were either one of two types: beautiful, satin-clad girls on the arms of well-dressed, important-looking men or tough-looking women, older mostly, wearing ill-fitting dresses.

"Get a load of her," said Ebbie and pointed. A woman in the next row down had her hair in a complicated bun and wore a man's suit.

"Well, I never," said Irene.

"I'll bet she has," said Ebbie.

As for the men, there were all types. Young and old, well-heeled and well-mended. Elegant men in evening dress and men in overalls. Irene felt breathless.

"So, you okay?" David asked her.

"Yes."

"Looks like all the market and Little Italy's here, too," said David. "Ain't it grand!"

In a few minutes a man climbed into the ring amidst a roar of applause and hooting. He held his hand up and a microphone was lowered from the ceiling.

"Ladies and gentlemen. Tonight's fight is a single bout, welterweight division, fifteen-rounder. And ... in this corner ... Frankie Genovese, weighing in at 145 pounds." Into the ring stepped a young man in red trunks. He danced about the ring, punching the air in front of him. "And in this corner ... Sammy Luftspring, weighing in at 142 pounds." This one wore a Star of David on his boxing shorts. David jumped up and cheered, his face lit with a big grin. Irene, Ebbie and Mike stood up too.

The two men met in the middle of the ring, where the referee, wearing a striped shirt, gave them their instructions.

David leaned over to Irene. "Okay, so this is what you need to know. Sammy's a counter-puncher. This means he only hits when the other guy hits, takes advantage of his mistakes, doesn't tire himself out trying to flail away. But Genovese's no bum, don't listen to what those guys said. He's about the most experienced boxer in all Toronto. This is going to be some fight."

Sammy Luftspring surprised everyone by changing tactics for the fight. From the opening bell he came out throwing punches. He tagged Frankie Genovese a couple of good hard whacks. And the crowd went wild. In the fifth round Genovese dropped to one knee, but didn't go down. In the sixth, he went through the ropes.

In the seventh, David yelled, "What the hell's Sammy doing?"

Luftspring seemed to lose energy. He became careful, cautious. Throwing fewer punches.

"Has something changed?" said Mike.

"You got eyes? Come on, Sammy, take the bum out! Don't quit now!" he yelled, his hands cupped around his mouth. "He's never gone more than six rounds before, he always knocks the guy out early. Maybe he's going to run out of gas."

Genovese waded into his opponent, landing uppercuts that looked like they were taking the other man's head off. Luftspring lay against the ropes and took body blows.

"Ah, shit," said David. The Italians in the crowd went nuts. After what seemed forever, the bell rang and each man went back to his corner.

"That's Doc Cooke talking to Sammy. He's a great trainer. He'll snap him out of it, if anybody can."

"It doesn't look good, does it?" said Ebbie.

"Not if you're rooting for Jews," said David.

The bell rang for the eighth round, and Sammy Luftspring came back into the centre of the ring with renewed energy. He pummelled Genovese.

Irene and Ebbie hid their faces, peeking now and then. It was bloody and it was terrible, but it was thrilling at the same time.

Genovese couldn't come out for the tenth round, so Sammy Luftspring won by a technical knockout.

"Sammy's the king!" shouted David, along with thousands of other fans. Even some of the Italians were cheering. It had been a hell of a fight. "Sammy's a god!"

The man next to David hugged him. "Mazeltov!" he said, and David hugged him back and said, "Mazeltov!" Then he turned to Irene and hugged her too.

As they followed the flow of people outside the arena, David's friends approached them.

"What did I tell ya?" said Lenny. "Hell of a fight!"

"We should live so long to see another like that," said Ben. "You gonna come down to the Grill? We said we'd meet up with Jimmy-the-Book down there."

"Yeah, yeah, sure," said David. "So, I'm going to see Irene home and then I'll join you guys."

"Don't take too long or we'll drink up all your winnings, pal."

Irene and David said good night to Ebbie and Mike, who wanted to know when the next match would be and would he promise to take them.

"Crazed fans I turned you into," he said, laughing, and they waved good night.

David and Irene walked slowly. It wasn't even a five-minute walk back to Irene's and she didn't want to rush. She felt as though she'd fought the fight herself, her hands shaking with excitement and adrenaline coursing through her veins. She'd never, never, sleep tonight.

"So, you liked it?"

"Yes! And no. I mean, it's so violent. Savage."

"So, you liked it," he repeated, grinning.

"Yes. I liked it. I don't know if I'd want to go again. But I liked it very much. It was exciting. And I liked your friends."

"They're good guys."

"How do you know them?"

"Here and there."

"You're so mysterious all the time, David. You're going to make me think you're a criminal or something."

"No, nothing like that, not really. Although I can't say the same about some of the boys. Lenny, for example, he did a stretch up at Kingston."

"Really? What for?" She found this didn't frighten her, as she supposed it should.

"He and his family got really down on their luck. Back in '32 when things were even worse than now. Lost his job, couldn't find another. He had a couple of kids to feed. He robbed a gas station up on the Danforth. Somebody saw him crawling through a window and called the cops. He didn't get three blocks. Did two years."

"That's awful. I mean, to have to steal because your kids are hungry."

"Are you kidding me? The jails are filled with guys down on their luck, Irene. This Depression's been good for the prison business."

"What happened to his wife and kids?"

"I'll tell you what happened. While he was in stir his wife got sick. Real sick, and she couldn't work. She'd been a maid for some rich lady in Forest Hill who fired her when she started coughing so bad. She probably had TB. She had to trudge through snow to stand in line for hours at the hospital's 'relief' entrance, then the doctors gave her a prescription for a medicine she couldn't afford. She died in a room on Augusta, and the kids were in the room with a dead body for two days before anyone came in to check. The boy, he was two, he died not long after, and the little girl, who was three, she was taken away by the social workers. When Lenny got out they wouldn't tell him where, because of his record. He never got over it."

"Oh my God. I'm so sorry. That's just terrible."

"Yeah, ain't it, though."

They walked a little ways in silence.

"So, how *do* you know him? Have *you* been in jail?"

"No, I haven't been in jail. Well, just for vagrancy, right? But that's nothing. A week here or there in the city lockup, maybe. But that's a question you shouldn't ask some of the guys. You sure want to know an awful lot of stuff all of a sudden." He shook his head and grinned at her. "All right, all right. I know them from some organizations I belong to. Clubs, like."

"What kind of clubs?"

"You are one nosy woman."

"I guess. What kind?" Perhaps he was like Uncle Rory and she wanted to know about that.

"Jewish Labour League. The Canadian League Against War and Fascism."

"Really?"

"Yes, Irene, really."

"Communists?"

"Some. Yeah. Communists. Anti-Fascists. Anti-goddamn-Hitlerites."

They had reached the corner of Homewood, and Irene made David turn back there, for she assumed her mother would be waiting and watching. It was after eleven, and she hadn't been out this long or this late since the Harry days. There was no light on in the house, not even in her mother's room. As she climbed the porch steps she listened for a sound from inside, something that would give her a clue as to what waited for her on the other side. She rooted in her purse to find her keys, dropped them, picked them up, fumbled with the lock.

Margaret sat on the third step of the stairs, her hands wrapped around her knees. She wore no slippers and only a thin night-gown. Irene could see up her thighs. She held two handkerchiefs, one in each hand, and her head was raised as though it had been resting on her knees. Her face was puffy from crying.

"Mum? Are you all right? I'm sorry I'm so late."

"Where have you been? Where have you been? I thought you were dead."

"I'm fine. What are you doing sitting there?" She went over to her mother and tried to lift her. "I only went out after work, Mum. I didn't go to China."

Margaret began crying again, her head in her hands. She mumbled something.

"What?" This quiet crying state was new.

"I thought you'd left me. I can't help myself. I try not to think, not to let go, but I can't, I can't."

"Stand up, Mum." Irene pulled her to her feet and started to help her up the stairs. "Did you take your medication?"

"Some."

"How much?" For she was frightened by this quietness.

"I don't think I can win. I thought I could."

Win what? "How much did you take?"

"Not enough, not nearly enough." She was still crying, and let herself be led to her room.

"Do you have to go to the toilet?"

"No. I just want to lie down now. My head hurts."

The bottle of sedative was on the nightstand. Some had gone, but not enough to do her harm, Irene thought.

"I love you, Irene. I wouldn't blame you if you didn't love me. I can't keep the crows away. Keep swatting at them. I can't help it."

Irene sat on the side of the bed and took her mother's hand. "Of course I love you. You're my mum." Irene felt like crying herself now.

Margaret's hand was suddenly tight on hers. "I don't want it to be this way. I don't want to be what I am. I don't want to say things. I can't help myself, Irene. Words fly out, they just fly. *I can't help myself!*"

Irene put her arms around her, her mother's body like an armful of cutlery, sharp and thin.

"It's all right, Mum. It's my fault. I should have come home on time."

"You're a good girl, Irene. I always said that. You were always a good girl."

• • •

The next morning Margaret watched Irene walk away to work, then she turned back in to the living room and looked around. Her eyes fell on a photo of Irene, taken years ago. In it Irene wore a white frilly dress with bloomers. She was posed in front of the hydrangea bush that had once bloomed at the side of the house. Such a long time ago, when she was a different woman. That had been when—1927, 1926?

A photographer had knocked on the door that day, so many summers ago, on a hot afternoon when Irene was down for a nap. Margaret had been in the cellar, running sheets through the wringer, and the knocking had annoyed her, for she was certain it would wake Irene up. She saw the top of a man's hat through the screen door. She hesitated. A woman alone in a house with a child needed to be careful. She stood behind the screen door with a scowl on her face, intended to intimidate the scoundrel.

A young man stood on the walkway, one foot on the first step. He touched the brim of his hat. He wore a vest and had taken off his jacket and slung it over his shoulder, in deference to the sticky August heat. He leaned against a tripod, and a heavy, square camera was looped across his back on a thick strap. His shirt-sleeves were rolled up and the golden hair on his arms sparkled in the sun.

"Yes?" she said, wiping her hands on her apron. A breeze reached her and she was aware that her face was shiny with perspiration.

The man began to speak quickly, his voice carrying the trace of an Irish accent. "Sorry to disturb you, ma'am, but I'm here to offer you a photograph of your children. A moment captured in time forever, like a piece of amber. I'm bringing the art of photography right to your door, missus. No need to book into a fancy studio. No need to even leave your home. No need even to pay if you don't like the photo. I'm in the neighbourhood for two days, ma'am. I only take a small deposit today and you pay the rest when I bring back your photograph tomorrow. If you don't like it, I'll gladly return your deposit."

"I don't think so. My little girl's asleep right now."

"Why, that's the perfect time. You just wake her up and put her into something pretty and she'll be as natural as can be. It'll be a picture you'll cherish forever. Like I said, if you don't like it, you don't pay." He smiled at Margaret, and his teeth shone white against his tanned skin.

"How much is it?"

"Only twenty-five cents. Quarter of a dollar, just a dime down. Copies three cents apiece. No better deal in all Toronto."

Margaret found herself staring at the young man's hands. He had the most beautiful hands she had ever seen. They looked like they could have been sculpted from marble, so fine yet strong looking.

"How do I know you'll come back if I give you ten cents now?"

"Shrewd. That's very shrewd. Tell you what, just for you, I won't take a deposit. You let me take the picture and I'll trust you for the money. That couldn't be fairer, now, could it?"

Did he think for a moment that he could talk her into doing anything she didn't want to do? She had agreed to the photo because she didn't want the young man to go. It was as simple as that. She wanted him to stay a while and she wanted him to come back the next day. She wanted to watch his hands on the camera.

Irene had been uncooperative at first, slow and cranky with sleep. Irene had been a difficult child. She was shy and awkward, not at all the sparkling child Margaret herself had been. But once she was dressed in a starch-crisp crinoline and a comb run through her unruly hair, she had been presentable enough. They posed her against the hydrangea. When the man put his hands on Irene's shoulders, turning her to face the mechanical lens, Margaret shivered as though he were touching her.

The next day when she heard his knock at the door she had pinched her cheeks before answering it. But instead of the young man with the Michelangelo hands, a boy stood there, his face a mass of freckles, his cap on back to front and the knee torn out of his dungarees. He held out an envelope.

"My brother said I was to deliver this picture to you, ma'am, and you was to give me what you owe. Says you owe him twenty-five cents."

Margaret was angry with herself when she realized how disappointed she was. She'd glared at the boy, then gave him an extra nickel to make up for it.

What had she hoped would happen? Anything. Something.

She now turned the photo face down. Then she stood it up again. She could see herself in Irene's face, in the expression, happy, excited, faintly bewildered and trying so hard to please. She had been a girl like that once, eager to make people happy. Eager to be in the centre of things. The Laughing Girl with shiny hair and party dresses and a future full of possibility. Not a wife and certainly not someone's mother. Well, she wasn't anyone's wife any longer. But she would stay a mother all her life. The world owed her that much, didn't it? For years of nothing at all? Didn't the world owe her one person who would stay and be with her and be for her and her alone?

30

August 1937

David watched Irene closely over the next few weeks. She went about her work, smiled at her customers, tallied up the day's receipts and ordered the necessary supplies like she always did. But he saw the pinched expression on her face when she thought no one was looking. When he asked her if she was all right, she simply said her mother was not doing very well and would say no more. In fact, she spoke to him only when necessary.

It made him angry, this submissive attitude of hers. He wanted his anger to be contagious, wanted her to catch it like a brush fire and let it burn away the crust of resignation and get down to the hard shine of steel he was convinced lay just beneath the surface.

He kept trying to draw her out, but she would have none of it.

He went to a meeting of the Canadian League Against War and Fascism on Thursday night to put the finishing touches on Sunday's plan. On Friday evening he said to Irene, "So, you going to church on Sunday?" He knew she'd started going to church again, as a way, he assumed, to have an hour away from her mother.

"Yes, I suppose."

"Why not skip it? I got a better idea."

It had taken some persuading, and some political educating, but David was pleased with himself. She had agreed to join him Sunday morning, even though it meant lying to her mother again.

"What did you tell her?" David asked when she arrived at his room above the shop at ten o'clock that morning. She wore a blue dress he hadn't seen before, with puffed sleeves and lace on the collar. On her head she wore a straw hat, with a sprig of silk lilacs on the brim. Quite suitable for going to church, but he wasn't sure it was right for where they were going. She carried white gloves. He looked at her shoes. At least they were sturdy walking shoes.

"I told her the church was having a tea after the service and I'd been asked to set up and serve. I hate lying to her. She can smell me out." Her mother had stood at the window watching her as she left, a hurt expression on her face.

"So, don't lie to her, then," said David. He pulled out his wallet, took a couple of bills and stuffed them in his pocket. He tossed the wallet on the table. "What do you have in your purse?"

"Just the usual stuff. Why?"

"You have any identification papers?"

"An ID card in my address book, but why?"

"Better maybe to leave it. I'm not expecting there to be any trouble, you understand, but just in case the cops do stop you, the less they can find out about you, the better. But, hey, there shouldn't be any of that. It's just a habit I have."

She paled, but took her address book out of her purse and put it down next to his wallet.

"Let's go," he said, grinning. "Come on, don't look so serious. You're doing something good here. Something important. Nothing bad's going to happen."

They stepped out into a fine August day, and walked quickly. The demonstration was to start at eleven in front of the German State Railway offices at York and Adelaide. David led her over to Yonge Street, and then south-west into the heart of the Ward.

The streets here were narrow and badly paved. There was no grass in front of the houses, just dry earth. Wooden houses leaned every which way, and from alleys came the acrid smell of the privies. Several times Irene put her hand over her nose. It was darker on these streets. Even though the sun was shining, it didn't seem strong enough to penetrate the gloom of deprivation. Behind an uneven, ill-mended and unpainted fence, five thin, dirty children played lethargically, one boy sifting dirt through his hands, a girl trying to bury her naked doll. Two men argued in an alleyway, their voices rough and filled with violence. Irene edged closer to David but didn't take his arm. She didn't want to let her discomfort show. A greasy gaggle of boys lounged, leaning on a wall, spitting on the street, leering at girls who passed. Here and there dull-eyed women in mended clothes stood on porches, staring at them. Whereas Kensington had had equal amounts of laughter mixed in with the tears, here the atmosphere was tense and edgy. They turned down Elizabeth Street, near the grim, grey structure called the House of Industry. A group of weary-looking men and women hung about, hoping to get a bowl of soup or a can of beans to take home.

In some places boards had been put down to form makeshift walkways from the edge of the road up to some small, wobbly-looking house. Cats were everywhere, presumably, Irene thought, to keep the vermin population at bay.

An old horse stood hitched up to a sagging wagon filled with a haphazard collection of bruised and mouldy vegetables, piles of rags, and several broken chairs. An old moth-eaten man with tobacco stains in his grey beard and a large mole on his face sat on the sidewalk next to the horse, who nuzzled him occasionally, but he seemed not to notice. The man smelled of wood smoke and mould. It rose off him like steam.

"You all right, Pops?" said David.

"Mind you own business, you own goddamn business," said the man, waving them away with an arthritic hand.

David shrugged. "So, suit yourself."

"The office is in this neighbourhood?" said Irene.

"Not exactly, but not far. York and Adelaide. Isn't much of a place, is it? Never been through here before, I'll bet."

"No." Her voice was small and she knew she sounded upset, which maybe was what he had been hoping for. "We didn't have to come this way."

"No, but maybe it's about time you saw the way really poor people have to live."

"I don't understand what this place has to do with the demonstration." She was ashamed to find she felt superior to these people, and at the same time too inexperienced to be attending this demonstration. There was so much about the world and poverty and suffering that she didn't know, could hardly imagine. And she was also slightly angered that David had chosen this route in order to manipulate her feelings.

"Oppression's the same wherever it is. Germany's just in the spotlight now, but don't for a moment think bad things don't happen right here at home, Irene. Don't ever think that. This squalor's the result of laissez-faire capitalism."

"And you think the Soviets are going to change all this?" She thought he was being naïve now, simply parroting the words he had been taught.

"Maybe I used to," he said, surprising her. "Now I don't know whether it's the answer or not. We're hearing bad things from there too. There was a time I maybe thought there'd be a real revolution. Now, I don't see it. Maybe there's some hope in socialism. There are some good guys in the Party, but no real leaders. They fight and fraction and push and shove and want power just like any other poor bastard. And, hell, I don't think folks outside the Party ever got as riled up as we thought they did. So, how are you going to get people to risk something when all they got is this and even this takes all you've got just to hold on to?" He waved his arm, taking in the whole street. "When you're bogged down in this sewer, how are you going to get the energy to fight?"

"Well, you're trying, aren't you? I mean, we are, today, picketing like this, aren't we?"

"Yeah, sure," he said, "I guess. It's something, anyway."

At the corner of York and Adelaide, a group of people stood outside the nondescript offices of the German State Railway. They held signs, and Irene read, "Arrest the Nazi Werner Haag!" This is what they were here for. David had told her that Werner Haag was a Nazi representative living in Canada. Reports had been written in all the newspapers about what was going on in Germany, and the anti-Fascist movement believed he should be hauled into court and tried for crimes against Jews.

"No Room for Nazis in Canada!" said one sign, and "No Canadian Nickel for German Bullets!" and "Spain a Base for Nazi Spies!"

People marched in a circle on the sidewalk, shouting out the slogans written on their signs. Several greeted David as they passed, giving his hand a quick shake. Lenny was there, and Simon. A girl with long black hair waved at David. Off to one side two men stood in front of a pile of picket boards. David and Irene went over to them. David picked up an "Arrest Werner Haag!" sign. Irene chose one that said "Nazis Not Welcome in Canada!" They took their places in the circle, Irene following David, and they began to march.

Irene felt bold and exhilarated and shouted "Arrest the Nazi!" with the rest of them. There were perhaps forty people, and although the majority were young, there were a few older faces. The men wore caps to shield their eyes from the sun, and some of the women wore straw hats. The men had their sleeves rolled up, but most wore ties.

They began a chant. "Arr-est the Na-zi! Arr-est the Na-zi!" She marched in step with the rhythm. David turned around to smile at her. She grinned back. The sun felt good on her skin. The smell of roses drifted over from a bush planted by the door of the office building and mixed with the smell of warm asphalt under her feet. She felt a part of something important, larger than herself.

There were not many people on the street today, not in this part of town, which was mostly offices, but the press was there. The *Toronto Daily Star*, the *Globe and Mail*, and *Der Yiddisher Zhurnal*. Sunday was a slow news day. A few pictures were snapped, which Irene made sure she was not in, for her mother would be sure to see it. A man from *Der Yiddisher Zhurnal* talked to one of the men handing out pickets.

They had gone on for perhaps twenty minutes when a woman said, "They're here," and pointed south. Down the street came the police, with three horses, a paddy wagon and their billy clubs at the ready.

"David?" said Irene, her palms suddenly slick against the handle of her sign. She felt a sliver enter her palm.

"Yeah, well, that was to be expected," he said.

As though fully prepared for this turn of events, people quickly abandoned the circle and formed into a solid square, four or five deep. As the police approached they sat down on the ground and became silent. David took Irene's sign away from her and laid it with his on the ground. He led her to the back of the group, but they did not sit down.

"All right, then," said one of the cops. "What the hell have we got here?"

No one answered him.

"You people gonna move along quiet like, or are we gonna have to move youse?"

David looked around, at the police, at the people on the ground and finally at Irene. She could see the struggle playing out on his face. His mouth twitched.

"Go on," called Lenny, sitting in the front. "It's all right. Go on."

"Shit," he said. "I better get you out of here."

He took her by the hand and started to jog up the street, pulling Irene behind him. She looked back over her shoulder. The police spread out around the tightly seated group. The horses danced and lifted their feet, as though unwilling to step on the humans on the ground. People had their hands up and their signs, protecting themselves from the sharp hooves.

"Just stay calm," said David, moving faster but not running.

The police seemed to pick out certain individuals. Lenny they went for right away, hauling him roughly by the arms, his feet trailing. They tossed him in the back of the van. Two cops picked up the girl with the long black hair and she squirmed, her face red. Irene could see one of them had a hand between her legs. An older man was roughly pushed and he fell to the pavement, losing his glasses. As he went to reach for them, a policeman kicked them under the hooves of a horse. The rest they shoved and pushed to their feet. David and Irene turned a corner and she could see no more.

"Oh my God," she said. "We could have been arrested."

"It's just a quick bust," said David. "They won't press charges. They don't want the papers squawking about it."

"But we could have been arrested," said Irene again.

"Yeah, I guess, but we weren't." And he sounded both relieved and slightly disappointed. "Would have been better, though, to get a bunch of us hauled into court. That's the only way to maybe arouse the public."

Irene didn't know whether to slap him or not. The problem was, she felt more alive than she had in months.

It was a week and a half since the Sunday Irene had come home flushed and distracted after being, she said, at a church tea. It had become Margaret's habit since then to sit in the window and watch Irene walk away down the street. She thought if she secretly observed her that Irene might give something away. She searched her daughter's mannerisms for some gesture that might hold the key. Did she swing her arms with anticipation? Did she touch her hair to make sure she looked pretty? Did she hurry away from the house, anxious to be away from her mother and nearer to David? Margaret wondered if Irene knew she was being watched and was controlling her actions.

She's become untrustworthy, murmured Mad Margaret. *A liar.*

Every night when Irene came home Margaret grilled her about David. "What do we really know about him? Have you seen the inside of his room? Have you made sure he isn't stealing? Don't you think there's something improper about you being in the store with him alone all day? Has he tried to touch you?"

But each question was met with a monosyllabic response, a shrug, a simple, slightly exasperated "Of course not, Mum."

The mystery remained unsolved. Ever since the night Irene had been out with David Hirsch and come home so late, Margaret was sure there was an omen she was missing. That night she had been sure Irene would not come home. Why was that? Irene always came home. Something evil was tracking her again, and it had to do with the sorrow-bearing Jew. *Watch out! It's near! Can't you hear it breathing?* It was getting more and more difficult to ride rule on Mad Margaret. *They're plotting together. Your daughter and the Jew.*

When Harry disappeared it had been such a victory. Margaret had felt sure Irene would be bound to her forever then, defeated by the loss of love. And then that David Hirsch arrived and contaminated everything. He was poisoning Irene, tainting her. *She's willing. She likes the forbidden fruit.*

Margaret had to know. She could not lose Irene.

It took three days for her to find the courage. Twice, on the second day, she made it out of the house. The first time only to the porch, the second all the way to the end of the street, propelled by a furious velocity, which failed her as a streetcar rattled past and she thought she saw the face of Mrs. Rhodes laughing at her from one of the windows. On the third day, however, with her nails digging half-moons in her palms, a floral scarf over her hair and a straw hat over that so she would not be recognized, she set out again. She decided she would not walk on

Homewood, where the neighbours might gawk at her, but would cut through the alley. She lifted the latch on the back gate and stepped out onto the dirt lane behind the houses. She scanned to the right and left. *Careful. Careful!* The lane was deserted and dusty. Nothing but blank fences and the green leaves from over-hanging backyard trees. She scuttled up to where she knew the lane led to a narrow passage to Sherbourne Street. Her heart thud-ded. This was her last chance. She knew she would not have the courage to attempt the journey again.

The path was clear. She slipped into the shaded light. A newspa-per, lying on the ground near a garbage can, flapped in the hot breeze and gave her a momentary start. She straightened her back and took a deep breath. *Go on! Go and see what they're up to. No good. No good.* She walked through the passage and out onto Sherbourne Street. It was quieter than she'd feared. A woman in a blue dress walked a dog and passed her without staring, without pulling away or making a face, which was a good sign. Carlton was busier. Streetcars rumbled by, and she was careful not to look at the windows. She found it hard to breathe. The air was full of the smell of gasoline and dust. She made herself walk more slowly and pulled the scarf over her mouth and nose. Her palms and the space between her breasts were damp with sweat.

On Parliament she kept to the west side of the street. She didn't even remember exactly where the store was. She knew Irene had repainted the window. Would she know it? Then, with a sharp contraction of her stomach, she saw it. It looked so tidy, so neat and friendly with the bright silver lettering on the window.

You can feel the foggy evil all around it. Crows roost on the roof.

Shut up.

Nasty things going on in there.

Margaret rubbed her temples and tried to figure out the best place to look and not be seen. She was a little surprised at how anonymous she was. No one stopped her. She saw no face she recognized. She wiped her palms on her hips. If she stood by one of the cars and pretended to look in her purse, she could see in perfectly.

Two girls went in the shop. A man came out carrying a bag. Margaret looked up and down the street, appalled at how quickly the cars rushed by. After several false starts she realized she must coordinate her movement to the traffic light at the corner. She waited for it to turn red and then, as a gap appeared in the flow, she cautiously crossed and took her place by a parked black Ford.

She opened her purse and pretended to search for something within. She glanced up, half afraid Irene would be standing in the doorway looking at her. She saw David Hirsch behind the soda counter, spooning ice cream into two glass bowls. He set them before the girls at the counter. She couldn't see Irene. David left the counter and went to the tables with a rag, started polishing the surfaces. He looked out onto the street and Margaret quickly turned away. She felt the skin at the back of her neck prickle. She held her breath.

Run! He'll catch you!

No.

Nothing happened and she turned back again. David had returned to the soda fountain. Irene was at the other counter, putting a book down. She must have been in the back. She looked hot and wiped her index finger across her top lip. Then David came over to her with a glass of something in his hand. He set it down next to her and said something. Irene looked up at him. The expression on her face seemed guarded, which pleased Margaret.

Yes, protect yourself, my girl.

Then David reached out.

He's going to put his hands on her!

He touched Irene's forearm and leaned over to say something in her ear. Margaret prayed Irene would recoil—*Slap him!*—would turn away, but she didn't, she angled toward his lips. Then she put her hand up to her mouth and smiled, glancing at the girls.

Get away from her! Get away!

David stepped away.

Margaret felt sick to her stomach. It was so obvious what was going on, and it was worse even than she had thought. He was a spider, that one. Where Harry Madison had been a rascal and a peacock, this one was a spider, weaving a silky web. Margaret could see that very clearly. He stood behind the counter, joking with the girls, but his eyes kept snaking back to Irene. Margaret knew what his intentions were; lust was written all over his dark face. Maybe not everyone could see it, but Margaret could.

We have such sharp perceptions.

Irene walked over to him and moved behind him. As she did she put her hands up on his shoulders, ever so gently, so that she might pass. The gesture told Margaret everything she needed to know.

31

"How about some fish? You feel like seafood?" David said one night as they were closing. "And don't give me that usual crap about your mother and all."

"It's not crap, as you so politely put it. It's just like that."

"We have to go through this every time, for God's sake? Call her."

"I saw a new bottle of bath salts in the linen closet last week," said Irene, sweeping up behind the counter. "I'm absolutely sure it was new. It must mean she's been out on her own, don't you think? Although when I asked her she got angry and said she hadn't been anywhere, that it had been there for years. But I'm certain that's not true."

"Geez, you'd think you were negotiating world peace. It's not that big a deal. Just call her. Tell her you have to work, maybe you had a late stock delivery."

David watched Irene make the call. She talked gently, her eyes closed and her bent knuckle softly tapping her bottom lip. She frowned when she listened. Then she put down the phone.

"Let's go," she said.

He steered her toward a little restaurant he'd discovered, run by a Greek who'd come to Canada fifteen years before. The evening was soft and ripe with late summer. The streetlights had not yet come on and children played in the street. A group of girls jumped double dutch.

Cinderella, dressed in yellow,
Went upstairs to kiss her fellow.
Made a mistake and kissed a snake,
How many doctors did it take ...

The iceman and his ancient horse plodded along toward Cabbagetown, and children ran after the cart, hoping to pick off a hunk of ice.

They strolled down to the juncture of King and Queen streets near the Don River. It was a working-class neighbourhood, full of families whose men laboured on the nearby docks. Hungarians, Macedonians, Armenians—the music of the languages swirled around them, as did the smells of cloves and cooking onions carried on the dusty breeze with the faint stench from the nearby abattoir.

The small restaurant was on the ground floor of a converted house and held only twelve tables, each covered with a blue-and-white-check cloth and filled with people. David was looking around for a free spot when an enormous bald man with a bushy moustache came out of the kitchen.

"David! My friend! You come here. Table for you here. Come, come!"

"Evening, George," David called back. The two men met in the middle of the room and slapped each other on the back. Irene was amazed to see this great walrus of a man move through the small room without knocking over everything in his path.

"Who you bring me here? Always you come in alone and now you bring such a pretty girl! Someone special I'm thinking, yes?" The man winked broadly at David and beamed at Irene.

"George Elytis, I'd like you to meet a very good friend, Irene MacNeil."

The man lifted Irene's hand to his lips and kissed it loudly.

"Oh, we gonna make a special meal for you tonight, oh yes sirree, Joe! You come, you sit."

He held out a chair for Irene. The big Greek lumbered back into the kitchen, where loud voices and laughter could be heard, their meaning obvious even if the words were foreign.

"He certainly seems to like you," said Irene.

"I think I remind him of Constantine, his son. He left a couple of years back, riding the rails. George gets regular letters, but he misses him."

Irene fussed with her napkin. Her eyes travelled this way and that, taking in all the bright noisy life around her. "I've never been in a Greek restaurant before."

"You'll love it. I come here a lot. Cheap and homey. George's a great guy and his wife, Sophia, she's a terrific lady."

Food began to arrive. Flaming cheese triangles, which frightened Irene at first. Phyllo pastry with spinach inside. Olives. Bread. Salad. And then a platter of strange fried things, some round like onion rings, some that looked disturbingly like deep-fried spiders.

"What is it?" said Irene.

"Calamari!" George Elytis announced proudly.

"So, taste it," urged David, who squeezed lemon over a piece and held it up to her mouth.

Irene opened her lips reluctantly. It was unlike anything she'd ever tasted before, crisp and rich with the taste of sea and salt.

"It's fantastic!" she said. "What is it?"

"Is squid!" said the big man, and then he and David burst out laughing. "David, he have same look on face first time. But is good, yes? Is very good!"

For a moment she didn't know what to do, and then she was laughing too, and it felt good, so good. Everything was light and clean and felt right and it was such a wonderful feeling, to be at a table with a blue-and-white cloth, in a room with white walls and sea-blue plates, among people whom she didn't have to watch all the time for fear they would change into someone else. But the warm light in the restaurant only made her see how dark and musty and tight her house was, the walls as close as skin, and her mother's need for her like paper glued over that. She realized she was crying.

"I'm sorry," she said, "I'm sorry." And hid her face in a napkin.

"Oh, I don't laugh at you," said George, wringing his hands. "David, you tell her."

"It's okay, George. It's not that. She'll be fine." Although he was stricken too.

"I'm gonna bring you some ouzo. Ouzo's good for this thing." And George returned with a bottle and two small glasses. He filled one up and handed it to Irene.

"Go on, you drink. Taste like licorice. You gonna like."

"Have some, Irene. It's okay," said David.

Irene wiped her eyes and took the glass that looked like a thimble between his fingers. She sipped. The liquor burned her throat, and she coughed, and laughed.

"Is medicinal," said George. "You okay now?"

"Yes, I'm fine. Thank you."

"Okay, I gonna leave you with David. You drink the ouzo, eat the calamari."

"So, what's the matter?" David asked.

"Everything," she said.

"Can't be that bad, can it?" He took her hand. She didn't pull away. "What do you need to make it better?"

No one had ever asked her this.

"I don't suppose you happen to have a new life lying around somewhere, do you? I could use that." It was easier to take this tone than to admit how much she would like for him to be able to make it better.

"No, I don't suppose I do. But you got a whole life ahead of you if you want."

"I just don't see how."

"Any way you want. Just make a start, for chrissake."

"I've been thinking about something."

"Yeah, what?"

"Maybe going back to school."

"So, go back to school." He chewed a piece of calamari. "What do you want to study?"

"Pharmacology."

"Yeah? Well, hell, why not? Women can do just about anything these days, I guess."

"It's just a dream, really. I mean, how would I afford the tuition? I don't have the money right now. But maybe someday."

"Why not? Maybe anything could happen, right?"

"Are you happy here, David?" If David were to leave before things got better, she'd never be able to hire anyone else. She couldn't close up the store every day to go to classes.

"I got enough. I live rent free, that's pretty good. A few dollars. I don't need more."

"Maybe I'm not very fair."

"So, let me be the judge of what's fair, okay? We can talk about other financial arrangements somewhere down the line. Listen. You go back to school if you want. For as long as I can, I'll be here, right?" He looked down at his plate. "We ... I think we make a pretty good team."

She frowned. Was he saying what she thought he was saying?

"Things change fast, though," he said, filling the uncomfortable gap. "I mean, you know, with what's goin' on in Europe. Things are bound to change. If war comes ..."

"And I don't even know if I could finish school."

"'Course you could. Don't be crazy."

She had a funny look on her face.

"What is it?" he said.

"I'm not sure how my mother would take it."

"So, why wouldn't she be pleased?"

"I don't know. I just ... Never mind." There were shadows in her eyes again.

"Listen, why not take one thing at a time. And the thing before us is this dinner, right? That's all. Just a dinner."

"Yes. And it's lovely," she said.

Seeing that Irene was smiling again, Mr. Elytis came over to the table.

"You having a good time yes?" he said.

"Yes, Mr. Elytis."

"You call me George, like David. And you," he said, thumping David on the shoulder, "you don't make her cry no more."

"Me! It wasn't me!"

"Sure, sure, all the boys say that, but the girls, they still cry."

David pulled on his ear.

"David here, he just like a son to me, like my own son. Connie, he travel around now, he has the fevers in his feet. Go, go go! All the time go! He come home soon, I got a good feeling. Marry a nice girl, yes? That's the way to go, pal." He took David by the scruff of the neck and shook him so he nearly fell off the chair.

"Don't you have something to do in the kitchen? Maybe slaughter a lamb?" said David.

"You want to be alone, eh? I find a hint. You don't have to hit my head. But, miss, he give you any trouble, you come to me. I gonna fix." George laughed, slapped David on the back and left to harass other delighted customers.

"He likes you," said Irene, trying not to laugh.

"Sort of like having a three-hundred-and-fifty-pound bear like you. It's a mixed blessing."

And maybe it was the ouzo, and maybe it was the calamari and maybe it was the laughter and the room, or maybe it was David himself, but the light feeling came back and she let it fill her up and push out the dark, at least for the moment.

32

September 1937

Irene sat at the table near the shop window making a list of pros and cons. In the long run, it would bring in more money. In the short run, it would cost money for books and tuition. It would be a wonderful challenge and a real profession with a future, but it would mean long hours of study and work too. Would there be time for all of it? What would happen if David left? She tapped the pencil's eraser against her tooth and stared out the window.

She'd made enquiries and found she could complete her high school requirements at night on an accelerated program the university offered for people just like her who had been forced to abandon their studies to work. If all went well, she could begin studying for a degree next year.

On the other hand, her mother had locked on her with a vengeance. Her questioning eyes followed Irene, intuiting, in that weird way of hers, that something was going on just outside the line of her vision. The miracle of Margaret's leaving the house earlier in the summer was clouded over now by her constant grilling and her belittling remarks about David.

"You can't fool me, my girl," she said. "I'm smart. I can see things. You can't pull the wool over these old eyes."

"There is no plot, for God's sake, Mum. What do you have against David?"

"I'll say no more. I'll say no more."

And Irene could see that she would try to keep quiet, slamming doors and rattling pots and pans to make up for her tightly clamped jaw.

"You'll come to a bad end, Irene, if you don't listen to me."

"Yes, Mum," she'd say, too tired to argue through another evening.

"We'll see. The truth will always come out in the end." Margaret's laugh was brittle.

Sitting in the shop, Irene thought of the impending winter and how the house always seemed smaller in the cold, dark days when she and her mother pushed up against each other, two grouchy bears in never-restful hibernation. She thought of the churning, restless, hungry world David had opened her eyes to, a world both tortured and yet beautiful in its struggle. She thought of Ebbie and Mike making their way in university and their eager enthusiasm for the future. Ever since the day of the demonstration and the walk through the Ward, she'd felt her life was at a crossroads. She had been part of something that day.

Irene sighed, put her papers away and headed home. It was Monday evening and she felt the tension in her shoulders as she walked up the path to her house, shuffling through the season's first yellow leaves. She wondered how many times she'd walked toward her house in this manner, sensing like an insect for any changes in the atmosphere, putting out feelers to pick up any subtle disturbances in the air. She had her own key, and yet her mother, by putting the bolt across the door, could still lock her out at will. This evening the door was unbolted. A good sign. Her mother could be heard singing "Sweet Leilani" with Bing Crosby on the radio. A very good sign. The house was rich with the smell of roast chicken.

"That you, Irene?"

"Smells wonderful in here."

"It's almost ready. Wash up."

"Yes, Mum. Be right there."

The table in the kitchen was set already. The salt and pepper shakers, the little Chinese man and woman, stood in the middle of the table, next to a red lacquered bowl full of green lettuce. Irene wondered, for the thousandth time, what this fixation was her mother had with red things in the kitchen, red and black wherever you looked. Irene sat down heavily on the chair near the window. Margaret, an apron around her waist and a scarf tied up like a turban on her head, had her back to Irene and was mashing potatoes in a pot on the stove. Then she turned to Irene, and her face was tight.

"I found this in your room," she said.

She took a pamphlet from the Pharmacy Department of the university out of her apron pocket and tossed it down on the table-top. The little Chinese man fell over, a few grains of pepper spilling from the top of his head.

Scream at her! Scream!

No.

"You went through my things?" said Irene.

"I was cleaning. I'm allowed to do that, aren't I? It is still my house, isn't it? Now you tell me, what's this all about?" Margaret struggled to keep her voice low. She had been filled with a powerful sense of vindication when she had come upon the pamphlet early that afternoon, because she'd finally unearthed the plot being hatched by David Hirsch and her daughter. Now, however, the feelings were mixed with fear.

"I was just making some enquiries. You know, maybe for the future."

"What sort of enquiries?"

"To be a pharmacist," said Irene, and the words sounded foolish even to her.

Her mother laughed. "Don't be ridiculous. It's not that you're not smart, dear, I've always said how smart you are. But a pharmacist? That's not going to happen." She turned away and bent to take the perfectly browned chicken out of the oven.

"Why not? Why couldn't it?" There was the feeling of stone in Irene's chest.

"Be realistic. You have to run the store."

"I've thought about that, and I've got an idea there, too."

"Oh, you have, have you?"

It was absurd, of course, but Irene wished she'd put down the carving knife. "It's not a big thing, Mum."

Margaret slammed the carving implements down on the counter and picked up a dishtowel. She began to wipe her hands, even though they were not wet. "It may not be a big thing to you, Irene, but it certainly is to me. I may try and put on a good face for your sake, but let me tell you, there isn't a day goes by when I don't feel like just packing it all in and crawling back upstairs to that bed. Well, I guess I should have expected this. You're your father's daughter, after all. Peas in a pod, the two of you. I can see that now."

We know about the Jew. We have discovered things, from the look on his face, the things we can hear between the words you say. You're both guilty of many things.

Not yet. Quiet.

"Mum, please, just listen to me."

"Why should I? You're all set to flit off to school every day and make me go out to work, are you? How do you expect me to be able to cope?" Margaret began scratching furiously at the back of her hands. "I wouldn't last a week stuck in the shop with that Jew." She looked at the chicken, the green beans, the mashed potatoes, all in their pots on the top of the stove. "This is all ruined. Completely ruined." She picked up the bean pot and threw it into the sink.

"Mum. You don't have to go out and work in the store. I never said that. None of this will probably ever happen, anyway." The words were tart with bitterness.

"Well, you certainly can't run the store and go to school at the same time, can you?" *Fool! Think!* Margaret's face paled. "Oh, don't tell me! You have some foolish idea in your head about selling, don't you? Well, I am not going to have you selling the store, selling our whole future, just so you can go off and waste money on a silly pipe dream."

"I wouldn't sell the store and it's not a silly dream, Mum." With every word it seemed more possible, not less. "I could turn the place back into a real drug store someday. I want to make something out of my life."

"I know I haven't made much out of mine, but that's hardly my fault, is it, now? You don't need to rub my face in it." She fished in the pocket of her apron for a handkerchief, and blew her nose.

"This is not a catastrophe, Mum. I don't know why you're carrying on so. I'm not going to sell the store. I'm not going to ask you to work there."

Margaret stopped crying and considered Irene. "So, you're going to forget about this, then?"

"No. I'm going to do this. I think I just might."

"Then, what are you talking about!"

"David will take care of the shop alone," she mumbled.

Margaret laughed. *Good! Let's get to the twisted root!* "That isn't even worth commenting on."

"Mother, nothing's been decided. But it is possible." She made every attempt to keep her voice even and reasonable, for she knew how the slightest tonal fluctuation could unhinge Margaret.

Margaret walked over to her and, before Irene could move away, reached out and grabbed her tightly by the jaw, her nails digging into her daughter's skin. She brought her face close to Irene's.

"Oh, you'd like that, wouldn't you? Well, I will not have that mangy little man insinuating himself in our lives. I knew the moment I set eyes on him he was no good. Look what news he brought with him. Not that we even know if he told the truth, of course. I've thought about that."

"Stop it!" Irene pushed her mother's hand away and slid her chair back into the corner.

Margaret stood in front of her, her hands on her hips. *Be careful! Lay it out. Show her, but be careful.* Her eyes became clouded and cunning. "We have only his story to go on, don't we? We don't even know if he's telling the truth. We have no way of knowing, do we? My brother could be very much alive, out there some-where. This could all be a con, and David Hirsch could be a cheap grifter. Or there is another possibility. I've thought of it, but I bet you never have, have you? It could be worse than a con. So much worse. You're still so naïve. But have you considered that Rory could have been murdered?" She tapped Irene in the chest with her finger. "That's right. Axed to death. Or hit on the head with a rock. Have you ever thought of that? And even you can see who the natural culprit would be, can't you? David Hirsch's hands could be very bloody indeed, my girl."

She hadn't thought about that! She hadn't considered it! That'll fix her. That'll bring her 'round again.

Margaret turned back to the stove. "No, I can see by the look on your face. When you're older, you'll see. People like that. They're not like us. You have to be cautious. I know what ideas he's been putting in your head. But it'll have to stop. He wants you, you know. Filthy things. You should thank me. I know how close you came. Almost turned against me, didn't you? Plotting with him,

I've seen you. But I wouldn't let that happen. No, my girl, I wouldn't let that happen. You'd be better off dead."

"Mum, don't say any more, please don't." All the air seemed to have left the house and there was only the pulsing pressure of her mother's words. She rubbed her cheeks, where her mother's nails had left half-moon marks. She saw Margaret with her sad, slightly askew turban on her head, a curl of grey hair sprouting from the side. She saw the attempts her mother made to create some sort of world where such a hat could be worn, in a red kitchen, while roasting a chicken, and it would be all right, it would be suitable, it would be appropriate. It was the kind of world you found at the end of a rabbit hole, and one her mother wanted to trap her in, just the two of them, gnawing on chicken legs, listening to the radio and forever picking each other's hairs off the white porcelain of the bath.

She said I'd be better off dead.

Where do you end and I begin?

Margaret carved the chicken, the knife slicing easily through the flesh.

"I know these things aren't easy to hear, Kitten. But we have to face facts. I could smell it on him right away. Hirsch." She chuckled, and waved the big fork in Irene's direction. "He hid his name from us at first. Did you notice? Didn't come right out and say he was Jewish. They're a sneaky people. I've said that before and you argued with me, didn't you? Your father was right in that. To think I used to disagree with him. But even you can see it now."

It'll be all right. Irene is a good girl. Now that she's been told the truth, it will be fine.

Margaret served potatoes onto the plates, then turned to the spilled pot of beans in the sink and spooned up some of those as well. She brought the two plates to the table.

"Don't be disappointed, dear. Don't look like that. Chief Thundercloud. Do you remember when I used to call you that? But really—" She patted Irene's hand, which remained in her lap, safely holding the other. Irene looked down at her mother's hand on hers, at the broad red scratches there. "I think it's for the best that things stay the way they are now. Except for David. You'll have to get rid of him right away. Eat up, dear."

Irene gazed at her plate. She knew that if she picked up the fork and began to eat, something dreadful would happen. It was very clear. If she ate this meal, here at this table with her mother, she would continue eating here every night for the rest of her life. She would remain in this kitchen, eating the same meal, day after day, too weak to fight the same repetitious battles, and eventually the walls she'd so carefully maintained—mortared with a little acquiescence here, a small agreement there—would crumble. They would fall and she would be invaded, overrun, occupied completely by her mother's unwell soul. There would be no boundary between them. They would be one.

You'd be better off dead.

"Irene? What's the matter, Kitten?"

"I'm going, Mother."

"Going where, dear? You have to eat your dinner. I made you this nice dinner."

Black wings! Feel the black wings!

Irene pushed herself up from the table. She walked down the hall. She walked up the stairs, each step feeling as if there were a concrete block around her foot.

"Irene! Where are you going?"

Idiot! Black wings! Do something! Do something!

Irene knew she must hurry. She climbed the stairs and reached her room before her mother could catch her. She put the chair under the doorknob. She pulled her suitcase from under the bed and began stuffing things into it. Her mother rattled the doorknob. A few clothes, not much would fit. The photo of her father, another of Uncle Rory. A book of poems by Auden. Her mother banged on the door. She felt like her father, leaving the house with next to nothing, leaving even less of herself behind. This will be, at last, her mother's house. Her mother, who terrified her.

"Irene! Let me in! Open the door!"

Irene opened the door.

"How dare you lock me out!" Her mother had taken the turban off now, tossed it aside in her anger, Irene presumed.

"I'm going, Mum. I'll call you." Irene put up her arm and moved her mother gently, but firmly, aside.

"Where are you going? Where are you *going?*"

"Maybe to a hotel. Then tomorrow I'm going to look for a room. Where I will live." She started down the stairs.

"*No!* I won't have this. No!"

Irene turned to look at her mother, although she did not want to. Women were turned to salt for actions just like this. She did not want to see her in this state, wanted to find some other way to part. Her mother stood halfway down the stairs. Her hands were in fists, raised above her head, her face full of dark fear and rage.

"I'm not leaving you, Mum. I'm just going. There's a difference. I'll see you. I'll pay for everything. You'll have to go outside now. But you'll be fine. I promise." She continued down the stairs and now her mother followed her, silently tugging at her, Irene pushing her away. With great effort she reached the door. She put her hand on the doorknob. The entire house seemed to echo and groan.

"I've known this would happen. I have always known what a devious girl you were. In my day children didn't fuck Jews, didn't abandon their parents, didn't leave them to die alone. I'll go mad, Irene! I will! And it will be your fault! I can feel it coming! You can't just leave me like this! I can't cope by myself. I'm not strong like you are! Irene!"

Listen to the sound of wings. Here they come. Goody.

Irene was so tired. It would be easier to just turn back, to let whatever might happen, happen—the two of them melding into one sad and festering wound, hiding together from the world. The two of them dying. She put her arms around her mother, who gripped her tightly. Every muscle in Irene's chest threatened to crush her heart. Then she pushed Margaret to arms' length and was surprised to see how much stronger than her mother she was. She picked up her bag again. She stepped out on the porch. Just a simple thing, a small step. A mere foot from one side of the door to the other.

"I might as well kill myself. I'm going to die alone," Margaret cried.

Death is a dark wing, too.

"Oh, Mum," said Irene, her own face streaming with tears. "You must stop, dear. Just stop thinking about yourself so much." Her throat was so thick the words were in a voice not her own.

Irene felt every step away from the house was a step walked on a bed of broken glass. She heard the door slam. The sound of her mother's yowling followed her down the street and a few of the neighbours came out to see whatever was the matter. She waved at them.

She saw her hand was trembling and she put it in her pocket. Then she took it out again and turned up her collar against the chill.

Eventually Margaret stopped screaming. She slammed her fist into her mouth again and again until she tasted the iron saltiness of blood. Then she was quiet. How long or how loud she'd been screaming she didn't know. Margaret stood in the dining room. She took her hand out of her mouth and ran it along the top of the table. It was as smooth and cool and reflective as a deep pool of water. Margaret had polished it herself. She bent down and lay her face against the surface, trying to flow into the dark cool world inside the wood. Then she rose again, because there was nothing else to do but rise. She sat in the chair in the corner. Her chair.

Irene would come back because she was a good girl. She would come back, and Margaret would wait right here. If she stayed here and did not move from this chair, then Irene would come back. Margaret gripped the seat with both hands.

She's gone. She won't be back.

Shut up. She will be back.

Gone, gone, gone, free as a bird, flown the coop, fly away, fly away, fly away home, your house is on fire and your children have gone.

"Shut up!" Margaret yelled. "Shutupshutupshutup!"

Fine. I can wait.

Margaret sat for a long time. She sat until it was clear Irene would not be back that night. She sat as darkness fell all around the house and did not get up to turn a light on, for if she moved ... Her teeth began to chatter and her legs cramped and all around her she knew something watched and waited. And still she did not move. She gritted her teeth so hard that pains shot up into her temples. Her back ached and burned with holding still, but still she did not move. She concentrated on the ticking of the clock on the desk in the living room, although she could not see it. She was frightened in the dark. The dark that would not budge. She began to cry.

Ready yet?

Shut up!

Go upstairs and get your medicine.

No. Shut up.

Stupid bitch.

She cried harder and gazed into shadows inside shadows.

It's just a shadow, just a shadow, she thought and she knew that was true. Just shadows on her mind. But there, curled into the darkness of the shadow-land, was another place, full of wild exultation. *Well, what do we have here?* Windswept and barren. A place of savage abandon. Land of the Crows. Margaret tried not to know that place; tried not to turn toward it. Her face contorted. *Come on, don't dawdle.* She felt herself sliding closer to the place-within-the-place. Margaret stood on the lip of the chasm and knew it did not matter if she flung herself into the breach. Nothing mattered. She could see that now, quite clearly. So simple. *Up you go.* And then she knew she was falling. A long and lazy turn upon turn, swoop and dive ... *Oopsy-daisy.* The Other Margaret stood erect and laughed peals of laughter that were not good to hear. Margaret's flesh goose-pimpled to hear it, so wild and terrible was it.

"Oh my God," said Margaret, and she fell from the chair.

When she woke it was daylight and she knew that Irene would not be back. She had fallen from her chair, failed to keep up her end of the bargain and had lost.

It's not so bad.

No.

Haw! Yes it is, yes it is, fooled you tricked you fooled you tricked you.

Margaret ran up to her room and slammed the door. Put the chair under the handle. Took it away again. She opened the door, spat on the threshold and laughed. She was Other now, abandoned in the windswept place. She could hear the wind under the floorboards. *Let it come.* Margaret let despair shake her, a rat in a bloodhound's jaw, and she fell upon the bed, her bones rattled with the force of her sobs. *The worst has happened now, nothing to worry about now.* She took her bottle of friendly pink sleep and put it to her lips. *I am so tired.* Margaret went to sleep. And woke. And drank. And slept some more.

She tried to open her eyes, crusted over with sleep, the eyelashes sticking together. When she pulled them apart, several eyelashes clung on her fingertips. She blew them away and looked at the room. Small room. Her room. Dark and close and comforting. It was like her own skin, enveloping and hiding her. Her house. It was hers.

Won't be ours for long. Money's all flitted away with the girl. They'll come and turn us out sooner or later.

The idea rolled over in her mind.

That makes it very simple, then, doesn't it?

How so?

We will stay alive as long as long as the house is ours.

Then we'll go?

Yes, then we'll go.

This seemed a sensible idea. All her worries would be over then, and an end would come. A friendly end. But until then. Until then the only thing she had to do was breathe in and out and in again.

Glittering things in corners can sneak up on you at any time. See? Do you see now?

Margaret saw.

What shall we do until the day our house is not our house?

Good question.

I think we'll sleep for now. And Margaret turned her head on the pillow, not bothering to take her medicine, for she was tired all by herself.

She came to slowly, in her bed, fully dressed, and for a moment could not think where she was and did not remember getting there.

Remember? We are alone now.

Ah. Yes.

Margaret stood then and felt her muscles protest. She did not know how long she had been ... what had she been?

We made decisions.

Decisions?

Yes, we will die when we lose the house. Friendly sleep.

Ah. Yes.

It came to her then that all the things she had ever craved, during a whole lifetime of fierce wanting, had fallen away. There was nothing left to want, since there was nothing left. And in the absence of wanting, she did not now know what disappointment felt like, although she tried to summon it. Or unrest. Or fear. She put her hands along her face to see if it was still her face at all.

Familiar bones held beneath her searching fingers.

I am so thirsty.

Drink something, then.

It was a place to start, while living until it was time to live no longer. Margaret would drink something. She was as weak as a baby sparrow and moved slowly. Then she passed Irene's door.

No.

Margaret would not, for just this moment, think of Irene.

She made her way to the kitchen and she poured herself a glass of water. She drank it and poured herself another and then one more.

She was hungry now, but something else more than that. She went to the front door and opened it. Newspapers were piled there. For how long? She picked them up, one at a time, for they seemed very heavy.

Two days.

No, three.

Risen from the dead, then?

Only temporarily.

Margaret took the papers into the kitchen and sat at the table.

She would not think of abandonment, of betrayal. She would not think of having to go out into the world and do things she did not want to do. See people. Go into a store. Margaret shut her eyes tight. She would not think of all the hopeless days before her. She would agree to not think of it for this particular minute.

Can we do that?

Yes. It think that might be possible.

If I think about it I'll slit my wrists now.

Don't think about it, then. Time for that later. Think about a drink of water.

And then what?

Think about eating an egg.

33

October 1937

David and Ebbie helped Irene move the last few things into her new room on Carlton. The proximity to her mother left David looking dubious, but Irene had insisted. David had offered to move out of the room above the store, but Irene had adamantly refused. He was a better deterrent to break-ins than she was, she said, and besides, she wanted a place that was her very own and was new, a fresh start.

Well, *new* was a relative term, she thought. The only reason she could afford it was because it was a run-down little place. But it had potential. They helped her paint the walls white. They hung pretty blue curtains, the same shade of blue as in the Greek restaurant. There would be nothing red, nothing black in this room. All must be clear and bright and airy. The three of them sat in the tidy kitchen alcove, pleased with the results of their labour. Irene's skin shone as though washed with light reflected from the Aegean Sea. When Mike joined them they all went to Syros, the restaurant named after George Elytis's island home.

David and Irene tried to convince Ebbie that squid was edible, and there was much laughter at the table, helped along by the bottle of retsina that George provided for the occasion, although Irene stuck to cola. The big Greek had proclaimed it a celebration and threatened to break plates.

Three men at the table next to them, in somewhat soiled working-men's clothes and surrounded by the remnants of their meal, drank beer and were locked in a discussion of European politics and the smell of war on the west-bound wind. George shushed them and chided them for ruining the atmosphere. Their voices dropped but the conversation continued.

Mike said, "Do you agree now that we'll end up at war?"

"I have no doubt of it," said Ebbie.

"Everything ends in war, it seems," said Irene.

"Uh-oh. Very gloomy," said David. "We all know how contagious that can be. All right, already, enough of this. Some battles have been won, eh? So, here's to Irene's new home!"

They raised their glasses and drank to her very good health.

"I do wish you'd taken a place a bit farther from the old girl, though," said Ebbie. "Given yourself a bit more breathing room."

"It doesn't really matter much at the moment, does it, since she's not actually speaking to me?"

Irene had called four times, and every time her mother had hung up the phone, which Ebbie said was a good sign.

"Well, she hasn't hanged herself, as threatened, at least you know that."

Irene would not talk about how frightened she had been those first few days on her own. She had stayed with the Watkinses, and Ebbie and David had persuaded her to remain away from the house for a while. David checked on her mother every day, and he assured Irene she was all right. He did not, of course, tell her he had been pretty scared himself when there was no sign of life for the first couple of days, not even the papers picked up from the front porch. And then, on the third day, they were gone, and he could see Margaret moving about inside. If he hadn't seen that, he told himself, he would have broken in the door.

Irene looked at her friends and knew they had her best interests at heart, that she could relax and be herself around them. Still. How could she tell them what it was like, how hard it still sometimes was to not go back? She had spoken to the lawyer who had handled her father's will and arranged for an annual allowance for her mother, but it hadn't quieted the worry, or the guilt. She arranged for groceries to be delivered weekly. She had done everything she felt she could do, and yet … It was impossible to explain to herself—how could she explain it to her friends? She hadn't told them how afraid she'd been that her mother might do her harm, and she never would.

"My mother is not to be despised, you know. If anything, she's to be pitied. The only thing worse than being around my mother is *being* my mother."

Mike and Ebbie laughed, but David did not.

"No, really, can you imagine how lonely it must be?" Irene shivered.

"You spend too much time worrying about what's going on in her head," said David.

"You might be right."

"Then, believe it. And live life. L'Chaim!"

"I'll drink to that," said Irene.

The evening is winding down now, as all evenings eventually do. Ebbie and Mike have gone off together, and David and Irene walk along Yonge Street. She has her arm through his. He has told her he'd like to go home soon, maybe early in the new year, to see his family, and this has frightened her. She has admitted to him that she does not want him to go and it has shaken her to admit her reasons for this are more personal than professional. He has said he will return, and Irene has chosen to believe him. She has said something that has made them both laugh.

She tucks her arm through his again and pulls herself close to the warmth and strength of him. She can smell the leather and soap scent of him—such good smells. She breathes deeply and closes her eyes. She lets herself float along beside him as she did that night last winter on the ice. She opens her eyes and smiles.

At her door he kisses her, a little awkwardly, which neither of them mind.

"I'll see you tomorrow," he says, feeling shy and a little foolish.

When he has gone and Irene has closed the door behind him, listened to his footsteps down the stairs, she begins to smile but the smile dies quickly as a surge of loneliness passes through her. She can sense her mother there, not far away, and imagines her feeling abandoned, despairing. Trying to put the image out of her mind, she begins to turn down the bed, but the image will not leave her and she knows she is in for another sleepless night.

She shrugs back into her coat and slips out of the apartment, along Carlton and up the street on which she was raised. She creeps along the long-forgotten flower bed and peers in the window. She expects the worst, but there Margaret sits, wearing her red dress with the white collar, her feet in slippers and a sweater around her shoulders. Through the window Irene can hear The Maxwell House Coffee Hour with George Burns and Gracie Allen playing on the radio.

Her mother sits with a cup of something at her elbow and a newspaper across her lap. She is doing the crossword puzzle, she reaches up with the eraser end of her pencil to push her reading glasses up her nose. On the radio the happy postman arrives at the door and her mother puts her pencil down to listen. She leans over and adjusts the tuning. She laughs at something as the postman sings in a fractured voice. Then the innocent chirp of Gracie Allen's voice and she laughs again. Slaps the paper with her hand and wipes her eyes.

Irene can't remember ever seeing her mother alone like this, when she thinks no one is looking at her. It is reassuring, yet unsettling at the same time. Her mother seems perfectly fine without her. Irene's heart tugs irrationally, to know she is neither as needed or possibly as cherished as she'd thought. She had expected to find her mother distraught, sitting in the dark, or upstairs in bed, or in her housecoat with tears in her eyes, and yet here she is, laughing at Burns and Allen. Her hair is combed and clean. After all the worry and the fear, what does it mean? She watches her mother take a sip of her drink, wrinkle her nose and add two heaping spoonfuls of sugar. Irene does not recognize the cup, a white one with a blue flower on it and a matching saucer. Margaret sips again, then picks up several small black medallions from a cut-glass bowl. The bitter licorice she is partial to. She puts a couple in her mouth and chews. Then she laughs again and wipes her lips on the back of her hand. She settles her hands in her lap and lets them sit there quietly. She does not scratch them. She gazes up at the ceiling as she listens to the radio, and Margaret looks satisfied, yes, that's the word for it, *satisfied*.

It's puzzling. Irene turns and walks away, shaking her head, baffled, relieved, and yet, something else. Made to believe her mother could not live without her, she now feels manipulated and betrayed. Margaret's world does not, apparently, revolve on the axis of her daughter's devotion. Irene feels unexpectedly hurt. It's too much to take in, too much to sort out. Perhaps this love is simply a stone she'll never be able to shake out of her shoe.

As she walks down the street toward her new home she is careful of where she puts her feet. She adjusts her step to the rhythm of the sidewalk.

Step on a crack, break your mother's back.
Step on a line, break your mother's spine.

Acknowledgements

Among the many people who helped me with the research for the book I would like to thank the staffs of the Metropolitan Toronto Research Library, the Albert J. Latner Jewish Public Library of Toronto and the City of Toronto Archives, particularly Karen Teeple; and Mike Brassard for early digging in the dusty stacks.

I am grateful to my agents Suzanne Brandreth and Dean Cooke for their belief in this book and their guidance as I learned to play with the big kids.

I also wish to offer my sincere appreciation to everyone at HarperCollins Canada: Iris Tupholme, Siobhan Blessing and the rest of the gang. You pushed me to a better book and taught me many things, including confidence in my abilities. Thank you.

The characters in this book are purely fictional. Some of the minor historical details have been altered in order to facilitate the narrative.

For those so inclined, here is a list of some of the books I found invaluable in my research:

Abella, Irving. *A Coat of Many Colours*. Toronto: Key Porter Books Limited. 1990.

Berchem, F.R. *Opportunity Road*. Toronto: Natural Heritage / Natural History Inc. 1996.

Berton, Pierre. *The Great Depression*. Toronto: Penguin Books. 1990.

Betcherman, Lita-Rose. *The Little Band*. Ottawa: Deneau Publishers. 1983.

Betcherman, Lita-Rose. *The Swastika and the Maple Leaf*. Toronto: Fitzhenry & Whiteside. 1975.

Biderman, Morris. *A Life on the Jewish Left*. Toronto: Onward Publishing. 2000.

Broadfoot, Barry. *Ten Lost Years*. Toronto: McClelland & Stewart Inc. 1997.

Davis, Minerva. *The Wretched of the Earth and Me*. Toronto: Lugus Press. 1992.

Hunter, Peter. *Which Side Are You On Boys …* Toronto: Lugus Press. 1988.

Levitt, Cyril H. and Shaffir, William. *The Riot at Christie Pits*. Toronto: Lester & Orpen Dennys. 1987.

Luftspring, Sammy. *Call Me Sammy*. Scarborough: Prentice-Hall of Canada, Ltd. 1975.

Meltzer, Milton. *Buddy Can You Spare a Dime?* New York: Facts on File, Inc. 1991.

Secunda, Victoria. *When Madness Comes Home*. New York: Hyperion. 1997.

Sharp, Rosalie, Abella, Irving and Goodman, Edwin. *Growing Up Jewish*. Toronto: McClelland & Stewart Inc. 1997.

West, Bruce. *Toronto*. Toronto: Doubleday. 1979.